COMMON GROUND

WENDY SMITH

Edited by
CREATING INK

Cover Design By
BOOKISH GRAPHICS

CONTENTS

This is a work of fiction. Names, characters, businesses, places, events, and incidents are either the products of the author's imagination or used in a fictitious manner. Any resemblance to actual persons, living or dead, or actual events is purely coincidental. Wendy Smith is in no way affiliated with any brands, songs, musicians or artists mentioned in this book.

This book is written in New Zealand English, and as such contains phrasing and kiwi colloquialisms unique to that dialect.

ISBN-13: 978-1-9-91130309-7

GLOSSARY

Te reo - Māori language
Wahine - Woman
Kuia - Grandmother
Dairy - Convenience Store
Hangi - Traditional Māori style of cooking underground
Whanau – Family
Piece of Piss - Easy
Boot - Trunk of car

CHAPTER ONE

JOSH

"YOU'LL HEAR FROM US."

Usually famous last words, but this audition has been something special. I've got a good feeling about this one.

Although, I've been wrong about that before.

Something has to come through before the end of the year. That's the target I've set, and there are only a few months left before I have to pack up and go home to Florida.

I've managed to pick up small jobs here and there, but nothing that's going to keep paying my rent for any length of time. My savings are nearly non-existent—I worked a year to fund the pursuit of my dream. It's not been long enough, and time is running out.

Fuck it. I'll treat myself to a decent coffee and go home. I deserve it for the long day I've had, and I just want to curl up in front of the television and chill for a while.

I walk to the coffee shop, enjoying the short stroll past Tiara Street Park on the corner.

The coffee shop can get quite crowded in here sometimes, but it's the middle of the afternoon and I timed this trip perfectly from the empty tables that greet me.

A brunette I haven't seen before is standing behind the counter, and I approach her, digging through my wallet for spare change.

"Latte, please."

"Sure thing."

I look up at the sound of a foreign accent, and into the deepest blue eyes I've ever seen.

"Let me guess. Australian?"

She scowls, narrowing her eyes at me, but still taking the money I'm offering her. "New Zealander."

I fist my hand in annoyance. "Shit. Sorry. You guys are real sensitive about that, right?"

She rings up the coffee on the register, and hands me the change before moving across to the coffee machine. "I don't sound Australian."

The machine whirs as it grinds the beans, and I breathe in the fresh scent of coffee.

"I'm sorry. I only had two words to make a guess."

"Do better next time."

I lean on the counter to get a better look at her. She's got long, chocolate brown hair that hangs in big curls just below her shoulders, and her light makeup doesn't hide her flawless complexion. I'm in love, and she's literally said ... twelve words to me.

"Are you new here? I haven't seen you before."

She nods. "I started last week."

My eyes drop to her name badge. *Dee.* "Live around here?"

She pours the milk into a metal jug, and starts frothing it. "You're just full of questions, aren't you?"

I shrug. "I'd have been here last week if I'd known you were working."

A small smile breaks through, and she shakes her head. With a roll of her eyes, she lets out a big sigh. "Well, I'm sure my day will be a lot brighter now you've been in."

I can't take my eyes off her, and when she shoots a glance at me through those long eyelashes, I'm gone for good.

She hands me the coffee, our fingers brushing, and for just a moment, our gazes lock before she lets go with a smile.

It's not until I'm out the door that I realise she's written something on the cup.

My favourite Canadian.

People turn and look at me when I laugh out loud.

I'm definitely coming back in tomorrow.

CHAPTER TWO

DELANEY

Six years later

"EXCUSE ME, MISS." A broad American accent calls me across the room. "Could I please get your help with something?"

I suck in a breath. Most customers are great, but we get the odd pain in the arse who wants more than just a breakfast. If he propositions me, I swear I'll kick him in the nuts so hard they'll retract into his body. *Permanently.*

"Sure." I smile brightly. "What did you need help with?"

"My friend and I are here to make a movie. You might have heard of it: *Twisted Hearts?*"

I shrug. We've had a couple of movies filmed locally a year since the whole *Lord of the Rings* craziness. I don't keep track of which movies are being made.

"Anyhoo, I just got this itinerary, and I was wondering if you could help me translate a word?"

Whew. "Sure thing."

"It says here they're planning a ..." He looks closer at the paper, as if it might reveal some hidden message. "What does that say? P ... po ..." He shoves the piece of paper toward me, and I cock an eyebrow in return. "Please, could you tell me what this says?"

I take the piece of paper from him and smile. "There's a *pōwhiri* organised for you on Friday," I say.

"What the hell is that? And how do you get the 'f' sound out of this word?" His confused expression is comical.

"The 'wh' is pronounced 'f'."

He nods, but he doesn't look that convinced.

"It's a welcoming ceremony."

"Well, why doesn't it just say that?"

"It does. That's the Māori word for it." I hand him back the paper.

He looks from me to it. "Well, I'll be damned."

"I would think they'll have a representative to help guide you through it. There'll be a challenge that will need to be accepted."

"A challenge?" the man sitting across the table says.

"Yes." How the hell do I explain this? "There'll be singing, maybe speeches, and a challenge. But like I said, someone should be with you to go through it as it happens."

"Can you be that someone?"

I smile and shake my head. "No. I'll be here. But enjoy. It'll be a lovely way to kick things off for your movie."

I'm not sure if he believes me, but I give him another smile and walk back toward the kitchen.

"What was that all about?" Pania asks.

"Something about a movie that's filming here soon. There's a *pōwhiri* on the main production site according to the paper they had." I grin. "He was trying to work out the word on his little sheet of paper. Maybe you should go out there next time. A Māori speaking *te reo* might just make his head explode."

Pania laughs. "I'd just confuse him. He could have looked it up on the net. Speaking of which ..." She pulls out her phone. "What's the name of the movie?"

"Uhh." For a moment, I'm blank. "*Twisted Hearts?*"

She taps something into her phone.

"Do you know who the star of the movie is?" Pania looks at me over her glasses.

My sinking stomach tells me I know what she's getting at. "No."

"No, you don't know, or no you don't want to know?" Her smarmy smile rankles me.

"Smugness is very unbecoming."

She laughs. "Should I tell you who the star is?"

I shrug, already knowing what she's about to say. She wouldn't be acting like this if it was anyone else on the planet.

"Let me guess. Josh Carter." My delivery of his name is flat, as it usually is on the odd occasion when I've been forced to acknowledge his existence.

"He's coming to town, Delaney."

I swallow hard. I've spent a lot of time thinking about how hurt I was that morning six years ago. He broke my heart in two.

"Delaney?" I shake my head as Pania says my name as if to shake me out of my thoughts. "If I find out where he's staying, we could go and egg his house."

I chuckle. "I thought you might have some idea to hook us up. I'm relieved you're only thinking of a little vandalism instead."

She cocks her head, giving me her sympathetic expression. "Why would I try getting you together with that arsehole?"

"Because you're a hopeless romantic who likes hot arseholes?"

She lets out a burst of laughter. "Oh, that is going in the Delaney smart mouth hall of fame."

"Even the thought of him gets under my skin. How long are they filming for?"

Pania shrugs. "How would I know? Maybe you should have spent more time talking to those customers. I bet they have all the details."

I blow out a breath. Based on prior experience, they'll be in town for at least two to three months. And if Josh is the star, chances are he'll be here the whole time.

Fuck my life.

I'M STILL BROODING about it by the time I arrive at school to pick up Melly. The sight of her breaks me out of my weird mood.

"Mummy," she calls out as she skips toward me.

"Hey, baby. Have a good day?"

She leaps into my arms, and I twirl her around, pressing a kiss into her hair. "The heater wasn't working in the classroom, so we were in room four today."

"Were you?" I walk out toward the school entrance and down the road a little until we reach the car.

She climbs into the back seat, and I fasten her harness before giving her a kiss on the forehead. "Love you."

"Love you too." She's so cheery, and it warms my heart.

My heart that's been as frozen as my feet since I left the diner.

The cold probably isn't helping my mood.

I drive back toward the diner, and my mind is not on anything other than Josh. I'm not sure how I'd cope if I saw him again. Time might have passed but the memory of how things went bad and the fallout afterward are raw.

I've got my daughter and my business to focus on, and I haven't had a man in my life for a while. And no one I've introduced to Melly.

Seeing him again adds complication to my life that I could do without.

But is it realistic to think we won't run into one another at some point?

AFTER MELLY'S gone to sleep for the night, I can sit and take stock of the day.

I have to stop worrying so much.

But it doesn't make thinking of the past hurt any less.

I smile as Josh's lips graze my neck. "Are you making breakfast?"

"I told you I would."

His dark eyes are so full of affection, and I melt just looking into them.

I knew Josh Carter would be trouble. The last thing I was looking for was any kind of romantic attachment in the weeks leading up to me leaving the US and going home, but when he walked into my life, he walked into my heart.

Even if he managed to accidentally insult me on that first day.

Somewhere on the floor on his side of the bed, a phone buzzes its way across the carpet.

Josh frowns. "Who the hell can that be?" He shrugs, kissing my lips this time.

"Get it. It might be important."

"You're important."

I grin. "I'm not going anywhere."

He leans over the side of the bed and plucks his phone off the floor. His face tells a me I was right.

"I have to take this call."

Smiling, I stretch, and his eyes darken as the sheet falls, revealing my breasts. His lips curl.

"I'm so back here as fast as I can. Promise."

"I'll be waiting."

I close my eyes. Sleep claims me, but when I wake, Josh is still nowhere to be seen.

There's a digital alarm clock on his bedside cabinet. It reads a little after nine, and as much as I don't want to, I need to get going.

My flight home to New Zealand is at some ridiculous hour of the morning tomorrow, and I need to work out if I can extend my trip at all or if I really do have to go home. The thought of the latter fills me with sadness. With another stretch, I roll out of bed.

His room is sparse. But I know he's a struggling actor trying to make it in a city full of them. I slip my shirt over my head, run my fingers through my hair, and make for the door.

The deep rumble of a man's voice comes from the living room, and I walk down the small hallway to see Josh. His back is to me, and his phone is to his ear. He's still on the phone?

"Don't worry about it. I'll ditch the bitch and come to you."

I freeze. Did I hear that right?

"She's history."

For a moment, I stand there, unable to move, unable to speak.

For weeks we've danced around, and I resisted him for so long because I knew I had to go home soon. But in the end I caved, and gave in to our mutual flirtation. We dated for two weeks before last night.

Last night—the best night of my life.

Now, in the cold light of day, I find myself mourning every kiss, every touch with his heartless words.

I open my mouth to speak.

"All I ever wanted to do was make you jealous." He laughs.

My stomach hurts. It's like I've been punched in the guts, and I want out. I thought I meant more to him. I thought we were the real thing.

I turn and go back to the bedroom, drag on my jeans, and stuff my phone and money card into my back pocket. Screw it. I'll be on that flight tomorrow and out of here, complete with my broken heart.

I tiptoe back down the hall. Josh still sits with his back to me, his ear pressed against the phone. Taking one last look, I pick up my shoes, open the door and quietly sneak out.

It's not until I'm half a block away that I let myself cry.

How could someone so sweet and genuine turn out to be such a monster?

How could I have been so wrong?

Josh destroyed me. Pania helped me pick up the pieces. If it hadn't been for her friendship, and her family around me, I wouldn't be the person I am now.

I would have constructed bigger walls around my heart.

Which is why I'm so worried. I'm not sure it'd take much for the walls I do have to crumble if Josh and I meet again.

The only question is how bad the fallout would be.

CHAPTER THREE

DELANEY

FOR THE NEXT FEW DAYS, I hold my breath every time the bell above the diner door rings.

Will he even remember me if I meant that little to him?

I'm torn between curiosity over seeing him and wanting the weeks to pass by with him not knowing I'm here.

On Wednesday afternoon, a short, blond man walks in carrying a tablet like a clipboard. A clipboard would probably be more effective. Mobile coverage is nothing much to speak of around here unless you're toward the mountain where the rich have holiday homes. While the rest of the world is moving to 5G, we're lucky if we have 3G.

"Are you Delaney?" he asks as he approaches the counter. He's American, but his accent is different to the guy who I spoke with the other day. It's much more gentle.

I nod. "Sure am."

"My name is George Wood. And I have a really big favour to ask."

"What kind of favour?"

"I'm working on the movie that's starting production next week. I don't know if you've heard of it. *Twisted Hearts?*"

Ugh.

"Yes, I've heard of it."

"There's a big welcoming party to kick things off on Friday, and I really need a caterer."

I raise myself up as tall as I can and eyeball him. "Don't you think you should have thought about this earlier?"

His sheepish expression tells me everything I need to know. "We do have in-house catering, but they're not going to be ready in time. And Mitch raved about the burger he had here the other day. So, he wondered if you'd be prepared to help us out."

"How many do you need catering for?"

Another sheepish look. "Two hundred. I'll make it worth your while."

Two hundred? I've no idea how I'm supposed to feed two hundred people with less than forty-eight hours' notice from my small kitchen.

"How much are we talking?"

He gives me a figure that makes me gasp. And then it turns out to be in US dollars, so I gasp even more. I'd have to be insane to walk away from this. "What kind of food?"

"The stuff you serve here. Most of the cast and crew live Stateside so appreciate home-cooked fare. But throw in some Kiwi delicacies as well."

For a moment, I ponder. Cooking two hundred sausage rolls would be a piece of piss. Throw in some hot dogs and burgers, and it'd be sweet. But I need to source all those things before the supermarket closes tonight otherwise I'm not going to get them from anywhere else. Not with this kind of notice.

"I'll do it. But I need to be paid upfront." I can cover it, but I'm not going to offer anyone credit. Especially when they're not locals.

"Agreed." He pulls out his credit card.

For a moment, I'm stunned.

"We'll have to do it in more than one transaction. My credit card floor limit isn't big enough," I say.

"Whatever works. You're a lifesaver."

I lead him to the other end of the counter, punching the numbers into the machine. One by one the transactions go through, and I hand him back his card with the receipts.

"Thanks again, Delaney."

"What address are we delivering to?"

"I'll confirm and email it to you if that's okay? I'm not completely sure of it myself."

I nod. "That's fine. Just make sure you let me know before ten-thirty tomorrow morning."

"No problem. I'll send it to you in around half an hour if you could give me your details." He taps them into his phone. "Thanks again. I was desperate until Mitch suggested this place."

I smile, assuming Mitch is the guy I spoke to the other day. "That's always great to hear."

"You have no idea what a relief it is to get this sorted out. I'd be dead if I didn't find an alternative."

"You're welcome. I'm glad to help." *And so is my bank account.*

With a promise to send me all the information I need, George leaves and I brace myself for Pania's reaction. We've done jobs at late notice before, but in a small town like Glenderry, it's never been one this big.

"You are going to kill me," I sing as I walk through to the kitchen.

"Who did you piss off this time?"

I laugh. Pania knows me so well. We grew up together in Whakatane, and her *whanau* took me in when I had nowhere to go. She's the McCartney to my Lennon, the Jay-Z to my Beyoncé, although in all fairness, she looks more like Beyoncé than I do with her flawless brown skin and long honey-blonde hair.

"No one."

"That makes a change." She pokes her tongue at me, and I roll my eyes.

"We just got a big catering job for Friday."

Her eyes widen. "How big?"

"Two hundred."

"Delaney, that's the day after tomorrow. From this tiny kitchen?"

I nod. "I know, but I think we can handle it. Burgers, hot dogs, and sausage rolls. The guy's sending me the breakdown, so I'm guessing we'll need vegetarian and vegan options too, and maybe gluten-free."

"Gluten-free." She looks at me like I've got two heads.

"It's for the movie people."

She gasps. "Really? I thought that would have been sorted ages ago."

"Me too, but apparently they're not ready. But we are, for the kind of money they've just thrown at me for it."

My phone dings as the email comes through from George. Sure enough, there are some specific requirements, but in terms of numbers, they're small.

"How much?"

I load up the banking app and show her the deposits. She grins. "You are one smart *wahine*. Do you think *he* will be there?"

"Who knows."

She nods. "It'll be interesting if he does show up. I haven't heard of any celebrities arriving, but he might have just sneaked into town."

"Well, if he has then he has. I can't do much about it, but I can say yes to making good money on food we can start preparing tomorrow. George's email says their on-site catering isn't ready to do the food, but their equipment's there, so we can grill the meat there, and boil the hot dogs, but have everything else ready to go."

Pania nudges my arm. "Sounds like you've got everything worked out."

"Getting there. We need to make a menu and list out what we need so I can raid the supermarket."

"This is insane, you know?" She laughs.

"We've dealt with worse. If they hate it, then at least we made the money. If they love it, maybe we'll get some more work out of them."

"I guess so. We'll pick up more custom if there are that many people in town anyway."

"You are very wise."

"You're pretty smart, too."

I snort and sit down at the table. In front of me is my laptop, which is the keeper of all the records, and I get to work.

This is going to be one hellish twenty-four hours.

AFTER PICKING UP AMELIA, I drive to the supermarket.

As I'm driving only one thought fills my head. What if Josh turns up tomorrow? There's been no news of him flying into town, but planes have been going back and forth at that private airfield just out of town.

At some point I'll run into him; Murphy's Law is good like that. But how soon will it be?

I need to try and put him out of my mind.

By the time we're finished, I've ordered so many bread rolls from the bakery, they have to start baking earlier than usual.

I've also raided the lettuce, tomatoes, pickles, frankfurters, and all the cheese I can get my hands on. The catered food won't taste quite the same as our usual diner meals. There are some ingredients I import from America, but the finished product will be as close as I can get to it.

At short notice, it'll have to do.

I hope it's enough.

CHAPTER FOUR

DELANEY

GEORGE GREETS me at the gate at eight a.m. on Friday morning.

Pania stayed back at the diner to cook, with Trina serving customers. I've brought Jo with me to help prepare everything. It'll be tight on both sides, but we'll make it work. At least food here will be spread out buffet-style and we won't have to do much once the final preparation is done.

"Here are your passes. Hold onto them afterward in case we need help during the production."

I laugh. "I appreciate that."

He hands us both a lanyard with a plastic tag that says *contractor* on it.

"If you park over there, the in-house caterers are setup nearby." He points to the right of us. "They're there to help if you need it too. I think they're feeling a bit sheepish about not being ready for this."

I shrug. "It's all good. We're mostly ready, but you said there were grills and hotplates?"

He nods. "Everything you said you needed is there."

"Thank you. Hope the rest of your day goes well."

He blows out a long breath. "I think it will."

Driving through, I park where he indicated and start the process of removing everything from the car.

It's all set up as promised, and the in-house caterers are really helpful.

By the time the food's laid out and people are ready to eat, I let out a long breath and just watch.

I don't want to look like a fangirl by asking about Josh, but I can't help but scan every person who approaches, doing a double take at anyone who looks remotely like him.

You have to get this under control.

"Delaney." George walks toward me with a big smile on his face. "Thank you so much again. This has been a real big hit."

"I'm glad to hear it."

"Can I ask you a question?" Jo speaks up from behind me.

"Sure," he says.

"Are the two stars of the movie here? Can we meet them?" Jo asks.

I grimace. George glances at me, his lips quirking up. "No, they're not here. They both fly in next week."

Turning, I see Jo's face fall, while I'm relieved but feel a tinge of disappointment too. I've seen Josh on the cover of magazines and occasionally on television, but I'm still a little curious about the man he's become. He's been in a bunch of blockbuster films, but I've avoided every one.

It's been an act of self-preservation.

"I'm sure I can maybe organise some merchandise or something for you. I'll ask them."

She smiles. "That would be wonderful."

"Thanks," I say. *"And sorry."* I mouth the last two words to George, but he winks at me as if to say it's okay.

"Hey, Delaney." The man I met in the diner the other day walks toward me. "I just wanted to say thanks. The food was great, and today went really well."

"Glad to hear it. Good luck with your movie."

"Thank you."

He walks away with a hot dog in his hand, and I let out a sigh.

"What did you want us to do with the leftover food, George?" I ask. There's not a lot, but I'm not about to leave any mess behind.

"I'll get it taken care of. You two have done more than enough for us. I'm so grateful."

"You're welcome. Just don't drop me in it again." I grin.

"You're an angel. And no offence, but we shouldn't need you again."

I laugh. "No offence taken. We'll clear out our gear and get going."

Packing up is easy, and I can't wait to get back to my daughter.

WHEN WE REACH THE DINER, I drop the boxes on the table and head through to the counter. Melly's eyes light up when she sees me.

"Mummy."

"Hey, sweet pea." I walk around the front and give her a hug. "Have you had fun?"

"Pania picked me up and she made me a hot dog."

"Did she?"

She nods as if I didn't organise for Pania to do that.

"Do you want to go home now?" My heart lights up as she buries her face in my chest.

"Yes, please."

"Let's get you down from there."

I help her off the stool and we walk back through to the kitchen.

Pania smiles. "Did everything go okay?"

"Really good. They had food warmers and everything ready, just no food. We didn't even have to clean up after ourselves."

"Was *he* there?"

I look over at Melly. She's picked up her schoolbag from beside the door and is waiting patiently.

"No. Apparently the stars of the movie fly in next week."

"An easy afternoon, then."

"It was good. I told George not to dump me in it again, but I think we need to be prepared just in case. I'm sure their in-house catering will be fine from now, but you never know." I shrug.

She grins. "If they pay as well as they did for today ..."

"Exactly. Anyway, I'm going to get this one home because we're both tired. I dropped Jo off on the way."

Pania sighs. "Some days, I'm really glad we close at five."

"Me too. Come over for a wine when you've closed up? I don't feel like cooking dinner, but I've got some leftover spaghetti and meatballs in the fridge to heat up."

"That sounds perfect."

"Come on, Melly." I take my daughter by the hand and lead her out the back door, across the small car park and over the road to our house.

We're quite lucky here. It's quiet, being off the main street, and we're the last house with a gap of about three sections between us and the nearest neighbour.

I'm grateful for the peace and quiet.

"Dodged a bullet, then," Pania says. She takes a sip of the sauvignon blanc we opened before dinner.

Melly fell asleep straight after eating, and I tucked her into bed still in her clothing. It's been a big day for her. She's used to going to the diner after school, but not so used to waiting there until nearly closing time.

"You could say that."

"I bet you're curious about him."

I smile, running my finger around the rim on the glass. "Of course I am."

"Are you still hung up on him? After all this time?"

I shake my head. "No. He killed that a long time ago. But I've been reminded of him every freaking day when I see Melly's eyes. She's so much like him in that respect."

"I'll have to take a look if I get a chance." She licks her lips. "You know, you could always take up Damon's offer. At least then you'd have the excuse of a boyfriend if Josh turned up."

I groan. "Nothing against him, but you know I'm not interested. He hangs around enough now. If I went out with him, I'd probably end up having to get a restraining order."

She nods. "I think you're right there."

"I've made it really clear to him that I'm not interested."

"And yet he's still there every day in the same seat waiting for you to serve him."

I roll my eyes. "He must have been disappointed today."

"Oh, he was. Today he even tried to engage your daughter in conversation. Melly just gave him the cold shoulder. Told him she wasn't allowed to talk to strangers."

My mouth falls open. She sees him nearly every day when he sits at the counter. "She didn't."

"You should be really proud of her. I told him it wasn't appropriate for him to try to keep talking to her if she didn't want to. He's trying to win you over through your daughter."

"I raised her well." I grin.

"You have, and don't you dare forget it." She takes another sip. "Today was good from what you said."

I nod. "Very good. I'm just really glad it's Friday and I don't have to work tomorrow."

Pania laughs. "I love you, my friend."

"Want to sleep over? We can open another bottle of wine."

She grins. "I like the way you think."

By the time I crawl into bed, I'm a little drunk and still thinking about Josh. He's never really left my thoughts, but now he plagues me even if he's not in the country yet.

But he will be soon.

I can't just run away from the life I've built here, and I refuse to hide.

This could be it—the moment I've been dreading for so long.

CHAPTER FIVE

JOSH

I WANT to broaden my horizons.

That's what I told my agent, Mac, when I said I wanted to do this movie.

It's the first movie we've fought over in six years.

I hated that it wasn't an action film, hated the concept, hated the script.

But when you get a call from an old friend who's convinced that this is her career launching pad, what do you do?

It had the added benefit of filming in New Zealand.

I could have come here years ago to look for Dee, but no amount of searching from the States had turned up anything. She'd simply vanished. It didn't help that I never got her last name.

It'd been lust at first sight, and me, the lovestruck teenager, had sat in the café where she worked all day every day when I wasn't auditioning.

Then I had two life-changing things happen in the same week. Dee and I slept together, and I landed the role that set me on a career trajectory that hasn't dipped since.

But I had no one to share the latter event when she left.

It's crazy to still be thinking about a girl I spent one night with six years go.

She disappeared the morning after without saying goodbye. She was due to fly back to New Zealand the day afterward, but for all I know she is back in the States, living under an assumed name.

So, now I sit in a rental house overlooking a view that I've been told 'will take your breath away'.

I flew in last night under the cover of darkness, and didn't get to see much of the vaunted landscape people talk about all the time. The nearby town is tiny, but it's a small-town romance we're filming, and the setting is perfect.

The house I'm staying in is huge. I think it's some billionaire's holiday home that he rents out. From this bed, I'm treated to a view of the lake, the stunning glass-like surface reflecting the golden rays of the early morning sun.

It's so peaceful.

Beside me somewhere, my mobile rings. It breaks into the stillness of my morning.

Clearly someone has other plans.

I feel the bed beside me until I lay my hands on the phone, and squint at the bright screen.

"Mac," I mumble.

"Good flight?" He sounds way too happy, but it's probably midafternoon in LA.

"Good sleep too until someone woke me up."

He chuckles. "Just wanted to make sure you got there okay. And to make sure your phone was working."

"Clearly, Mindy did her job. But I might still grab a local SIM while I'm here. Fuck paying roaming charges."

He laughs again. "You can afford it."

"That's not the point." He makes fun of me all the time for my miserly ways, but I've been stone broke before and never want to be there again. I'd rather save my money and donate to charity where I can to help other people in that position.

"House okay?"

I scan the room. "Looks good. I walked in the door and crashed last night, though."

"I'll leave you to it."

"Thanks. I'll give Mindy a call now and see what else she's organised."

"Good idea."

Mindy answers on the first ring. I wouldn't expect anything different from her.

"How's the house?" she asks.

"Big and in the middle of nowhere." I laugh.

"Good. It sounded fabulous. I've got an email from Richard to send you."

"Who?"

"Richard Baker. The guy whose house you're renting. I'll forward you the welcome email he just sent me. He's got some local food recommendations that you might enjoy."

I grin. "That'd be great. I'm starved."

"I'm not sure if you've taken a look, but the kitchen is apparently fully stocked if you feel like cooking."

Laughing, I walk down the stairs. "I'm not sure I'd go that far. Though, it depends on whether anywhere around here delivers. I appear to be tucked away up a mountain."

"I'll send this email through and you can take a look. If you need anything, call me."

"Of course."

Mindy's Mac's sister-in-law, and while she takes her job as my PA seriously, sometimes she's a little too serious.

My phone dings as the email comes through.

Josh,

Please feel free to treat my home as your own. It's to my

eternal regret that I don't get more time there, but it's good to know it's being put to good use.

I'm not sure if you'll have time for sightseeing, and this time of year will be pretty cold, so the usual tourist things won't be very attractive. There aren't a lot of restaurant options, but there's the pub which offers snacks during the day and bigger meals in the evenings and on weekends. Lafontaine has French cuisine, and Delaney's Diner serves American-style food. I think you'll like it; it'll be like eating back home.

There's no UberEats, but Delaney's delivers between midday and five, Monday to Friday. Small-town New Zealand has a thing about being open later and on weekends, which is a bit of an inconvenience, but I'm sure you'll work it all out.

Please email me directly if you have any issues.
Don't be surprised if it snows down as far as the house. The road gets black ice on it this time of year, so be careful.

Kind Regards,
Richard Baker.

I NOD AS I READ. The guy sounds decent enough. And his food recommendations leave my mouth watering. I load Google and search for "Delaney's Diner".

The website comes up.

I click on the online ordering tab. Pictures of food pop up, and I zoom in on the combo options. I'm sure they won't look how they do on the website, but right now, I'd kill for a burger.

Selecting a combo with fries and a thickshake, and then adding another burger to it, I go to the page where I have to fill in my information.

I'm not ordering under my real name. The last thing I want is to bring attention to myself here. I like a quiet life.

What's this guy's name? Richard Baker. I type that in, retrieve the address from the earlier email Mindy sent me, and fill the rest of the form in before paying for it.

Delivery time is approximately thirty minutes.

I nod. That's fair. My stomach grumbles at the thought of food.

It can't arrive fast enough.

CHAPTER SIX

DELANEY

"DON'T FALL OVER, but we have a delivery order," Pania calls across the kitchen.

I sigh. We have a delivery option, but most locals come here to eat. I should probably get rid of it, but there aren't a lot of places around here that offer the service. And any business is good business.

"I can take it. I've got to go and pick up Melly anyway."

She nods. "I'll get it cooked and ready to go."

"Where am I going?"

"The Baker estate."

"Richard's there? It's not like him to be staying and ordering food from us. Doesn't he usually get gourmet shit flown in from Auckland?"

Pania laughs. "He has ordered in before. Maybe he felt like slumming it today?"

"Maybe. I hope he knows again that he'll be paying a premium for delivery. That road probably has black ice this time of year."

She frowns. "If you're worried about it, why don't I take it?"

"I'll be fine. I'll just drive slowly. Besides, I'll have to swing by and grab Melly first."

"I'll get the sale processed. It's just a couple of burgers, fries, and a thickshake so won't take long to throw together."

"Sounds good."

I head out to the front of the diner. Damon, who spends more time here than his printing business down the road, waves at me from a stool at the end of the counter

"I'm heading out to get Melly and take a food delivery. You two okay?" I ask Trina and Jo who are both out serving customers. They nod, Trina walking toward the counter to cover for me.

"Delaney, could I have another coffee?" Damon asks.

"I'm sure Trina can help you with that." I smile.

"I like it better when you do it."

I bristle. "Well, Trina's good at making coffee and I have to get Amelia. The school bell doesn't wait for anyone."

Before he answers, I turn on my heel and walk out the back. "Food ready?"

Pania nods. "Just about. The fries have another thirty seconds or so. Damon give you grief out there?"

"He wanted me and me alone to make his coffee."

She sighs. "That man has it bad. But he needs to find someone else to moon over."

"Can't you go out and flirt with him for a bit?" I flutter my eyelashes at her.

Laughing, she shakes her head and returns to the deep-fryer. "Here's your meal. Have fun, and don't forget your jacket. It'll be freezing up there."

By the time I get to school, the bell's rung and Melly's waiting near the gate. I let out a sigh of relief because while we have the standard delivery time on the website as approximately thirty minutes, Richard's house is on the outer limit due to its location.

She jumps in the car, and I buckle her into her child seat.

"We're going for a drive," I say.

"Where?"

"Up the mountain. I have a delivery to make before we go to the diner."

She claps. "Can we see the snow?"

"It's not cold enough for snow, honey."

Melly pouts.

"We'll come back when there is, and maybe we can make a snowman."

"Like Olaf?"

I bite down a laugh. Children's movies have a lot to be answer for. "Maybe. I think he'll have to stay on the mountain, though."

That seems to be a good enough answer as she settles back in her seat and smiles.

Thankfully, the path seems quite clear. The ice can be dangerous, but I know the road well and where there are problems.

Before too long, I make a right turn into the driveway and Richard's house looms ahead. It's a beautiful two-storey place with huge windows and high ceilings. I bet anything it's toasty warm inside, unlike my car, which has what I refer to as a 'sometimes heater'.

Pulling up outside, I grab my jacket from the passenger seat and slide it on. The car's warm, but up here it'll be freezing. After zipping it right up, I pull a woollen hat down over my ears and slide my gloves on.

Melly laughs when I turn to talk to her, the collar of my jacket zipped up over my mouth.

"Be good. I'll be back in a minute."

She nods, the pompom on the top of her hat waving around. I really need to stitch that damn hat back up before she loses it. She's so attached to it because I made it for her, but while the knitting's solid, my sewing is apparently not too hot.

I open the door of the car, reaching for the insulated bag and sliding the contents out. Grabbing the thickshake from the drink holder, I walk the short distance to the front door.

Ringing the doorbell, I pray that he hears it. Last time I was here, he didn't at first and this stupid house is so big, it takes an age for him to walk from one end to the other. I also have no patience being up here. There's a marked difference in temperature between the mountain and the town.

"Come on, Richard." I stamp my feet to try and get warm. The sooner I get back to the warmth of the diner, the better.

"Sorry."

I hear him before I see him, and his voice causes me to catch my breath. It's so familiar.

It still takes a moment for it to register once the door swings open. *That's not Richard.*

He has a towel wrapped around his waist, and nothing else. I drag my eyes up from his towel to see a dark trail of hair up to his navel, and I know I'm still staring as I make my way over a very impressive set of abs, to an even more impressive pair of pecs covered in a light dusting of dark hair.

And there it is. That handsome face with stubble and those dark eyes—eyes I've drowned in before.

"I ... I ..."

Josh.

His tired gaze looks down, and his expression slowly changes as if he's just noticing that he's half-naked.

"Shit. Sorry. I should have thrown a robe on. I just flew in last night and I'm jetlagged to hell, which is why I need this. Do you have a phone number I can just call if I need more? I've only got my phone and I hate ordering online with it. Fat fingers." He grins.

"More?" *Jesus, Delaney. Get it together.*

I hand him over the thickshake and bag. Raising them as if to say thanks, he smiles a cheesy smile that makes my knees knock together. "I've heard your food is like being home, and I'm sure that's what I need right now."

My mouth's so dry, I'm not even sure I can form any more words, and an awkward silence falls over us. This is not how I pictured a reunion, but then again, I never expected to see Josh again.

"It's ... it's on the side of the bag. We can take phone orders." My words are muffled by my jacket, but I don't care.

He nods. "Great. I promise I won't make a nuisance of myself."

When he smiles, the dimples in his cheeks make my stomach flip. Why on earth am I this way? I thought six years would make a difference to the way he makes me react. Apparently not.

"It's no problem."

He takes a sip of the shake. "Damn, that's good. I'm sure I'll be back to feeling like myself after this."

My throat constricts, and my heart thrums about a million miles a minute.

He yawns, gathering the bag into the same hand as his shake and then scratches the back of his neck.

The abs move.

I swallow hard.

"Thanks for that."

I nod, and turn back toward the car.

"Wait. Do I tip you? I'm sorry. I just arrived here last night and I don't know the custom."

Tension pools in my stomach at the smooth sound of his voice. He always had that, even six years ago. It's one of the things that drew me to him.

"No." I croak. "No tip needed. We don't do that here."

"Oh. Okay. Thanks again."

My heart thuds as I walk toward the car. For once I'm grateful that I'm clothed in a thick jacket and beanie. He didn't recognise me.

After I open the car door, I slip off my jacket and tug the beanie off my head, shaking out my hair.

Relief floods my system when I slide into the driver's seat and start up the car.

"Are we going to work now, Mummy?"

"We're going to the diner." I nod.

She lets out a dramatic sigh. "Good. It's warm there."

I laugh. "I know it's been a long week. Want Mummy to make you a special burger when we get there?"

Melly claps. "And fries?"

"And fries. Then we'll leave the others to it and go home and watch a movie if you want."

"Can we watch *Zootopia* again?"

I sigh. "Yes, we can watch *Zootopia* again."

Me? I just want to go home and have a much stronger drink than the ones we sell at work.

After my afternoon, I think I need it.

CHAPTER SEVEN

JOSH

I DON'T CLOSE the door right away.

The icy blast coming from outside should be enough to make me, but there was something about that woman, and I can't put my finger on it.

I couldn't see her face, and her voice was muffled, but she seemed familiar.

It's probably just because I'm so tired.

When she reaches the car, she pulls off her jacket, and then her hat, shaking out her hair.

Brown curls spill out.

I catch my breath. The simple action brings back memories of an earlier time.

Saturday night at our local nightclub is good for two things: Cheap drinks and getting laid. Since I met Dee, the latter's not of any interest to me. I'm here for the alcohol.

One drink later, and my best friend, Reece, has disappeared with a blonde. I'm left with Jessie and Clarke, two of our older acting class buddies. Jessie wants more. She always did.

"Come home with me," she says.

I shake my head. "It wouldn't be fair on either of us. I like you, Jessie, I really do, but ..."

"His heart's been stolen by an antipodean barista." Clarke pretends to swoon, and all I do is roll my eyes at him.

A flash of brown curls catches my eye. It can't be. I guess she's staying somewhere in the neighbourhood.

Dee scoots around the outside of the dance floor, a drink in her hand and her eyes scanning the room. I assume she's looking for a seat.

"I'll be back."

I stand and smile as I walk up behind her.

"Dee!" I yell.

Despite the loud music, she still jumps, her drink spilling over her hand and onto the floor.

"Oh my God. Canadian boy." She grins.

"What are you doing here?"

She pokes me with her index finger. "I could ask you the same thing."

I shrug. "This is where I come to blow off steam."

Her nod is slow as she seems to take me in. "That's why I'm here. I've only got a few weeks left and I've barely done any partying since I arrived. The drinks are so cheap."

I laugh. "That's why we come here, too."

"We?"

"I'm with some friends of mine." I suck in my bottom lip. "Want to dance?"

Indecision crosses her face, but she nods. "Sounds good. I'll just finish this."

She gulps down the rest of her drink, leaving the glass on an empty table. "Come on."

Taking my hand in hers, she pulls me onto the dance floor.

As we make our way there, Katy Perry's "Firework" begins to play. I roll my eyes.

Dee laughs. "Come on. This is a fun song."

"It wasn't quite what I had in mind," I yell.

We both rock to the music, not touching each other even though I long to feel her in my arms.

"I think I should warn you that I can't dance at all."

She laughs. "I noticed. But I can't dance either, so you're in good company."

"No way. You're amazing."

She grabs my hand. "Thanks. You're a good liar."

"I'm not lying." I tug her the rest of the way to me. She hooks her arms around my neck as I slide mine around her waist. "That's better."

"You're so much trouble, aren't you?"

"Not at all."

The moment catches us both by surprise. I can see it in her eyes. And without thinking, I lean in and kiss her.

She doesn't freak out.

She kisses me back.

It's not long and passionate like I want it to be, but when we do pull apart, she's got the same goofy look on her face as I'm sure I do.

"Come home with me."

She shakes her head. "I can't. I shouldn't have even let you kiss me."

Her words are like a knife to the heart.

Dee places her palm on my chest. "It's not that I don't want to, Josh. It's just that starting something now would be unfair to both of us. I go home soon."

I capture her hand in mine. "I've never met anyone like you."

"I've never met anyone like you." She echoes my words with a sad smile. I'm not alone in the way I feel; I'm sure of it. Her kiss ridded me of any doubts I had about that.

"We could find a way. I want to try."

For a moment, her eyes search mine. She likes me. I know she does.

"Can you make a promise not to fall in love with me?" she asks.

I hold my hand up, fingers crossed. "Of course I will."

"It doesn't count when you do that." She squeezes my hand. "I just don't want either of us to end up with a broken heart."

"We'll spend the next few weeks getting to know each other and see how it goes. This isn't impossible, Dee."

We're shouting over the music, despite standing so close to one another. I take her hand in mine and lead her off to a corner of the room.

"Why do I think I'm going to regret this?" she asks.

She's so close. I lean even closer.

She nods and gives me her final permission. I kiss her, softly to start with, but then her arms slide back around my neck and she opens up to let me in.

There's no way I want this kiss to end.

She tastes faintly of bourbon and Coke. My body's against hers, and I let out a moan when she drops her hands and slides them around my waist.

When the kiss ends, I press my forehead to hers.

"You are trouble. I knew it." She's breathless.

"Let's get out of here. It's too noisy. I'll grab my jacket and walk you home."

With her hand still in mine, we make our way to the table.

"Where have you been?" Jessie glares at me.

"I'm going home. Are you okay to get back to your place?"

"I'll take her." Clarke smiles at Dee. "Is this your Kiwi goddess?"

Dee laughs. "Is that what you call me?"

"Maybe." I lift my jacket off the back of the chair.

Her grin lights up her whole face. She's so freaking gorgeous, and I know she's scared to start something, but I've never felt so comfortable around another human being before.

She gives Clarke and Jessie a little wave, and we turn and head out the door.

We're halfway down the street when she comes to a stop.

"Wait. Were you with that woman?" she asks.

"Who? Jessie?" I shake my head. "She's a friend from my acting *class, and we sometimes all get together for a night out. Clarke'll make sure she gets home okay."*

Dee nods. "Alright."

"We're just friends. I don't like her the way I like you."

She pauses. "I like you, too."

"Are you sure you don't want to come home with me?"

She's torn; I can see it. "I don't sleep with guys I'm not dating."

"When are you free to go on a date?"

She laughs. "I'm not working tomorrow. That's why I came out tonight."

"I can do tomorrow. I'll take you to one of my favourite places."

Dee rests her palm on my cheek. "You're not making this easy."

"That's the plan."

She sighs. "One date."

"To start with."

With a shake of her head, she drops her hand. "I don't know, Canadian boy. One date could lead to all kinds of trouble."

"To be honest, I hope it does."

She holds her hands up in surrender. "I've got to give you an A for persistence. And if I wasn't so close to leaving the country, I wouldn't hesitate." Dee licks her lips. "But sure. Show me what you've got."

Her gaze fixes on me, and I lean closer.

This time, our kiss is long and slow. I linger on her lips, my chest pounding at the thought of making sure tomorrow's perfect.

That was it. I walked her back to the hostel she was staying in, and the next day we had our date.

I thought that would be that. She'd fall in love with me and we'd live happily ever after.

But that's not what happened.

All this time, and my memories of our time together are triggered by the little things.

What we had was short, intense, and it ended abruptly.

I've never met anyone like Dee again.

I'm not sure I ever will.

CHAPTER EIGHT

DELANEY

WHEN WE REACH THE DINER, I lead Melly through the kitchen and to her favourite seat at the counter.

"I'll just get you a burger, honey."

Melly nods. "A special one."

Special to her means a burger patty and sauce. Nothing else. And it has to be barbecue sauce because she's going through a phase of only liking that.

"Be back in a minute. Trina, can you make Melly a thickshake, please?"

She nods. "Sure thing, Delaney."

I turn and walk back into the kitchen. If I know Pania, she's already got Melly's burger underway.

She smiles as I approach. Sure enough, the patty's on the grill and Melly's favourite sauce is on the bench.

"You look like you've seen a ghost."

"I think I just did." I sit at the table, staring at the wall.

"Are you okay?"

I nod slowly. "That house? It's been rented out."

Pania shrugs. "I guess I shouldn't be surprised. Richard Baker's spent, what, maybe a couple of months there since he bought the place?"

"He rented it to Josh."

"Josh ...?"

"*That* Josh."

Her eyes widen. "Oh my God, Delaney. Did he recognise you?"

I blow out a breath. "If he did, he didn't give any indication of it. Mind you, I was wrapped up like Ernest Shackleton about to explore the Antarctic."

"What about Melly?"

I lean back in the chair. "She was in the car. They didn't see each other."

"Are you okay?"

I knit my fingers together, placing my hands on the table. "Yes. No. Maybe?"

"What was it like? You know, seeing him again?"

"My stomach hurt. Does that sound right?"

She rounds the table and places a hand on my back. "I'm not sure there's a right or a wrong way to feel."

"I guess he looks a lot more ... grown up."

Pania laughs. "Six years is long enough to make a difference. And if you ask me, he has got hotter with every movie."

I pull my hands apart and bury my face in them. "I don't want to hear that." Reaching behind me, I slap her thigh. "What am I going to do?"

She wraps her arms around my neck and lowers her head beside mine. "I don't know. But if he didn't recognise you, no harm done, and you've got some time to think about your next move. I doubt anyone who stays in that house will deign to visit the diner."

Laughing, I lean my head against hers. "I guess you're right. Remember that one time when Richard came in?"

"How can I forget?"

As nice a guy as Richard is, he's on a whole other planet. He came in once with his girlfriend, who glittered with precious stones and looked down her nose at all of us.

"I really did assume that he'd ordered delivery. Gave me one hell of a fright when Josh answered the door half-naked."

Pania pulls away. "Half-naked? Did you get a picture?"

"No." I cross my arms. "I did not get a picture. Do you think I go around taking photos of men I'm delivering food to?"

Her mouth falls open. "He's not the first answering the door like that?"

"Well, yes, but the answer is no. No pictures."

She lets out a sad sigh. "Shame. That man is fine."

I just shake my head. "He is, but we're so not going there."

She walks back to the hot plate, flipping the burger. "At least with him not recognising you, it'll buy you a bit more time."

I nod. "I really thought I could go the whole time without seeing him. Instead, I see him on the first day he's here."

She turns her head. "How do you know it's his first day?"

"He said he was jetlagged and that he arrived here last night."

Pania laughs. "You're in so much trouble. Fate might just keep bringing you two together."

I shake my head. "I think the universe has other plans for us."

"Yeah, but this seems like too good an opportunity to miss. Especially for Melly." She smiles. "I'll just finish off this burger for her."

I shake my head. "No, I'll sort it out."

Josh being here brings up a whole lot of unwanted memories. Not just of the day I left.

He wasn't the only one to break my heart. My mother did that too when she kicked me out.

Tears prick my eyes. I moved out to stay with Pania, and never went back. I haven't spoken to my mother since, and I doubt I ever will.

Melly missed out on so much not having her father around, and her grandmother, but I'll be damned if anyone's going to screw with our lives now.

She's my priority. She always has been. I tried to let Josh know about her, but he was too hard to get in touch with.

And then I watched from a distance as he grew more famous.

I never could bear to watch his films, but I didn't have to as stories about him appeared in the media, and on social media he was hard to avoid. At some point, when I'd had a few drinks and was feeling generally sorry for myself, I even liked his Facebook page.

But what we had was over, and I was left with a daily reminder of him in our daughter.

Once again, I'm at war with myself over telling him about her. This is my chance to do that, but at the same time, he's got the wealth to take me to court and maybe even win custody of my little girl.

I'm not sure it's worth the risk.

CHAPTER NINE

JOSH

MY STOMACH RUMBLES.

I just gulped down that thickshake, both burgers and fries, and I'm still hungry. That was some unexpectedly good food. And Richard was right. It really was like being back home.

But I'm not about to ask that woman to deliver any more food. There's a reason she was dressed up so warm.

I can't believe I answered the door in a towel.

She must have thought I was a real tool.

I bury my face in my hands. It's not always easy to keep my feet on the ground with all the praise and adulation my work gets. But at the same time, I'm the same guy who moved from Florida to LA and worked my ass off auditioning to get to the position I'm in. And I won't ever forget that.

After cleaning up the rubbish, I open my suitcase and pull out a fresh set of clothing. It's cold out there, but jeans, a T-shirt, and a thick jacket should be enough.

Parked outside is a rental car for my use, and I roll my eyes at the sight of a late-model BMW. I really don't need anything this ostentatious.

But a car is a car, and I unlock and open the door.

It is nice. The new-car leather smell hits me as I slide into the driver's seat. I've driven enough times in England to be used to driving a right-hand car on the left-hand side of the road.

Sliding my phone into the mount, I sync up the Bluetooth and take a look at Google Maps to see where I'm going.

Delaney's Diner.

Not only am I going to get another mouth-watering burger, but maybe I'll also get to meet the woman who delivered the first one. After her action conjured up that memory, I'm curious.

I take the road slowly down the mountain. Last night, someone from the production picked me up and drove me up here, so I'm completely unfamiliar with the road. But I remember what Richard said in his letter about the black ice, so the trip is slow.

The town is picturesque set against the background of the lake. And the diner stands out in an otherwise colourless town.

It looks like something that walked out of 1950s America, and I love the authenticity, even from a distance. This is owned by someone who's worked out their market and nailed it. And I bet they do a roaring business while we're filming here.

I park the car outside and lock it before heading toward the door.

The tables are mostly full with customers, their hands wrapped around their coffee cups as if they're trying to suck all the heat out of them into their skin. I don't blame them with how cold it is outside, but it's toasty warm in here.

The stools by the counter are empty, bar two. They're occupied by a dark-haired man, and a little girl eating a burger.

There's one person being served, and I walk over to wait behind him.

"That burger looks good," I say to the little girl.

She turns to me and smiles, her whole face lighting up. "My mummy made it."

"Did she? I hope she makes mine."

"Want a chip?" She holds up a fry, and I shake my head with a grin.

"No thanks. I'm just about to order my own. Are you having a thickshake too? They're so good."

She nods, the plait in her hair flying. "This is my second one."

"Really?"

"I was soooo hungry after school."

"That's because you didn't eat your lunch. Again."

A voice comes from the door into the kitchen.

The man in front of me moves, and I get a clear view. My heart skips a beat.

It can't be.

"I don't like my lunch."

My heart's in my throat as she comes closer.

As large as life, Dee—*my* Dee walks out of the kitchen until she stands on the other side of the counter to the girl. Her focus is entirely on the child—she doesn't even glance at me.

"There's nothing wrong with your lunch."

"Did you want to order, sir?" Another voice knocks me out of my stupor, and I turn to the woman at the cash register.

I swallow hard. "Uhhh yeah. I had a couple of burgers and thickshake delivered earlier, and I was wondering if I could get two more burgers and another thickshake."

She nods. "We only had one delivery order today, so I can bring that up on the system and sort that for you. Just give me one minute."

"Thanks."

My eyes drift back to Dee and the little girl. Dee's either ignoring me or hasn't recognised me. I find that hard to believe, but it's a possibility. I'd never forget her face. She's grown up, as I have, and she's filled out with curves she didn't have back when I fell for her. But she's unmistakably the same woman.

"Did you want fries?"

I snap back to my order.

"Yes please."

"That'll be thirty-four dollars." She frowns. "Oh, shit. I mean. I can make a combo out of one of those. Give me a second."

"No problem."

A short, dark, well-built man waves his hand despite Dee standing right in front of him.

"Hey, Delaney."

Her name's Delaney? It's her diner. No wonder I couldn't find her when I searched on social media. I don't know if just knowing her name was Delaney and not Dee would have been enough, but it wouldn't have hurt.

"Yes?"

"Could I get a mac and cheese?" He beams. I know that look. It was almost permanent on my face in the weeks when I tried to convince Delaney to go out with me. A simple look from her, and my whole body reacted.

"Wasn't the hot dog enough?"

He pats his stomach. "You know how I feel about your food."

She turns back toward the kitchen. "Trina, can I get a mac and cheese for Damon?"

"Sure thing."

Delaney smiles at him, and I know that look too. It doesn't hit her eyes, and she gives him much, much less than the full smiling experience I remember.

"Sir?"

I turn back to the woman serving me. "Sorry. I was miles away."

One end of her mouth quirks. "I understand. I was saying that's thirty dollars."

I reach into my pocket and pull out my wallet. Mindy arranged some New Zealand dollars before I left the States, and as my stomach grumbles, I'm incredibly grateful once again for her.

"Give me a second. I'm not really familiar with these."

"If you've got a green note and a blue note, that'll do."

I nod, pulling out the coloured notes. For the first time, her gaze hits mine, and I know the moment she recognises me because her mouth falls open.

"Shit. Forget it. It's on the house."

"Jo? Everything okay?" Delaney turns from the little girl and heads toward us.

Jo hasn't dropped her gaze from me, but she nods as Delaney approaches her.

"I'll pay for it. You're one of my favourite actors ever." Jo's breathless.

Delaney seems completely focused on Jo, and ignores me.

"You really don't have to," I protest.

"I do." Jo's chest heaves as she looks at me. I'll never get used to this.

"Put it through, and don't worry about it. I'm not going to let you pay for it, Jo," Delaney says.

I lean closer. "I'll pay for it."

Finally, Delaney's eyes meet mine. "You probably should. If you still eat as much as you used to, you'll send me broke if I feed you for free."

I laugh at her unexpected humour, and she gives me a smile—that smile. The smile that ol' Damon didn't get.

"Here." I hand her the bills.

"Thanks." She completes the transaction on the register. "Where are you sitting? We'll bring it out."

"I thought I'd just sit at the counter."

She swallows hard, shuffling uncomfortably. "Sure. Take a seat."

Damon's sitting on the far side of the little girl, and I take a seat closer to Delaney.

"So you did notice me."

"I noticed you earlier today when I delivered your first meal. I'm not surprised you're here for more. You always did eat like a hobbit."

Frowning, I run my fingers through my hair. "What do you mean?"

"First breakfast, second breakfast, elevenses ..." Her laugh doesn't sound the way I remember, and I'm sure she's holding back. But this is probably an awkward situation for her.

"Oh yeah. I still do that too. Growing boy that I am."

She nods. "I can see."

I want to tell her she's beautiful, and that I can forget that she disappeared on me but being right in front of her, everything goes from my mind except how good she looks.

"Sorry about earlier. I was a dumbass and went straight to sleep jetlagged when I should have tried to stay up to try and get in sync. When you rang the doorbell, all I could think about was my stomach."

If I'm not mistaken, her cheeks flush pink.

"It's okay. I wasn't expecting to see you at all. I thought you were Richard."

"Richard?"

"It's his house you're staying in. And his name was on the order."

I nod slowly. "Of course. I should have put my name on the order I guess, but I was trying to keep things low-key." I lick my lips. "Sorry to see me?"

Before she can answer, a little voice speaks up beside me. "Finished, Mummy."

Delaney gives one of those breathtaking special smiles to the girl. "Good girl. Let me wipe your face."

She pulls out a napkin and cleans the smears of sauce from around the girl's lips.

"Your daughter?"

She glances at me. "Amelia, this is Joshua."

"Call me Josh." I extend a hand to Amelia and she gives me the sweetest smile before sliding her small hand into mine. Giving it a shake, I smile right back.

"Hi, Josh."

I know I shouldn't feel it, but jealousy wells in me. Delaney came back to New Zealand and had a kid. Is she married? Who is he? "Hello, Amelia."

She lets out a dramatic sigh. "No one calls me Amelia. My name's Melly."

I smile. "Well, I think I'll stick with Amelia. It's a very pretty name."

"Can I get another coffee, Delaney?" Damon says.

I bristle. I don't know why he bugs me. Maybe it's the way he looks at her.

"Sure thing. I'll check where that food's got to."

She turns back toward the kitchen. I've spent six years with this image in my head of her, but Delaney now just blows all that out of the water. I shoot a glance down the counter at Damon. He's got his eyes on her ass, and I clamp my lips together at the sight.

I have no right to judge him. But I'm going to.

Unless ...

My gaze drops to her left hand. It takes a moment to get a decent look, but there's no ring on her finger. That tells me all I need to know.

Unless she doesn't wear a wedding ring.

Or she's not married but she lives with Amelia's dad.

Or ...

Fuck. I'm not that horny nineteen-year-old pursuing her from the moment I laid eyes on her. Am I? Maybe I'm just the twenty-five-year-old version. Which, given my behaviour right now, isn't really all that different.

"Josh. Do you like burgers?" Amelia asks.

I grin. "I sure do. I've got two coming."

"Two?" Her dark eyes are so wide. "I can't eat anything more and I had one."

"Burgers for you." Delaney slides my plate in front of me. "And mac and cheese for you."

She takes Damon his plate and turns. "I'll just get the fries and your thickshake."

"Thank you."

I don't know what's going on in that head of hers, but the small, sad smile she gives me does funny things to my stomach.

This wasn't supposed to happen. And I can't act like some immature boy in front of her. For years I thought about the day when I'd finally find her, but I didn't expect things to be so, so easy between us. But then again, she's always been good at putting people at ease.

"Here you go. Enjoy your meal." She places the fries and shake in front of me and turns to go to the coffee machine.

I want to eat slowly so that I can spend more time, but my stomach grumbles again and reminds me why I'm here. Besides, at least I know where she is. This isn't finished.

"Do you think I can eat all this, Amelia?"

She shrugs.

"You'll have to save the answer to that for another day, because it's time for us to go home," Delaney says, as she hands Damon his coffee.

No.

"Noooooo." Amelia makes me smile.

"You're lucky you had dinner here, miss."

"But I want to know if Josh can eat all that food."

Delancy leans over. "I'll tell you what. Pania's coming out here to take over until closing. How about I ask her to keep an eye on things?"

Amelia nods.

"Before you disappear." I swallow despite the huge lump in my throat. "Can I see you again?"

"You know where I am."

I nod. "Guess I do. Can I get your number?"

She hesitates. "I'm not sure I want to do that yet."

Yet. She said yet.

"Hey, dude. Leave her alone. What makes you think you can just ask her for her number like that?" Damon speaks up, and I turn my head to look at him.

"Six years of waiting to catch up with her."

I don't miss Delaney's gasp. I'm not giving this guy a minute of my time. I meet Delaney's gaze. "Okay, then. You know I'm coming back. We need to talk."

Her demeanour shifts, and she seems to withdraw into herself. "I know we do."

Amelia waves at me. "Bye, Josh."

I smile at the miniature Delaney as she jumps down and ducks around the counter. She's so much like her mother.

Delaney's a mother.

In my head, she's always been frozen in time. I guess I never thought of how her life might have changed in the past few years. At least she fulfilled her dream of becoming a chef, if her business is anything to go by. I'm happy for her.

But seeing her hasn't quenched the thirst I had for knowledge.

I want more.

And as Amelia disappears into the kitchen with her mother, I smile at the realisation that she didn't wave goodbye to the guy down the counter.

She only waved goodbye to me.

———

AFTER EATING MY MEAL, my stomach is finally satisfied, and I head back out toward the car.

I know he's behind me. I can feel eyes burning a hole in my back.

When I reach the car, I turn. Damon's standing right behind me.

"Sorry. Did you want something?" I ask.

"Delaney's not that kind of woman."

I raise my eyebrows. "How do you know what type of woman she is?"

"Someone who's not interested in some fancy pants actor swanning into town."

Smacking my lips together, I take a breath. There's no point getting upset about a guy who's pissing around a woman who's clearly not interested. Amelia didn't even acknowledge him.

"Not that it's any of your business, but we have history. So, I'd appreciate you dropping the guard-dog thing because she's not yours either."

He recoils, and I know I've hit a nerve. I'd bet anything his next step is to run to Delaney to tell her what he's done. That's what guys like him do.

He turns and walks away, and I open the car door and step in. For a moment, I close my eyes, picturing her behind the counter. She still has that curve to her lips, and the smile in her eyes that always made me feel like I was the only man on the planet. That look was for me.

Even six years later, she shared it.

And it was all mine.

CHAPTER TEN

DELANEY

FROM THE MOMENT I heard Josh's voice, I knew I was screwed.

How else would I have greeted him? The last thing I wanted was a scene in my own diner.

So, I treated him like I would have anyone else I know. I teased, but tried to keep things business-like.

But I'm still shaking like a leaf by the time I get back into the kitchen. Melly holds my hand as we walk through, and I find Pania by the back door, waiting.

"I heard you-know-who was out there." She laughs when I shoot her a death glare. "You okay?"

I nod. "I have no idea how, but I think I dealt with it alright."

She smiles. "You don't look alright. Go home and have a drink after the munchkin is in bed."

"I think he knows." My voice is barely more than a whisper, but I don't want anyone else to find out.

"What? How?"

I shrug. "He said we need to talk."

"Maybe he just wants to compliment you on your delicious food."

I shake my head. "I doubt it. I mean, I know he liked the food, but his tone said there was more to it." Biting down on my bottom lip, I press Amelia to my side, covering the ear that's not stuck against me. "What if he does know? What if he tries to take her?"

Pania sighs. She places her hand on my arm as if to steady me. "Then, talk to him. Find out what he wants. If anyone can talk him into being reasonable, it's you."

"Mummy, can we go?" Melly's full of food and tired.

If she falls asleep now, it means I have lots of time to sit in the quiet and think at night. That's the opposite of what I want today.

We walk out the back. There's a small car park, and we live right across the road behind the diner.

My car's already parked up at home.

We cross, and as we reach the front gate, I let out a sigh at the sight of Damon walking toward me.

"Delaney."

I turn to Amelia. "Why don't you go and wait for me at the front door? I'll be there in a minute."

She nods, and I watch as she walks up the path toward the house.

I turn to Damon. "Yes?"

"I just wanted you to know that I had a word with that guy who asked for your number."

My eyebrows rise right along with my temper. "You did what?"

"I told him you're not that kind of girl. Men like him, they roll into town and expect girls to just drop their knickers after knowing them for five minutes."

I resist the urge to roll my eyes. That's not Josh. At least, it wasn't when I knew him. He and I spent weeks just being friendly with some gentle flirting before we even went out on a date. And even then, he was the perfect gentleman, and in the end, it was me who initiated sex.

"You don't have to defend me. I've known him more than five minutes."

He hesitates. Damon's made it clear in the past that he's interested. I'm not. As confused as I am about Josh's arrival, I'm not about to let Damon think that goading Josh is the way to my heart. Not when Josh could so easily turn my life upside down. He has the money and the means to insert himself into our lives. I've always known that.

"Josh is an old boyfriend. We haven't seen each other in six years. He's never been anything but good to me." *Except for that one time that he broke my heart.*

Damon frowns. "I thought you'd appreciate me sticking up for you."

"He did nothing wrong." I've been avoiding this conversation for a long time. He's a customer, but he's got a nerve taking a shot at Josh when he's asked me out for himself. "Look, Damon. It's nice that you want to look out for me, but I get guys asking for my number all the time. I give them a smile and serve them more food. I'm not interested in dating. I have Amelia to look after."

He takes a step forward. Without thinking, I move back to maintain distance. His expression tightens.

"I always thought I'd persuade you otherwise."

"I'm flattered, but I don't need a minder trying to scare anyone else off."

"I see." He nods. "Bye, Delaney."

For a moment, I stand there, making sure he's moved away before turning back toward the house.

A long time ago, a teenage Josh got so deep into my heart, I never thought I'd shake him loose.

And seeing him today just clarified one thing for me.

I still haven't.

CHAPTER ELEVEN

JOSH

DELANEY'S still on my mind days later. I haven't been back to the diner yet, but it's hard not to spend every moment I can trying to reconnect on some level.

We have unfinished business.

In the meantime, I have work to get on with.

My early scenes are few and far between, but I sit in that house, overlooking the town and learn my lines. I'm glad Jessie's really the leading actor on this. She has way more scenes than I do. But my name will bring in the crowds.

I head to the set where my trailer awaits. Filming doesn't start for another few days, but I'll get settled in and meet the cast I haven't yet met.

It doesn't take long to find my co-star, and when I see her, I suck in a breath.

Jessie and I have history. And it's not romantic. She wanted it to be, but I wasn't interested in her in that way. And then Dee—or Delaney, consumed my thoughts to the point of obsession for a while.

We did the chemistry test back in the States. Apparently we sizzle on screen, which is about the opposite to what we do off.

"Are you excited about filming? I can't wait." She flicks her strawberry-blond hair over her shoulder.

"Yeah, should be good."

She frowns. "Don't sound so enthusiastic."

I laugh. "Sorry. This is my first romantic comedy and hopefully my only one."

"So, you're not up for making a sequel?" She runs her fingers through her hair, curling the ends around her fingers.

"I don't think these movies have sequels. Boy meets girl. They fall in love. Something bad happens to split them up. They get back together. Isn't that how these things go?"

She frowns. "Oh wow. I didn't think you were so cynical about love."

"I'm not. It's a trope. Although, in this case, it's a hilarious series of events that also leads to them not even kissing right until the end of the movie." I shrug.

"It's such a shame." She giggles, and I bristle. "I always thought we were destined to film a romance together."

"Anyone want coffee? I'm heading into town because Mitch wants a burger, so I thought I'd do a coffee run." A face I haven't seen before looks expectantly at me. I've never been so relieved to be interrupted.

"Yes, please." Jessie speaks up. "Soy latte, no sugar."

The young woman writes down her order and looks at me again.

I shake my head. "No thanks."

Her interruption gives me a chance to head off to my trailer and hide until I have to come out. Jessie's not a bad person, but I'm surprised after all this time she's still flirting with me. I know she's had a few high-profile romances, and it's been forever since we've spent any time together.

Doing this was a bad idea.

Only, I can't say that because Delaney's here.

I've had her on my mind since I saw her the other day. Truth is that in some ways, she's always been on my mind.

I have so many questions.

Six years ago, I thought the feelings I had for her were mutual. How could she have come back here and have a baby with someone else?

I loved her from the start.

Settling in, I read through my script again. There's just one scene I'm rehearsing today and it's not that long or with Jessie. I'm looking forward to getting back to the house and some time to myself.

I'm not sure how long I'm reading for, but the sudden knock on my trailer door makes me jump.

I open the door to the assistant who did the coffee run.

"Josh. This one's for you?" The puzzled expression on her face leaves me just as confused.

"I didn't order coffee."

"The woman in the diner said to give this to you."

I reach for the cup, and laugh when I see what's written on the side.

My favourite Canadian is Ryan Reynolds now.

Maybe talking to Delaney won't be so bad after all.

CHAPTER TWELVE

DELANEY

I SHOULDN'T HAVE DONE it.

But on Friday when making a dozen takeaway coffees, I had to make just one more. I never did know when to keep my mouth shut, or leave something alone.

He doesn't want me. He can't do.

Part of me expects him to walk in the door later in the afternoon. That same part is a little disappointed when he doesn't. It's so weird to have all these conflicting emotions when how much I was hurt still plagues me.

Thankfully this time, Melly doesn't sleep in on Sunday morning. I've got a party to cater with the food being picked up before midday. There are thirty sandwiches, thirty burgers, a bucket of fried chicken, and four large apple pies to make before then, and I'm doing it by myself.

I completed a lot of the preparation yesterday, and just have to cook the meat and put it all together this morning. Pania goes to church on a Sunday, so she's not available to help. But I can handle it as long as I don't have any interruptions.

Melly spreads out her colouring book and pencils on the

counter. There's a perfectly good table in the kitchen, but she loves the dark leather stool to sit on. I think it's because she likes climbing up.

"I'll make you breakfast and get started. You know where I am if you need me."

She nods.

"If you get bored, let me know. I'll turn the TV on."

In the kitchen, I pull everything out that I need, and drop some bread in the toaster for Melly. When it's done, I grate a little cheese over it and microwave it for a few seconds. She loves it.

I place it in front of her and head back out to the kitchen. Working quickly, I roll out the pastry, pull out the apple pie filling from the fridge and put them all together. Four pies. There's enough for a fifth, so I make another one to sell in the diner.

I like working by myself sometimes. I can get around the kitchen with ease and move as quickly as I can. It's all in the preparation.

When I'm done and everything's in the warmer, I just have the pies to come.

I walk out to check on Melly again, just as she drains her milkshake.

"Nearly done. Now we just have to wait for Dave to come and pick it all up."

A sharp tap on the door makes me look up.

Josh.

His eyes follow me as I walk to the door and unlock it.

"I saw Amelia through the window. I didn't think you were open on Sunday."

I shake my head. "We're not. I just came in because we're catering a party today and the food's being picked up soon."

He takes a step closer. "I've just been for a run. Any chance of a drink?"

I move back to let him in. "Only a cold one. I'm not turning the coffee machine on."

He nods. "That'd be great."

"Everything in the fridge is cold." *Oh my God, that is up there with all the dumb things I've ever said.*

Josh shoots me a little smile, but doesn't point out that what I've said is pretty obvious. Instead, he walks to the fridge and pulls out a bottle of water.

"Take it. The till's closed and I'm not opening it for one transaction."

He grins. "Thanks. I'll come back and pay you. Promise."

My chest tightens. Last time he made me a promise, he ripped my heart out instead.

I don't care, but I wish he'd leave with the water.

I hate how good he looks.

I hate that even wearing sweaty clothes, he looks better put together than most people I know.

I hate that perfect hair.

I hate those brown eyes that seem to pierce my soul.

And I hate that despite everything, I could so easily love him again.

Instead of leaving, he makes his way to the counter and sits on a barstool next to Melly. And right along my chest being tight, a lump forms like a golf ball in my throat looking at the two of them.

"Do you help your mother cook?" he asks.

Amelia nods. "Sometimes."

"I bet you do all the important jobs."

She looks at me with the dark eyes she shares with her father. "Mummy said I could have a piece of apple pie when it's cooked."

"Really?" Josh turns his gaze to me. "Any chance of a slice for me? If it's anything like the other food here, it'll be fantastic."

"Well, I ..." Truth is, there's plenty for him to have. I have a pie to spare, and while I'd planned on selling it, one slice won't break the bank.

"Two pieces of pie, Mummy."

I narrow my eyes as I look at the little traitor to the left of Josh.

The smug look on his face tells me he knows just how I feel about being betrayed. "I'll go and check on it."

Everything else is packed. I remove the burgers from the warmer and slide them into the insulated cases to keep them warm. I'll take the chicken out at the last minute.

The last thing is the apple pie.

Opening the oven, I slide out the tray. They're cooked to perfection and I draw a deep breath. Packing four of them, I leave the lids open on the boxes to let them breathe before taking the fifth back out the front.

Leaving the pie to rest for a moment while I grab crockery and cutlery, I then cut two slices of apple pie and place them on two plates with a dollop of ice cream.

Josh smiles as I place one in front of him.

"Yummy," Amelia says.

"It really looks yummy." Josh nods.

"It's still hot, so be careful."

"Yes, Mum," they both chorus.

The door opens. I smile at Dave as he walks toward me. "Good timing. I just took the apple pie out of the oven."

"Brilliant." He nods toward Josh and Amelia.

"I'll go and get it."

"Did Maggie pay you? She was sure she did, but ..."

I smile. "She paid me on Friday. We're all square."

Dave turns to Josh. "It's my granddaughter's birthday."

"Happy birthday to your granddaughter," Josh says.

"I'll pass that on. She's a fan of yours."

I suppress an eye roll as I turn back to the kitchen. Of course she's a fan. Everybody loves Josh.

Stop being so bitter, Delaney.

One by one, I take the boxes out to the front counter.

"Do you need help taking that out to the car?" Josh asks Dave.

"I think I'll be fine. Maybe if you could grab the door?"

"Sure thing." He flashes the smile that worked on me so long ago.

It seems genuine, and I'd like to think that it is, but I'm not so sure. He is an actor. And I'd thought I was special to him once only for him to stab me in the back.

Josh crosses the room with Dave, and holds the door open for him before heading back to the counter.

He sits on the stool and picks up his spoon. "Do you know what I like about your mother's apple pie, Amelia?"

She screws up her nose. "What?"

He runs his spoon across the crust. "Well, the crust is nice enough. It's not too tough, and it's perfectly cooked. And the apple's not mushy; it's soft and yet firm. But the best bit?"

I want to look away, but he fixes his intense gaze on me.

"The best bit is that it's sweet, but just a hint of sour. I love the sweet. Don't get me wrong. But the sour is what keeps me coming back. I love the way it gently bites and keeps you wanting more."

I suck in a breath, and he holds me in his sights for the longest time.

"I like the ice cream." Amelia beams.

Josh chuckles. "You know what? I do, too."

He ruffles her hair, and she laughs, and all it does is infuriate me.

His gaze shifts back to me, and I look away. I can't watch them together. It hurts way too much.

We could have had all of this. A life together. A family. Instead I dealt with all the blows alone while he grew rich and famous.

And now he's waltzed in here as if nothing's happened.

I want him to leave.

I want him to stay.

What will happen when he leaves town? Will he forget we ever existed?

I should intervene and make him go before Amelia gets too attached. But how can I do that with the way she watches him, entranced by the sight as he joins her eating pie and ice cream?

She's twisted around his little finger. I always knew she would be.

"Hey, Delaney," he says.

I meet his gaze. "What?"

"Are you sure your favourite Canadian is Ryan Reynolds?" he asks.

I shrug. "What can I say? *Deadpool* won me over."

"Huh." He smiles. "Guess I'll have to work at regaining my title."

"I'm not sure that's possible." I sigh. "Ryan is pretty damn hot."

His eyebrows rise.

"Very, *very* hot." I shoot him a smug smile, all the while knowing it won't be Ryan I'm thinking about tonight in bed. But he doesn't need to know that.

"I'll work really hard then."

Our gazes lock, and I'm just so lost. I want to hate him, but I always knew if I saw him again it'd be like this. It just always was like this between us. We had this way of slipping into easy conversation even if it seemed like we were sniping at each other.

"Mummy, I'm finished."

Melly's voice shakes me out of my stupor, and I focus on her. "Good girl. I'll get these plates washed and we'll get out of here."

"What are you doing for the rest of the day?" Josh asks.

"As little as possible."

"Want to come up to the house? Richard's got this pretty kick-ass entertainment system and about a billion movies. I'm sure there's something we can all watch."

It's tempting. But then I look at Melly and steel my resolve. How can I be sure I can trust him? If he hasn't worked it out already, then spending time with us will only bring that moment closer to him.

And I'm not ready for that.

"Thanks, but no. I've got so much to do at home before school and work tomorrow. I've already lost half a day working."

His expression falls, and I almost cave, but this isn't any good for either of us. Once the movie's finished, he'll move on and leave us behind. There's no point in getting too attached.

No matter what my heart tries to tell me.

"Another time?" he asks.

"Maybe. We'll have to see."

"I guess I should make my way back." He says it, but doesn't move, his hand lingering on the bench.

I look at the door. "You didn't run all the way from the house, did you?"

He shakes his head. "No, I parked about two miles away. Just wanted to get some exercise."

"Fair enough."

An uncomfortable silence falls over us. I don't know why he's hanging around or wanting to spend time with us, and I don't really want to ask him. I'm well aware that I'm sending him mixed signals, but when he's nearby, my brain cells up and run away leaving me to fumble my way through our encounters.

"I'll see you again soon. I'd really love to catch up properly with you," he says.

I nod. "Sure."

"Bye, Josh," Melly says.

"Goodbye, Amelia. Have a good day at school tomorrow."

She beams, and with a nod he turns and walks out. Part of me wants to run after him and tell him that we'll come with him, but instead I grip the counter and just watch.

"I'll just lock up and we'll get out of here," I say.

Melly climbs down off the stool.

I walk to the front of the store to lock the door and I spot it. Right outside on the ground is a plastic drink bottle.

"Damn it." I hate litter, and it's been left there deliberately from the way it's tucked against the building.

I push open the door, and pick up the bottle. It's full of water, which is still pretty cold.

"That's mine. Sorry. I forgot to grab it."

I turn at the sound of Josh's voice. He's running back toward me with a grin on his face. *What the hell?*

"You conned me out of a bottle of water when you had this?" I wave the bottle in the air.

"Maybe I just wanted to see you."

Damn it. He's using the dimples against me. Again. "You are the single most frustrating person I've ever met."

"That's a compliment, coming from you."

I hand him the bottle. "There you go."

When he takes the bottle, his fingers brush mine. And just like the first time that happened, there's electricity between us. It tears at the heart he shattered six years ago. I spent so long putting it back together.

Without another word, I turn, closing the door behind me and leaving him on the other side. The last time I cried over him was not long after Melly was born, and he's not going to make me cry again, even if my eyes prick with tears.

I lock the door and walk away. If I look back, I'm so scared I'll cave. I'm not sure what he wants, but it sure as hell isn't me.

It never was.

FORGET SELLING IT TOMORROW. I take the rest of the apple pie home to eat for myself. It's the least I can do after my day.

How does he make me feel like this after all this time?

If he didn't want me then, why is he hanging around now?

It's so confusing. Right when I thought my life was sorted out.

Melly climbs up onto the couch with me. She's had dinner and her bath, and she's in her pyjamas while I eat a big plate of pie and ice cream.

"Want some?" I ask.

She nods, and I pick up a spoonful and hold it to her mouth. She chews, and I wait until she's swallowed.

"Do you like Josh?"

Melly nods again, snuggling up to my side. "He's funny. And he likes pie, too."

"He sure does." I feed her another spoonful, stroking her hair with my free hand. "I love you, Amelia Carruthers."

She beams up at me, still chewing, but her arms wrap around my waist and when she's finished, she buries her face in the side of my chest.

I'm such a mess. I can't let him in, but I can't stop myself. And I need most of all to protect her.

I've been all tied up in knots and slipped into that familiar banter with him as if the years apart never happened. Nothing will ever come of it. I know that.

So why am I full of hope?

CHAPTER THIRTEEN

DELANEY

ON MONDAY, just after one, Jessie Lane walks into my diner.

I've never forgotten the way she sneered at me when Josh and I were dating. He had three close friends back then. Reece was always with some girl or other, and I never got to meet him. Clarke was a sweetheart, more interested in Reece than me or Jessie.

And Jessie was the one who made heart eyes at Josh whenever we saw her, completely ignoring me. Josh just never seemed to see her in that way, which left me a little surprised when I heard he was making this type of movie with her. It's an odd move, unless they are actually seeing each other.

The thought of that leaves me frustrated and angry.

And it's clear she has no idea just what she's walked into as I step out from behind the counter and walk over to her booth.

"You." The word is so filled with hatred that it even takes me by surprise.

"Jessie, isn't it?" I can be bitchy too.

"You know it is."

I shrug. "I can't keep track of every extra they hire for these films."

Her eyes narrow. "I'm the star of the movie."

"I thought Josh was. Did you want something?"

She draws in a breath and raises her nose in the air. "I want a Caesar salad. No cheese, no croutons, no anchovies. I don't want any oil in it."

"Should I just get you a lettuce? It might be easier."

Her scowl makes me clamp my lips together to stop myself from laughing.

I nod. "Got it. One Caesar salad missing all the flavour."

I turn and head toward the kitchen. Trina stares at me as I walk past her, and Pania's right inside the kitchen door, snickering.

"What was that?" she asks.

"What?"

"Jo just came in here and dragged me out the door. You're the one who's so big on customer service."

I laugh. "She's not a customer. She's a parasite who should have detached a long time ago." Fluttering my eyelashes, I clasp my hands together. "Oh, Josh, you're so big and strong, and I want you to be my boyfriend even though you're clearly not interested in me."

Pania chuckles. "Like that, is she?"

"I met her in LA. She instantly disliked me because Josh liked me. And she made her feelings really obvious. I'm not about to kiss her arse when she's in *my* house."

She grasps my arm. "This is why we get along so well."

"Anyway, she wants a salad without any ingredient that might actually give it some taste. So, I'd best get onto that."

She just shakes her head, but I go to the fridge and take out all the ingredients, snapping on a pair of disposable gloves after I've placed them on the bench.

I grab a bowl, pick up some of the romaine lettuce and drop it in.

As I add the ingredients she does want, I'm cast back to an earlier time.

"Jessie doesn't like me."

Josh runs his fingers down my arms. "I don't care what Jessie thinks. You're the one I want, Dee."

My breathing grows ragged just at the heated look in his eyes. I've done the thing I vowed not to do on this trip. Fall in love.

"I'm so crazy about my Australian barista."

I laugh. "I'm surprised you are. I've been told I never stop talking."

"Maybe I like to listen."

I splay my hand on his stomach as he leans over. When he kisses me, Jessie's irritation is forgotten. She's just not important.

Time disappears, and our hearts are in sync.

He growls when I palm his cock through his jeans. "I thought you didn't want this."

"I changed my mind. My prerogative."

I'm not sure if it's fair on either of us, but I've never wanted anyone like this before.

"Delaney."

I look up to see Pania staring at me. For a moment, I'm a bit lost, and then I look down into the bowl and laugh.

"Whoops. Got a bit distracted. Her salad's tossed."

"Give it to one of the others to take out."

I shake my head. "Oh, no. This one's mine."

Tipping the salad into a serving bowl, I strip off my gloves and pick up a set of cutlery. It takes everything to muster a smile, but I do it because I'm not about to show any weakness in front of this woman.

I walk to her table, place the bowl in front of her, and lay the knife and fork, wrapped up in a napkin beside the bowl.

She looks closely at the salad. "Is that it?"

"I removed all the things you didn't want. That's what's left." I smile sweetly. "How about a drink to go with that?"

Pania's going to have to keep me away from the rat poison.

"A Coke would be nice."

"Is that Coke, Diet Coke, Coke Zero, or Coke No Sugar?"

She glares at me. "Just a Coke."

"Righto."

Turning on my heel, I take a Coke from the fridge, drop some ice into a tall glass and pour the drink.

Dropping it off at the table, I look at Jessie. Her expression is still all screwed up, and she's forking the lettuce one piece at a time.

Deep down, I actually feel sorry for her.

She seems miserable.

I go back to the counter and retrieve a bottle of salad dressing.

Without saying a word, I deliver it to her table and walk away.

I'm not sure if she uses it, but life's too short to not eat dressing on a salad.

GEORGE WALKS in a little after two.

Jessie's long gone, and I'm in a much better mood. But the expectant way he looks at me tells me that there's something coming.

"Hi, George."

He smiles. "Delaney, big favour."

I let out a sigh. "Is that a question or a demand?"

His eyebrows shoot up. "Can I beg?"

"If you really want to, but maybe you should just tell me what this is about."

He claps his hands together. "Well, we have a little problem. And by little, I mean really big one, and I'm hoping that you can help me?"

"It depends on what it is."

He sighs. "I screwed up and I need dinner for an evening shoot on Friday. Your food went down so well, and I thought maybe we could try some Kiwi delicacies."

"It's awfully short notice."

Nodding, he holds his palms up. "It's totally my fault. I had it in my calendar for the wrong date, and I thought I had two more weeks."

We could do it, especially if they pay as well as they did last time.

"How about you email me the details and I'll take a look? What kind of Kiwi delicacies do you want? You know we don't eat actual Kiwis, right?"

His tense expression disappears when he laughs. "I did know that. And whatever you feel is a good fit. As long as we have gluten-free, vegetarian, and vegan options."

"Sure. We could do a good old-fashioned barbecue or something similar. Plenty of meat, but different salad options. That would be reasonably simple to do in bulk. I'd have to order the meat in though, so the sooner you can get me those details, the better."

His relief is obvious as he lets out a long, loud breath. "Thank you. You're a legend."

"Don't thank me yet."

He smiles. "You're still the best. Thanks for even trying to help me."

"If I can't get enough meat, you can help me make sandwiches and salad."

He laughs.

He thinks I'm kidding.

When I don't laugh too, his laughter comes to an abrupt stop and his face drops.

"Get that email to me ASAP and I won't need your help in the kitchen."

His smile's still tight as he leaves, and I blow out a breath. What I should be doing is staying clear of anything to do with that production, but at the same time, it's all money in my pocket.

And with things as tight as they are, it's hard to argue with that.

* * *

AFTER THE DINER'S closed for the night, Pania makes her way to my house.

George got his email to me right before five, but if we put our heads together, I'm sure we can get something together for Friday.

"What have we got?" she asks.

"He's sent me the numbers. It's not as big as the other day that we did, but they'll be working into the night, so they'll need something to keep them going."

She looks over my shoulder. "Where are they filming?"

I look at the email. "Trevor Jenkins' land by the lake."

"Why don't we do a *hangi*? If we can get permission from Trevor, then Wiremu can dig a pit the night before and we can get it started in the morning, put the food down early afternoon, and then we just need to pull it out at dinner time."

I nod. "It fits with George's requirements. Make some different green salads, potato salad—maybe even do a spit roast because you know that there'll be people who aren't keen on *hangi*."

"That's a really good idea. We could do chicken, beef, lamb, pork, potatoes, kumara, and pumpkin. And as an alternative, pig on a spit and maybe a couple of rotisserie chickens."

I type the ideas into a spreadsheet to do the calculation on how much we'll need. "I'm really liking this. It's good money, and also not too much effort."

"Just put the food in to cook and leave it for a few hours."

"While we make all the other bits and pieces to go with it."

She smiles. "This is why we make such a good team, Delaney."

"We sure do. And your cousin. Do you think he would help us?"

Pania nods. "He's the one who knows all about how to prepare a *hangi*. I'll talk to him, and I'm sure he'd do it for a few dollars."

I grin. He's been staying with her these past few weeks while he works out what to do with his life. Young and keen to work, I'm sure he'll be glad for the work, even if it is just for a day. "Whatever works. We'll need everyone onboard for it, but I'm sure Trina and Jo will love to hang out on the film set."

"We could light a bonfire on that tiny bit of beach he has. We don't need a permit this time of year. It'd be nice to have an outdoor meal."

Forget it being a job. It's beginning to sound like a nice night out with my friends.

Will Josh be there?

I'm jolted out of my thoughts by Pania's hand landing on mine. "You know Josh will be there, right?"

I laugh. "I literally just had that thought."

"Maybe you should screw him and get it out of your system."

Shaking my head, I save my spreadsheet to look at later and close the laptop. "I'm not sure I could ever do that."

"What? Screw him, or get him out of your system?"

I shrug, but the reality is that Josh will never be out of my system.

I've known that the whole time.

CHAPTER FOURTEEN

DELANEY

AT LEAST GEORGE has given us more time for this meal. And Pania's idea has made the evening a lot easier.

My mouth waters as the food is taken out of the ground. Pania and Wiremu make a show of it as there are a lot of people here who haven't had *hangi* before.

I can already taste the smoky-flavoured food.

"That smells so good." Melly squeezes my hand. Against my better judgment, she's here because I don't have a babysitter. Keeping her away from Josh is proving to be difficult. Not that I've seen any sign of him. He's filming, but no doubt will be here at some point to eat.

"We'll have some very soon." There's a ton of food, and there'll be leftovers too, but they're filming into the night so I'm sure it'll be all gone by the morning.

Once the cast and crew have eaten, I grab two paper plates and get a little bit of everything for Melly and me before we sit down on the stone beach by the fire.

"This was such a good idea," Pania says.

"Really good. At least it's not too cold tonight too. It's like the weather knew what we were up to."

I sense the moment Josh and Jessie arrive for their dinner. The chatter behind us increases and people greet them as they walk to the tables.

My stomach churns seeing them walking together, but it's not like they're holding hands or anything.

I'm not even sure if Josh sees me as he sits with some of the crew, talking with them while they dig into the food.

Melly cleans her plate and then leans back. "I'm so full."

I laugh. "It was good then?"

"It was so yummy."

I finish my food and get up, then walk to the nearest bin and throw the plates in. Josh catches my eye as I turn and the look he gives me is so intense, I shiver.

Dropping my gaze, I head back to my seat.

"Come for a walk, Amelia?" Trina says.

Melly looks at me, and I nod. "Go on."

"We won't go far."

"It's okay." I give Melly a kiss, and she skips away with Trina, hand in hand.

"Delaney."

I swallow hard as Josh walks toward me. There's that arrogant swagger in his step that wasn't there when I first met him, and I hate it, but I love it too. He exudes confidence he didn't have six years ago.

"Hey," I reply. "Josh, this is Pania. Pania, Josh."

"Hi." My traitorous best friend shoots him a flirtatious wave before standing. "I think I might go and join the others."

I narrow my eyes. "Fine."

She disappears down the beach as Josh sits on the log beside me. "That dinner was amazing."

"I'm glad to hear it. I was worried that it wouldn't fit everyone's tastes, but I didn't have to."

He leans back a little—enough that in the firelight, I can see the golden flecks in his irises. They're the same as Melly's, and cause my heart to skip a beat.

"It was great. I liked how you did the spit roast too as I can see how *hangi* might be an acquired taste." The way he pronounces it makes me smile, and of course he doesn't miss a thing. "Did I say something funny?"

I shake my head. "It's not what you said. It's the way you said it."

He grins. "I seem to remember you teasing me about that once before."

That's a punch to the gut. I remember that too, but it was when we would laugh and joke with each other. Before the night he broke my heart.

"Some things don't change."

He seems to study my expression. "And some things do. A lot. What happened to you, Delaney? What happened to Dee? She was so carefree and just having fun. You're still the same deep down, I can tell by the way you give me shit, but something happened."

I drop my gaze. "Life happened."

He nods toward Melly. She's playing on the beach with Trina and Jo. There'll be no problems getting her to sleep tonight—she hasn't stopped since we got here. The fresh air and exercise will knock her out. "She looks just like you."

This conversation is getting a little too close to home.

"That's what people tell me. I should probably get her home to bed."

I stand, but Josh grabs my hand. "I looked for you. As hard as I could. I didn't get very far because I didn't know Dee was Delaney."

Tugging my hand from his, I take a moment. "I was going through a phase."

He nods. "I guessed as much. I always wished you were with me when I got my big break. That role changed my life." His brows knit. "Sometimes, I wish we could go back."

Anger ripples through me. "Stop it. I fell for your lines last time, and I'm not falling for them again."

"What are you talking about?" The gold flecks seem to disappear. It's stupid but I miss them the instant they're gone.

"Just forget it, Josh." I turn and walk away. Melly sees me and runs, her face lit up with so much joy it makes me want to cry. God, how I love this kid. Nothing and no one is going to take her from me. I'll fight until my last breath if I have to.

I'm not telling Josh the truth. Not when he can't give me the same courtesy.

She leaps into my arms, and I laugh with her.

"We're going home now, baby."

"Do we have to?" She leans her head on my shoulder, and her body flops—ready for sleep.

"It's time."

"Here comes Josh," she whispers.

I turn. Josh is approaching, his gaze fixed on Melly. His brows are knitted, like he's focusing on something.

"Come on. Time to go."

Setting off at a brisk pace, I manoeuvre around the bonfire and head toward the car park. I'm grateful that for once I'm not cleaning up because I can just get out of here.

When we reach the car, I buckle Melly into her seat.

Josh isn't far behind me, and I climb into the driver's seat and start the engine.

"Delaney, we need to talk," he calls.

"I've got to get home. Talk to you later." I drive off, leaving him behind. It's not until I'm at the end of the road that I realise just how much I'm shaking.

He can't have worked it out. Can he?

CHAPTER FIFTEEN

JOSH

WHAT THE HELL WAS THAT?

It was a moment, a fleeting moment when I looked into that little girl's eyes and saw myself. Would Delaney keep something like that from me?

Maybe I saw things in the firelight that weren't there.

"Josh."

I sigh at the sound of Jessie's voice. "What?"

"Is everything okay?"

There's an emotion in her eyes that I can't quite place. I'm used to her looking at me like a piece of meat, but there's some actual feeling behind that look.

"Yeah, it's fine."

"She's not interested."

I narrow my eyes. "What would you know?"

"If she was, you wouldn't be chasing after her. She's not worth it. She'll only hurt you again."

"You don't know anything about us." Turning, I walk back toward the lake.

She runs after me, grabbing my arm. "I know enough to know she broke you when she ran out on you the first time. I'm not sure what hold she has over you, but—"

I shake her off. "There is no hold. You have no idea what you're talking about."

"Yeah, I do. You cut all of us off except for Reece. We were friends, Josh, and you just threw it away because that bitch decided she didn't want you anymore."

Coming to a complete stop, I turn to look at her. "Don't you ever call her that again."

She flaps her arms. "And now you're defending her. Do you know who's always been there for you? Me. I thought maybe you'd get over her last time and see what we could have, but instead you mooned around and then ignored me." Tears well in her eyes. "I thought this was my chance for *us*."

"I'm sorry if you had that impression, Jessie. I only ever wanted your friendship. Nothing else."

She won't look at me now, and I do feel sorry for her. But not enough to give her what she wants.

"I thought ..." She sniffs.

"If anything was going to happen between us, it would have happened a long time ago," I say as gently as I can. "Delancy and I have a connection that I can't explain. We did back then, and ..." I sigh. "It's still there. For me, anyway. And I'm almost certain it's there for her too."

Jessie sucks on her bottom lip, still not meeting my eyes and looking like she wants to cry. "So, there's no chance?"

"No. I'm sorry, but no."

The bright production lights shine behind us, and all I can see now are the tears falling on Jessie's face.

"Jessie, I ..." I stop myself before I inadvertently give her hope.

She wipes her cheeks with the palms of her hands, smearing her makeup. And then she runs back toward where we've been filming, and all I can do is watch her leave.

I feel like shit, but at the same time I'm not sure what else I'm supposed to do.

I looked forward to coming to New Zealand. But I never expected to find Delaney and still feel that pull toward her.

And Amelia. How did I never see that before? I've sat in that diner right beside her, and all I saw was her mother.

Could she really be mine?

CHAPTER SIXTEEN

JOSH

THERE'S no filming for me the following day, and I'm glad of it as I nurse my hangover from the night before.

I spent all night working out the math of Amelia being mine, which is ridiculous because I have no idea exactly how old she is. Delaney needs to tell me the truth.

Pania's standing at the counter when I walk into the diner. And that little cockroach, Damon, sits on a stool in front of her. Seriously, the guy must spend all his time here.

"Hey, Pania. I was looking for Delaney."

She straightens up. "She's not here. It's my Saturday."

I nod. "Can I get her address?"

"No."

Pania stares me down, and I give in and blink first.

"Please? I need to talk to her."

"Then you come back when she's here. I'm not giving you her address." She narrows her eyes.

"If she hasn't given you her number or address, she's not going to do it now." Damon actually has the nerve to smirk at me.

"You know you can butt out any time you like. This isn't really any of your business."

He stands up, which is laughable because I have a good foot and a half over him. "I'm trying to look after my friend."

It's my turn to smirk. "No, you're just trying to piss out your territory and it's a pretty small circle from where I'm standing."

"Ahem."

We both turn to look at Pania.

"Both of you need to leave because I am not having this place turn into Testosterone City." She looks at me, then at him.

"You can't kick me out," Damon says.

"Just watch me." She gives him what I can only describe as a death stare, and he visibly shrinks in front of her.

"Oh, you're good." I grin.

Damon glares at me, and all I do is shrug.

"Delaney's not going to waste her time with you. She's too good for that," he says.

Pania rolls her eyes. "Don't you start that shit again. Get out of here." She turns to me. "You too."

"Yes, ma'am."

Her lips twitch, but she doesn't budge an inch. "Don't you pile on the charm, actor boy. Get out of here."

"I will. Could you please let Delaney know I'm looking for her?"

She nods. "Of course."

I make the first move, but I know Damon's right behind me. He grumbles all the way out. Something about arrogant Americans.

Reaching the door, I hold it open. "After you."

He glares at me while I wave him through, but thankfully he heads in a different direction to where my car's parked.

I let out a sigh, walking down the street toward the car.

"Josh Carter."

It's an older voice that says my name, and I turn to see a woman approaching me.

She smiles. "I thought that was you. I'm Maureen Randell."

I nod. "It's nice to meet you." For a moment, I hesitate, but it's not going to hurt to ask. "Can I ask you something? Do you know where Delaney lives?"

Her smile grows. "I do. But I'd really like a favour from you first."

One of my eyebrows inches up. "What kind of favour?"

"My niece Hannah. She loves Reece Evans, and I understand you're friends with him."

I chuckle. "I am. He's one of my best friends."

"I was wondering if you could get him to send her a message? Just to say hello. She would love that."

"Sure thing." I pull my phone out of my pocket. "I'll call him now."

Her eyes widen. "Really?"

"It's no problem."

I dial Reece and smile when he answers, his southern drawl coming down the line. "Josh. What's up? It's two in the morning."

"Where are you?"

"London."

I laugh. "Sorry, I thought you were in New York."

"Filming shifted a few days ago."

"Thanks for answering. I really need a favour."

He sighs. "What is it now? Who do I have to kill?"

I laugh again. We've been tight for seven years, and he's one of the few people who I know really has my back. That's why I know he'll do this for me.

"If I give you a phone number, can you call this woman and just say hello to her? In exchange her aunt is giving me Dee's address."

He gasps. "*Dee?* You found her?" Of all my friends, Reece was the one who never met Delaney when we were together. He has the attention span of a goldfish when it comes to women, and at nineteen he was never around because he was either auditioning or getting laid.

"I did, and I've spoken to her, but now I need to go visit."

"That sounds stalkerish."

"Dude."

He sighs. "Fine. Just text me the number and I'll do it right away. I'll chat to her for a bit and then try and get back to sleep. You're lucky I'm still feeling like shit from the jetlag and not working in the morning."

"Thanks. I really appreciate it."

"You owe me now, Joshua. I want nudes if this woman is everything you made her out to be."

"Not a chance. Please just make this call."

"Have I ever let you down?"

I pause, but can't find anything in my memory to suggest he has. "No. Which is why I looove you."

"Oh, stop it and go get your woman."

Mrs Randell's face is lit up with anticipation as I hang up the call. "If you give me her number, I'll text it to Reece and he'll call her now."

She grins. "Oh, thank you. Delaney lives in the next street over, directly behind the diner. I'm not sure of the number, but the street is Tui Street and hers is the last house."

She hands over her phone with the number showing, and I tap out a text to Reece.

"All done. I'm sure she'll let you know when it's happened."

"I'm sure she will. Thank you so, so much."

"Thank *you*."

I jump back into the car, bring up the town on Google Maps and trace a path around the block to what looks like Delaney's place. I guess I'll know it when I see it. Maybe.

It's a small house, with brick cladding, and although the lawn looks freshly mown, the garden's a little overgrown. Delaney's blue Suzuki Swift sits in the driveway.

That's the place.

I pull up outside and just look at the house. What if Amelia is my daughter? What happens to us then? Is there a chance we could be a family, or am I reading way too much into the easy interactions I've had with Delaney? And how do I protect them both from the media attention they'd get just by being associated with me?

I've got to try.

Jumping out of the car, I head to the front door and before I can second-guess myself, I knock.

"Just a minute." Her voice comes from inside.

The door opens.

I catch my breath.

She's dressed in a pair of figure-hugging jeans, and a tight white shirt. *Holy shit*. It's like she's been poured into her clothing, and she looks incredible.

"Josh?"

I do jazz hands. "That's me."

"How did you get my address?" She leans against the door, the side of her face pressed against the edge like it's giving her comfort.

"Well, I went to the diner, but no one would tell me."

She nods. "I'd expect that."

"Your friend Damon was there. Oh, he doesn't like me. Pania threw us both out."

At that, she straightens up and draws a deep breath. "Ignore him. I already told him to leave you alone."

"You did?"

"He seems to think if he acts like some kind of white knight that I'll fall into his arms. But real life doesn't work that way."

I can't help my smile. "It did once."

"You were different." She sucks in a big breath. "Anyway. How did you find my place?"

"Out in the street, I ran into a friend of yours. Mrs Randell."

She smiles and nods. "She's a regular coffee customer."

"Yes, and she's got a niece who's apparently a huge fan of Reece Evans. Remember Reece, the friend you never met?"

"Oh, I know all about Reece." She grins, and I'm almost hurt by her reaction. Reece has that effect on women.

"Anyway, he's going to call her, and in return—"

"She told you where to find me."

I shrug. "I'd have done almost anything to get your address. If it wasn't her, I'd have sweet-talked someone else."

"Could have looked in the white pages. My name's on the website you ordered your burger through."

I hesitate. Not once did that even cross my mind. "I'm a dumbass."

"Well, yeah, but you did find me. So maybe not so much of a dumbass after all." She says *dumbass* with an exaggerated American accent.

"Gonna let me in?"

"Depends on what you want."

"I think you know."

She clamps her lips together, and gives me a small nod, standing aside to let me through.

The first thing I lay eyes on is the fridge, covered in Amelia's artwork. There are so many pictures of two stick people, one smaller than the other, hand in hand. All she seems to have had is her mother.

"Do you want a coffee?" Delaney asks. "I was just making one."

"Sounds great."

"Amelia's not here. She's having a sleepover with a friend tonight and I've already dropped her off."

I nod. "It's probably good that she's not."

Delaney hesitates, then nods too. "Go through to the living room and I'll bring you a coffee in a minute."

She points at a door, and I walk through to a cosy room which again is adorned with Amelia's artwork. These must be the pictures that are special to her because there's a wall full of framed pictures, with photos of the two of them in between.

If my instincts are right, I missed all this, and I swallow hard just thinking about it.

"How do you take it?" she calls. "Sorry, I can't make you a latte. It's instant."

"White, one sugar."

It's a moment later that she walks through, coming to a stop beside me.

"There are some beautiful photos here of the two of you." I can't stop looking. Amelia laughing with her mother, hugging her, kissing her—it's all there.

"This is our memory wall. Every so often, Amelia has a drawing that she's worked extra hard on, and we hang it up."

"You need a bigger wall." I smile as she hands me a mug.

"One day." She turns and sits on the sofa. I join her, looking around the rest of the room. Amelia's everywhere, from the toy pile in the corner, to the discarded pink jacket on one of the chairs.

I take a sip of coffee. "That hits the spot."

"Whoever thought. Josh Carter, Hollywood superstar, in my living room drinking instant coffee."

Shrugging, I smile. "Coffee is coffee. I've drunk far worse than this. I always did like the way you made it."

"This is pretty different to that old coffee machine I used to have to slap into submission." She laughs. "Having a decent machine that didn't need a kicking every day was one of my top priorities when I started the diner."

"Is it doing well? Your business, that is."

She nods. "We have a lot of local regulars, and pick up quite a bit of the tourist trade. It's not huge, but it's enough."

"I'm glad. Ever thought of extending your hours for visitors who want food in the evenings?" I shoot her a sly grin.

With a shake of her head, she seems to study her coffee. "When Pania and I moved to open the diner, we realised there's a way things are done around here. After five, the pub serves meals, and they don't like anyone treading on their toes. We're not staffed to run seven days either. It works."

"That's a shame."

"Small towns are very difficult to change. But I could never have afforded to set up somewhere larger. The costs were just too prohibitive. And we love it here."

I place the cup on the coaster that sits on the coffee table, suddenly unsure about how to approach this. She must surely know I'm going to ask.

There's no point in beating around the bush.

"Is she mine?"

Delaney tries so hard not to give anything away, but it only takes a moment before her expression crumples. She places her cup on the table, closes her eyes. "Yes."

"You kept her from me?" Pain sears my body. All it took was a glimpse in the firelight of that little girl's face and I knew. But there was still a part of me that thought there was no way Delaney would be capable of hiding her. Not when we'd had what I thought we did.

"Why?"

She buries her face in her hands and sobs. I'm right beside her with hot tears blurring my vision. Amelia is my blood. That sweet little girl who befriended me straight away is mine.

"We were over." She sniffs and raises her gaze. Her eyes are already red, and I'm torn between walking away and pulling her into my embrace to comfort her.

Instead, I cross my arms to stop myself from touching her.

"I don't even understand that, Delaney. We fell in love, and we had one magical night that I never wanted to end. And then you were gone. I tried to find you, but I didn't know what your real name was."

She wipes her cheeks with the palms of her hands. "You didn't want me. And I tried to tell you. I tried to get in touch when I found out, but your phone was disconnected and the letter I sent came back return to sender."

I swallow hard. She's right about that. When I got the part, I left behind the apartment and went home until filming started. I had no money until I got paid for the film, so disconnected everything, including the phone.

She had no real way of getting in touch with me. Not directly. But that still doesn't explain why she left.

"What do you mean I didn't want you?" I ask.

Delaney sniffs again, clamping her lips together like she's fighting more tears.

"I heard you." Her voice is so small, I nearly miss the words.

"What did you hear?"

She looks everywhere but at me, and tears continue to roll down her cheeks. "You were on the phone. And you were making plans with someone else. It hurt so much, Josh. You used me to make someone else jealous and then—"

"What the fuck are you talking about?" I take a deep breath, blowing it slowly out. "Sorry. You didn't deserve that. I've just been mystified for all these years about why you left, and now ..."

"You said you were going to ditch me. That I was history."

Understanding hits me like a ton of bricks. I should have told her that morning what that phone call was about. She must have walked in at the wrong time.

I pull out my phone. "I want you to see something."

She's quiet as I navigate to YouTube and pull up the clip I want.

"Come here." I grasp her arm and pull her around until she's cradled against me. She doesn't fight, and I wrap my arms around her, my chest to her back, and hold my phone in front of us.

"What are you doing?"

"You never saw any of my movies, right?"

She shakes her head.

"Not even my first one?"

She shakes her head again, and I press play on the clip. I'm an undercover cop in the movie, who's trying to find a way into a crime family. And I do it by making the daughter of the bad guy fall in love with me.

And when I struggle at that last hurdle, I use another woman to make her jealous.

Mission accomplished, she calls me.

"Don't worry about it. I'll ditch the bitch and come to you. You know it's always been you, baby."

Delaney stiffens in my arms, and I let the clip finish.

I laugh. "She's history."

I stop the clip.

"Was that what you heard that morning?"

She lets out a sob. I can't be angry with her. How on earth would I have reacted if the shoe was on the other foot? I had no idea that morning when Mac called that I was so close to landing the part. That all they wanted was for me to run some of the lines in character with one of the actors I'd be working with.

I'd already run through two scenes when I got to that part.

"Oh, baby." I turn her around in my arms and don't wait for her to say anything in response. Wrapping her tightly, I stroke her head while she cries on my shoulder. What else can I do? She hurt as much as I did.

"I screwed up." She sobs.

She pulls away. Her eyes are red-rimmed and all I want to do is make sure she never has to cry again. I was so in love with her six years ago, and seeing her again has woken up my heart.

I cup her face. Her eyes search mine, and there's no anger in me, only the sorrow over the life we could have had together.

"What do we do now?" she asks.

The day of that phone call was the day all my dreams came true. Except for one. The woman I wanted to share it all with disappeared. Delaney was my dream then, and I can't deny that I have feelings for her now.

Her lips twitch.

I lean in and claim her mouth, my lips caressing hers. She lets out a whimper, and it spurs me on as she opens up and my tongue meets hers for the first time in six years. This is what we both need, what we always needed. She's my one who got away, and I'm not making that mistake again.

But the discovery we both just made about what happened six years ago has made any union between us so fragile that any attempt to push her right now might make it all collapse.

I can't stop myself from kissing her, and the way she slides her arms around my waist tells me she's feeling the same way.

The strokes of her tongue are tentative, mine forceful, and she falls the rest of the way back into my arms with a moan that rolls down to my toes.

I close my eyes, not wanting this to end, and feeling like I'm righting a wrong that's gone on far too long.

When it does, I open my eyes and all I see is her. Her expression's a mix of confusion and need—that aching need I have to the bone.

"Josh," she whispers.

"Don't know about you, but I needed that." I press my forehead to hers. I should have done more. I should have chased her to the ends of the Earth to find out why she left.

"It was ... unexpected." She has the softest laugh, but at least she's not crying anymore. I don't ever want to make her cry again.

"You're a part of me, and it doesn't matter how long we've been apart, you burrowed into my heart a long time ago." I straighten up. "I've been wanting to do that since I first saw you again. The second time."

A smile breaks through the sadness just for a moment before her eyes cloud over. "You should hate me."

I shake my head. "I could never hate you. I'm pissed that you didn't stop to talk to me, or even confront me over it. And when you left, it killed me inside. We had something so special."

She drops her gaze, but I slide my index finger under her chin and raise her face until her eyes meet mine.

"But I also can't help the way I feel. I'll give you the time and space to think about how to do this, but I want to see Amelia and get to know her. With you."

She swallows hard. All this time we both went through so much unnecessary pain. Her feelings of betrayal. My feelings of abandonment.

We've already lost more time than we ever should have.

"All I wanted that morning was for whatever the producers

wanted to end so I could make breakfast and join you in bed. I hope you know that."

It's small, but she nods. "I do now. I feel so foolish."

"If the roles were reversed, I'd have been devastated to hear that. No wonder you didn't want anything to do with me."

"It hurt." Those two words are all she gets out before she tears up again.

"I swear I'll never hurt you again." The urge to kiss her is back, but I need to leave her to think over what's just happened and make a decision about our daughter.

She says nothing, but blinks a few times before giving me a gentle nod.

"I'll get going and give you some space." I pause. "But I want you to know that the ball is completely in your court. Whatever you decide, I'll go along with. You know our daughter better than I do."

I don't mean that to sound bitter, but Delaney flinches and I take a breath to stop myself saying something else equally stupid. "Delaney, I didn't mean anything bad by that. I'm trying."

She nods again. "I know."

I give her a tender kiss on the lips and stand up before I take it further. While I want nothing more than to drag her off to the bedroom and show her exactly how I feel, this isn't the way to handle the situation.

We can't use sex to avoid the conversations that are no doubt to come.

We need to take the time to decide our future together.

"Come and find me when you work out what we're doing. You know where I am."

I give her my number. She's been to the house, and I'll make sure she has access to the set.

I'm not afraid that she won't be able to contact me.

Not this time.

CHAPTER SEVENTEEN

DELANEY

WHEN I WAS A LITTLE GIRL, my mother used to take me to church every Sunday.

I haven't been since I moved to town. I'm usually so tired by the end of the week, and I love my sleep-ins. But after a night of tossing and turning with next to no sleep last night—I feel so lost.

I'm not sure if this is the right thing to do, but it can't hurt.

Pania gapes as I walk toward her pew and sit next to her. The service is about to start, and people are sitting quietly waiting.

"What are you doing here?" she whispers. "I was always sure you'd burst into flames if you stepped into a church."

"I'm not a churchgoer, but that hardly makes me the antichrist." I shrug. "I don't know. I guess I'm just looking for some guidance."

She laughs, and at least a dozen heads whip 'round to give us dirty looks.

"Are you okay?"

I let out a sigh. "Josh showed up yesterday. He knows."

"Oh my God. What are you going to do?"

"What can I do? He wants to spend time with her."

Pania nods. "I guess that's natural."

"He wants to spend time with me too."

She squeezes my forearm so hard that I cry out. Those same people who gave us dirty looks before do it again. *I give up.*

The minister steps up to the lectern.

His eyes go straight to me, and I take a seat before I'm chastened. Not that he would. Would he? I mean, I know he usually comes in on the days we have seafood chowder, and that hip flask in his pocket he uses as a little additive doesn't contain holy water.

The smile on his face is so awkward, and I guess it's because I've never come into his territory before. I give him a polite smile in return and he seems to straighten up.

"Good morning," he says.

That's the point where I tune out.

Now I've spoken to Pania about it, all I can think about is Josh's request. I can understand him wanting to spend time with Amelia. But me? I made a big mistake not confronting him that day.

With the arguments my parents had before my dad left echoing in my ears, I ran rather than confront him. And I've been running ever since. Maybe we settled in Glenderry, but it was partly because it was quiet and so far away from everything and everyone.

I never thought Josh would find me.

Love is patient. Love is kind ...

I look up at the broad wooden beams that make up the church roof and sigh. I've even managed to pick a week where all I feel is guilt from the text the minister's reading. I don't know what for. It's not like I've done anything wrong.

Melly's never had her father in her life all because I mistook that phone call for the real thing. Josh is right—it's not my fault, but knowing that doesn't make me feel any better.

Pania nudges my elbow. "Want to go out for a drink after this? Seeing as you don't have to rush home?"

I stare at her. "It's not even eleven in the morning."

"It won't kill you."

I nod. "Fine. Just one. As long as we can get something to eat too because I'm starving."

She smiles. "Of course."

"THIS WAS SUCH A GOOD IDEA." I cut into a slice of beef and fork a piece of roast potato, moaning as I take in the flavour.

"Told you. We should make a date for the Sunday roast more often. They start serving it from eleven." She picks up a potato with her fork. "You don't even have to come to church with me."

"I didn't mind this morning."

She laughs. "You weren't even paying attention. You've got Josh on the brain."

I sigh. "That's hardly surprising." Playing my bottom lip between my teeth, I study her for a moment. "He kissed me."

Pania puts her fork down. "Wait. What? You missed that bit."

"Apparently the things I heard him say about me? It was a misunderstanding." I wince. "They were lines from a movie. *The* movie."

Her mouth falls open. "Oh my God. You thought ..."

"The casting director wanted to hear him run through some of the lines. All this time. If I'd seen the damn movie, I would have known."

Pain crosses her features. She's the one who held me when I cried over him, who stood by me when every pregnancy test I bought was positive, and who gave me a home when I needed it. I wouldn't be where I am without my best friend.

"Oh, honey. I'm so sorry."

I shrug. "Josh was remarkably calm about the whole thing. But I think a big part of it is that he wants me back."

"He said that?"

Nodding, I pick up another potato. "He did. He's still an amazing kisser too. That tongue of his ..."

"I hate you." Pania laughs.

"It's true. I can't help it if it's true."

She grins, and I let out a long, slow breath. When I've finished here, I need to go and talk to him. Regardless of what happens between us, he's entitled to see his daughter.

The thought of them having a relationship warms my heart.

It's the second chance I never got with my father.

And no matter what, my daughter deserves that opportunity.

CHAPTER EIGHTEEN

DELANEY

MY HEART'S in my stomach all the way up that mountain. Seeing the house Josh has rented again just emphasises the massive gap between us. It puts my tiny rental to shame. This is the lifestyle he's used to now. We're worlds apart when we were once so similar.

He opens the door before I get to it.

"Where's Amelia?" he asks.

"She's still at her friend's place. I'll pick her up on the way home."

He shoots me a smile, but it's missing the magic it usually has. "I hope she had fun."

"Me too. I wanted to talk to you about her without her around."

He stiffens. The Adam's apple in his throat bobs as he swallows before licking his lips. "Come in."

I've never been inside this house before, and it's surprisingly sparse. I guess Richard doesn't store a lot of personal stuff here, but the room Josh leads me into just has a lounge suite and a television in it.

It's such a lonely house; in that respect, my tiny place puts it to shame.

I think of our wall, covered in photos and Melly's artwork. There's more space here than I'd know what to do with. And it's all bare.

"Come and sit down. Did you want a coffee?"

I shake my head. "No thanks. I won't be too long."

We sit on the couch together. His expression is filled with so much hope. "Did you think about me seeing her?"

I nod. "I've not thought of anything else. And I didn't want to keep you waiting because I know you're not in New Zealand for long." I'm not trying to hurt him, but the way hope gives way to a wounded look tells me I've hit a nerve.

"I'll be back, though. I can't stay away now."

I hold up my palm. "I'm not trying to start anything with you. The last thing I want to do is to piss off the one person who could take my daughter from me."

Josh's jaw drops. "I'd never do that to you."

Taking a deep breath to stop myself from tearing up, I nod. "Anyway, I'm happy for you to see Amelia. But I don't want to just tell her upfront that you're her father. She needs time to get to know you first."

He nods. "Agreed."

"No games, Josh. It's going to blow her mind when she finds out her father's some Hollywood star, and I don't want her to get any big ideas."

"I understand."

"I know you're busy, but if you could let me know when you have some free time, we can arrange something. Maybe you can come over for dinner."

His lips curl into a smile, and I can't look because he still makes my heart flutter. Every single time.

"I like the sound of that. I'll check my schedule, but I think I'm good on Saturday if that's okay."

"Send me a text to confirm. I'll be at home anyway and there's rugby on, so Melly will be in fine form."

His eyes meet mine. "She likes rugby?"

"Adores it. Doesn't really get the rules, but she likes yelling at the television."

Josh laughs. "Sounds like fun."

"Yeah, we'll see how you feel after eighty minutes of it." I grin.

"I'll be with my girls. That's all that matters to me."

I take a deep breath. "Well, gotta go and pick Melly up. But let me know. I'll cook a lamb roast or something."

"Now that sounds good." The look he gives me is so intense, I'm not sure I can move anymore because I'm just a puddle on the floor.

"Okay."

He walks with me to the front door. I step outside, and into the cool afternoon.

"Thanks for coming to see me. I promise I'll take it easy. The last thing I want to do is push you away," he says.

"I know you missed out on a lot of time with her. But maybe we can put some things to rights." I shrug. "See you later."

"You bet."

It's not until I'm halfway to get Amelia when what Josh said registers.

I'll be with my girls.

Except, I'm not his girl.

There is such a big part of me that wants to be. It's confusing. Only yesterday, I thought our prior relationship was built on a lie. And despite how hurt I was back then, I still found myself drawn to Josh.

Now I know the truth; there's nothing standing in my way except my fear.

I knew for years that I could have got his attention through the media. Melly and I could have had a life of luxury with what I could have sold my story for.

But her life would have been turned upside down along with mine.

Whatever happens, she comes first—then *and* now.

CHAPTER NINETEEN

JOSH

WE'RE FILMING SOLIDLY through the week. But there's a lot of waiting around in my trailer, and all I can think about is my upcoming visit with Delaney and Amelia. We'll be together as a family, even just for the evening.

This was the last thing I expected when I came here, but I couldn't be happier. If I could only persuade Delaney that I'm serious about both my girls, and that they are my girls, then I'll be a very happy man.

Midway through the week, I can't contain myself. I wanted to keep discovering Amelia to myself as the more people who know about things between us, the harder it will be to keep a lid on it. But I can trust Reece.

"Dude. I've been waiting for an update." He doesn't even say hello, and I laugh at the way he answers the phone. "Did you see her?"

I can't help but grin. I'm not sure if we've put the past behind us completely, but we're on the way. "I did."

"And ...?"

"It's still there. The magic, I mean. She's the woman I fell in love with, and I'm on the way there again."

"Why did she leave?"

I sigh. "It was a misunderstanding. But I'm hoping we can put it all behind us now. Especially when it turns out that ... we have a daughter."

"Wait. What?"

I'm grinning again, but that's what happens every time I think of Delaney and Amelia. "Delaney had a baby."

"Who's Delaney?"

"That's Dee's real name as it turns out. You should see her, Reece. She's gorgeous. Both of them are."

"You sound happy. And that makes me happy. I hope things work out." He blows out a breath. "I have to get going, but let me know what happens. I'm glad you found her."

"Me too. I still can't believe it. Talk to you soon?"

"Sure thing."

The call disconnects, and I'm left smiling to myself.

Saturday can't come fast enough.

BY THE TIME Saturday comes around, I'm anxious to see both of them.

I catch my breath when Amelia opens the door. She grins. "Josh."

"Hello, Amelia."

She grabs my hand and pulls me into the house and straight into the living room. *My heart.*

"Hey." Delaney walks into the living room. "I didn't hear you at the door."

"I did." Amelia beams. She's still holding my hand and it's giving me this tingly feeling I hope never goes away.

"I can see that. We talked about opening the door, didn't we?"

Delaney shoots her a pointed look, but the smile on her face takes the sting away.

"I saw it was Josh from the window."

Delaney meets my gaze. "She's been waiting all day for you once I told her you were coming to dinner."

"Really?" I squat beside her. "I'm honoured."

"We don't get a lot of visitors. Mostly Pania, and she drinks wine with Mummy."

Out of the mouths of babes.

I laugh. "Wine's good."

"Let's just end this conversation and move on." Delaney places her hands on Amelia's shoulders. "Dinner's nearly ready, and then the rugby will be on."

Amelia lets go of my hand and reaches for my face, pulling my gaze back to her. "The All Blacks are playing tonight, Josh."

"Are they? I've never watched rugby before."

Her small mouth forms an *o*. "It's my favourite."

"Wait until she does the haka for you."

While I haven't watched a game, I have seen a haka before. I grin at Amelia. "Really?"

She nods. "When they do it."

"I can't wait to see it." Straightening up, I look at Delaney. "Want some help with dinner?"

"No, it's almost all done. I'll just bring it in here to eat. I cooked roast lamb, so I hope you like it."

"Sounds great."

For a moment, I just watch as she leaves the room. I really need tonight to go well. The smell of the cooking food makes my mouth water, but all I care about is where we go from here.

Amelia grabs my hand and pulls me to the couch. "I was just watching Disney. Do you like Disney movies?"

I nod. "I've seen a few."

"My favourite is *Zootopia*. Mummy says we've seen it a million times."

"A million and one," Delaney calls from the kitchen.

Amelia giggles.

There's some cartoon playing on the television, but I barely pay attention as my girl climbs up beside me and watches it. She's what I look at. Her dark hair curls like Delaney's, and she has her mother's delicate features. But her eyes are all mine.

"Here we go." Delaney carries in two plates laden with food. "I'm not really one for making everyone sit at the table. We usually sit in here and eat dinner together."

"I don't want to disrupt your routine."

"You're not." She walks back to the kitchen and returns with her own plate. "Are you ready to change channels, Melly?"

"I'm not changed yet." Amelia pouts.

"You've got plenty of time."

"Changed?" I ask.

"She's got an All Blacks shirt she wears for every game. It's tradition."

"I love the All Blacks," Amelia says it so matter-of-factly.

"I got that." I laugh.

She returns to eating and again I find myself just watching her. Amelia abandons her fork and picks up each piece of potato, each floret of broccoli scooping them into her mouth. I shoot a glance at Delaney who just shakes her head and smiles.

"I should tell her off, but she's eating her vegetables and that's a win," Delaney says.

"I'm not much of a vegetable fan either." I sigh. "But I do what I have to do."

Delaney grins. "She takes after you in that regard, then."

After dinner, Amelia races to her room to change, and I'm left on the sofa with Delaney.

She's switched channels already, and the game build-up is on. But I'm not paying any attention to that either because there are so many distractions in this house. Those legs, that smile, the love in her eyes for *our* daughter.

I have pangs over never being a part of this.

Amelia comes running back in and tugs on my hand to pull me to my feet.

"Wait. What? What's going on?" I ask.

"It's the national anthem," Delaney says. "Melly takes it very seriously."

I smile. "Oh, well in that case ..."

Amelia squeezes my hand as I stand. Delaney stands beside me, her hand drifting near mine. I take it, and turn my head to look into her eyes.

I clamp my lips together as Amelia bellows out the song.

"*E Ihowa Atua. O ngā iwi mātou rā. Āta whakarangona. Me aroha noa.*"

"Melly, we don't have to yell." Delaney puts her finger to her lips.

But saying that has the opposite effect as Amelia takes a deep breath.

"*Kia hua ko te pai. Kia tau tō atawhai. Manaakitia mai.*"

She turns to me. "*Aotearoa.*"

I smile at her before turning to look at Delaney's bemused expression. And despite the little girl to my left now belting out the English words of the anthem, I can't take my eyes off her mother. She's so quiet in Amelia's wake, but she sings the words soft and low.

I'm already under her spell again, and she has no idea.

But her hand in mine leaves me thinking she's feeling the same way.

WATCHING the game is the most fun I've had in a long time.

But that's not because I'm watching the screen.

Delaney tries to explain the rules as they play, but Amelia roars every time a try is scored, and yelps with every kick. It's the cutest thing I've ever seen.

She's in my face for the whole eighty minutes, but I don't mind at all. I'd much rather watch her.

My daughter.

I loved Delaney when we were together, and I know we can grow that love again. But I'm also head over heels in love with my little girl.

Her dark curls fly as she jumps up and down in excitement, and she really does have an insane amount of energy for the entire game.

"She'll crash when this is over." Delaney smiles at me.

"I'm not surprised." I laugh.

"Not long to go," Delaney murmurs.

I spend the last few minutes, watching the clock, all the while knowing that as it ticks down, my time with these two is running out. It's just one night, and there'll be others, but every second I get with them is precious.

The final whistle blows.

"The All Blacks won." Amelia's eyes are wide, and her smile is the most beautiful thing I think I've ever seen. This is *my* little girl.

"I saw, sweetheart."

She claps, wiggling her hips in an exuberant dance.

"Maybe if you're here in summer, she can introduce you to cricket," Delaney says.

"Cricket?"

"We love cricket, Josh. I play at school."

"Do you?"

Amelia rolls her eyes. "But it takes so long."

Delaney shakes her head. "You have no idea. Your school games are so short."

"How long does it usually take?" I ask.

"Depends on the format, but the international games can last five days."

"Five days?" I gawp at her. "Why so long? How do they play that it takes five days?"

"They play slowly."

I narrow my eyes at her until she breaks into a laugh. "Stop teasing me. You know I'm going to look this up."

"I know. It's fine. I'm not lying." She raises her chin, but I don't miss the smile on her face.

"Never said you were. I want to see this now."

"I can teach you." Amelia cups my face and moves it to look at her.

"Okay. That means I'll have to come back and visit again when it's warmer."

"You will, and now it's time for bed for one tired little girl."

Amelia pouts, but it's clear she's fighting a yawn.

"How about we go and get you into your nightie and your teeth brushed, and then Josh can read you a story."

Amelia stares at me. "Could you?"

I nod. "Of course."

As Delaney gets up to guide Amelia out of the room, I touch her arm.

"Thank you," I murmur.

"You're welcome." She gives me a warm smile, and my heart swells. I never thought I'd feel so fulfilled, but just being in their presence does that.

This is my family.

Or at least, it will be.

***

"SHE'S READY FOR HER STORY." Delaney stands in the door of the hallway, and I walk to her. She places a hand on my chest.

"I want to tell her."

"I know you do. I do too, but give her a chance to get to know you a little."

Nodding, I place my hand on hers. "I know. You've done an incredible job. She's so much like you."

"I'm not sure that's a good thing." Delaney laughs.

"I am. She's not afraid of anything, is she?"

Her lips twitch. "Very little. You'd better get in there and read her that story or she'll riot. Second door on the left."

I laugh. "I'll be back soon."

She lifts her hand, and I make my way up the hall.

Amelia gives me a sleepy smile as I walk into the room.

"Okay. What am I reading?"

She hands me the book as I sit on the bed. "*Hairy Maclary from Donaldson's Dairy.*"

"Does he live on a farm?"

She laughs. "No. He lives in a dairy."

"I thought that was where cows live."

Amelia shakes her head. "It's like the supermarket."

"Oh." I nod, but that's another thing I'll have to look up. Opening the book, I start reading. "Out of the gate, and off for a walk ..."

She's well asleep by the time Hairy Maclary has gathered all his friends together, but I read to the end just in case.

I reach down and stroke her cheek with my knuckle. She shifts in her sleep, her little lips pursing. She's so beautiful, and she's mine and Delaney's. I've missed so much of her life, and I don't want to miss another minute.

But that's going to be difficult.

My schedule is busy—perfect for a single guy with no children. After this movie, it'll be another two months at least before I have any time to spend with Delaney and Amelia. Negotiations are happening with projects beyond that too, which I'll have to rethink.

And then there's the knowledge that the press will be all over this if they find out—and that's only a matter of time. I have to protect my girls.

She shifts again, and I know it's time to get out of here before I accidentally wake her. I'm sure Delaney would kill me if she has to deal with a grumpy, tired little girl.

Delaney's sitting on the sofa when I walk back into the living room, the TV remote in her hand.

"She's a whirlwind."

"Just wait until she finds out you're her father. You won't stand a chance." Delaney laughs.

"She's so much you. But I can see a lot of me in there. My mother is going to flip."

Delaney blanks. For a moment, she just stares at me.

"Did I say something wrong?" I ask as I sit beside her.

"I never thought about grandparents." Despair crosses her face. "Oh, your mother's going to hate me for keeping Melly from her."

I shake my head. "She won't hate you. I'm sure she won't be happy, but the minute she meets Amelia, she'll be over the moon."

"I'm so sorry, Josh." Delaney looks up at the ceiling.

"You have nothing to *be* sorry for. You tried to tell me. That's what matters."

"Will she believe that though?"

I blow out a long breath. The truth is, I don't know. Dad'll be fine. He's really easy-going, and just the knowledge that he has a grand-daughter will be enough. But my mother won't be so impressed. She's the one who had to encourage me to follow through with the role in *Gauntlet* when I wanted to throw it all away. Delaney leaving broke my heart and it took everything to pull myself together and keep on pursuing my dreams.

"Honestly, I'm not sure. But she'll get over it. She has no other option." I trail my fingers down Delaney's arm. "There's something else we need to talk about. Is my name on Amelia's birth certificate?"

"No. I would have needed you to fill it in with me. There's no father listed."

"If you're okay with it, I want to add my name."

Delaney nods. "I'm assuming you want a DNA test?"

"I don't need one. I can see for myself, and I trust you."

Her eyes search mine. "Are you sure? I don't have any objection. I can understand if you want to do it, and it's not a big deal."

I take her hand in mine and squeeze it. "I don't have any reason to think you're lying to me. Hell, you didn't want to tell me in the first place because you were scared I'd try taking her."

Emotion seems to overwhelm her as she shakes a little. "You're being way too reasonable. I can't even find anything about this situation to take the piss out of."

"You're losing your touch."

She smiles, but it's faint. "Are you sure you want to add your name to her birth certificate?"

"Why wouldn't I?"

She pauses, seeming to be getting her breathing under control. "Well, I just thought that it means you're responsible for her in a way you're not right now."

I nod. "I know. If it's about money ..."

The pained expression her face warps into tells me everything I need to know. This must be incredibly awkward for her. They've survived just fine without me all this time, and I can't just swoop in and buy their love. Not that I would want to.

I want both her and Amelia to love me for me.

"I don't want your money, Josh."

"Well, that's too bad because I plan on making sure neither of you want for anything ever again. And I want something from you too."

She swallows hard. "Like what?"

"I want us to start again. That day when we first met. I've replayed that in my head a million times. That's what I want us to find our way back to."

Delaney shakes her head. "It was a long time ago. We were both different people."

"I'm still Josh. The guy who made you laugh. The guy you used to make fun of." I pause. "Scratch that. Still make fun of."

Her lips twitch. "It's so easy to make fun of you."

"See? We're halfway there already."

I reach out, pushing a lock of her hair back behind her ear. "I was crazy in love with you back then, and we could have that again. But I need to know how you feel."

She sighs, dropping her gaze. "I thought I was over you. Even if I still can't watch any of your films, I thought that any romantic feelings were dead. But just the thought of being near you makes me nervous."

I run my fingers down her cheek. "You don't ever have to be nervous around me. Like I said. I'm still the same Josh you met six years ago."

"But you're not." Her eyes meet mine again. "You're the big Hollywood star, and I'm a nobody."

"That's not true."

"It's okay. I'm fine with that." She smiles. "You didn't even recognise me the first time you saw me here."

I hold up my palms. "In all fairness to me, I was heavily jetlagged, and you were dressed like you were off to explore the Antarctic."

Delaney snorts. "That's exactly what I said to Pania when I got back to the diner."

"I can still make you laugh. That gives me hope there's something between us."

She places her hand on my chest. "There'll always be something between us. We made Amelia, didn't we?"

I take a deep breath. "I want another chance, Delaney. With you."

She blinks rapidly as if she's fighting back tears. "Are you really sure? I don't know if I fit into your world."

"You were my world. I want that again."

"Josh," she whispers.

I kiss her. Soft and slow at the start, but I claim her mouth with mine with an intensity that builds to a crescendo as she opens up to me.

There's no way I ever want her to leave my life again. This time, I'm playing for keeps.

The past falls away, and all we're left with is the here and now.

We're no longer the teenagers who fell in love—we're the adults who never got to indulge in it.

She lets out a soft moan against my mouth, which wakes a part of me that I thought long dead.

As the kiss ends, I press my forehead to hers, and close my eyes.

It's been so long since I've been this content.

Her blue eyes drink me in as I pull back.

"I'm here for a couple more months. If it's okay with you, I want to spend some time with Amelia and with you. And some alone, adult time with you while we get to know each other again," I say.

It seems like we sit in the silence forever. She seems to be taking it all in, and I know it must be overwhelming. But this is Delaney, the girl I never stopped thinking about. My one who got away.

Finally, she nods. "I'd like that. But there's something you should know before we spend any more time together."

"What is it?"

"I'm not the girl you met six years ago. So much of me has changed. Both mentally and physically."

"You've been raising our daughter alone. I'm sure that's been tough at times."

She licks her lips. "I'm blessed with good friends." For a moment, she pauses again. "I gained a lot of weight when I was pregnant. And I've never been able to get rid of it. I have stretchmarks. And I'm pretty sure I have stretchmarks on my stretchmarks. My body's so different to when we were together. I don't have that flat, tanned stomach anymore."

I slip my arm around her shoulders. "Are you telling me you're self-conscious?"

"Around someone like you? You've only got better-looking."

Smiling, I lean my head against hers. "You're beautiful. Even more than you were when we met."

"Stop it."

I lift my head. "Do you really think I'd lie to you? I'm trying to put back together what should have been. But it's going to take both of us to do that."

Slipping my fingers under her chin, I raise it until she's looking in my eyes again. Her lips part as her breathing speeds up. She's inches away.

"I really want to kiss you again."

She takes a sharp breath, but after a moment, she gives me a quick nod.

It's with such a sense of relief that I claim her mouth with mine. I thought she might push me away, and there's a long road back, but we're on it. Starting slow, I relish the feel of her warm, soft lips against mine before she opens up to let me in.

And then, I'm lost. Kissing her is like travelling back in time to when everything was so simple. We were just a boy and a girl falling in love.

We could be that again.

Sure, it's a little more complicated this time, but Delaney always had a part of my heart and it's just a matter of handing over the rest.

Isn't it?

I DON'T STAY LATE because I'm working tomorrow, but two hours of movie-watching with Delaney in my arms is the best thing that's happened to me in years.

I'd forgotten how good it felt just to hold her.

She seems content, snuggling against my side, but we're both careful that's as far as it goes.

"I should leave," I murmur as the end credits roll. "Not that I want to."

Delaney looks at me with those big blue eyes I always loved. She doesn't have to tell me she feels the same way. "I'm not ready for you to stay."

I nod. "I know."

Standing, I entwine my fingers with hers and pull her to her feet. This whole situation is weird for both of us, where Amelia just seems to have taken it in her stride.

"I still don't know what to think. About everything." Her smile is strained. "But for so long I was afraid of telling Amelia about us. I thought I'd have to lie to her about you loving me."

"Oh, baby." I pull her into my arms, closing my eyes as she snuggles in tight against me. "I was so crazy about you. Amelia was definitely conceived in love."

"I know that now."

"You don't have to be afraid. We could have it all back, Delaney. You, me, and this time, Amelia. I know we can."

When she lifts her head, I see the hope in her eyes. I feel it too, but I have to go at her pace.

"Are you going to be okay?" I ask.

Delaney nods. "I'll be fine. Talk to you tomorrow?"

"I'll text you. If that's alright."

She nods.

We walk to the door, hand in hand.

I dip to kiss her goodbye. It's soft and slow, and I don't miss the small sigh she lets out when it finishes.

"You addle my brain," she says.

I smile, raising my hand to her cheek. "Listen to your heart. I know what mine's telling me."

More than anything, I wish we had more time. If I wasn't shooting back-to-back movies, I wouldn't leave after I finish this one. But once this is done, I'll be leaving the country, and while I know I could always come back, I want my family together before I leave.

Because if I don't, there's no way I'll be able to convince them that where they belong is in the States—with me.

CHAPTER TWENTY

DELANEY

I'M SO CONFUSED.

Josh has made his feelings obvious.

All this time, we both hurt over that day and for very different reasons.

But since Amelia was born, my path has been clear. All I've wanted was to make sure she had the upbringing I didn't have. My mother resented me over my father leaving. Amelia just needed to know she was loved.

Seeing Josh again conjures up both good and bad feelings. Can we really put the past behind us? My cheeks heat every time I think of the way he so calmly showed me that movie clip. If I'd only put my pride away and gone to see the damn movie, I might have understood years ago.

We've lost so much time.

I'm not sure that Josh has genuine feelings for me, or if he's living off a memory. For my part, I'm still frustratingly attracted to him. Any red-blooded, straight woman would be.

And then there's the issue that played in the back of my head ever since Melly was born, and that's the attention we'll get from the media. Josh can't shelter us from everything."

Pania knows better than to go anywhere near the topic, and manages to avoid it for two days before she approaches me about it.

"How did it go on Saturday?" she asks.

"Fine."

"Do you want to talk about it?"

I shoot her the side-eye. "Do you want to know about it?"

"You know I do. Yes, I'm being nosey, but you're my best friend and I'm worried about you."

For a moment, I play my bottom lip between my teeth. "He wants us to be a family. He wants me."

Her eyes widen. "And you want ...?"

"I don't know what I want. That's the problem." I sigh. "When I'm around him, my insides are twisted up, and I can't help myself. But when we're apart ..."

"You second guess yourself and think you're not good enough."

If it was anyone else, I'd slap her, but Pania's right. Maybe I left him, but he left me behind a long time ago. We didn't get the chance to grow together, and we're in such different places in our lives.

I nod.

"Delaney, you loved him so much. And you hurt each other, even if it was unintentional. All this time, I've hated him on your behalf, but he really does seem to be making a big effort. And you look different when you're around him."

"Look different? How?"

She pauses as if thinking for a moment. "Remember when we were in the last year of high school, and you started seeing Greg Cook?"

I grimace. "Of course I do. What's that got to do with anything?"

"You were so happy, and everyone hated you for scoring the captain of the first-fifteen. And then you had sex in the back of his car and it was terrible and you broke up with him."

I blow out a breath. "Pania, I'm real happy to take this trip down Memory Lane with you, but again, what's that got to do with this?"

"Well, when he told everyone that he wasn't your first, and that you were sleeping around—everyone believed him and you were devastated." She pauses. "That was nothing compared to when you came back from America. And even after Melly was born and we opened the diner, there was always such a sadness about you. I saw it because I knew what you were like before all of it. I'm not sure anyone else did."

I nod. No one knows me better than Pania. She's the keeper of my secrets, and the one person I trust with everything.

"You were always a smart arse, but once you and Josh happened, you became so hard and defensive. And I know you had to." She holds up her palms. "Don't get me wrong; I love feisty Delaney who takes no shit. But sometimes it's like something is missing."

I pick at my fingers. "For a long time, cutting Josh out of my life felt like I'd lost a limb. We weren't together long, but he was it for me. I always thought I'd grow out of it."

"Want to know what I think?" She's got that look in her eye that tells me I'm going to hear it no matter what.

"Do I have a choice?"

"Forget Greg. Josh was your first real love. And everything happened so fast, neither of you caught your breath. And then this stupid misunderstanding broke you apart before you got the chance to really explore things." She shrugs. "Maybe it's time to get this out of your system. Either way."

I swallow hard. "I really need to go and see him."

She nods.

"The last two times we've seen each other, he's kissed me."

Her lips curl into a smile. "Well, I think that's got to tell you something."

"I just wish there was a way of talking to him without having to talk to him. You know?"

Pania laughs. "I've never seen you this twisted up over anyone."

"No one ever made me feel the way he did." I sigh. "Does."

"Have you heard from him since Saturday?"

I nod. "We've been texting."

"And ...?"

"It's nothing too crazy. Good morning, goodnight, I want to fuck you until neither of us have any bodily fluid left. The usual stuff."

She stares at me. "You're kidding."

"Yes. I am. He doesn't text me goodnight." I laugh.

"You're such a bitch. Won't even give me the real goods."

"He's just being really sweet. That's all. He wants to be a part of his daughter's life, and I'm the way to get to her."

Her eyebrows creep up. "It's more than that, and you know it."

"I'm still struggling to believe it." My phone buzzes, and I pull it out of my pocket. "Speak of the devil."

"It's the middle of the day."

"He's bored. I had no idea how much sitting around actors do on set."

Josh: Dinner Friday? I really need to see you.

Pania looks over my shoulder. "There's no mention of Melly."

"No, but I'm not going to have dinner with him and not her. We're kind of a package."

Josh: *If you want, you could come up here to have dinner with me? Do you have a babysitter for Amelia? I'd love to see her too, but I'd really like to spend some time just with you.*

"Oh, he wants you. I'll babysit."

I glare at her. "Traitor."

"You need to sort this shit out once and for all. I'll prepare to stay the night on Friday."

I narrow my eyes even further. "So you're assuming I'm going to sleep with him?"

"Damn right." She laughs. "He's hot and he wants you."

"I don't know what to do."

She shrugs. "Follow your heart, Delaney."

"That's what Josh said. Have you two been talking?"

Pania smiles. "No. But if it was me, we'd be doing more than talking."

I gape at her. "That's my ..."

"Your what?" She crosses her arms, one eyebrow popping up.

"My Facebook relationship status it's complicated. That's what he is."

She drops her arms to her sides. "Just go to dinner and see what happens. What harm can it do?"

The truth is, I'm not exactly sure what harm it can do.

I look at my phone.

Me: *I've got a babysitter. What time do you want me there?*

Josh: *Around seven?*

Me: *It's a da...*

I pause. *Delete.*

Me: *See you then.*

CHAPTER TWENTY-ONE

DELANEY

IT'S the longest half-week ever.

Why am I so nervous?

We've had a first date before. How will things go tonight?

I change four times before I settle on a simple black dress Pania made me a while ago, and I've never worn. It's not too revealing, but I like the way it sits on my hips, and my cleavage looks amazing in it.

"Hello?" Pania's voice comes from the front door.

I step out into the living room.

"Pania." Melly runs to Pania.

"You just saw her a few hours ago." I laugh.

"I'm staying with you tonight, my sweet little girl."

Melly's eyes widen. "Really?"

"No. Like I told you, I'll be home later." I shake my head and shoot a glare at Pania.

Pania looks me over. "I don't think I've seen you wear a dress in forever. Is that the dress I made you?"

I grin. "It is. Fits like a glove because you're so clever. This is a special occasion. He didn't tell me how I should dress, so I took a punt."

"Well, you look beautiful. He won't be able to resist."

"Mummy's going to see Josh," Melly announces.

Pania nods. "I know, sweetheart."

"He loves Mummy."

I stare at her. "What?"

"He held her hand so he loves her."

I bite my bottom lip and try not to laugh. "I'm not sure about that, Melly. But I do like him."

"So do I. He watched the All Blacks with us." She turns to Pania for that last bit, and Pania smiles, running her fingers through Melly's hair.

"That sounds like fun. What are we going to do tonight?"

"She's had dinner. I wouldn't worry about a bath, but bedtime is ..."

"She'll be fine with me. I know the rules. Go and have fun with your man."

I open my mouth to correct her, but I smile instead. He is my man. If I want him to be. It's just such a fantastical thought when I think about who he is. Back when we first met, we were equals. Now, it feels like he's unobtainable. But that's not true. *He wants me.*

"Get out of here, girl."

I give Pania a hug before bending to kiss my little girl on the forehead. "Be good for Pania."

And when I'm out the door and on the other side, I take a deep breath of the cool night air and steel myself before seeing Josh again. Because his intensity scares the crap out of me.

I pat my bag, having retrieved the letter I sent him all those years ago. The letter that told him he was going to be a father.

It's time he read it.

IT'S a beautiful night to drive up the mountain.

The air is crisp, and the sky is cloudless. I've never been up here at night before, and the view must be incredible.

I'm still relieved to pull up outside the house, and a little afraid of what's inside.

Despite saying I'm not staying the night, I still wore my best underwear. Just in case. I'm prepared for anything. At least, that's what I tell myself.

Josh answers the door dressed in jeans and a T-shirt. I look down at myself. "Am I overdressed?"

He shakes his head. "You look beautiful. Come in before dinner burns."

I take a sniff as I walk in the door. "It's a bit late by the smell of it."

"Shit." He runs, but I follow behind him into a large kitchen. A large *shiny* kitchen. Forget the man—the appliances in here are new and look virtually untouched, and I could seriously orgasm just at the amount of bench space.

This. This is the way to my heart.

"It's okay. It's just a little brown in the centre."

I walk over to where Josh is standing by the cooktop, frypan in hand. In the centre are four slices of bread, and if I'm not mistaken, cheese between them.

"You made me a toasted sandwich for dinner?" I clamp my lips together.

His brows knit. "I know it's not much, but you know how bad I am at cooking."

I laugh. "Nothing's changed."

"There's plenty of food. I'm sure I can make something else."

He turns, and I grab hold of his hand. "Josh. It's okay. I'm happy to eat whatever you make."

"Are you sure?"

"You cooked for me, and it's the sweetest thing ever. I love it."

His eyebrows quiver. Uncertainty crosses his face. "Are you sure?"

"Completely. Let's eat before it gets cold." I link my fingers in his. "Everything's perfect, Josh. I don't want to change a thing."

I take a deep breath before leaning over to kiss him. He opens up, his tongue sliding over mine, but I pull back before it goes too far.

"Are you okay?" he asks.

"I'm fine. I just need something to eat."

He grins. "Give me one second."

He tips the frypan. The sandwiches slide onto a plate sitting beside another plate with an identical meal on it.

Picking up the two plates, he leads me through the dining room and into a soft-lit room with a big couch and an even bigger television.

"What are we doing?"

"I thought we could watch *The Fellowship of the Ring*. It's been a while since I've seen it, and it's the extended cut so it's the longer version." His lips curl. "And the longer I get with you, the better."

I nod slowly. "That's a great idea. But if you've got it, why don't we watch *your* movie?"

"Which movie?"

"*The* movie."

Josh smiles. "You might be in luck. I think it's on Netflix." He licks his lips. "You know, if things had been different, you would have been on my arm at the premiere, and we would have celebrated its success together."

I let out a sigh. "I know. I wish things had panned out that way."

"Me too." He places the plates on the coffee table in front of the couch. "Did you want a drink? There's literally everything here."

"Juice or something fizzy would be nice."

Josh nods. "Coming right up."

I take a deep breath as he leaves the room. He's being so sweet. I'm not sure what I expected, but him cooking cheese on bread in a frypan wasn't at the top of the list.

It takes me back to when we first met. It's the kind of meal we shared when we were dating.

"Here we go. Two orange juices." He places the glasses on the table and sits beside me. "This takes me back. Grilled cheese used to be the only meal I could afford on the menu of the coffee shop."

I laugh. "Is that why you ordered it so often?"

"That, and I got to spend time with you. I borrowed off Reece to pay for it most of the time."

"Really?"

He shrugs. "I needed an excuse to spend time with you, and at that stage you hadn't said yes to going out with me."

All I do is smile. I liked him so much too. He came in daily, always with the same order, and spent every minute until he got his food chatting to me. I knew he was interested, and I was too.

I pick up my plate. "Let me critique this meal."

"Please don't." He laughs.

"It'll be fine. When the weather's cold like this, Melly and I snuggle down on the couch with a blanket and some cheese toasties and watch movies."

His lips twitch. "Does that mean we get to snuggle? I've got plenty of blankets."

"Maybe. Depends on how good this is." I pick up a sandwich.

"That's harsh, Delaney."

I laugh. "That's me."

WHEN WE'VE FINISHED EATING, he takes my plate and disappears, returning with a wool blanket and a hopeful look on his face.

How can I say no?

Spreading it across us, he slips one arm around my shoulders, and starts the movie.

I steal glimpses of him, only to find him looking at me.

"What?" I ask after the third time I catch his eye.

"I like looking." He cocks his head. "I'd like to be kissing you, but this will have to do."

I shrug. "I wouldn't say no."

His eyes search mine for a second before he leans in. I cover the gap and our lips meet. Kissing him takes me back, and I don't want to stop. Ever.

He pulls back. "You're supposed to be watching my movie."

Laughing, I turn back to the screen, leaning my head against his. "I was, but someone distracted me."

"Good distraction, I hope."

"Always."

Josh is amazing in the movie. He's a good man undercover, and pretending to be bad is hard on his character. I find myself in tears when we reach *that* point of the movie.

He holds me in his arms, kisses my tears away, and his care of me during that tiny little scene is what finally makes me believe this is real. All of it.

Everything I've felt for so long—the hurt, the sadness over Melly not having her dad in her life, the loss I felt for the man I'd come to love—that will never change. But it's in the past because I finally start to see a future.

A future with Josh.

I'm sorry when the movie ends, but still resolved to not spend the night. I hate being away from Melly. And there's still a lot of ground for Josh and I to cover.

"What did you think?" he asks.

I smile. "You were amazing. I should have seen that movie a long time ago."

"I understand why you didn't."

"It would have left me feeling foolish, but I would have guessed at the truth."

He's back to searching my eyes, and my vulnerability is probably written all over my face. I want what we had, and so does he.

"We can't recreate the past. It's too late for that," I say.

"I don't want to do that. I want to start over."

His lips twitch, like he's fighting a smile. "I was so nervous about our first night together. All I cared about was making sure you wanted more. I even googled to make sure I knew where the clitoris was. I know now."

My heart leaps. "I was nervous back then, too. But that was a long time ago." *Wait.* "What? You did what?" I clamp my lips together to stop myself from laughing, but it's too late and despite my best efforts, I let out a choked laugh.

"Don't. I mean, I was sure I knew where it was, and you weren't the first girl I'd slept with, but ..."

I hold up my palm, letting out a snort-laugh. "Stop it. I'm not sure whether you're digging yourself a bigger hole or telling me the most adorable thing I think I've ever heard."

"Can we go for the latter?" Those dimples light up and my heart flutters at the sight.

"Damn it, Josh. You need to stop being so cute."

He grins. "That's a good sign, right?"

"I don't know what it is."

"You keep letting me kiss you. I want more than just your friendship, Delaney. You know that."

I shrug. "I know what you think you want, but I wonder if it's just after finding out you had a daughter you have some misguided feelings for me."

He grasps my arms. "Nothing about how I feel is misguided. I mourned losing you for so long after you left. It feels right to have you back."

"One step at a time. Okay?"

His loving smile makes me want to take back those words. I want to jump his bones and ride him like a rocking horse.

Get yourself together, Delaney.

"I should go," I say.

He nods. "You're worth the wait. I know that."

I swallow hard.

Together, we get up and walk to the front door.

"I've got something for you." Reaching into my bag, I pull out the letter. I never opened it when I got it back—there was some finality in the writing on the envelope that said *gone, no forwarding address.*

"What is it?"

"I'd always thought I'd give this to Melly if she ever asked about us. I had this plan to explain to her that her daddy was very famous, and that I'd tried to tell him about her, and that it wasn't his fault that he didn't know." Tears well in my eyes, and I bite my bottom lip to try and stop them. "So, take this because it's yours, and when we're both ready, we can tell her our story."

His Adam's apple bobs as he swallows, but he takes the envelope. "Thank you."

"I should have tried harder to get hold of you. You just seemed so out of reach."

His eyes turn so sad. "I probably was. My assistant helps me handle my social media, and any queries go to her and my agent first. There were barriers between us, Delaney, and I know that."

I take a step closer. "I don't know what this is between us. Not yet. But I wanted you to know how sorry I am for everything. I'm not sure I'll ever be able to make it up to you."

He smiles, and takes me by the hand. "All we can do is move forward. I hope you know how much this letter means to me."

"I never wanted you to not know. And I know that's a double negative, but you know what I mean."

He laughs. "I know what you mean."

"Goodnight, Josh."

Squeezing my hand, he raises it to his lips. He closes his eyes and kisses it softly. "Goodnight, Delaney."

"Thank you for a lovely evening."

And then he lets me go, and I walk to the car without looking back because I know if I do, I'll stay.

Maybe that wouldn't be a bad thing, but I need some fresh air after that reminder of the past.

I need to be home with my girl.

CHAPTER TWENTY-TWO

JOSH

MY HANDS TREMBLE as I look at the envelope.

What would my life have been like if I'd received this? What would I have done back then if I'd found out about Delaney's pregnancy?

There's a good chance I would have thrown away my film career just to be with her. I'm not sure if I ever would have had another opportunity like the one I got.

Regardless of my success, it's a high price to pay for the family I should have had. Delaney and I could have worked everything out years ago.

I walk back into the house and sit on the couch.

Taking a deep breath, I break the seal on the envelope and pull out the piece of paper from within.

Dear Josh,

I'm sure you're surprised to hear from me. Well, surprise!

I was a coward that morning, and ran before confronting you, but I heard you on the phone. At least you didn't have to worry about dumping me, or letting me come home and breaking my heart then. And I am heartbroken. Why? I fell in love with you, but why did you do it?

As much as I want to know the answer, this letter isn't about me.

There's no easy way to tell you this, but I'm pregnant. It's okay. I don't expect you to take responsibility for the baby. I'm not sure what I'm having yet, but I wanted you to know, and I'll contact you again when the baby arrives just in case you do want to know.

I'm not living with my mother anymore. She gave me an ulti-matum that I get rid of the baby or leave, so I left. My friend Pania, who I told you all about, and her mum have taken me in. She's got a huge family, and our baby will be a part of that family now, so he or she won't want for love.

I wish things were different. I tried to call you, but your phone isn't in service. Then I saw the casting news and realised things are on the rise for you. Maybe it doesn't mean much, but I'm so proud of you, and one day our son or daughter will be just as proud.

I'll tell them all about you when they're older, and let them make up their mind if they want to find you.

I've dialled back my studies and am doing a shorter course to become a cook rather than the chef studies I had planned. My focus is going to be on this baby and making sure they

have the best life I can give them, whether you're a part of
that or not.

I also wanted to let you know how much you hurt me. I didn't
want to fall in love, but I couldn't help it because you are
perfect. I'm not sure I'll ever not love you because even
though my heart is broken, I still want us.

And I just realised that I said this letter wasn't about me, but
I've made it about me. That wasn't intentional. You know
how much I talk.

Anyway, I don't want to make this letter too long. I'm happy
that you're going to get to live your dream, and I hope your
film does crazy well. I'm not sure if I'll be able to watch you
on screen, but I'm sure you'll soon be the star you were
always meant to be.

All my love,
Delaney

I STARE at it for a moment. This is her through and through. She's
in pain, but talking through it. It's her answer to dealing with
everything.

She tried to tell me, and I can understand her frustration in not
being able to reach me.

The reality was that despite how crazy we were about each other,
we'd barely scratched the surface.

Delaney was left without many options, and she could have sold
her story to the press a long time ago. But she didn't.

This letter fills a big gap, and I'm so grateful that she gave it
to me.

She always loved me. As I always loved her.

I place the letter on the coffee table and stand. She'll be halfway home by now, but I can't wait any longer.

I'm going to claim my family.

CHAPTER TWENTY-THREE

DELANEY

PANIA LOOKS up as I walk in the front door.

"I didn't think you'd be back tonight."

"I told you I would be."

Flopping on the couch beside her, I lean my head on her shoulder.

"How did it go?"

"Tonight was perfect. You should see the kitchen in that house. Brand new, top-of-the-line appliances, marble benches—"

She laughs. "Girl, shut the fuck up and get to the romance."

"He made me a toasted sandwich for dinner." I raise my head. "He burned the bread a little, but it was the best toasted sandwich ever."

Pania cocks her head. "So, not much of a cook."

"He never was, but he tried."

"And then?"

"Then we sat in front of this ridiculously big television and watched his first movie."

She smiles. "Did you *just* watch the movie?"

"No?" I shrug. "And then before I left, I gave him the letter I wrote him where I told him he was going to be a father."

Her mouth falls open. "You kept that?"

"I always thought it was an important part of Amelia's story. Now it's in the hands of the person it was meant for."

"It's good of you to do that."

I let out a sigh. "It felt right. We don't have much time before he leaves again."

"But he'll come back."

"Will he? Or will he move on with his life once he leaves?"

Pania's eyes fill with sympathy. "Oh, honey. I'm sure he won't. Tonight meant something."

"I'll be okay. I just worry about letting Melly down."

"Delaney, you could never let that girl down. Everything you've done for the past six years has been for her. You've taught her to be strong, and she'll roll with the punches just like you had to."

I lean back on the couch. "I never wanted there to *be* any punches. It was bad enough she was growing up without her dad. That's the one thing I never wanted for her."

"I know, but her dad's here now, and it looks like he wants to be a part of her life. So that's something, isn't it?"

Meeting her gaze, I smile. "You've become his biggest fan."

She grins. "I just love seeing the difference in you when he's around. You practically floated through that door tonight."

"He makes me happy. I can't deny that." I let out a happy sigh. "And it's not because he's Josh Carter, movie star. It's because he's the Josh I fell in love with in the first place. Even down to the slightly burned toasted sandwiches."

She places her hand on my arm. "And there it is. You look better than you have in years, my friend. He's still the one."

"You know, I think he is."

My heart races at a sudden heavy knock on the door.

"Who on earth is that at this hour?" I stand, and cross the room.

"Delaney, it's Josh. I need to see you."

I swallow, turning back to look at Pania. "I guess he read the letter."

Pania waves franticly. "Don't just stand there. Open it."

She stands, picking up her bag as I pull open the door. I can't decipher the emotion on Josh's face, but whatever it is consumes him as he just looks at me.

"I'm making myself scarce." Pania pushes past both of us. "See you on Monday, Delaney."

"Sure." I barely hear myself say the word with all the blood rushing in my ears. "What are you doing here?"

His eyes are wild, searching mine. "I read the letter."

"I guessed you would. Why are you here?"

He swallows hard. "I want you. I always did. Things got fucked up, but it doesn't matter."

"Josh ..." I press my palms to his chest. There's nothing more to say, and I get lost in those dark eyes. I've dreamed about them so many times, and now they're looking right at me.

There's a moment, just one, where nothing happens and we're just frozen. But it's only a moment.

He cups the back of my head with one hand, his mouth closing down on mine. This time, there's no holding back. I sink into him, and even though we've kissed a few times, this is different. This is us, Josh and Delaney, the way we were always meant to be.

When we finally come up for air, he presses his forehead to mine. "Bedroom?"

I gulp. As much as I want him, I've been terrified of this moment.

"I don't want to wait any longer," he whispers. "We've already wasted so much time."

He's told me several times, but it's taken this long for it to sink in. He wants *me*.

We're still standing in the doorway.

Thank heavens I don't have any neighbours.

But as I pull him into the house, I catch a glimpse of Pania over his shoulder. She's standing by her car, giving me the big thumbs up.

She'll want every minute detail of tonight.

Looks like there'll be a lot to share.

CHAPTER TWENTY-FOUR

JOSH

"I'M SO sorry I never got the letter," I say as Delaney closes the door.

"I just wanted to show you that I tried to tell you."

I slide my arms around her waist. "I never doubted you when you told me. But I really appreciate you giving me that. It means so much."

Her smile quivers. "I'm glad."

"You went through so much, and I wasn't there for you. I should have been, and I am so sorry."

"I'm the one who's sorry." Her voice cracks.

"We're both here now. That's all that matters."

"Are you sure this is what you want? You can have a relationship with Amelia without being with me."

I swallow hard. "Do you think I don't know that? I want you."

Delaney is beautiful.

I see it, but she doesn't. It's frustrating. The years we were apart have done some damage. Maybe if we'd been together the whole time, she wouldn't feel so awkward.

She nods, taking me by the hand and leading me down a hallway until we come to a stop before Amelia's open bedroom door.

"Look," she says. "We made her."

The hall light spills into the bedroom. Fast asleep, under a duvet cover covered in cartoon characters I really should look up so I know who they are, is my daughter. *Our* daughter.

"She's perfect. Just like her mother."

Delaney buries her face in my shoulder. "I don't know about that."

"I do." I squeeze her hand. "Do you think she'll be okay if I'm here in the morning?"

"She adores you. She'll love it."

"Are you ready for this?"

Her eyes give her away before she says the words. "I want you, too. I've been holding back, and ..."

"I know you have."

"You scare the shit out of me, Josh Carter."

I stroke the back of her hand with my thumb. "We're just Josh and Delaney. As we always should have been."

She smiles. "I like that idea."

"Let's go."

With a nod, she leads me a little farther down the hallway to another room. A large bed sits against one wall, and there are more photos around the walls of Delaney and Amelia.

She comes to a stop, but doesn't turn.

I take the hint and step up, slowly dropping the zip on the back of her dress. She sucks in a breath. I'm so aware of her nervousness, but I know all we have to do is find our rhythm together again.

She drops her head forward when I plant kisses on her shoulders and push her dress down her arms.

"Turn around."

Delaney hesitates.

"I want to see you."

She looks over her shoulder at me, blinking a bunch of times as if trying not to cry. "I'm scared."

"Of what? I've seen you naked before." I stroke her cheek with my knuckle. "You were beautiful then, and you're beautiful now. We've both changed, but my attraction to you hasn't."

"Yeah, but when you changed you became an Adonis. I'm more like Quasimodo."

My mouth falls open. "Stop it."

"Promise not to scream if you see something you don't like?"

"Delaney. I like everything about you. Turn around."

She moves slowly, but I catch my breath when she stands before me in her bra and panties. I like everything. She has nothing to be afraid of when it comes to me.

Her lush curves encased in white lace make me hard as a rock. All I want to do is touch her soft skin, and make her cry my name.

I reach for her, pulling her closer until her breasts are pressed against my chest.

"Josh," she whispers.

"Don't you ever worry about how I feel about you."

We kiss slowly, growing deeper as we take our time. There's no hurry, but I ache to be inside her—to return home.

She relaxes into me, and I reach for the hooks on her bra. I kiss her until I have to stop to release them.

"Just kissing you makes me so fucking hard," I murmur.

After working the clasp with my fingers, I slide her bra straps down her shoulders and throw it to the ground.

She crosses her arms. I shake my head, wagging my right index finger at her. "Nuh-uh."

It takes a moment, but she drops her arms to her side.

"Do you hear me screaming?"

Delaney shakes her head.

"Lie back on the bed."

She gives me a slight nod, backing up, but pulling me along, her hands on the hem of my shirt. I help her lift it over my head, closing my eyes as she runs her palms over my pecs.

The contented sigh she lets out leaves me opening my eyes to watch her.

"You're pretty beautiful yourself, Josh Carter."

"Nothing compared to you."

Her eyes meet mine, and her cheeks flush with colour. I'm so in over my head with her, just as I was from the day we met. I need her.

"Scoot up the bed."

She does as she's told, and I unbutton my jeans, dropping them to the floor. Her gaze never leaves mine, but I don't miss that her chest is rising and falling faster as her breathing becomes erratic.

Flicking my boxers to the side of the bed, I reach for the waistband of her panties and pull them down her legs.

For a moment, I just take in the sight of her.

Her breasts are fuller than I remember them being, but I guess that comes with having a baby. And those curves ...

Delaney's the most beautiful woman I've ever seen.

She shrinks under my gaze, and I shake my head. I lie on the bed beside her, and trace a finger between her breasts to the stretchmarks she seems to hate so much.

"Don't," she whispers.

"This is where Amelia grew."

She nods.

"This is where you nurtured our girl until she was ready to come out into the world." Her expression softens. "You're so beautiful, Delaney."

She looks away.

I love the gasp that comes from her when I suck a nipple into my mouth. Her skin is soft and warm beneath my palm as I explore her, trailing my hand down over her stomach.

Delaney laughs. "That tickles."

I raise my head. "Some things don't change."

Her breathing speeds up, and I gaze at her mouth as her lips part when I reach her pussy.

"I want you so much, I can't even begin to tell you." I nuzzle her breast, lapping at her nipple while I slide my fingers into her pussy and back over her clit.

She's so tense, but as I tease her body, the tension eases out of her, and she relaxes into it.

"Josh." Her voice is so soft, and she reaches behind me, stroking my shoulder blades.

"Ever since I saw you again, you're all I've thought about."

"Seeing you confused me at first."

"I'm sure. But I'm here now, and you've got me for good. If you want me."

Her hand shakes a little. "I want you."

"I'm yours, Delaney. I don't want to waste another second of my life without you."

Her eyes are so full of emotion. This is it. My heart's on the line for her, as if it's ever been off. The truth is, no matter how much time passed, it was always Delaney.

I move my hand faster, and she catches her breath.

A strained moan escapes her lips, and I capture them with my own, swallowing down the sounds of our passion. I want it all. Now and forever.

Delaney arches her back, pulling away and crying out as she comes, her whole body trembling against me. It's the most beautiful thing I've ever seen.

"That didn't take long." I tease.

"Sue me. I'm a little out of practice." She smiles.

"Spread your legs for me."

I move between them as she complies. Nothing's changed. She's still shaved, but with a little landing strip. I thought it was cute back then, and now I grin.

She giggles as I drop my head to taste her.

"What's so funny?"

"Well, it's just that I'm not sure what to call you anymore."

Confused, I lift my head. "What are you talking about?"

Her face is lit up in a smile. I love seeing her so happy. This is a moment I want to capture forever.

"I'm not sure whether to call you my favourite Canadian or Mr. Google."

I laugh, planting a kiss on her thigh. "Right now, you could call me anything and I wouldn't care."

"Are you sure?"

"Delaney, do you want me to come back up there and find something to occupy that smart mouth of yours, or do you want me to eat your pussy?"

She lets out a contented sigh. "Please continue."

"I don't know if you ever stop talking."

I look up from between her thighs at the hottest woman I know.

"Maybe I keep talking so you can shut me up."

The thought of what I could do to keep her mouth busy makes every ounce of blood race to my cock.

Instead, I run my tongue up her slit.

"Ooooh," she says.

Ignoring the smart tone of her voice, I tongue her clit until she's arching her back again. I've only ever done this with Delaney once before, and now I revel in the renewed acquaintanceship with her body.

Back then, I had no idea what I was doing, but I managed to make her come.

Now, she's wriggling under my tongue, and when I look up, her fingers are locked firmly in her hair as she pushes and strains against me.

I've got her right where I want her.

Returning my attention to her pussy, I give her clit a gentle suck. She gasps, then lets out a moan that reverberates to my soul.

If I don't get inside her really soon, I'm going to come all over her sheets like the teenage boy I used to be.

The sound of a drawer opening makes me look up.

She reaches into the nightstand and pulls out a condom.

"I think you want this."

Her cheeks are flushed pink. She's as ready as I am from the heated look she gives me.

I take the condom from her, tear the packaging open and roll it down my cock.

Delaney nods, and I don't hesitate, pushing into her and dropping over her body until I can claim her mouth with mine.

She's every bit as tight and hot as I remember, and it's a strain now, just as it was the first time to control myself. But this is our first night together again—a night to remember.

I have to show her how I feel about her because I know she still has doubts. Our lives have just progressed in different ways and now we need to come together. In more ways than one.

"You feel so good, baby," I say.

"I love you being inside me."

I kiss her again and again, pressing my tongue against hers, knowing she can taste herself on my lips. Each movement inside her brings me closer to the brink, and when she tilts her hips slightly, I angle in better and rub against her clit.

"Ooooh."

When she makes that sound in the back of her throat, I'm done for. My body jolts as six years of love and loss come to a climax, and I'm fully reunited with the woman I've always wanted.

Delaney might not think much of herself at times, but I'd do battle for her any time she needed me to.

We might have to work out the logistics, but I'm never letting her go again.

I LOVE her curled around me, the feel of her naked body against my skin.

All we've done is talk and fuck for the past three hours, and I'm content to keep on going.

"I'm sorry if I seemed a little insecure. You're a big deal," she says.

I shrug. "We're not much different than we were."

"I'm not sure about that. You went and grew these."

She runs her fingers over my abs. I shiver at her touch. She's the only one I ever want to touch me again.

"I can get rid of them if you want. You just need to keep feeding me that comfort food." I laugh.

"Don't you dare."

"Those take a lot of work, I'll have you know."

"I'm sure they do."

With her index finger, she traces around them. My cock's rock-hard again, and she's completely oblivious to what she does to me.

"Delaney, you really need to stop that."

Her eyes are wide when she looks at me. "Why?"

"Because if you don't, I'm going to roll over and fuck the shit out of you."

She laughs.

"When you touch me, I lose all sense of myself."

Her expression grows serious. "Really?"

"You still have no idea just what you do to me."

Her eyes are so full of affection that it warms my heart.

"Well, I don't know about you, but I'm not sure I have any energy left, so if you want to fuck the shit out of me, don't expect much in return."

Laughing, I kiss her hair. "Maybe we should just talk for the rest of the night."

"That sounds good to me."

I lick my lips. "Why did you name her Amelia?"

Delaney's expression softens. "Remember our first date?"

"How could I forget?" I'm still confused, but she takes a breath and continues.

"You took me to see the Los Angeles Maritime Museum, and then we got lost because you were too stubborn to look at your GPS. And you wouldn't listen to me."

I laugh. "No, I told you then, we were looking at houses we might live in one day."

She cocks an eyebrow. "Whatever. Anyway, we realised it was a cul-de-sac, and you finally pulled over to look for directions. And when they came on screen, you were so excited, you leaned over and kissed me. It was so hot."

I remember that day. She was so frustrated with me, but I was being the big macho I-don't-do-directions man. And by the time we pulled over, her nose was all scrunched up, she was so pissed, and it was the most adorable thing I'd thought I'd ever seen. I was already smitten, but her angry face was so cute.

So, I'd leaned over and kissed her before taking her home.

"What does that have to do with Amelia's name?"

Delaney palms my cheek. "We had our first argument in Amelia Avenue. And our first make-up kiss."

For a moment, she takes my breath away. I pride myself on having a decent memory, but all I can recall from that day is how nervous I was, and how good it felt to kiss her.

"Josh, maybe we weren't together, but you have always been a part of Amelia in more ways than just biological. I made sure of that."

"Why do you call her Melly then?"

Delaney grins. "She couldn't say Amelia when she was little. It frustrated her that I called her that when she called herself Melly. So, I adopted it and it stuck."

"It's cute, but I think I'm gonna stick with Amelia."

"She'll love it and hate it all at the same time. I usually call her by her proper name when she's in trouble."

I try my best mock-horror face. "Why would my little girl ever get into trouble?"

Delaney laughs. "Oh, you just wait." She pauses. "Maybe tomorrow we can tell her you're her father."

I look at her for the longest time. This is what I want more than anything, but I trust her to make the decision about telling Amelia the truth. "Are you sure?"

"Regardless of what happens between us, she deserves to know." Delaney places her palm on my chest. "But we'll also have to prepare her for when you leave. It's important that she not wake up one day to find you gone."

I squeeze her arm. "We'll work together on it. You'll have to help me with this parenting thing."

She sighs. "I'm not sure I'll be any help. She's five and I'm still fluking my way through it."

"Your letter said your mother kicked you out. I hate that she didn't help you."

"I had Pania's mother. She was my day care while Pania and I studied, and she took on the role of grandmother. I'm not sure what I would have done without her."

I stroke her arm. She should never have gone through it alone. While she was doing that, my career was starting. If I could, I'd have given it all up to be with her and Amelia.

It's not too late for us, but I missed so much.

"Is she here in town? I'd like to meet her."

Delaney shakes her head. "When I turned twenty-one, I got my inheritance from my grandmother. She left me part of the profit from the sale of her house. So, I ended up finding a run-down diner in a small town, and the rest is history."

I close my eyes, nuzzling her temple. "Why here?"

"I could afford to buy the business and still have a little money left aside. Pania agreed to come with me, and we started off doing all kinds of different things. But I noticed that we had more American tourists through than anything else. And I'd learned a lot in my time in LA. So we took the chance and rebranded doing USA-type food." She laughs. "Even the locals loved it because it seemed exotic."

"It's good food." I open my eyes and meet her gaze. "Everyone on set who's eaten at the diner praises it."

She smiles. "I'm glad to hear it."

"And you found your guard dog, Damon."

The breath she lets out is audible. I know he frustrates her just as much as he annoys me. "When I first came to town, I dated a couple of guys. I think he thinks that I'll do the same with him if he hangs around. One of them got kind of serious. There wasn't the same chemistry as we had, but he was nice and he had no problems dating a single mother."

At her words, I suck in a breath. As much as I hate the thought of Delaney being with anyone else, and another man taking my place in the family, she's a grown woman and we weren't together.

"In the end, I was glad I never introduced him to Melly. I'd have had to meet someone really special for that to happen."

I stroke her arm. "It didn't end well, huh?"

She reaches for my chin and pulls my gaze to hers. "Let's just say only one man has ever used Google for me."

I laugh, pressing my forehead to hers and planting a kiss on her lips. "It's just you and me from here on in. And I don't even need to refer to Google anymore."

She grins. "You did alright."

"Alright? I think I did better than alright."

Delaney lies back and looks at the ceiling. "I think you might have to try again. Just so I can compare."

I nuzzle her neck. "Is that a challenge?"

"You bet it is."

IN THE NIGHT I wake twice, still in disbelief that she's finally with me.

I tried to move on, but I never had the chemistry with anyone else that I shared with Delaney.

Now I have a second chance to love her.

And I will.

She's my love, the mother of my child, and my muse.

"Josh." She smiles as I approach the counter.

"What time do you get off today?"

"Two. Why?"

"I thought we could hang out." I look at my feet, suddenly shy. *"I really enjoyed yesterday."*

"Me too." She frowns. *"Didn't you have the call-back this afternoon?"*

I shrug. "I'm not getting the part. They want someone older."

"But they called you back. That's got to mean something." She wipes the counter down with a wet cloth. *"Call me afterward and maybe we can go see a movie tonight?"*

I lean over the counter and peck her on the lips. Yesterday, we had our first date. Today, all I want to do is keep kissing her.

"You're right. Mac thinks I've got a good chance."

"That's your agent, right? You have to listen to him." She cocks her head.

"I guess."

"You told me if you don't get a job you have to go back to Florida at Christmas. Grab whatever opportunities you can while you're here. You don't want to leave with any regrets."

Memories flood back while I watch Delaney sleeping. If she'd let me slack off that day, I would have skipped the call-back and never got the job.

And I do have regrets. Not about the job, but about what happened between us.

But now I have to be philosophical about it. My job led me back to her.

We lost six years, but I don't plan on losing any more.

CHAPTER TWENTY-FIVE

JOSH

THUD. *Thud. Thud.*

The beat of the music fills my ears, and I reach out to touch Delaney. The bed's still warm, but she's not there.

Memories of the night before wash over me. I never thought being with her again was possible, but here we are in a small town in New Zealand, piecing it all back together.

I reach for my boxers on the floor and tug them on.

Slipping out of bed, I open the bedroom door. The music's coming from the living room, and if I'm not mistaken it's "Raise Your Glass" by P!NK.

What I see makes me grin.

Delaney's dressed in a tank top and shorts, and she's holding Amelia's hands as they dance around the living room. They break apart, and Amelia giggles as they keep dancing up a storm, Delaney's hips swaying to the music.

I get heart pangs at the sight.

Slipping up behind Delaney, I place my hands on her hips, moving with her as she laughs loudly.

"Josh!" Amelia squeals.

"You two look like you're having all the fun," I say. Grabbing Delaney around the waist, I pull her onto the sofa. Her grin lights up her whole face. She lunges forward and pecks me on the lips.

"What about me?" Amelia asks.

Delaney grabs our daughter and pulls her toward us, covering her face in kisses in the process. More giggles fill the air, and my heart.

"Good morning, Amelia," I say.

"Good morning." She jumps up on the sofa between Delaney and me. "Can we have breakfast?"

"I'll go and make something." Delaney stands and switches off the music. "Why don't you show Josh your favourite morning cartoon?"

"I should get dressed," I say.

Delaney shakes her head. "Nah. You're just fine as you are. Super fine even."

I laugh.

"You're in your underwear." Amelia's eyes are wide.

"I am, but that's okay apparently. What's this cartoon?"

"*Paw Patrol.*"

"Show me."

Amelia sits beside me as we watch, and soon the aroma of bacon and another scent I can't identify floats through the air.

"What are you making, Delaney?" I call out.

"French toast and bacon."

"Smells great." I turn to Amelia. "I should at least put on a shirt."

She nods. "I'm wearing my nightie. I don't sit in my underwear."

I laugh. "No, you don't. Give me a second."

Heading back into the bedroom, I tug on my shirt, and pick up my jeans and jacket before turning around and going back to the living room.

Amelia pats the cushion beside her. She's so welcoming, and doesn't seem at all bothered that I'm here. Does she suspect? There's an ease between us that will help when we do tell her the truth, and my stomach's churning over the thought of it.

Whoever thought a five-year-old could make me so nervous?

"Here we go." Delaney carries in two plates and puts them on the coffee table. "I'll just grab mine and the coffees."

"I'm *so* hungry," Amelia says. Delaney shakes her head.

"She's such a show-off when you're around. Must be trying to impress." She laughs.

"I'm already impressed. By her and her mother."

Delaney grins. "You've already got all the brownie points after last night."

I shrug. "Just telling the truth."

She gives me one last look before disappearing into the kitchen again.

I'm so crazy about her.

WE LAZE AROUND ALL MORNING, watching cartoons with Amelia before Delaney makes lunch.

This time, I follow her into the kitchen.

"Let me help."

"You don't have to. Spend more time with your daughter." Delaney smiles. "She adores you; she really does."

"She doesn't really know me."

"She knows enough to just be fine with you being here. Did you see her freak out this morning?"

"No, but ..."

Delaney pecks me on the lips. "But nothing. Let's have some lunch and then tell her. If it were anyone else, I might be wary, but she's shown just how much she likes you."

My heart leaps.

Amelia knows me, but I'm still nervous as all hell. How will she react? Will she wonder where I've been? Will she hate me? Will she just turn back to her cartoons without a care in the world?

"Josh. She's going to love it. Trust me. We'll sit down and tell her. If we beat around the bush, she'll just get confused."

I nod. I'll back off and let Delaney steer this ship. There's no one who knows our daughter better than her.

Delaney grasps my arm. "Go and spend a little more time with her while I make some lunch."

"Are you sure? I'll help."

She shakes her head. "I'm fine. I enjoy cooking for my family."

Her family. The words leave a lump in my throat, and I'm unable to speak for a moment.

"Go."

She pecks me on the lips again, and I turn, a little drunk on the overwhelming emotion. I guess this will be like a roller coaster for a while.

"Josh," Amelia calls. I grin.

Maybe soon she'll be calling me Dad.

AFTER LUNCH, we clear away the plates and Delaney joins me on the couch. Amelia's been on the floor with some of her toys while she's been eating, and isn't paying any attention to either of us.

"There's something we need to talk to you about, Melly," Delaney says.

She looks at Delaney. "Can we watch a movie with Josh this afternoon? I know where the popcorn is."

It's like a punch to the gut. Six years of work, and there are no movies of mine that she can see. I never once thought about that. I'm not sure I ever had to. But it's definitely something I need on the to-do list. I doubt my manager will like the idea, but I'm over doing what he thinks is right.

"Sure we can. But I need you to come here first."

Delaney pats the sofa between us, and Amelia climbs up. Tears well in my eyes as she gives me a hug.

"There's no easy way to say this, so I'm just going to tell you. Josh is your daddy."

She shoots a wide-eyed glance at me. "My daddy?"

Delaney nods, her gentle smile so reassuring.

Amelia turns to me. "You're my daddy."

I stroke her hair. "Yes, sweetheart. I am."

"Are you coming to live with us?"

I meet Delaney's gaze. "We have a lot to sort out. But I'm here for a few more weeks before I have to go and work somewhere else. And we'll spend some time together and get to know each other better."

Delaney smiles, and it tells me she's okay with that answer.

Amelia hugs me again, and I wrap my arms around her.

"Do I call you Daddy? Or Josh?"

I look at Delaney again, but she just shrugs.

"Whatever you feel comfortable with."

"I'm going to call you Daddy. But I might forget sometimes and call you Josh."

I chuckle. "I understand, sweetheart."

"Can we have popcorn now?"

"You *just* had your lunch," I say.

"Growing girls need endless supplies like food, apparently. She's inherited your hobbit ways." Delaney laughs. "How about you two choose a movie, and I'll make some popcorn partway through it."

"I love that idea," I say.

***

TWO MOVIES AND DINNER LATER, we've spent the whole day lounging around together.

Our time together has been perfect.

The thought of having to work tomorrow is a real kick in the gut, but at least I have my girls now.

"It's time for your bath and then bed, sweetheart," Delaney says.

Amelia pouts. "Do I have to?"

"You have school and I have work tomorrow. And I think your dad has work too." Delaney smiles. "How about after we're ready for bed, Daddy reads you a story?"

Amelia's eyes widen. "Could you read me Hairy Maclary again, Daddy?"

I nod. "Of course I can."

She follows Delaney up the hallway to the bathroom, and the sound of water running echoes down to the living room.

I lean back on the sofa and take a long breath. That went even better than I'd thought it would. Apparently children can be so accepting. More so than adults.

But now I have both my girls in my life, and for that I am grateful.

This is the life I never thought I'd have. At least, not with Delaney. I thought that eventually I'd find someone, fall in love, and have a family. But I never felt that spark with anyone else, not to the extent I did with her.

Having her back is everything I ever wanted.

All the wind's sucked out of me as a weight hits me in the stomach, and I laugh at Amelia throwing herself onto my lap.

"I'm ready for my story."

"Come on then."

I stand, pulling her up with me, and she hooks her legs around my hips as I start to move with her.

Delaney stands in the hall doorway, shaking her head with a bemused smile on her face. She moves out of the way to let us pass, and doesn't follow into Amelia's bedroom.

I drop Amelia gently on the bed and she lets out a tired laugh before lying down so I can tuck her in.

She yawns, and I plant a soft kiss on her temple.

"I don't want to go to sleep. I want to play with you."

I stroke her forehead. "I'm not going anywhere. I do have to work, but I'll be here every minute that I can."

"Goodnight, Daddy."

My heart.

"Goodnight, my beautiful girl."

I pick up the book from beside the bed, and this time I don't get anywhere near halfway through before she falls asleep.

"You know it's the reading that does it. I used to sing her to sleep and rock her, but that stopped working when she was four. Now I read her a story and she's out like a light. I'm enjoying that while it lasts." Delaney leans against the doorway.

I stand and walk toward her. "I've got to be on set early tomorrow, but I can stay the night."

Delaney wraps her arms around my waist. "Good. I think Mummy and Daddy need some quality time."

"That's going to take some getting used to."

She rests her head against my chest. "You did so well. She's so happy."

"I love her calling me Daddy."

"I'm glad."

I take a breath and kiss the top of her head. "Do you mind if I keep sitting in there with her for a while?"

Delaney pulls back. "Of course not."

"It might sound weird, but I just want to look at her. While she's not jumping all over the place."

She smiles. "I think that's a lovely idea. I'll go and clean up the kitchen and get ready for bed."

"Meet you there?"

Delaney raises her face and I give her a tender kiss.

Today has only made me love her more. She's the one who's given me the whole world. Right when I thought I had everything.

DELANEY'S in bed when I reach her room. I strip down to my boxers and slide into bed beside her. Spooning her, I pull her tight against me.

I love how normal this feels. My life has been anything but

normal for years. But in this little house, in this small town, I'm content and settled.

This isn't what I'm used to. In LA, I have a house. It's huge and private, but it's not a home. Home feels like this.

I'm not sure what I'm going to do when I'm away.

"Delaney," I whisper.

She turns her head far enough that I can make up the distance and kiss her.

"You alright?" she asks.

I nod. "Thank you."

"For what?"

"For her. For all this." I take a breath. "Come with me when I leave."

"We can't."

"Can we talk about it tomorrow?"

"Of course."

She turns back, and I press myself against her, my arm over her waist. Once filming is over, I'm travelling to the UK and then the Philippines for my next project.

It was all arranged before I knew I had a family here.

I don't want to go.

CHAPTER TWENTY-SIX

DELANEY

JOSH IS GONE in the morning when I wake.

I knew he would be. He has to head over early for costume and makeup and whatever else he has to do before his day starts.

Pania opens the diner in the morning at seven-thirty and I drop Melly at school an hour later before heading over there.

It's late morning when the order comes through.

"Someone has it bad." Pania grins as she gets off the phone.

"What?"

She dangles a piece of paper in front of my face. It's so close that the writing's all fuzzy.

"Order for Mr. Josh Carter. Omelette, salad, and thickshake to be delivered to set. He's requested a particular person to do the delivery."

I grin. "He's so naughty."

"Bet he is. You look much happier lately, and I'm sure it's all tied up with an appendage of his."

I nod. "It really is. He has the cutest nose."

Pania slaps my arm. "I'm just proud of my girl for getting some.

And sorting all that historical shit out. I bet that's a weight off your shoulders."

Letting out a long breath, I nod again. "Amelia adores him. Though she did before she knew he was her dad. And things between us are really good." I bite my bottom lip. "He wants us to go with him when he leaves."

Her eyes widen. "No way."

"I'm not ready for anything like that. Besides, I can't just walk away from you and the diner. He has to understand that I have commitments here."

"Delaney, I don't think anyone would begrudge you for putting your family together. I'll put this order together now, but at some point we need to sit down and talk about it."

I nod. I guess it's inevitable now that at some point things will change. When? I'm not sure. What I am sure is that it's up to me.

"I'm guessing this delivery could take a couple of hours?" she teases.

Shrugging, I turn my back to hide my grin from her. "Maybe."

"Grab the chance before he does leave. I'll get this food cooked."

"No, I'll do it."

"Cook it with love." She laughs.

"Something like that."

I love cooking, especially for my family, and Josh is a part of that now. He deserves my best. Especially after what I put him through.

It doesn't take long to fill his order, and I throw it all in the insulated bag to take to him.

"Have fun. Don't do anything I wouldn't do," Pania calls.

"That doesn't leave a lot," I call back.

And still, I grin all the way to the car because Josh can't go a day without seeing me. Which is good, because I'm not sure about going the whole day without him.

GEORGE WAVES as I pull up to the set.

"Josh told me you were coming. I'm to take you to him."

"Well, aren't I special?"

He grins. "I hear you are. Park over there, and I'll walk with you. He's filming right now, but he won't be long."

"He'd better not be. His food will get cold."

George laughs. "I'm not sure he's too worried about that."

I drive over to where he indicates and park the car. Climbing out, I grab my bag, the food, and his shake out of the cup holder.

"Lead me to him."

We walk side by side through another gate, and I see the cameras and crew before we get close.

George nudges my arm. "You never told me you had history with Josh."

"I didn't tell anyone. How do you know?"

He shoots me a sheepish look. "I saw him go after you the night you catered. He looked upset. I know he argued with Jessie."

I come to a stop and turn toward him. "You're a good source of gossip, then?"

He chuckles. "Not usually, but you've been good to me and it involves you, so ..."

I take a deep breath. "Josh and I were involved a few years ago."

His eyes widen. "Ooooh."

"Yes. And Jessie's going to shit a brick when she finds out we're seeing each other again. She never liked me."

He nods slowly as if everything's falling into place.

"Come on then, let's get you to him. Maybe it'll help her shit some bricks." He grins and I think I've taught him something new.

"I'll make a Kiwi out of you yet, George."

After a short walk, we round a corner and I'm confronted with a wall of cameras and lights. Josh and Jessie come into view.

"Over there. We'll just have to wait until they're finished," George says.

I swallow hard. It feels like an intrusion.

Josh has his arms around Jessie in a romantic embrace.

"Cut."

I clamp my lips together in amusement as the second the word comes out, Josh drops his arms and takes a big step back. Jessie frowns.

She really does look like someone's shit in her cornflakes. But I forget about her when Josh links eyes with me.

"There's my girl." Josh beams.

"I heard some guy wanted food?"

He takes the bag and thickshake from me, and hooks his arm around my shoulder. "Only from the best delivery person in town."

"I'm probably the only delivery person in town."

"I had to see you," he murmurs.

"Couldn't wait until tonight, huh?"

"Nope. Have you got a bit of time?"

I shrug. "I'm the boss. Besides, Pania has everything covered. Why?"

He gathers everything in one hand and slips his free arm around my waist. "Jessie's got scenes to film this afternoon. I don't. I thought we might sneak off to my trailer for a little while."

"Oooh, did you now?" I laugh between kisses as he pulls me tight against him.

And then he kisses me, long and deep, and I'm lost as his tongue claims mine. At first, I'm a bit self-conscious, but then I don't care if there are cast and crew around. Josh is showing everyone how he feels about me and leaving them in no doubt who he wants. He clearly trusts them.

And his body's leaving me with no doubt *what* he wants.

"Let's go to my trailer." He nuzzles just below my ear, sucking the lobe into his mouth.

"You're a bad boy, Josh Carter."

"No, just a man who's crazy about you. And super frustrated that I have to work because I want to spend every available moment with you."

I palm his cheek. "Okay. I take part of that back. You're also a very sweet boy."

He grins.

"Food first, then love."

I roll my eyes as he pulls me toward the trailers. "You'd better make this worth it."

"You know I will."

HE SIGHS as I pull the food out of the bag and place it on the table up one end of the trailer.

"Thank you. I could eat your cooking all the time. I really wanted a burger and fries, but I need the protein."

"Don't they feed you?"

He shrugs. "Nothing as good as this."

Cutting off a piece of omelette., he takes a big bite. His eyes roll back in his head as he chews. "Oh damn, Delaney. This is so good."

I laugh. "As much as I love praise for our cooking, I kinda hope that's a euphemism."

"Well." He talks with a mouthful of food. "I am eating you next."

"Promises, promises."

He smirks between bites, and when he's done gets up and washes his hands in the basin. "Now for part two of this lunch break."

I smile. "Which is ..."

He leads me through the curtain that partitions the trailer. A bed fills the far end, and I shake my head.

"Who would have guessed?" I say.

He kisses me softly. "Get on the bed, Delaney."

I link my fingers in his and lead him the short distance to the end of the trailer.

Lying on the bed, I pull him behind me, and he cups the back of my head, giving me a gentle kiss.

"Are you supposed to have me in this trailer?"

He cocks his head. "I'll have you wherever I can."

"No. I mean, I thought this was for work."

"No one's going to tell me off if that's what you're worried about." He kisses me again.

"I can't take time off work for sex." I raise my eyebrows at him.

"I know. But I don't have much time left here, and I don't know if you're going to take me up on coming with me. So, if we're going to do this long-distance to start with, I want every moment I can get." His eyes are so full of emotion. This is such a messy situation in a lot of ways, and I understand where he's coming from. I want this with him, but I can't just leave town. We are going to be apart.

I wrap my arms around his neck and kiss him harder. He slides his arms around my waist and kisses me back. There's so much tenderness in his kiss, and I sigh against his lips.

"I need you naked," he whispers.

The blinds are down, but I still feel a little uneasy at his request.

"I locked the door on the way in. Not that anyone should be intruding." He slides his hand up my shirt, freeing one breast from my bra and gently squeezing the nipple. "I need my mouth on these."

My strangled laugh surprises even me. "So needy."

"Always when it comes to you. I have a lot of time to make up for."

"Let me sit up, and I'll take it all off."

He grins, backing away as I sit and tug my shirt over my head. Reaching behind me, I unhook my bra, and I don't even have it all the way off before he ducks under my arm and sucks a nipple into his mouth.

"You're so impatient. It's like you weren't in bed with me last night."

I lean back, and he chuckles against my skin, his hand caressing the other breast.

He laves at my hardened peak, and I close my eyes. I swear my nipples are directly connected to my clit. He barely needs to touch me and I'm melting underneath him.

"Delaney," he whispers. "All I want to do is touch you."

Raising his head, he meets my gaze. Those dark eyes of his are filled with so much love that he doesn't need to tell me how he feels. It's all happening again so fast, and this time I just give in to it. We're not nineteen anymore, and I'm not fighting this attraction off. We might be apart soon, but for now, being together is all that matters.

I sink into the mattress as he claims my mouth with his. His tongue caresses mine, his hand sliding down my torso until he finds the button of my jeans.

"Wait." I'm breathless.

Confusion crosses his face. "What?"

"Are you sure you don't need to Google anything?"

Josh's eyebrows shoot straight up. "I'm pretty sure I'll be fine. Has your clit moved since last night?"

I grin. "Not that I know of."

He gives me a tender kiss on the lips.

"Well, I'm pretty sure I'll find it just fine. Over ..."

Kiss.

"And over ..."

Kiss.

"And over again."

"Is that a promise, Mr. Carter?"

Desire crosses his expression. "Oh yes, Ms. Carruthers. That's a promise."

I laugh again as he undoes my jeans and pulls them off, along with my panties. Moving back beside me, he slides his hand up my thigh and strokes my clit with his fingers.

"Ooooh you found it by yourself," I tease.

"Is that some kind of challenge?"

I bite my bottom lip. "Maybe."

"I like a challenge."

I let out a long sigh as he slides a finger inside me.

"I'm not sure I'll ever be able to get enough of you," he whispers.

I cup his cheek. "I feel the same way."

His eyes search mine. "Damn having to work. I want to spend every day like this." He rubs my clit, and I arch my back to push against his hand.

Josh rolls onto his stomach, and I spread my legs to let him in. I let out a long moan as his mouth engulfs my pussy.

Long gone is the teenager who fumbled with me. Here's a man who's sure of himself. And he's mine, all mine again.

A warm glow spreads through my body as I grow closer to coming. Josh sucks gently on my clit, and I throw my head back, crying out despite my paranoia that someone might hear.

He rolls on a condom. There's so much I want to tell him, so much I want to say. But I hold back because this is still so new even if it feels like we've waited for this for so long.

He slides inside me, and his mouth is on mine in a moment, and I can't talk anyway.

The emotion is overwhelming. So long ago, we did this and made our beautiful daughter.

"You feel so good," he says.

"So do you." Josh kisses me again as he thrusts into me. He's all urgency and need, and I don't want this to end, but it will. At least until tonight when we'll cling to each other all over again.

The clock is ticking on our time together, and we both know it.

I thrust my hips up to meet him and he moans. As much as I love him being inside me, I also love the deep groan he makes when he comes.

I'm rewarded with that sound as he slows and drops his lips to my neck. I let out a sigh of contentment, and he nibbles on my earlobe.

"Tonight, we're going to bed after Amelia's gone to sleep." He chuckles.

"No argument from me there."

Josh rolls off me, pulling me onto my side. "Glad to hear it."

"And now I have to do the walk of shame back to my car."

His brows twitch. "Do you think anyone heard us?"

"Probably. But I'm sure no one's going to think any the worse of the handsome Hollywood star who lured me into his trailer."

Josh grins. "Lured?"

I run my fingernails over his stubbled cheek. "That's my story, and I'm sticking to it."

"You're such a temptress, Delaney. How could I resist? I always behave badly when I'm with you."

Laughing, I drop my hand. "I should go."

Josh groans. "Do you have to?"

"I can't abandon Pania all day. Besides, we'll see each other again tonight."

He pouts, and I just roll my eyes.

"Stop being so cute, Josh."

Chuckling, he squeezes my hand. "I'll do anything I can to get more time with you."

"Well, it worked." I push myself down to the end of the bed, and pick up my clothes.

Arms reach around my waist and pull me back.

I laugh. "Enough. I have to go. As it is, it'll be time to pick up Melly from school soon."

When I say that, he drops his hands and plants a kiss on the back of my neck. "I guess I could let you go for a few hours."

A few hours. When he leaves town we'll be apart for longer than that, but I don't have the heart to bring that up right now.

It only takes a minute to pull on my clothing, and I stand, turning back toward the bed.

Josh pulls off the condom, throwing it in a bin before he pulls on his boxers and pants. "I'll walk you out."

Jessie's standing a few metres away, giving me a filthy look as I step out of Josh's trailer. He walks out behind me, still shirtless with all the love in his eyes for the world to see.

"See you after work?" he asks.

"You bet."

He kisses me, running his hand down my spine until it rests on my arse. "Thanks for coming to see me. Best lunch delivery ever."

I laugh. "Any time. Only not any time, because some of us have to work for a living."

He pouts. "Ouch."

"Later, 'gator." I peck him on the lips again, and walk away toward the exit and my car. I smile sweetly as I pass Jessie. "Have a good day."

She crosses her arms like the diva she is, and with a flick of her head, storms off

I don't care.

I have *him*.

———

I KNOW Josh is home when Melly squeals.

He walks into the kitchen where I stand at the cooktop, stirring the sauce for dinner.

I close my eyes as he nuzzles my neck. "Welcome home."

"I love it when you say that," he murmurs.

"My home is your home while you're here. You don't need that fancy house." I slide the sauce from the heat to a vacant hot plate and turn to face him.

Josh slides his arms around my waist. "No. All I need is you. Thank you for coming to see me today."

"I don't think your co-star is too impressed."

He blows out a breath. "She's quite something, isn't she?"

"If you mean she waltzes into my diner and talks to my staff like shit? Then yes."

He shrugs. "Try and ignore her. Some people let all this stuff go to their heads."

"You're so normal. I don't think you've changed at all. You're still a pain in the butt."

I yelp as he slaps me on the arse before laughing.

His eyes shine with amusement. "I've tried not to let it change me. It's nice, but at the same time, there's so much pressure. But now I have you back in my life, I'm sure you'll keep my feet firmly on the ground."

"I'm not sure if that's an insult or a compliment."

Josh laughs. "You're not capable of bullshitting me. If I'm being terrible, I doubt you'll hesitate to tell me."

"Oh, you know it." I lean over and peck him on the lips. "I doubt you know how to be terrible." Licking my lips, I continue. "I used to think you were, but after finding out the truth, I don't think you have it in you."

He lets me go. "I'm so glad we found each other, Delaney. And that we can both put the past behind us. I still wish you'd come with me, but it doesn't take a genius to understand you can't just walk away from everything you've built."

I swallow hard. "We just need time. I need to know that you're one hundred percent with me and Amelia. I need to know we're solid before I can consider moving with you. How else will I know we'll last or just fall apart?"

"It won't. I swear."

"We've been together five minutes, Josh. Trust takes time. And I'm not talking about me trusting you; you have to trust me too."

He nods. "I know. I'm sorry I'm impatient. Sometimes, I feel like I've waited six years for this."

My heart weeps when he says that. It's all my fault for rushing. But I was never patient, and even less so back then. And I'm not one to back down from confrontation either, but those simple words he said hurt me.

But I can't back down from this. I need to know Melly and I have that security.

Even if it means delays in being together.

CHAPTER TWENTY-SEVEN

DELANEY

SOMEHOW, I'm not surprised when Jessie turns up in the diner the next day.

I know it's personal between us. It doesn't take a psychic to know it's all about Josh.

It has been from the night in the club when she realised I was in the picture.

I'm at the counter, and Trina is out serving customers when she arrives. She sits in a booth not far from the counter and smiles as Trina approaches.

I can't hear what she orders, but the next part is much louder.

"Don't take all day about it. Last time I was in here, the service was so slow."

Trina shrinks, but I'm not about to take that.

"If you think the service is that bad, you're welcome to take your business elsewhere," I call out.

Those green eyes fix onto me. "What did you say?"

I take a deep breath. "I said, 'You're welcome to leave'. There are other food places in town. Maybe the pub would be a good choice if you want your food faster. They sell packets of potato chips. You get given them as soon as you pay. Novel concept. I know."

Walking around the counter, I don't stop until I get to the table. I smile at Trina. "It's okay. I'll take it from here."

"Back home, the customer's always right," Jessie says.

I take a look around. Every single eye in the place is on me. I can't let my temper control me, but I sure as shit am not going to put up with her any longer.

"In case you hadn't noticed, Jessie, you're not back home anymore. You're in my diner. And I'm telling you to get out."

With a flare of her nostrils, she stands, and storms toward the door. "This isn't over. At least I'm not whoring it up on the set with any man who'll take me into his trailer."

"If whoring it up means having sex with my boyfriend who's also the father of my child, then I guess that makes me a whore."

Behind me, someone starts to clap. I don't want to drop my gaze, but I bet anything it's Pania.

Jessie scowls. The door opens, and of all people to walk in ...

"Uhh everything okay?" Josh looks between Jessie and me.

She barges past him out the door, and I'm left breathing heavily, still watching the exit.

"Good on you, girl." Dave pats me on the shoulder as he passes me to leave.

"That was awesome." Pania's voice comes from behind me.

Josh reaches me, and takes my hands in his. "Are you okay? What happened?"

"Jessie diva happened. She's just so awful."

"Delaney, take a breath." He's so close, and I throw my arms around his neck and squeeze him tight.

"I'm fine. She was just a complete bitch to Trina, so I told her to leave. She had a tantrum."

"Mummy said the B-word." A little voice comes from behind me. *Shit.*

"Sounds like it's the right word to use." He grimaces. "I'll be glad when this is all over. I'm never making a romantic comedy again. It's so not funny."

"She called Mummy a whore. What's that?" Amelia asks.

"It's a not very nice thing to say and you are never saying it again." I let go of Josh and walk to Amelia, wrapping my arms around her.

"She was such a bully, Mummy. Just like Oscar at school He's a meanie."

"I hope he's not a meanie to you."

She shakes her head. "No, but he's mean to Lucas sometimes."

"Do you want me to talk to Lucas' mother and let her know?"

Melly shrugs.

I look over my shoulder at Josh. "The whole town knows you're Amelia's father now too."

His eyebrows rise. "I thought we ..."

"I lost my temper."

"It was a thing of beauty," Pania says. "Jessie did accuse Delaney of W-H-O-R-I-N-G herself out."

I could kiss her for spelling it while in front of Melly.

"She what?" Josh says.

"Apparently I was with any man who would take me into their trailer. I told her only my boyfriend and the father of my child." I cock my head. "Maybe I should have specified that you're both of those."

He smiles, reaching for my cheek and running his thumb down it. "I'm sorry."

"It's not your fault. We'll be fine if she stays away. Which she should do because apparently the food is terrible and our service is slow."

It's Josh's turn to scowl.

"Just leave it, Josh. She's not worth worrying about. She'll be leaving town soon enough."

He frowns.

"Honestly, don't worry about it. She won't be back in, and you'll be finished working with her soon enough."

"She shouldn't treat you like that, though. No one should."

I shrug. "You're a bit biased. She's not the worst person I've ever dealt with."

He's conflicted. His brows waver, and I just know there's something cooking in that brain of his.

"Why don't we all go home and pretend none of this happened?"

It takes a moment, but he nods.

"Daddy." Melly reaches for him, and he scoops her into his arms and plants a kiss on her forehead.

It doesn't matter anymore if people know about us.

That cat is well and truly out of the bag.

CHAPTER TWENTY-EIGHT

JOSH

DESPITE DELANEY WANTING me to leave her confrontation with Jessie alone, I can't see how I can.

As it is, I need to tell Delaney something tonight, and she's not going to like it.

But it wouldn't sit right with me if I didn't tell her.

I've never mixed my private life with my professional, but I want to spend my forever with Delaney, and we haven't had the conversation about my career and the things I do to make a living.

I love what I do, and while love and sex scenes aren't really my thing, I do them without too much of a complaint. It's my job. And I'm relieved that this rom-com at least isn't big on either. While my character does fall in love with Jessie's character over the course of the movie, we only get one big on-screen kiss. Which is a relief.

Maybe I wouldn't have cared so much if I hadn't found Delaney. She knew what I was when she met me, only then I hadn't been half-naked on the big screen with a beautiful woman. At least the kiss with Jessie is fully clothed.

I'm a professional. But Delaney undoes me. And after losing her once, I can't be dishonest with her, especially after her run-in with Jessie.

The thought of what I have to do tomorrow makes me sick to my stomach.

Amelia's in the living room in front of the television. I would be in there, but instead, I follow Delaney into the kitchen while she sorts out plates of food she brought home from the diner. I could eat those burgers every night— they're my favourite as Delaney makes them. Maybe I shouldn't but I'll work out a while longer tomorrow if it means indulging with her. Besides, I've filmed the one shirtless scene I had in this movie.

"There's something I need to tell you," I say.

"What is it?" She turns to face me.

"Tomorrow's my big kissing scene with Jessie."

Delaney's expression stays surprisingly neutral. "Oh. I was trying not to think about that. I figured you'd have to kiss her, seeing as it's a romance movie."

"Are you jealous?" I study her expression closely. Delaney's pretty good at hiding how she feels, and I don't think today is any exception.

"No." But she doesn't hide it fast enough. I see a flash of irritation in her eyes.

"Liar." I laugh.

"Maybe I wouldn't feel so bad if she wasn't so annoying."

I slide my arm around her waist and pull her to me. "It might make you happier to know that because this is a romantic comedy, I almost kiss Jessie much more often than I actually kiss her. We kiss once at the end."

Delaney bites her bottom lip before letting go and laughing. "I guess those are the rules."

"They so are. Boy and girl meet. Boy and girl fall in love, but both are too stubborn to get their shit together. Boy and girl screw it all up. And then finally ..." I pull her the rest of the way into my arms and she squeals as I dip her. "They kiss."

I lean down and kiss her. She tastes of ice cream, and when I finally pull away, I scowl. "You and Amelia had ice cream without me."

"She wanted a slice of pie when we were at the diner."

"Oh, she did, did she?" I raise her to a standing position. "What about me?"

Delaney's eyebrows dip. "Aww you're so cute when you pout."

"That's the idea."

"I saved a piece for you too. It's in one of the bags."

"Have I told you just how much I love eating your pie, Delaney?"

Her cheeks redden, and she laughs again. I love making her laugh. It's the best sound in the world. "I'm pretty sure I know."

"Well, once I've eaten the food, I'll show you just how much."

She rolls her eyes and pushes me away.

"I love you." I study her reaction. It worries me that she'll get scared because life with me is going to be nothing like it was before. There's a lot that both Delaney and Amelia will have to get used to.

"I love you, too."

For a moment we stare at each other.

Delaney breaks first, laughing. "You should see your face. Were you scared to say it?"

I shrug. "Maybe just a little."

"No more being afraid, Carter. You and me were meant to be." Her eyes shine with happiness.

"Glad you see it that way. Does that mean you're coming with me when I go?"

The light that was in her eyes disappears. "Not yet. I mean, long term we will, but there's a lot I need to work out here. Pania's not just my friend; she's my business partner."

"I understand."

"I hope so, because this is something we have to be careful with. It's going to turn our worlds upside down whenever we do it. Especially when you're travelling around on location."

Running my hand down her arm, I take her hand. "I'm going to stop doing that so much."

"Really?"

"I've been thinking. I've got this movie and the next one that I'm filming basically back-to-back. And then I'll focus on jobs based in LA. I've got a house we can live in there, and it seems like the perfect place for us to be based."

She takes a moment, but she nods. "I thought that would be the case."

"Reece has been talking forever about us setting up a production company of our own. Maybe it's time for us to spend some time doing our own thing."

Delaney's smile shows me I'm on the right track.

"You think that's a good idea?" I ask.

"Does that mean I get to meet Reece Evans?"

Laughing, I squeeze her hand. "Are you using me to get to Reece?"

"Maybe." She places her index finger on her chin as if she's seriously thinking about it. Cocking her head, she laughs. "No. I just want us to have whatever stability we can get. We both owe it to Melly."

"We do. I want that for her too. Her life's about to change in a big way, but I think as long as the three of us are together, we can do anything."

Her whole face lights up. "I like the way you think. Now, let me get this dinner served and we'll talk after Melly goes to sleep."

I leave the kitchen feeling like we've taken a step forward.

I'll take it.

CHAPTER TWENTY-NINE

DELANEY

DESPITE THE SITUATION being very different, there's a feeling of déjà vu that comes over me when Josh leaves.

We've been together for such a short time and soon we'll be apart. Separated by oceans.

This time it's different, but the way my heart aches thinking about him leaving makes me feel somewhat the same.

"I'll call you every day," he murmurs in my ear.

"I'm not holding you to that. I know you could get busy and forget."

He shakes his head. "If I'm not going to be able to call you for any reason, I'll tell you."

My eyes fill with tears as he grasps my arms. It's not fair. I swore I'd never cry over him again, and even though it's for a different reason than last time, I've already broken my promise to myself more than once.

"Delaney. You're it for me. You always were."

He kisses me with so much tenderness, the tears escape and roll down my cheeks.

How can he make me any promises when he's so far away?

"Talk to me."

His eyes search mine.

"I love you," I say. It's all I have left in me right now.

"I love you too." He wraps his arms around me and I close my eyes. I'm just glad Amelia said her goodbyes before she went to school today. That was emotional enough, but she has far more confidence than I do in this situation.

I'm feeling guilty just for doubting our relationship. Since we got back together, we've been solid. There's nothing that should cause me any doubt. But we haven't yet agreed on anything to do with the future.

Finding common ground is so hard.

"I need to go. But I want you to know just how much I do love you. You and Amelia are my whole world, and I'll do whatever it takes to make this work."

"I know," I whisper.

"More than anything, I wish you'd come with me, but I understand why you're not." He lets me go, and looks at me with so much pride it hurts. "You've built your life here, and it's hard to walk away when you've worked so hard. I'll give you all the time you need, but we have to work this out."

I nod. "We both need to do a lot of thinking."

Josh just shakes his head. "I'm just thinking about when I can be with you again. Now, I have to go or I'm never leaving."

"I wouldn't complain if you stayed."

He gives me one last hug, and a deep kiss that takes my breath away.

"Josh," Mitch calls to him. "We've got to get going."

"Later, 'gator," I say.

He smiles. "See you, my favourite Australian barista."

"You might just have inched in as my favourite Canadian again."

After a peck to my lips, he turns and walks toward the plane. I let out a sigh and watch until he reaches the foot of the stairs.

Jessie stands in the door to the plane, and I can feel her evil eye from where I'm standing.

It doesn't deter Josh.

I turn, and start my long walk across the airstrip back to the car.

"Delaney!" he yells.

I look back over my shoulder. Josh is halfway up the stairs.

"What?"

"Send nudes."

I flip him off.

He just grins at me.

"I love you!" I yell.

"Bye, beautiful."

I get one last glimpse before he disappears inside and I run back to the car, so I can watch the plane take off.

As it does, my heart goes with it.

This time, it's not torn apart. But it's far from whole.

CHAPTER THIRTY

DELANEY

IT'S BEEN six weeks since Josh left.

Despite his vow to call me every day, he's been filming in a jungle in the Philippines for the past week and unable to call.

He knew going in it'd be difficult, so at least he warned me, but it's been tough. Especially when some gossip site has photos of him on set with his new co-star.

Another romance for Josh Carter the headline screams at me. We don't get a lot of reporters hanging around our town that I know of. The fact these photos leaked out of the jungle tells me there's someone on the cast or crew who did it.

I know better, but it hurts.

He looks happy, and it doesn't help that the actress he's working with is a former model and stunningly gorgeous. Jessie Lane is a good-looking woman, but Gabby Reynolds puts all us mere mortals in the shade. It's like she was created by Zeus himself.

The photos show them laughing and joking, and then there's the icing on the cake: her heading into Josh's trailer right behind him.

I know he loves me. I know there's an explanation.

But right now, I'm lying in bed watching *Grey's Anatomy* and cramming a bag of potato chips into my mouth as fast as possible while trying not to think about it.

When my phone buzzes beside me, I pick it up and look at the screen.

Josh.

"Hey, baby," he says.

"Hi."

"I've missed talking to you. We were in this damn jungle, and the reception really was non-existent. I tried to get a satellite phone, but that proved to be too hard. I'll make sure we have one when we go back."

I swallow. "You're going back?"

"Yeah, we had a permit to be there that expired. So, we've got a week here and then we'll take a break for a couple of weeks while that gets sorted out. It's ridiculous." He yawns. He sounds so tired, and I think he's called me before having the sleep he so desperately needs.

"Where are you now?" *Where's Gabby?*

"Manila. There are a few scenes we can shoot here."

"Okay."

"Are you okay, Delaney?" Concerns bleeds through his tone, and it brings tears to my eyes.

"I'm not sure."

"You're usually talkative, but you're so quiet."

I wipe a tear rolling down my cheek with the palm of my hand. "Are we okay?" I ask.

"What do you mean?"

"I mean, you couldn't call me all week, but photos of you and Gabby Reynolds made it out of the jungle. Are you with her?" I sniff.

"What photos? She's here with her partner. And damn it, Delaney, as much as I'd love you to be with me here, I wouldn't want you to witness all I had to."

I snort. "What do you mean?"

"The man oozes sexuality. And him and Gabby are real hot for each other. The air-conditioning in her trailer broke down, and I invited her to share mine while it was fixed. I couldn't turn my head without seeing them practically having sex around the trailer."

I clamp my lips together to avoid laughing while I wipe my cheeks again. "Really?"

"Really. If anyone's trying to link me and Gabby Reynolds, they are way off the mark. Hell, Antonio's enough to confuse *me*."

"Well, she does share the last name of my favourite Canadian."

Josh chuckles. "Oh, not this shit again. That's my title."

I laugh.

"I love you, Delaney. There's no way I'm fucking this up for a fling. I'm living for the day when I can see you again. Which is another reason why I'm calling."

"You didn't just want to hear my sexy accent?"

Josh sighs. "That too. Reece has offered me his holiday home in Hawaii while we're on break, and I know it's late notice, but I want you to come and spend my time off with me."

My heart seizes. Hawaii? I haven't had a holiday since before Melly was born. Lying in the sun and relaxing sounds more like a pipe dream than reality.

"Melly has school. It's only halfway through the term. And neither of us have passports."

"If Amelia is in school, then maybe you could come over by yourself? Would Pania look after her?"

I blow out a breath. "I'm sure she would."

"I'll pay for an emergency passport, and get Mindy to book your tickets. You won't have to do a thing other than apply for it."

I groan. "It's so tempting."

"Then do it. I'd give anything to kiss you right now."

"I'd give anything to jump your bones."

He laughs. "That thing you do when you squeeze my balls ..."

"That thing you do with your tongue." I sigh.

"What thing?"

"Anything." I laugh. "I just want your tongue."

"I'm sorry I couldn't leave it behind with you." He pauses. "What are you wearing?"

I laugh. "I'm in bed, but I've got my winter pyjamas on. Nothing too exciting."

"You're in bed; that's a start."

"Without you."

"Then get online and order that passport. When you've done it, let me know and I'll get your tickets booked. Just think about it. Two weeks on the beach."

I laugh. "We'd never see the beach. I'd be pinning you to the bed."

"Even better. I miss your tits."

Oh, we're going to play that game.

"I miss your cock more."

"Believe me, he misses you."

"He?"

"He has a mind of his own when it comes to you. My hand's not cutting it."

I look down at my crumb-covered shirt. "I don't think I'd cut it right now. I look like a slob. Maybe you should use moisturiser."

Josh laughs. "I'd rather be inside you. You drive me crazy. I can't wait to see you again."

"I miss you." I brush the crumbs off to the side of the bed where they fall on the floor, and snuggle down under the covers.

"I miss you. And I need you to trust me. There's no one on this earth I want to be with. Only you. I hope you know that."

Cradling the phone close to my ear, I move until I'm comfortable. "I do. It's just … those sites are ruthless."

"They are, but this is me telling you that you never need to doubt how I feel about you. We're owed our happy ending, Delaney."

He's right. Deep down I know he wouldn't put us at risk, but after not being able to see him or speak to him, that story hit a nerve. I need to steel myself for worse. It's not ever going to get better.

"I'm sorry. It's just a bit much."

"No. I'm sorry. I should have warned you about this kind of thing. The media will do anything if they get a sniff of what they think is news."

I sigh. "So, this isn't a one-off?"

"They'll try and link me with anyone when all I want is to be with you. Please try and remember that."

"I will." I stare at the ceiling.

"What have you been doing? How's Amelia?"

"Work and school. She's good. She's missing you too."

"Next time I'll try and call earlier. Give her a kiss for me."

"I will."

"I guess I should let you go and get some sleep. I love you."

"Love you too. Goodnight, Josh."

"Still wish you were here. Goodnight."

When we terminate the call, I look at the clock by the bed. It's only nine-thirty, so I scroll to Pania in my contacts and press call.

"Yo."

I laugh. Even that short word tells me she's eating. She's probably in bed watching TV and stuffing her face like me.

"If I wanted to go away for two weeks, would you come and stay here to look after Amelia?"

"You know I would." Her words are muffled. "Why?"

"Josh just asked me to spend a fortnight in Hawaii with him."

"I hope you said yes." I hear her swallow. "You're insane if you didn't."

"Are you sure? I don't want to dump you in it."

She laughs. "My best friend's Hollywood boyfriend has just asked her to spend two sex weeks in Hawaii, and you think I'm not going to bend over backwards to make it work for you? You'd do the same for me."

"You're the best."

"Don't you forget it."

"I promise I'll find you your own Hollywood boyfriend."

She lets out a dramatic sigh. "Oh, Delaney, that's what I'm counting on."

CHAPTER THIRTY-ONE

DELANEY

"EXCUSE ME."

The very tall man in the aisle seat looks me over. "Yes?"

"Could I squeeze past you? That's my seat." I point past him to the middle seat in the row. The thought of having to bug this guy if I need to use the toilet while we're flying tightens my chest.

In the diner, I can handle social situations—I know my customers. But I'm not a fan of being surrounded by people, and that's how this feels.

I hated flying economy to the US last time, and although the flight to Hawaii isn't as long, the thought of being sandwiched between two guys is not exactly awe-inspiring.

All I want is a bit more space and a comfortable seat.

At least at the other end of this flight, Josh'll be waiting and it'll be worth it.

The man in the aisle seat eyes me and lets out a loud sigh as if I'm asking for the moon. Slowly, he stands and steps out to let me in. He grunts as I make my way past.

"Thank you."

There's no acknowledgement as he sits back down.

I tug off my jacket and tuck it into the seat pocket in front of me. Sitting down, I buckle my seatbelt, lean back, and close my eyes.

This brings back memories. I was a nervous eighteen-year-old last time I flew long-distance, and I've been through so much since then. But I thought I could conquer the world, and I travelled alone for nine months before I met Josh.

My flight home I barely remember; I was still shell-shocked by what had happened.

Mum had picked me up, grumbling about how it wasn't fair that the flight landed at some ridiculous hour of the morning. Within weeks, she'd cut me out of her life completely. Everything fell apart.

But this trip will be different. Josh and I need time together to finish rebuilding things between us, and I'm confident it'll go well.

I'm going to miss Amelia like crazy. But she's in her first year of school and still making friends and establishing routines. I don't want her to get the idea that because Josh is her dad we'll be flitting off whenever he calls.

I watch the safety video, and soon the plane rumbles on its way to take off.

Here we go.

The first couple of hours of the flight, I flick from show to show on the in-flight entertainment. Nothing keeps my interest, and my mind keeps wandering. If it's not Melly I'm thinking about, it's her father.

I don't care if she has school. The next trip, we'll do together.

Maybe I need to find a movie to keep my mind off things.

Selecting *Magic Mike XXL*, I smile. I don't get to watch a lot of grown-up movies at home. By the time Melly's asleep, I'm lucky if I don't fall asleep in front of the television most nights.

Channing Tatum gyrates on my screen. *Does Josh know him?*

My life really is about to turn weird.

The man to the left of me snorts. "The movies get worse every time on these flights."

I turn up the sound, cross my arms and block him out.

It's just me and Channing for the next couple of hours.

The time passes pretty quickly, and as the credits roll, the smell of hot food fills my nostrils. My stomach grumbles even though I had a snack at the airport as I knew my ticket didn't come with a meal. At least I'll get a cup of coffee to tide me over for a while longer.

The men either side of me are served a meal. It looks like a beef wellington with mashed potato, but I try not to look because my mouth is watering.

"Coffee or tea? Or maybe a cold drink?" the flight attendant asks me.

"Coffee would be lovely."

My neighbour glares as the attendant reaches over to hand me the small tray with a cup full of coffee in it. I pour in the milk, stir in some sugar, and open the wrapped chocolate chip biscuit. At least I've got something to eat.

Flicking through the movies, I find one that stars Josh. I've only seen the one movie of his so far, and maybe this'll distract me while I'm waiting for this flight to end.

Settling in with my coffee and my movie, I gaze at the screen and smile. This'll all be worth it when I'm in his arms and we can forget about the outside world.

My stomach clenches when Josh appears on the screen. Watching him is a revelation.

Before my eyes, he transforms into an action hero. This movie's so different to the last one I watched, which was moody and dark. This one is full of running and explosions, and he's the good guy who's been betrayed and has to rescue the girl.

Even when he kisses her, I swoon before the jealousy hits me.

It makes me think of him in the jungle with Gabby Reynolds, and even though he told me she's there with her partner and they're crazy in love, the thought of her in his arms drives me a little more than crazy.

By the time the movie's over, I feel empty.

There are still two hours left on the flight. At least I haven't had to pee yet.

Of course, the thought of that gives me the urge to.

I let out a long breath and stare at the ceiling of the plane.

The urge to pee builds.

I should have two choices. But the guy to my left is snoring, and Mr. Grumpy on the right is in the middle of his own movie.

Shit.

I have to do this before it ends up being urgent. Taking a deep breath, I tap Mr. Grumpy on the shoulder.

He glares at me.

"I'm sorry, but could I please get past you? I just need to pop to the bathroom."

He scowls, sighs dramatically, and tugs off his headphones. For six and a half hours he's not been disturbed, so he could just do it.

With another big sigh, he stands, and I move past him.

The plane bathroom gives me a few moments of peace—as much as you can get on a plane anyway—and then I'm back with the knot in my stomach, asking him to move again.

He's still grumbling when I'm back in my seat. I swear, Melly is more adult than this guy.

I only hope the flight home's better.

IT'S a bit of a miracle I make it through border security in one piece with my knees knocking the way they are. Not that I'm doing anything wrong, but it's one of those things that's enough to make you nervous.

As it is, I worried I'd accidentally leave something in my handbag that I wasn't supposed to carry on the plane, so I shoved my phone, passport, and purse into my jacket pockets and stuck my handbag in my checked bag. At least I'm not about to be separated from the things I need.

I cast my gaze over the rows of people waiting.

No sign of Josh.

But then a tall, grey-haired man in a black suit catches my eye. He's holding up a sign that reads *Delaney Carruthers*.

He smiles when I walk up to him.

"Ms. Carruthers?"

I nod. "Josh isn't here?"

"He apologised for not being able to make it himself. It's my understanding he was called into a meeting with the production team for the movie with all the issues they had in the Philippines. But I'll take you to the house and he'll be there as quick as he can."

"Thank you." It's not ideal, but at least my feet are on the ground and surely I'll be able to find something to eat soon.

"Just the one suitcase?" he asks.

"That's right."

"Come this way." He takes the case from me, wheeling it as I follow him through the airport and out to a black stretch limousine. For a moment, I just stare at it because I've never ridden in anything like this.

After opening the door for me, the driver smiles as I step inside the car. I blow out a long breath as I sink into the soft leather seat.

"Good flight?"

I look up to see an older man sitting opposite me.

I don't answer for a moment.

"I'm Mac."

I know of Josh's agent, but we've never met. "Uh, hi. Flight was as okay as a flight that long can be."

He chuckles. "You'll have to get used to flying long-distance if you and Josh stay together."

My ears tingle. Why is he in the car to pick me up, and why is he talking about my relationship with Josh? It's none of his business.

"It's been a while. I'm sure once I'm used to it, it'll be fine."

The limo starts moving, and I'm relieved that soon I'll be with Josh and away from this guy. Something's not right.

"You're probably wondering why I'm here while Josh is busy. I needed to talk to you."

"Me?"

His expression gives nothing away. "I'm here to make you an offer, Delaney. I'll give you a million dollars if you leave now and get on the first plane back to New Zealand."

I swallow hard. This is far from the welcome I expected. And now I'm pissed. "I'm not interested. Josh invited me here for us to spend time together, and that's what I'm planning to do."

His eyes narrow. "You're a smart one, aren't you?" He leans forward. "Make it ten million dollars."

"Why are you so scared of Josh and I being together?"

For a moment, he says nothing.

"You nearly killed his career the first time around. He's twenty-five and hasn't peaked yet. You'll bring him down before he gets his chance to really soar."

Tears prick my eyes, but I'm not about to let this man win. Even if I'm still unsure how this is going to work. But I was the one who walked away all those years ago when Josh did nothing wrong, and I owe him the chance to love both me and Amelia.

Amelia.

It's not just me that Mac is trying to get out of the way. It's Josh's own daughter. Josh would never condone this.

"Well, Delaney? Just think of what you can do for your daughter with that money." He sneers as if my hesitation means he's won.

"I'm not remotely interested in your offer. What I want is to put my family back together the way it should have always been."

He shrugs. "I hope you remember that when Josh leaves you behind."

"That's a chance I'll take."

I fold my arms and lean back in the seat.

Because even if in the end it's Josh who walks away, then I did my best to give Amelia what I never had.

A second chance to have her father in her life.

IT'S NOT A LONG DRIVE, but the rest of it is spent in silence.

I pretend Mac doesn't exist. Tears prick my eyes as I look out the window, and I don't take in any of the scenery until we come to a stop.

Muffled voices come from outside, and I lean forward to see a guard talking to the driver.

We're nearly there.

The light fades as we head into evening. But there's still more than enough for me to see a Hawaiian woman standing outside the house.

The incredibly large, blue-with-white-trimmings house. It's beautiful, two storey with large verandah running around the outside.

Of course Reece Evans owns a freaking mansion.

She smiles widely at me as I step out of the car.

"Aloha, Delaney. I'm Leilani, the housekeeper. I'll show you to your room and arrange some food. You must be starving after your flight. I know the airplane food isn't that great."

I smile. It's nice to meet someone who seems happy to see me.

"That would be wonderful. I'd kill for a cup of coffee."

She laughs. "You won't have to. We'll go to the kitchen and I'll make some."

"Thank you. Thank you so much."

"Come this way. Let me show you around."

I don't look back at Mac as we walk into the mansion. I'm not going to allow him to continue any conversation about paying me off. It's absurd. And Josh will know about it.

If the outside of the building was impressive, the inside is even more so. A wide, sweeping wooden staircase leads to the second storey, and the rooms that are visible are massive. My whole house is about as big as the living room.

"How about we do coffee first and then I'll show you to your room? I'm sure I know what I'd want first," Leilani says.

"You read my mind. Sounds perfect to me."

She leads me down behind the staircase and into a huge kitchen. All I can do is stare with wide eyes at how beautiful it is, from the built-in appliances to the marble benchtops. A grin lights up her face.

"Josh told me you were a cook. He said you had a thing for kitchens."

"It's lovely. I like shiny appliances. Shame they don't stay that way."

Leilani laughs. "The kitchen's recently been renovated. I'm hoping these will stay like this for a little while. Take a seat."

I walk to the large table and pull out a chair. This is the most comfortable I've felt since leaving home. I close my eyes and take a deep breath. The air is scented with fresh baking and coffee, and my stomach grumbles.

The sound of something being placed in front of me makes me open my eyes. It's a platter freshly baked rolls, cheese, different spreads.

"This looks amazing. Thank you so much."

"Anything else you need, just ask." Leilani smiles before she goes back to the bench to pour me a coffee.

I dig right in, slicing open a roll and filling it from the platter. I moan as I sink my teeth into it.

"Hungry?" Leilani asks as she places the coffee down.

"Starving. I had a chocolate-chip cookie on the plane. And that's it. This is amazing."

She frowns. "I'm sorry to hear that."

I shrug. "It's okay. I'm just really glad to be here now. Do you know how long Josh is going to be?"

She shakes her head. "He wasn't sure. But he left crystal-clear instructions that you were to be well looked after."

I grin. That's so Josh. It's what left me so confused over the plane seats. Although thinking that leaves me feeling like I'm being ungrateful when he's paying for everything. It's hard to wrap my head around.

"Are there many staff here?" I ask.

Leilani seems to think for a moment. "Not usually. It's just me and the driver. We have a company that comes in and takes care of the gardens, and while you two are staying here, security has been ramped up."

I widen my eyes. "Really?"

She nods. "We have a security firm that watches the place, but whenever Reece stays, or in this case Josh, we get in extra security. Can't be too careful."

That feels a bit weird to me, but I guess I understand.

This is the life I'm going to have to get used to.

AFTER I EAT, Leilani leads me upstairs to the bedroom I'll be sharing with Josh.

It's incredible.

The pale blue walls with white curtains leave the room looking so bright and airy. A large bed sits at one end of the room, and there's a walk-in wardrobe opposite. My single suitcase looks wholly inadequate in comparison.

"I'll leave you to it. There are fresh towels in the en-suite if you'd like to take a shower or a bath, and just pick up the phone if you need me and dial zero for the kitchen."

"Thank you so much." I want to hug her. She reminds me a lot of Pania's mother. The two of them would probably get along great.

"You're welcome. Hopefully Josh will be back soon. I'm so happy that he found you, Delaney. I've been taking care of this house for four years, ever since Reece bought it, and Josh looks happier than I've ever seen him."

I grin. "I'm pretty happy too."

"You have a beautiful little girl. I've seen the photos. Next time, you bring her to come and see me."

Laughing, I nod. "I will. Promise."

"I'll leave you to settle in, and remember, call me if you need me."

"I will. Thank you."

She closes the door behind her, and I head straight to the bed. All I want is to shut my eyes for a little while.

The mattress is the most comfortable one I've ever lain on. This is the luxury I expected from this trip. Today's been exhausting, so it doesn't take much to fall asleep.

When I wake, it's dark, and I slide off the bed and venture downstairs just in time to see Josh walk in the front door.

His whole face lights up at the sight of me.

"I'm sorry I'm so late. Have you been taken care of?"

I nod. "Are you hungry?"

He grasps my arms and pulls me toward him. "I'm starving, but I want a taste of you first."

All the tension in my body disappears when I'm in his arms, and he gives me a soft, but needy kiss.

"Fuck food."

I squeal as he bends and scoops me into his arms. All is right with my world again, and I'm where I need to be—with Josh.

Fuck Mac and his attempt to get rid of me. I'm stronger than that. *We're* stronger than that.

Josh carries me up the stairs and back toward the bedroom. I laugh the whole way.

"I'm too heavy for this."

"No, you're not. You're perfect."

I bury my face in his neck for the rest of the way, and he sets me on my feet inside the door which he closes behind us.

"How was your flight?" he asks.

I pause. There's no point in lying, and Josh knows me well enough to read me. "Not fun, but I'm here now."

"What happened?"

I shrug. "Nine hours stuck next to a very tall, muscular guy who took up a lot of space and did not want to move when I needed to use the bathroom. I just hope I have an aisle seat on the way back."

"Wait. What?" He stares at me, and I smile.

"Like I said. I'm here now with you; that's all that matters."

"No, it's not. You were supposed to fly first class. Or business class if that wasn't available. No one should have been blocking your seat."

I shrug. "I was in economy. It's how I flew to the US the first time, but an aisle seat would have been much easier. I survived."

His nostrils flare. "I'm calling Mindy. I gave express instructions for your fare. This is my time to try and impress you and convince you that you need to be with me. I wanted to give you the best."

I reach up and stroke his stubbled cheek. "Josh, it's okay. You don't need to impress me."

"But I wanted to."

"You're so cute when you pout." We can worry about this later. Right now, I just want him.

He shakes his head and chuckles. "You disarm me every time. I can't get angry around you. You're the charming one."

I laugh. "I'm not sure I deserve that honour."

He takes my hand in his, raises it to his lips, and kisses my palm. "I love you so much. And I'm pissed that my grandstanding has been made ineffective by Mindy. She's never screwed anything up like this before."

"At least you're acknowledging that you were grandstanding."

"You'll be in a much better seat on the way home, I promise." He wraps his arms around my waist and pulls me in tight against him. "That's if I let you go home."

"Is there something in your pocket, or are you *really* pleased to see me?"

"Stop trying to distract me."

"I shouldn't have to distract you. You wanted me here, and you got me. Alone. For two whole weeks." I run my tongue slowly across my upper lip. "Question is—what are you going to do with me, Joshua Carter?"

"Oh, I can think of a few things."

I squeal as he bends, and throws me over his shoulder. We fall in a heap, unceremoniously on the bed, kissing and laughing.

"Seriously? Your way of getting me into bed is to throw me on it?"

He nuzzles my neck. "Do I really have to try to get you into bed?"

"Are you saying I'm not virtuous?" I clutch at my chest in mock horror.

"I'm sure you are. At times." He grins. "You make me laugh. It's so hard to focus when you're around." He kisses me hard.

"It's not exactly easy for me either." I cup his face and look into his eyes. It doesn't matter how I got here. I'm with him and that really is all that matters.

Being with him again is everything.

CHAPTER THIRTY-TWO

DELANEY

A GENTLE BREEZE wafts through the windows and across the bed, and I arch my back, enjoying the feel of it licking my bare skin.

Josh is warm beside me, sleeping on his stomach, his arm flung over my waist. This makes up for yesterday.

"You're really here," he mumbles.

"Yes, I am." I smile, and roll toward him.

He looks at me with sleepy eyes. "I'm so glad you came. I missed you like crazy."

"I missed you too. What are we going to do while I'm here?"

His lips snake into a smile. "I can think of a few things."

"I'm going to see the sights, and not just the inside of this bedroom."

Josh laughs. "We'll go for a drive in the next couple of days, get some shopping done. Let's load up those suitcases for your return trip. I want to spoil you and our daughter."

"Uh, suitcase. I travelled light."

He shrugs. "You'll be travelling in luxury on the way back. I'll get all that shit from yesterday sorted and find out what the fuck Mindy was thinking."

I sigh as he slides his hand up and cups my bare breast.

"I love waking up naked with you," he says.

"I just love waking up with you."

He kisses my shoulder. "We could do this every morning."

"One day, we will. Depends on how well you behave while I'm here."

"Is that right?"

I squeal as he kneels, then launches himself onto me. He uses his knee to spread my legs, and then he's right there, his erection pressed against my leg.

"I can feel how happy you are right now."

"Let me show you." He scoots down my body, and I close my eyes when his tongue hits my clit. "I don't need any other breakfast than you, Delaney."

"Really? My stomach is grumbling." I sigh.

Sighs turn to gasps as he taunts me, teasing me with his tongue.

"I love you," he says as he reaches for the condoms in the bedside cabinet.

"I love you too."

His slide into me is torturously slow, and I meet his gaze as he lowers himself onto me.

"Two whole weeks of this." He kisses me again, and I'm lost in the sensation. Josh always knows exactly what I need.

"I know. How are we both going to survive?" I tilt my hips to take him a little deeper. "I'll even deal with your morning breath for this."

He lowers his head to my breast, sucking on the nipple.

"Oh." It's all I've got left to say.

"It's not often that I render you speechless." He laughs.

"Make the most of it."

He shifts to the other breast, while moving slowly inside me. I didn't realise just how much I missed sex until we got back together, and how hard the last six weeks have been.

It'd be easy to become addicted to it with Josh.

I close my eyes again, just enjoying that breeze across me while

Josh worships my body. He's right. We could have this every morning.

I have some very big decisions to make.

AFTERWARD, I roll to my side and Josh spoons me from behind.

"Come and live with me in the States when this movie's finished. We'll make a fresh start—the three of us."

I shuffle over and roll onto my back to look at him. It's what he wants. And I do too. But I vowed a long time ago not to be dependent on anyone.

"I need to think about it. It's not as simple as us just up and moving."

"It could be."

"I have a career, and obligations to take care of. There's something I should tell you about too."

His jaw tics as if I'm about to tell him his dog died, or I've been sleeping with Damon. I'm sure he can tell it's not good from my tone, but I can't hold it in.

"Mac offered me money to leave you."

Josh doesn't need to say anything. The look of disbelief that crosses his face stabs me right in the heart. "What? When?"

"Yesterday when I arrived." Tears prick my eyes. "He offered me a million dollars to get on the next plane out of here. When I said no, he upped it to ten."

Josh's eyes search mine. "I ..."

"You don't believe me." I fist my hands in exasperation.

"It's not that, it's just that ... he's been so good to me. He knows how much I love you. Why would he ...?"

I hold up my palms. "I'm going to get dressed and go for a walk. You can work that out while I'm gone."

He reaches for one of my wrists. "Delaney, don't."

"I've told you what I needed to. Now I'm giving you space to wrap your head around it. The flight attendant said there are markets not far from here. What I need is fresh air." I pull away, slide off the bed and open the wardrobe. After slipping one of my dresses off the hanger, I throw it on the bed while I grab some underwear out of my bag.

"We need to talk about this. I'm sorry if I didn't react the way you expected," he says.

"What? Like believing me?" I tug on a bra, hooking it behind me.

"Of course I believe you, it's just—"

"And that's why I'm going for a walk."

I know I'm being pissy, but we promised to be always open and honest with each other, and with that comes an expectation of trust and belief. I should have told him last night, but we got so carried away.

Pulling my dress on, I slather myself in sunscreen. Josh stays silent, and every time I glance at him, he seems to be brooding over what I said.

Grabbing my bag, I storm out the door, hurt and angry at the expression on his face.

What if he doesn't believe me?

What if Mac denies it and Josh chooses his word over mine?

I never wanted to get in the way of anything to do with his career. Never in a million years would I have taken the money.

For six years, I had a hole in my heart. Now it's been filled and someone's trying to tear us apart again?

No fucking way.

CHAPTER THIRTY-THREE

JOSH

I DON'T KNOW what to do.

Delaney thinks I don't believe her, but it was the shock of hearing what she had to say that sent my head spinning.

Reece has been telling me to ditch Mac for years. I'm his only client—at least, the only one that's stuck around, and the most successful. But I keep getting the jobs, and his advice always seems sound.

The only time I've broken away from that was when I went to New Zealand, and I have no regrets over it because it led me back to Delaney.

I pick up my phone and FaceTime the only person I know I can talk to.

Reece answers almost straight away with a big smile on his face. "Hey, what's up? Enjoying the house?"

I nod. "It's great."

"Is your lady with you? I need to meet the woman who has you tied up in knots."

I don't even need to say anything.

"What happened? You look like the sky is falling."

Letting out a sigh, I shrug. "It might be. We had a fight this morning."

He frowns. "Didn't she only just get there? What on earth did you argue about?"

"Mac."

Reece rolls his eyes. "Dude. Don't let that asshole come between you two. What did he do?"

"He offered Delaney money to leave me."

Reece's eyes nearly pop out of his head. "Whoa. That is a huge line to cross. Isn't your contract coming up for negotiation soon?"

I nod. "Sure is. The new one's with my lawyers."

"Don't you dare sign. He's trying to get rid of anyone who might see through his bullshit."

"Do you think so?"

His brows twitch. "Do you not believe it happened?"

"I do. Delaney wouldn't lie to me. But I owe Mac so much."

Reece grunts. "You owe him jack shit. He might have got you the first audition, but your success sells you. Not him. He's flying around the world on your dime, and wants to interfere enough to drive the mother of your kid away. Don't let him."

I nod. "I won't. I guess I just needed to hear that."

"You spent years wondering what happened to Delaney. Now you know and you have her back. Don't let anything get in the way of that."

I smile. "When did you become such a big advocate for love, Mr. Love-Them-and-Leave-Them?"

Reece grins. "I always figured she must have been something special from the way you were hung up on her. Never thought you'd get another opportunity with her. I'd never let a woman go who had that kind of impact on me."

I give a little sigh thinking of Delaney. Reece stood by me when I was so miserable over her leaving, and our friendship was one of the reasons I kept going.

"Don't give her a reason to walk away again. She clearly doesn't give a shit about money or she would have been after you years ago for child support."

"I never had any doubt about that. She loves me for me."

"Then kick that asshole to the kerb and start your life with her. And give Sara a call."

I chuckle. Sara's Reece's agent. She's solid, and she doesn't take shit from him. He's been trying to get her into bed since they met, but she's focused on his career and her other clients. And she's the perfect person to sign up with. "Even if I do, she still won't sleep with you."

"Maybe not, but it'd be worth some brownie points. She's good at her job and she won't rip you off." He pauses. "Anyway, where is Delaney? I need to meet her."

"She went for a walk this morning to the markets. She was pretty pissed at me."

"At you? Why?"

I hesitate for a moment. Just like I did this morning. "She told me about Mac and thought I didn't believe her. I did, it was just hard to hear."

"And you let her go?"

"She was steamed. I couldn't forbid her from going."

"Yeah, but she thinks you think she's a liar."

I shake my head. "I told her I believe her."

"You'd better sort things out. I'm living vicariously through you right now." He laughs.

"I will. But I need to give my lawyer a call and catch up with Mac. While Delaney's cooling down, I need to get this fixed."

"Huh," he says. "You really do love her. I've been trying to talk you out of staying with him forever."

I nod. "I know. Sometimes you just need the right wake-up call."

"I'm glad you had it then. Talk to you later, dude."

"Speak soon."

I terminate the call and stare at my phone for a moment. There's another call I have to make first—one that I should have made last night when alarm bells began to ring.

Dialling Mindy, I take a deep breath. I've never had any reason to get angry with her before, but her personal relationship with Mac is about to make our working relationship very difficult.

"Hey, boss," she says when she answers. She's so cheery, which just makes this more difficult.

"Hi. I have some questions around Delaney's plane tickets. I gave instructions that she was to fly at least business class."

She laughs nervously. "Mac told me to book economy."

"Who pays your wages?"

"You do."

"Did you not think that maybe you should have done what I asked you to do? I know you're Mac's sister-in-law, but I'm your boss."

There's silence for a moment. "I just thought—"

"My personal life has nothing to do with Mac. It's none of his business. Is that clear?"

"Yes," she whispers.

"If Delaney's ticket is economy for the trip home, I want it upgraded. And I want the updated ticket sent to me."

"I'll do it now." She sounds stunned, but I wonder now how often I asked for things to be done only for them to be run past Mac. How many commitments have I missed when I've promised people things? What else don't I know?

I end the call with her, and flick through my contacts. The next call will be to my lawyer, and then I'll probably give Sara a call.

Last, but definitely far from least, I'll confront Mac.

I START with the wing of the house that Mac's sleeping in. He arrived here not long after I did to catch up and go over upcoming opportunities while I had some downtime. There's no sign of him inside.

I find him out the back, sitting by the pool and finishing up a meal.

"Josh. Good meeting yesterday?"

I nod. "Yeah. Hey, Mac. Did you fly first class out here?" I ask as I take a seat.

He nods. "Might have been business class. I'm not completely sure. Why do you ask?"

"What about Delaney?"

His eyebrows rise. "I'm not sure. Whatever Mindy booked."

"Mindy booked what you told her to book." I pause. "When you offered to pick Delaney up from the airport, I thought you were helping me out. Is she really that much of a threat to you?"

Understanding crosses his expression. "I just wanted to make sure she was loyal. You don't even know for sure that the kid is yours."

"Amelia's mine."

"You haven't had a DNA test done. Are you really going to take that risk?"

I draw in a deep breath. "She's mine. I have zero doubts."

He shrugs. "Well, if you're prepared to take that risk."

"The only thing I have doubts about is you."

Straightening up in his chair, the icy look he fixes on me would have stopped me in my tracks early on in my career. But Reece is right. It's time to cut myself loose from Mac.

"I've just spoken to my lawyers, and I won't be renewing my contract with you."

In all the time I've known him, Mac's never been angry with me, and now I know for sure why. I'm his meal ticket, and he's trying to plant a seed that that's how Delaney sees me.

But I know better. I have faith in what Delaney and I have.

"Josh, I know you're pissed with me. But ..."

"I've already found new representation. The way you treated Delaney crossed a line, Mac."

He hesitates. "You're really going to cut your most important business relationship for a piece of pussy?"

I fist my hands, but I won't be taunted into punching him. I'm sure that's exactly what he wants. "If that's the way you're going to refer to Delaney, then all you're doing is confirming my decision for me. Get the fuck out, Mac. My lawyers will be in touch."

"You'd better believe I'll be consulting my lawyers."

"Go for it. Just get the fuck out of my face. And you need to find a new job for Mindy too. I can't have her working for me anymore."

Six years ago, Mac had seemed like a god to me. But now, when he stands before me, he's a mere mortal. But he made a big mistake thinking he could get rid of Delaney.

She's the one woman I'll never let go of.

CHAPTER THIRTY-FOUR

DELANEY

LEILANI FUSSED WHEN I LEFT.

She wanted the driver to take me, but I wanted to walk.

The directions she gives me are easy to follow, and I set off. The guard lets me out the gate, and I walk down a long road that leads toward the markets. The road is lined with trees in parts, that give way to show the impressive houses on either side.

Warm sun on my face makes me smile. While the weather is changing back home, it's nothing like this. Despite what happened this morning, I'm glad I came.

Josh and I will survive this. I know it. But he needs time to process what I've told him, and I need some fresh air after that plane trip and then dealing with Mac.

Mac's bullshit won't tear us apart.

Leilani said the walk would be about half an hour, and the sun makes me glad I slathered myself in sunscreen before I left.

I walk until I reach the end of the road and then turn right until I see the market stands, just as I was told.

Bright stalls fill a large carpark, and even at a distance it's clear there's a huge variety of things for sale. The scent of hot dogs and chips fills the air, and pop music plays which gives it a party atmosphere.

I'm not really sure where to start, but it's a wonderful distraction.

I'm not there long when I hear a voice behind me.

"Delaney."

A familiar voice with an English accent comes from behind me. I don't know anyone here, so God knows who it could be.

I turn.

Gabby Reynolds, as large as life, comes swaggering toward me. As she draws closer, it's clear she's even more beautiful than her photos would suggest. Her brown hair shines in the bright sunlight, and her blue eyes dance. She smiles.

"I'd have recognised you anywhere. I'm Gabby."

"I ... I ..."

She nods. "You're surprised I recognised you. It was easy. I've seen a million photos of you. Josh is a very proud boyfriend."

I beam. "Really?"

"He has so many photos of you and your daughter on his phone. I think I saw them every chance he got."

I blush, and her smile widens.

"Are you out shopping?"

"I came for some fresh air. It was a long flight yesterday."

"I can imagine." She grimaces. "I hate flying. If I could film everything in the UK, I would just stay there."

There's silence for a moment, and she seems to study my expression. "Do you want to sit down and talk somewhere? I'm waiting for Antonio to finish his shopping. That man is worse than I am."

Nodding, I take a look around. No one seems to be paying much attention to us, which makes me feel a bit better about being seen with Josh here. There are picnic tables and benches all around the market, and I could do with being off my feet after that walk.

"Here." She points at a nearby table. I follow her, and as we sink onto the seats, she lets out an audible groan. "My feet were killing me."

"Mine are a bit sore too."

"It's a decent walk from Reece's house. Do you need a ride home?"

I shake my head. "I really just wanted to get some fresh air. I'm going to take a look around the markets before I go back."

She gives me a knowing smile. "Make him sweat it out."

"Something like that."

"Are you okay?"

The pain of Josh's disbelief comes rushing back at me, and I blink away tears. "I will be. Josh and I had some words, and I came out to clear my head."

Her eyes are full of empathy. "I'm so sorry to hear that. I know he's been so anxious to see you. But I'm sure the separation has been hard."

I nod. "It certainly hasn't helped."

"And I'm also sure those ridiculous articles saying we were fooling around didn't help either. The media can be arseholes."

Despite my hurt, I smile. She's clearly not backward in coming forward.

"What's really stupid was that Antonio was with me the whole time. We'd never been to the Philippines before, and we wanted to share the experience. When the air conditioning broke in my trailer, Josh gave up his for the two of us. There's never been anything between Josh and me except on-screen."

I blow out a breath. "Despite what it sounds like, I do trust him. But it's hard."

She nods, reaching across the table and placing her hand on mine. "I know. Antonio was separated when we met, and the media ate it up, making out I was sleeping with a married man. But him and his wife were well and truly over before I came on the scene. Try not to let it get to you."

"I will."

Gabby's face lights up. "Do you want to meet Antonio? He's walking this way."

I turn my head to see a ridiculously hot man walking toward us. He's dressed in white shorts with a white shirt that only highlights his deeply tanned skin and dark hair. And his eyes are trained on Gabby.

Turning back, I can't help the little smile that crosses my lips at the dazzled way she's looking at him. That's love.

"Every time," she mutters. "He just looks so good."

"I'm glad you found someone to talk to," he says in a thick Spanish accent. "Sorry I took so long."

She beams. "It's fine. Delaney, this is my Antonio."

He extends his hand, and I reach out thinking he'll shake mine, but he raises it to his lips. "I would have recognised you anywhere. Josh has a million photos of you."

"So I hear." I grin.

"We're going to get some lunch and then go to our rental. Want to join us?" she asks.

I pause before shaking my head. "Thank you, but no. I think I'll just have a bit more of a wander and then head back to see Josh."

We stand, and she rounds the table to hug me. It's familiar, but she clearly feels like she knows me, and I have a whole new appreciation for her. She's not just some random woman I've seen snuggling up with my boyfriend in a magazine, and she very obviously adores her man.

"I hope we see each other again, Delaney. I'd love to meet your little girl sometime." She smiles.

"I'd like that."

Antonio winks at me. "She's so clucky."

"Hush, you." Gabby shrugs. She raises her palm so that she's talking to me behind her hand. "He's not wrong, though."

I grin. "It was really nice to meet you."

"You too. Maybe we can meet up for dinner before we go back to filming."

"That sounds really good."

They walk away, hand in hand, and even my heart skips a little just watching them. There's no doubt about the state of their relationship, and now I'm even more sad about those stupid articles. How must it feel for Antonio to read that while he's right there seeing there's nothing going on?

It's so not fair.

I SPEND the next hour walking through the market, picking up a crocheted doll and running my fingers through the feathers of dreamcatcher. I could spend a fortune on Melly here, and I'm glad she's not with me. Everything would be catching her eye.

And then I spot it.

It's a white summer dress with large purple hibiscus flowers. It's similar to the one I'm wearing, but I couldn't find anything like it in a child's size back home.

She'd love it.

I open my bag, and dig my hand around in the cluster of receipts. It's not there.

Shit.

Closing my eyes, I see myself yesterday sliding my purse, my passport, and my phone into my pockets. Where they've stayed. I was so flustered this morning that I have nothing on me.

"Did you want me to gift wrap it?" the smiling lady behind the table asks.

"I'm sorry. I'll have to come back. I've managed to leave my money at the house."

She nods. "It's fine. I can put it away if you want me to? We're here tomorrow as well."

"Thank you. I really appreciate it."

My cheeks burn as I walk away, and not just from embarrassment. I need to get back to the house and out of this sun. There's not a cloud in the sky, and very little respite from the heat until I do.

Retracing my steps, I'm relieved to reach the point where I turn, but I know there's still a long way to go.

I come to a stop at the side of the road. I'm lost without my phone. I can't even summon an Uber. Which would be pointless anyway as I'm not sure of the actual address of the house.

Rubbing my forehead to try and ease the headache that's building, I sigh.

The only way is forward, so I take a deep breath and plod toward the house. *What the hell was I thinking?*

But the image in my head is of Josh's expression this morning. The one that screamed how uncertain he was when I told him the truth. It was hurtful after we've come so far, and I've been the one who's needed to trust him. He needs to trust me too.

Hot tears sting my eyes, and I'm sure this walk is much longer than the one I went on this morning. The temperature's risen since I left the house though, and it's a dry heat. I'm glad I put sunscreen on, but not so happy about not having a hat.

My headache grows as I get closer to the house. There's foliage at least on both sides of the road to give me some shade. But it's not enough.

I've never been so glad to see anything in my life as I am at the sight of the gates.

The guard's different to the one that let me out this morning.

"Hello. Could you let me in, please?"

He narrows his eyes. "Do you really think it's that simple?"

His voice. This is the guy who was on the gate yesterday who spoke to Mac. I breathe a sigh of relief.

"I came in the limo yesterday from the airport. Travelled with Mac Brown?"

He rolls his eyes and points across the road. "Pull the other one. You think you're the first person who's tried this today? That group over there all saw Mr. Brown arrive yesterday, and you were definitely not in the car."

"Yeah, I was. Now could you please give Josh a call, as I don't have my phone on me, and let him know I'm here. He'll want you to let me in."

"I wasn't born yesterday."

"Please. I'm not feeling well, and I need to get inside."

He crosses his arms. "That's not going to happen. You give me some ID to show who you are, and I'll think about it."

My stomach rolls.

"All my ID is inside the house. Please, can you just call Josh and tell him I'm back?"

The guard literally rolls his eyes.

I swallow hard. The last thing I need is to lose it. It's just going to make the situation worse.

"Stand back from the gate. I won't warn you again."

Hot tears spill down my face. My head is thumping already, and it feels like I'm burning up from the inside out. "Please, just call Josh."

"I'll be calling the police if you don't leave."

I puff out my chest. "Go on then. At least then I'll get a phone call and be able to talk to Josh."

He laughs, turning away. My cheeks blaze in a combination of sunburn and humiliation. I need to lie down, but I have nowhere to go.

At least the spot across the road where the others seem to have camped out has some shade.

I walk toward them. My heart thuds in time with my pounding head.

A cheer goes up, and a woman near the front chants, "Josh, Josh, Josh."

Well, I guess I know why they're here. I knew he had fans, but this is crazy.

As I reach a large rock to lean on, I stumble.

"Hey, are you okay?" The young woman who chanted for Josh looks at me with a concerned expression.

"I've got a pounding headache, and I feel …"

Turning back toward the bush, I lose the contents of my stomach. It almost immediately lightens my headache a little, but I still feel gross.

"Want some water?"

I nod. "Please."

She hands me a water bottle. The cap's a little chewed, but I'm past the point of caring about someone else's germs.

"Have the whole thing. I haven't had anything out of this one yet. I filled a ton of bottles this morning with ice and water."

"Thank you."

"You're welcome. First day here?"

I nod, and take a long drink from the bottle. It's not ice-cold, but it makes me feel a little better.

"I've been here for the past three days. Ever since I heard Josh Carter was staying."

"Three days?" I croak.

"I'm his biggest fan. Although, I'm sure you want to argue that with me."

"No, I think you've got that over me right now." I look back over my shoulder and glower at the guard.

"I'm not sure about that. Your accent tells me you're not from around here." She smiles. I'm sure she wouldn't smile if she knew who I was.

"I'm from New Zealand."

"New Zealand? I've always wanted to go there. I'm Becky."

"Delaney."

"You're not looking too good. Are you staying far from here?"

At her question, my eyes sting with tears. I can't take much more.

The pressure in my head builds again. I hold my hand to my forehead, as if it makes any difference. What I need are painkillers and a long sleep.

"Delaney?"

I look up to see two Beckys in front of me.

"I ... I ..."

She's shouting as my legs go out from underneath me, and the last thing I'm aware of is hitting the gravel at the side of the road.

Hard.

CHAPTER THIRTY-FIVE

JOSH

DELANEY'S BEEN GONE for hours, and the longer she's away, the more anxious I become.

She said she needed some space, and I've been happy to give it to her. I never meant to make her think I doubted her word; it was the shock of hearing what Mac had done that hit me hard.

I love her. I trust her.

And now I have to make sure she knows that.

I toy with my phone for about the fiftieth time since she went for her walk, and finally take a deep breath and dial.

Her shrill ringtone echoes through the quiet room, and I spin in the direction it's coming from.

I lift a cushion on the chair in the corner of the room. The jacket she wore yesterday sits underneath it, and through the fabric, the glow of the ringing phone tells me I'm wasting my time calling.

Fuck.

She had a bag when she left. I guess she didn't transfer her things to it.

Picking up the jacket, I search the pockets. Inside are her phone, her purse, and her passport.

My stomach sinks.

What on earth has she been doing all this time with no money and no phone?

Where are you, Delaney?

Running my fingers through my hair, I look down at the bed. *Think, Josh.*

I need to go looking for her. She said something about the markets, and maybe she got a little lost on the way back.

Making my way downstairs, I find Bradley, Reece's driver.

"Could you help me please, Bradley?" I ask.

"Of course, sir."

"Delaney's not back, and I'm worried about her. She's left her things behind by accident. I need to borrow one of Reece's cars to go and look for her."

He nods. "Of course, sir. I'm happy to help."

"We can cover more ground with two of us."

"Come this way, and I'll find you what you need."

I follow him down to the kitchen.

There's a locked cupboard on the wall, and he retrieves a key from his pocket to open it. The cabinet's full of keys as Reece is a lover of cars. He's got a few in the garage.

While I'm waiting, one of the security guards walks in. I hate needing security, but it's a no-brainer to keep Delaney safe.

What a joke. Then I let her walk off by herself.

When I find her, I owe her the biggest grovel ever.

"Sit down and I'll make you a drink," Leilani says to the guard. "It's hot work out there today."

He nods as he sits at the table beside a couple of others from the security team. "Tell me about it. Big drama down at the gate. One of the girls out there fainted and someone called an ambulance for her."

"An ambulance?" One of the others asks.

"Pretty sure she had heatstroke. She looked quite pink, and threw up before she fainted."

One of the other men at the table laughs. "Damn. It was only a matter of time before it happened to one of them."

"This was a new one. She tried the whole 'Josh Carter is my boyfriend' line to get in the gate. Gave up when I made it clear she wasn't getting in."

I freeze. The way they're talking pisses me off. I'm aware there's a small group who have camped outside the gate, but Delaney's my priority. I've done a shitty job of that, and it sounds like the situation outside the gate isn't much better.

"What did you say?" I ask.

The guard turns toward me. "Just one of those fans trying to get in to see you, sir. I took care of it."

"What was her name?" Prickly heat runs up the back of my spine.

He shrugs. "No idea. Pretty little thing she was, but I wasn't born yesterday. Looked sweet, but I'm sure that's just another tactic to get inside. Tried to tell me she came in with Mr. Brown yesterday."

For a moment, I stare at him. He turns back toward his friend.

"What did she look like?"

"Curvy little brunette."

"Was she wearing a dress? White with big blue flowers?"

When he turns back around, his wide eyes tell me everything.

"You fucking idiot." Anger swells within me.

"Josh," Bradley says. "We know where she is now. I'll get the car and pick you up out front."

My jaw tics, but I have more important places to be. My girl is ill and I need to know she's okay. I give him a curt nod. "This isn't finished."

I storm from the room. I'll deal with the guard later. Right now my focus has to be on Delaney and cleaning up this mess I've made with her. As it is, I'm on the back foot, and I need to make things right.

How the fuck do I convince her she belongs in my world when she can't even get back into the house we're staying in?

I'm not sure I'm worth forgiving.

She's so convinced that there's this gulf between us and this has just amplified it.

Fuck.

THE RECEPTIONIST at the emergency room looks up as I approach.

"I'm looking for my girlfriend. She was brought in with heatstroke."

She nods. "What was her name?"

"Delaney Carruthers."

"If you'd like to take a seat, sir ..."

"No, I want to see her. Now."

She raises an eyebrow like she's heard this shit a million times. "It'll just take me a moment to find someone who can help you."

"Thanks."

I'm way too wound up to sit, so instead I lean on the desk while she picks up the phone. Without even thinking about it, I tap my fingers on the hard surface of the desk until a man in a suit approaches me.

"You're looking for Ms. Carruthers. Are you her next of kin?"

"Boyfriend. Why?"

"There were questions she couldn't answer when she arrived. Mostly about insurance."

I roll my eyes. "Who gives a fuck? I'll pay for any expenses if she doesn't have any."

"So you don't know either?"

"I didn't book her tickets, so I'm not sure about travel insurance, which I'm guessing this would fall under? Either way, she's covered. Now, can I please see her?"

He nods. "Sure. Someone will be in to sort it all out with you."

"Whatever it takes. Please, just get me to Delaney."

SHE'S LYING in the bed, her eyes closed. I follow the cannula in the back of her hand up to an IV drip beside the bed.

"Delaney."

"We gave her something for the migraine, and it's made her drowsy. It'll pass."

I turn to the doctor. "When can I take her home?"

"She should be okay to go when she wakes up. There's no damage, but she was dehydrated. She'll need to rest and keep out of the sun for a couple of days."

I nod. "That's no problem."

If I have to wrap her up in cotton wool, I will. I'll do whatever it takes to show her how much she means to me.

After approaching the bed, I sit in the chair beside it and take her hand in mine. I've already lost Delaney once, and it caused us to be apart for six years. I don't want to spend another minute without her.

The minutes tick by—the only sound in the room is the analogue clock on the wall. But I sit and wait because it's all I can do.

"Josh?" she croaks.

"Hey."

"You found me."

"I'm so sorry, baby. I'm sorry for everything."

"I want to go home," she whispers.

I nod. "I'm getting you out of here."

"No. I want to go home to Melly." She blinks, but tears still escape her eyes and roll down her cheeks.

"Let's just get you out of hospital first. Then we'll talk."

"I don't belong here." Her sad tone hits me square in the chest. This is the very thing I'm trying to get past, but now ...

"You belong with me. I'm going to prove it to you."

"How?"

"I'm not sure yet, but I promise you nothing like this will ever happen again. It shouldn't have happened this time."

She sniffs. "He wouldn't even call you. And he threatened me with the police. I was already feeling sick, but this was just humiliating, Josh."

I reach over and stroke her cheek. "I'm so sorry, babe. And I'm sorry about our argument. I never once thought you were lying about Mac. It was just such a slap in the face from him."

She says nothing else for the moment, but closes her eyes at my touch. I love this woman so damn much, and I've been the cause of her misery. If I'd handled everything better this morning, she would never have ended up here.

"I love you, Delaney. And our family is my priority. I got rid of Mac."

Her eyes fly open. "What?"

"We were in the middle of contract renegotiations anyway. We already fought over me doing the movie in New Zealand, and Reece has never liked him. What he did to you was the last straw."

She seems to search my expression, her eyes so full of sadness that it breaks my heart. "You said he got you your big break."

I shrug. "Maybe he did. Maybe I would have gone down the same path with someone else. But no one disrespects my lady and gets away with it. I've got another agent in mind, and I think she'll be good at finding the balance for me."

"As long as you're happy." She looks around the bed. "Can you help me up?"

I look for the bed control and press the button to raise it until she's sitting up. Delaney gives me a weak smile. "That's better."

Reaching for her, I wrap my arms around her neck and close my eyes as I hold her tight. "I'm so glad you're okay. I'd be lost without you."

She sighs, sliding her arms around my waist. "I love you."

For a moment, we're stuck in place, just holding each other. I'd stay here forever if I could, with Delaney in my arms, safe and sound.

There's a knock on the door, and I look up to see a nurse standing in the doorway.

"Mr. Carter, there are some papers for you to sign."

I nod and let go of Delaney. "Of course."

She approaches with a clipboard, and I look them over before signing at the bottom. With a warm smile, she addresses Delaney. "I'll just free you of the IV, and you can go home any time."

"Thank you," Delaney says. Exhaustion haunts her voice, and I'm not sure I'll ever forget that. I need to take her home to rest.

It only takes a moment for the nurse to remove the cannula. "I'll go and get a wheelchair."

"I'm sure I can walk."

She wags her finger at Delaney. "Hospital policy. Besides, he can push you."

Delaney's laughter is music to my ears. "That sounds good to me. Although you are risking me running him over."

Her eyes dart between Delaney and I as if she's not sure about how serious Delaney is.

"Oh, she's serious. I probably deserve it too."

She disappears without really reacting, but I'm sure our exchange will turn up on social media at some point. Things like this usually do.

"Mac messed with the flight booking too. I asked Mindy to change it, and I've got the new ticket. No one will be blocking your seat on the way home, and you'll get fed."

Her smile is weak, but it's what I need to tell me things might just be okay.

Once I get her to the limo, I hold her in my arms again and close my eyes. Nothing has ever felt so good.

"You scared me," I whisper.

"I scared myself. I'm sorry for getting shitty with you this morning."

I shake my head. "I'm sorry for my reaction. You know I believe you. Always."

She nods.

"It might take a while, but we'll get this right, Delaney. Together."

She curls in tighter. "As if I'm ever letting go now."

I laugh and kiss her on the forehead. I lean my head against hers as the concrete high-rises of the city spread into sprawling mansions and hedged estates.

A sense of relief settles on me when we go through the gates.

Outside the car, I scoop her into my arms despite her protests, and just like the night before, carry her up the stairs to the bedroom. At some point, she slumps and rests her head in my neck. After all she's been through, this is the least I can do.

Leilani fusses, and I love her all the more for it. She's become more like Reece's second mother than just the housekeeper, and her care for him appears to extend to us.

"The bed's freshly made, and I'll bring in some cool face cloths. I've had a dash of heatstroke before, and that'll help make Delaney feel better."

"Thank you."

Delaney reaches for Leilani's arm. "Thank you so much. I'm sorry to be a burden."

"No such thing. It's wonderful to have you two to look after. I told you that you should have gone by car." She wags her finger at Delaney and I chuckle.

"Lesson learned," Delaney says.

I've learned a big lesson from this too.

I can't let anything like this happen to her again.

CHAPTER THIRTY-SIX

DELANEY

I'M NOT GOING to lie. Being pampered makes me feel so much better. My body still feels like it's on fire, but at least my headache has faded, and I am no longer queasy.

What a mess.

My pride is wounded more than anything. I understand the guard not believing me, especially when I had no ID on me, but what I don't get is why anyone would find being such an arsehole so funny.

Josh has been back and forth, getting me drinks and making sure I'm okay. I'm just happy to be inside with the air conditioning cranked and getting some of that cool air.

He sits on the bed.

"There's one more thing I want you to do," I say as the golden rays of the afternoon stretch into the bedroom.

His hand in mine gives me comfort. "Anything."

"You need to go out and see your fans."

His dark eyes focus on mine. "I don't want to leave you."

"I'm fine. Some of them have basically camped out for days waiting to get a glimpse of you."

He grips my hand tight. "*You* are my focus right now."

"One of them helped me out there. A woman named Becky. She gave me a bottle of water." I lick my dry lips. "She's your biggest fan."

For a moment, he hesitates.

"Josh. I'll be fine. I'm not going anywhere. Can you do it? Please? For me? I don't want anyone else collapsing."

He nods slowly. "For you. I'd do anything right now if it made things right between us. I fucking love you."

"I love you, too. Fighting with you sucks."

Josh stands, raising his free hand to my cheek and grazing his knuckles down it. "When I get back, we'll talk. Are you sure I'll be safe?"

I shrug. "I have no idea."

"I'd better kiss you goodbye then."

His kiss is soft and gentle, and when I close my eyes, all I feel is his love.

The thought of not belonging here still circles me like a vulture, but when he just shows me he loves me, the barrier between us crumbles.

"I won't be long. Make sure you have something to drink."

"Yes, boss."

His grin makes me laugh. "That's right. I am. So stay here and do as you're told."

"Oooh I hope you know what it does to me when you're being all dominant." I laugh harder as his eyes widen. "It's a joke. You know I'm in charge."

He shakes his head. "I should have known that was too good to be true. Be back soon."

I do as I'm told and take a sip of water before settling down on the pillows.

Closing my eyes, I enjoy the cool air flowing over me. Sleep pulls at me, and even though I don't want to, I slide into its grip.

"Delaney?"

I open my eyes to see Becky approaching the bed. She's as white as a sheet, and her mouth is hanging open.

"You really are his girlfriend."

"I thought you might like to see her," Josh says as he follows her into the room.

"Yes. Thank you."

He walks to me, leans over and kisses the top of my head. "I told Becky how grateful I am that she helped you. I'm not sure she really believed it."

Becky sits on the side of the bed. "I thought that was a story to get past the guard. What an asshole, not letting you in."

"Reece got rid of him. I was ready to kill him, but Reece spoke to the big boss at the security company and had that guard moved on."

"Do you mean he lost his job?" I ask.

Josh shrugs. "He's nowhere near you, and that's all that matters. I'm sure they just moved him somewhere else. Hopefully he loses that attitude."

"I hope so. He was nasty. The guard earlier in the day at least flirted with me," Becky says.

I laugh. "I could have handled that."

Wriggling over, I make space for Josh to sit beside me. I lean my head on his shoulder. "I'm just glad it's all over. What about you, Becky? Are you going home now you've met Josh?"

She laughs, nodding. "I haven't been home in three days. It's time. I still can't believe I'm here."

"Well, I'll follow up as we agreed, and get some signed merchandise sent to you," Josh says. "And like I said, I'm so grateful you were there when you were and that you helped Delaney. I don't know what I'd do without her."

"I'm just glad Delaney's okay. That must have hurt when you hit the road."

I shrug. "I can't even remember it."

"Your face does, judging from the bruises," Becky says.

I raise my hand to the side of my head. It is tender, and there's a lump that'll take a while to go away.

Josh kisses my hair. "I hate seeing you hurt."

"A bit of rest and I'll be fine."

"I should be going and let you rest," Becky says.

"Thank you again." I smile.

"You're welcome. I can't speak for everyone out there, but I'll leave you two alone. Have a good holiday, Delaney."

"I'll walk you out," Josh says.

He pecks me on the head again. "I'll only be a minute."

Becky pauses in the doorway. "If you're ever back in Honolulu, give me a call. I gave Josh my details so he can send me some posters."

I nod. "I'd like that."

I close my eyes again as they leave. I'm vaguely aware of the bed sinking soon afterward.

"Now I've got you all to myself."

"I'm too tired to do anything."

Josh laughs softly in my ear. "That's why we're going to sleep."

I snuggle back against him as he spoons me.

His warm hand on my stomach is the last thing I remember.

CHAPTER THIRTY-SEVEN

JOSH

BY MORNING, Delaney's feeling a lot better.

The colour's back in her cheeks, and her eyes aren't as sunken as they were last night.

She's propped up in bed, eating breakfast, and no longer talking about going home.

I dodged a bullet. And I have to make sure that she feels comfortable in this life with me before I stand a chance of her and Amelia being with me full-time.

"I've got a treat for you this morning," I say.

Her smile lights up her whole face. It's a far cry from the miserable Delaney I brought home from the hospital. It does my heart good to see it.

"What is it?"

I lick my lips. "I got a text from Reece. He wants to see you're okay for himself. So, I'm going to FaceTime him."

"You're FaceTiming Reece Evans?"

I laugh. "If he hadn't been such a man whore, you would have met him back in LA. I don't know why you're fangirling over him."

She pouts. "I'm allowed. Besides, I didn't think I could fangirl over you."

I laugh. "If you'd met him back in LA, you'd be giving him the same shit you give me. At least this way I get to keep that all to myself."

"You're crazy."

"About you."

I sit on the bed beside Delaney and dial.

Reece's smiling face fills the screen. "Dude. Took you long enough."

I laugh. "I had to warn Delaney what I was doing so she didn't die of shock."

He chuckles. "Introduce us."

I grin. "Delaney, this is Reece."

Her eyes widen as I turn the iPhone toward her. "Reece Evans, this is Delaney."

"Damn, Carter. You done good."

Delaney blushes. "Can we keep him?"

I scowl. "Hey."

"I've seen all his movies."

"Your girl has good taste." Reece laughs, and the sound of Delaney joining him makes me smile.

"You've seen all his movies, and never watched mine?" I stare at her.

She shrugs. "There's a reason I never watched yours. Him, I never had a problem with."

Reece lets out a low whistle. "She's got you there, Josh. It's very nice to meet the famous Delaney after all this time."

Delaney shifts her gaze to me.

"He's been talking about you for years. You were the one who got away. But I guess there's no chance of that happening again. Such a shame."

His eyes drift down the screen, and I look from the phone to

Delaney. One of the straps of her nightgown has slid down her arm, and ...

I tilt the phone up.

"Dude."

"That's my girlfriend you're perving on."

Delaney giggles, and I arch an eyebrow at her.

"She's cute." Reece winks and I just shake my head. "Anyway, Delaney, I wanted to make sure you were okay after yesterday. I heard all about it from my housekeeper. She was very upset."

Delaney nods. "I'm okay. Another day or so out of the sun and I'll be fine."

"That should never have happened. The security company is usually so good at keeping track when I have guests stay. They really dropped the ball with you, and I'm sorry. Any time you need somewhere to stay in Hawaii, you're welcome at my place."

"Thanks, Reece. I really appreciate it."

"I've got to run, I've got a scene to shoot. Go look after our girl, Carter. I will definitely call you another time. Hope you're enjoying your holiday otherwise."

Delaney shoots me a heated gaze, and I damn near drop the phone.

"I'm sure the rest will be fantastic," she says. I suck in a breath as her hand lands in my lap.

"Gotta go, Reece. Bye." I terminate the call and Delaney giggles when I launch myself at her.

"So, you've seen all his movies?"

Delaney nods. "Every one."

"Do you want to see more of mine?"

She runs her tongue slowly over her bottom lip. "Maybe."

"I'll pick something out for tonight."

With a sigh, she lies back on the pillow. "I like that idea. What are we going to do today seeing as I'm not supposed to get any sun?"

I grin. "Oh, I can think of a few things."

Delaney captures one of her curls with her index finger and twists. "What kind of things?"

"Let me show you."

She laughs as I brush my lips over her neck. "Oh, I like the way you think, Mr. Carter."

"I won't stop until you tell me you're still mine."

"Josh," she says softly.

I raise my head. "I know you're struggling, but I want this to work more than anything. I'll make things better, Delaney. I swear."

She nods, but the sadness in her eyes tells me she's not sure if she believes me. "I know you will."

"You're my whole world."

Her lips twitch into a smile again. "I'm yours, Josh. Always was. Always will be."

I trace my fingers down her cheek.

"Thank you for calling Reece. It was fun." Her smile widens. "I also met Gabby when I was out."

It takes me a moment to register what she's said. "Gabby Reynolds?"

She nods. "She was shopping. Or, rather, Antonio was."

I laugh. "Those two are joined at the hip."

"They're really something. Gabby recognised me from the apparently million photos of me you had in your trailer."

"I might have gone a bit overboard."

"Josh, I know you love me. I don't ever want you to think I doubt that."

"As long as you remember that whatever happens. Life with me won't always be easy, but I will always do my best to protect you."

I mean what I say. I'll do whatever it takes to keep Delaney and Amelia safe.

But it only takes a few days to feel like some of that unravels.

CHAPTER THIRTY-EIGHT

DELANEY

MY DAD WAS a big fan of Joe Jackson.

It's one of the few things I know about him.

Mum played his *Look Sharp* album a million times when I was a kid. Apparently they were both fans. The refrain of *"Is She Really Going Out With Him"* played throughout so many of my childhood memories.

It's the song I hear in my head now as I look at the headline on this story. I really shouldn't be reading it, but it's hard not to.

The headline reads: *Is he really going out with her?* And there's a photo of us leaving the hospital, my hand in his as he helps me into the back of the limo. I'm leaning toward him, my head against his shoulder. It's actually a really nice photo of me. I bite my bottom lip as I open the image in a new tab and save it as Josh's wallpaper.

The column's written by some nasty, bitter gossip columnist who probably wants a piece of him for herself. And I could let it drag me down, but I've already learned I need to harden myself against the bad stuff. It's hard when it's right in your face.

"What are you looking at?" Josh walks into the room, towelling his hair dry. The humidity is pretty high today, and we've both been trying to cool down. Not easy when we end up tangled in the sheets right after showering most times.

"This lovely photo someone took of us."

He leans over my shoulder to look at the computer browser. "What the fuck? She's got your name and everything."

"You know, you did just fire Mac. He doesn't like me." The words are out before I can stop them, but Josh just nods.

"You're probably right. I'll get my publicist onto it. I thought we might have more time to ourselves before the world caught wind of us. I'll ask her to watch out for stories about Amelia."

I turn in my seat, looking up at him. "I'll call Pania too. She'll keep Amelia safe."

"I've been on the receiving end of her glares. I have faith in her."

This was what I always feared, but at the same time, I knew it would come at some point. "Are you okay with this? I mean, if they go digging ..."

He leans forward so his face is inches from mine. "They'll find a pair of teenagers who just had some things to work out before they got their lives together. And they'll also find a pair of adults who don't give a shit what anyone else thinks because they're crazy in love."

I grin.

"Where's your phone? You have social media, right?"

I nod. "Mine and the diner. Twitter, Facebook, and Instagram."

"You should turn off all your notifications. There'll be people who have already tracked you down. I wanted to protect you from all of this." He sighs. "There'll be some nasty messages and posts aimed at you."

"I'll turn off my messaging everywhere. Facebook's already locked down to friends only."

"Oh, you'll have friend requests. I don't need to tell you to be careful."

I pick up my phone.

"Clear them. There's no point in trying to keep up with that."

"Reece Evans friend requested me."

Josh laughs. "Typical. Just let me double check that it's actually his account."

It takes a moment for him to check. I just stare at my phone. Reece Evans wants to be my Facebook friend. What planet am I living on?

"That's him alright. There's a request from Gabby too."

"You can accept that one. She suggested we get together for dinner before we all leave."

Josh nods. "We should. I'll give her a call later to organise something. Do you use lists for your Facebook friends?"

I shake my head.

"Maybe you should start. Then you can keep posts just for us."

"Well, there aren't any nudes."

Josh laughs. "Save those for me."

I lean over and peck him on the cheek. "They'll only be for you. I'll sort the lists out later."

I rub my face with my hands. "This is all so much."

"This is my life, Delaney. I'm not known for dating, so my friends, the ones who want to be friends with you, know that it's serious."

My phone pings a bunch of times, and he sighs. "I'll turn your notifications off too. I didn't want it to yet, but your life is going to change. You know that, don't you?"

"I do."

"Still want me?"

I take the phone from his hands and throw it on the bed. Wrapping my arms around his neck, I push myself against him and give him a kiss that'll leave him with no doubt just how much I want him.

"We are never going to leave this bedroom again, are we?" he asks.

"Another week and I'll be going home, so yes, we will at some point."

He looks at me with so much love it takes my breath away.

"Why don't we see if we can FaceTime Amelia and then I'll take you to dinner. If our relationship is out there, we've got nothing to hide."

"Are you sure?" He has his own world to protect—especially now he's cut ties with Mac.

"Am I sure I want to take my beautiful girl out, and not hide her from the world? Yes. Reece told me about a great place to eat. Let's try it. But first, Amelia."

After checking the time, I FaceTime Pania. She grins when she answers.

"I've just been reading this really terrible story about you. The photo's hot though. You two are on fire together."

I laugh. "That's what I just told Josh."

"I'm guessing you want to talk to this girl who went crazy the second she heard your voice?"

"Yes please."

Josh leans over me as Melly's face fills the screen.

"Daddy!" she shrieks.

"Hey, baby."

"I miss you." She pouts, and my heart melts at the sight.

"I miss you too, but I'm coming to see you soon. Just gotta finish this movie, and I'll be all yours for a few weeks."

Turning to him, I shoot him a look that I hope says *really?*

"My plans have changed a little during the past week. I got rid of something that was holding me back, and now I can pay some attention to you."

Melly claps, and I swallow hard. He'd better come through for her.

"I'm going to take your mother to dinner, but I just wanted to say hi and tell you that I love you very much."

"I miss Mummy." She sniffs.

"I know you do, baby, but I'll be home in a week. And then it sounds like we're getting ready for Daddy to come and stay with us." I nudge Josh's arm.

"Pania makes nice pancakes. We have them every morning for breakfast," Melly says.

"Do you? Better than silly old cereal." I smile. My heart pangs seeing her. This is the longest we've been separated, and I can't wait to get home to her. Especially if Josh is following me.

We make small talk for a bit, and then Pania calls her in the background.

"We gotta go to the diner, Mummy." She purses her lips.

"Okay. Be good for Pania. Love you, baby."

My heart lunges as the screen goes blank and I lose sight of her. That little girl has been my whole life for the past few years. I feel like I'm missing a limb without her.

"Next time we come here, we'll bring Amelia."

I shoot Josh the side-eye. "Were you just reading my mind?"

"Something like that." His smirk is unbearable.

"And what's this about coming to stay with us for a few weeks? Don't you have another project after this?"

He captures one of my curls and loops it around his finger. "Nothing that's going to stop me being with my girl."

I sigh. "I'm right here. Give a girl a warning, will you?"

"I'm sorry. Amelia was right there, and—"

"We're her parents. We need to discuss this first. You can't just come and go out of her life like that."

He drops his hand.

Letting out a sigh, I take his hands in mine. "And I love you for it, but I'd appreciate it if you didn't just drop the news without talking to me first. If something happens and you can't make it, how hurt do you think Melly will be?"

He searches my expression. "I won't let you down, Delaney."

"You won't let me down—but you're not in charge of your schedule. What if it changes again?"

His face falls, and I know I've made my point.

"Why do you think I never got serious about anyone else, Josh? She can't have her heart broken. I won't allow it."

He nods. "Are we okay?"

"Of course. But please, if you're going to announce your plans, let me know first? I don't want to build her up only for her to be hurt."

Josh lets go of my hands and wraps his arms around me. "I promise. And I'll be there for her, and for you. It'll be a lot easier if I can move you two to LA."

"Will it? You haven't been back to LA since you left us last time."

He nods. "I know, but I've been thinking a lot about how after this next movie, I don't have any firm commitments. Reece and I have been talking about working on our own project, and I thought I might take a couple of years off to do it."

My mouth falls open. "You haven't stopped working since your first movie. Are you feeling okay?"

He buries his face in my hair. "Being with you again changed my life. All I could think about was work before, and which projects were worth my time. Now, all I want is to be with my family and do what I want to do."

We're more important to him than anything else.

I'm speechless. What the hell do I say to that?

"Get dressed, and let's go and enjoy the night." He pecks me on the lips and turns to the wardrobe.

I spring out of bed and pick a dress out of my bag. Time for a shower and the good underwear. Might as well go all out.

Tonight, we'll be seen in public properly for the first time, and my stomach's a mess of butterflies just thinking about it.

But I deserve this. And so does Josh.

We can't hide forever.

THE RESTAURANT TAKES my breath away.

It's not crazy fancy, but it's all candlelit with what look like very comfortable chairs. That's all I care about apart from the food.

"Mr Carter." The maître d' greets Josh as if they're old friends. "This way, please."

People turn and stare as we're shown to a table. It's weird, but I hold my head high and Josh grips my hand tight as we walk.

The maître d' pulls my chair out, and I take a seat with Josh sitting opposite.

"Like it?"

"It's lovely." I lean over a little. "People are looking at us."

"They will. They'll see my beautiful girlfriend and they'll all be jealous."

My cheeks burn. "Stop it."

"It's true. I'm so crazy about you, Delaney. I'm not sure I can ever show you how much."

"You do all the time." I sigh. "We hit a bump in the road, but it doesn't mean we're going to fall apart. We're too solid for that. And I think if you come and spend that time with us you told Melly about, it'll help too."

"I'll be there. Wild horses wouldn't keep me from the two of you."

"Your menus." A waiter hands them to us, and gives Josh the drinks menu.

"Delaney? What did you want to drink?" Josh asks.

"Something sweet and bubbly would be nice."

He nods, making some selections from the wine list, and the waiter disappears while we look at the food menus. My eyes nearly pop out when I realise there are no prices. The thought of that makes me hyperventilate.

"Are you okay?" Josh asks. "Choose whatever you want."

"There aren't any prices."

He smiles. "It doesn't matter. We won't be washing dishes."

I laugh. "That's not what I mean. It's just ... weird."

"Next time, I'll take you somewhere not so weird."

"Oh, I'm not complaining." I can't help the grin on my face. This whole thing is crazy. We haven't actually been on a date since we first went out years ago. But it's nice, and it's sweet, and this is Josh's way of telling the world that I'm his girl.

Which just makes me want to jump across the table and straddle him.

But I don't think this is the kind of place to do that.

CHAPTER THIRTY-NINE

JOSH

DESPITE BEING PREPARED, our restaurant visit manages to escape the press, and I'm glad for the reprieve because saying goodbye to Delaney at the end of the week was the hardest thing I've had to do in forever.

I hate being apart again. And I'm already counting the days until we'll be together.

I'm back on set when my phone rings. At least we're not in the middle of nowhere this time, and I can receive the call.

"Josh." Tonya's tone is clipped. "We've got a situation."

At least I didn't lose my publicist when I ditched Mac. She and Mac used to disagree about literally everything, but she's never done me wrong. And she and Sara are tight which made the decision to switch to Reece's manager really easy.

I wave to Aaron, the director, and step inside my trailer.

"What's going on?"

"I'm trying to squash a story about your daughter."

My heart pounds. It was only a matter of time, but I'd hoped that we'd be able to ease into it.

I grab a chair and sit down, wishing I could hold Delaney. It's been three weeks, and I miss her like crazy.

"Is it about Delaney too?" Maybe someone from Glenderry said something. It was always possible.

"The headline is Josh Carter's Secret Love Child. What do you want me to do? I've spoken to a lawyer already and we could argue that they're putting a minor at risk. They have photos."

I nod. "Do whatever you have to do. Delaney's going to kill me. She knows what's coming. Amelia isn't fair game. I haven't even told my parents yet."

She lets out a sigh. "I suggest you tell them in case we can't get this pulled."

"You're right. Of course. I'll call Delaney first and let her know too. Please keep me updated."

"Will do."

Shit.

Every time I think we've hit a rough patch, I think that's as bad as it's going to get. I should have had a better plan for this, but I thought in their small town they'd be safe. When I find out who's been digging ...

I dial Delaney.

"Hey. Haven't I already heard from you today? I'm not complaining, but we're going to have to talk about your clinginess." She teases.

It takes a moment for me to gather my thoughts. It takes that long for her to figure out something's wrong.

"Josh? What's going on. You're still coming to spend time with us, right? Because I don't want you to let Amelia down, and—"

"I'll be there. There's something else I have to tell you."

She lets out a sigh of relief. My gut clenches knowing that'll be short-lived.

"The media have got hold of a story about Amelia. And photos."

Delaney gasps. "What?"

"My publicist called me because she got wind of it. She's working with—"

"I don't want her picture up there, Josh. I've seen some of the shit people have said about me. I'm a big girl. But she's five." She lets out a strangled sob and it damn near breaks my heart to hear.

I close my eyes. The last thing I ever want is for either of my girls to hurt, and Delaney's one hundred percent right.

"My lawyer's trying to get them to stop publication. I don't know how anyone got hold of this, except ..."

"I know it's not you." She's still upset, but at least she's not crying. I don't ever want her to cry.

"I agree. I'm so sorry. I wish I could undo all this."

She sighs. "I guess it was only a matter of time. Doesn't make it any easier. How bad is it?"

"I'm not sure, but they're headlining it as my secret love child."

I know she's back to being Delaney when she snorts. "I guess it wasn't much of a secret when I lost the plot at Jessie in the middle of the diner."

And then she does such a turn-around that it makes my head spin. "You know what? Fuck them. Let them say their worst. We're your family even if some narrow-minded arseholes get all pissy about it."

I'm not sure what clsc to say. "I love you."

"I love you, too. And I know we've still got to work everything out, but nothing is going to stop us all from being together. One way or another."

"You're so hot when you're angry."

"I'm hormonal because it's that time of the month, and I'm in bed with a hot water bottle. But still, fuck them."

I grin. "You're the best. I'm not sure what my parents are going to say. I haven't told them about us yet. Or Amelia. I wanted to be us for a while before I did that."

"Well, if they're not happy with me or your daughter or both of us, fuck them, too."

All I can do is laugh. "What would make you feel better?"

"A large block of chocolate and no arseholes putting my daughter in the media."

"I can help with one of those. Trying to stop the other."

She lets out another loud sigh. "You can only do your best."

"That's what I'm trying to do. I'll go order a shipment of chocolate for you and call my mother."

"Let me know how it goes. Love you."

"Love you, too."

AFTER SENDING the biggest bouquet of red roses with a gift basket full of chocolate, I dial my mother. I try not to call her constantly with updates. And with so many things changing in my life, there are a few I need to catch her up on.

"Hello?"

"Hi, Mom."

"Joshua. It's so good to hear from you." There's a touch of sarcasm in her voice, and I know it's because I haven't been in touch as regularly as she'd like.

"Sorry I haven't called. I've got something I need to tell you about. I wanted to tell you this in person when I got back to the States, but the media have hold of it, and I don't want you to find out via the tabloids."

She laughs softly. "Is this about the girl you're seeing? She looks lovely."

I close my eyes. "Do you remember right before I got my first big film that there was a girl I was really interested in?"

"The one who disappeared?"

"Yeah."

She huffs. "I do. She nearly derailed the opportunity that launched your career with that little stunt."

Shit. She's right. I was a confused mess between getting what I always wanted, and losing the person I thought I'd share it with. I'd moped for weeks.

"Well, that's Delaney. The woman I'm with now."

"Oh, Josh."

"It's a long story, but I need you to know it really wasn't her fault back then. It was all a big misunderstanding."

There's silence for a moment. "I hope she doesn't do it to you again. Lord knows, you don't need it with the stress I'd imagine you're under splitting away from Mac."

"Mac can go to hell. He tried to buy Delaney off, and she refused. And there's something else you should know. Something I need to tell you before you read it online."

She doesn't answer, but I'm sure she's processing what I just said. And I don't want to wait any longer to tell her because it's only a matter of time before some arsehole journalist contacts her.

"I have a daughter. Delaney and I do."

"What?"

"Her name is Amelia, and she's as cute as a button. I'll send you photos. She's five."

"You have a daughter?" she whispers. "What? How?"

"Delaney had a baby."

"Are you sure she's yours?"

"You only have to look at her to know. Trust me on that."

"Josh." There's so much emotion in her voice. I hate dumping this on her from so far away, but if Tonya is right, the news is about to drop and I can't have my mother finding out about Amelia that way.

"I'm so sorry, Mom. A reporter's got hold of the story, and I'm trying to stop it to protect Amelia, but I really needed to tell you in case they run it."

She lets out a long breath. She's used to the crazy things happening to me, but this has to be the most out-of-the-blue thing I've landed on her.

"Please send me the photos. We'd love to see her. I'll work out how to tell your father."

"Thanks, Mom."

"Oh, this is not over, Joshua. We will be having further conversations about how you hid this from me."

I swallow hard. Here comes the even harder part.

"I didn't know. I've only found out these past few months. And I wanted to see how things went with Delaney before pulling her into my insanity."

Her sigh says everything. "I'm not sure how to feel about it. She kept your baby from you and she almost ruined your career, but now you want to be with her?"

"She tried to tell me, Mom. I have all the proof of that I need."

"Oh, Josh."

"Anyway, I have work to do and I'll call you later. But I'll just text you through a couple of photos of Amelia. You'll fall in love with her. I swear. She's amazing."

"I can hear how much you already love her. Please send them. I want to see my granddaughter."

After ending the call, the first thing I do is pick out some photos of Amelia. One by herself, one with me, and one with both Delaney and I. Pania took that one. The three of us are holding hands with Amelia in the middle, and while she's looking straight at the camera, Delaney and I are sharing a smile.

There's so much love in that photo, and it's one of my favourite photos of us.

I press send and Mom texts me back moments later.

Mom: *She's beautiful. And that last photo is wonderful. I'm looking forward to hearing the rest of your story.*

At least that crisis is averted.

But there's still the story to come if that runs, and dealing with any fallout.

THE STORY RUNS before the end of the day.

They don't muck around with putting it up on the web, and it'll be in print by morning.

Clear as a bell, there are three photos of Amelia. She's so beautiful. There's a big smile on her face, and in one of them she's skipping along beside her mother.

Fuck.

I'm so close to us being a family, and this is Delaney's biggest fear.

I can't blame her. I've seen some of the comments on social media over the story about me and Delaney. I don't know what motivates people to be so mean. This time around, I'm sure a lot of the bile will be aimed at Delaney rather than Amelia, but that doesn't make me feel any better.

Tonya puts out a brief statement in case anyone else comes knocking.

Josh is upset and angry that his family has been used in this way. There is no secret love child, but a family that he didn't want the limelight focused on. Delaney and Amelia should be entitled to their privacy, and no more interviews will be granted to any news organisation which publishes this story.

It's simple, but who knows how effective it will be?

I do want to know where those photos came from.

CHAPTER FORTY

DELANEY

THE WHOLE WEEKEND is an emotional rollercoaster.

There's a part of me that says Josh and I can't be together. Not if the cost is our daughter. But I can't walk away. I'm in way too deep, and there's an equal part of me that thinks that staying will keep her safe.

It's so hard to think when we're apart, but equally hard when we're together.

I'm glad Josh got me to turn off my social media notifications. Every man and his dog wants a piece of our story. He's got people to handle this stuff, but if Joe Blogs reporter from another trashy rag tweets me again, I'm going nuclear.

He got off lightly in the article. I'm made out to be some kind of gold-digger who's come back for what she can get. I know it's not his fault, but I think if I wasn't this strong, I'd be a puddle of tears on the floor.

Maybe the angry hormone surges help rather than hinder me right now.

I feel under bombardment, and I'm not sure how I'm going to face the week ahead, but I have to push through this because our family is worth it.

Early Monday morning, there's a knock on the door, and I smile when I see the courier with a huge bouquet of roses and basket full of all kinds of chocolate goodies. *Josh.*

"Mummy, look at all the chocolate." Melly's eyes are huge.

"Your father sent them."

"They're from Daddy?"

I gather her into my arms and hug her tight. "They are from Daddy. Want a little bit before you go to school? Just don't tell anyone you had chocolate with breakfast."

She giggles.

I start pulling things out. This didn't come cheap. I pick up my phone and flick off a quick text to Josh.

Me: *I got the flowers and the chocolate. Thank you. Love you xx*

"Which one do you think we should open?"

Melly's index finger goes straight to her mouth as if it's the most important decision she'll ever have to make. She examines each box and bar before picking a brightly coloured bar.

"This one."

I laugh, peeling back the wrapper and snapping off a piece each.

"Mmm, thank you, Daddy," I say.

She laughs. It's only one piece, but she's already managed to smear it around her lips.

"You're a mess. We're going to have to clean up before school."

"Do I have to go? Can't we see Daddy?"

I shake my head. "Sorry, baby. He's working. But he's coming to see us really soon."

"I miss him." Her lower lip wobbles.

"So do I. But he'll be spending some time with us in a few weeks, and maybe he can take you to school in the mornings and pick you up. That's what I think he should do for a while, anyway."

She beams. "Really?"

"He's going to be here for a few weeks, so we need to make the most of it. And he'll want to be with his little girl for as much time as possible."

Melly flings her arms around my neck. "I can't wait for Daddy to get here."

I swallow down the lump in my throat. "Neither can I, baby. Neither can I."

THE SCHOOL PRINCIPAL smiles when I walk into the office.

"Delaney. I thought we might see you today."

I nod. "Stacey. I guess you've seen the story."

She sighs. "I did. We talked about it in the staff meeting this morning. There have already been calls into the office."

My mouth drops. "I'm so sorry."

Stacey shakes her head. "Don't be. I can't say we've ever been through this before, but we all want to keep Amelia safe. No one will be able to get near her who shouldn't be."

"Thank you." I tear up.

She walks around the front desk and gives my bicep a squeeze. "The good thing about being in a small-knit community is that we all know each other. You and Amelia are family. And we take care of family."

"Thank you."

"I will call you myself if anything unusual happens. And until this settles down, we'll keep a closer eye on her during breaks. Maybe pick her up from the office instead of the gate for a while. I'll tell her to come here when the bell rings."

"That's a good idea. I really appreciate it." I sniff.

"We all know the truth, and what was in that article was far from it. Amelia's safe with us."

I smile and nod.

"I've got to get to work. Thank you so much for everything."

By the time I reach the car, I'm in tears. At least this time, it's because of the kindness of others.

Pull yourself together, Delaney.

I take a deep breath and start the car. Work at least will keep me busy and hopefully keep my mind off everything else.

I'll still worry about Melly, but she's in good hands.

THE DAY DRAGS.

I'm a bit crampy all day, and my head hurts. I could go home, but being away meant Pania carried the load, and I need to make up for that.

The highlight of my day has to be the flowers and chocolate.

My phone buzzes.

Josh: *Glad you got them. Sorry they couldn't get there sooner. Hope the chocolate's still of some use. Love you too. FaceTime me after school. I need to see you. xx*

Damon walks in just after one and sits in his usual spot.

"What did you want today, Damon?"

He visibly shrinks when I address him. It's so unlike him, and I spot it straight away. What the hell?

"That story wasn't fair on you. I wanted you to know that."

After a hugely emotional weekend, I blink back tears. Again. "Thank you."

"I ..." He gulps. "I thought that it would focus on how he abandoned you. Not paint you the way it did. I'm so sorry, Delaney."

The floor falls out from underneath me.

"What did you say?"

He hesitates. "He's not good enough for you. And I thought that article would be about him. You have to believe me."

"They were your photos?" I croak.

Damon nods. "I sold them. You can have the money."

"You fucking bastard," I scream.

"Delaney. I'm sorry."

The smell of Pania's perfume alerts me to her presence behind me.

"She's five, Damon. Do you know how much damage you've done? Get out of my diner and my life," I yell.

He holds up his palms. "I'll sort it."

"You can't. You've taken the last bit of privacy she had and you destroyed it. Did you ever think once about what this would do to me and my daughter?"

Pania steps around me. "Get the fuck out of here before I slap you. Don't you dare ever come back."

He stands and backs away. "I never meant to hurt you. I swear."

"It's way too late for that."

Pania turns me around. "Go sit in the kitchen. I'll be there in a minute."

My feet are like clay, but I move them, one in front of the other. But it's like I've forgotten how to walk as I force each step all the way to the table.

We've planned so much at this table—and had so many conversations. Now it's the support I need as I collapse in tears face first.

"Oh, honey." Pania's beside me minutes later, pulling me into her arms. "I've got rid of him. We'll have him served with a trespass notice. That man's not stepping foot on this property again."

"I never thought anyone from here would do that to Melly." I sob.

"Neither did I. I guess when there's money involved, it pays not to trust anyone." She hugs me tight. "Except me. I've always got you."

"I know you do."

She rubs my back. "You have to tell Josh."

I nod. "I'll do that when I get a grip."

"He loves you. He'll take care of this."

Pulling back from her, I struggle to breathe at first. "Will he? I'm the one getting the tweets and the nasty comments and having to make sure Amelia's safe."

Pania brushes my stray hair off my face. "He'd climb mountains for you. Anyone can see that. Give him a chance. Did you tell him about the comments and tweets?"

I shake my head. "He's got enough to deal with."

"Then give him this too. He's your partner, and he deserves the chance to protect you."

She's right. Josh has to know everything. I can't bottle it all up and hide it from him. If we're doing this, I need him.

Especially where our daughter's concerned.

I PULL myself together before school pickup and drive down to get Melly.

Instead of parking outside, I drive in the gate and use the visitor's park outside the office. I get a few odd looks, but I ignore them and head inside where my girl waits.

"Mummy." She flings her arms around me.

"Come on, sweetheart. Let's go home."

"Are we going to the diner?"

I shake my head. "Not today. We're going home to call Daddy."

Her whole face lights up, and she jumps up and down on the spot.

"Thank you," I call out to anyone who can hear me.

I've never been so relieved that the day is over as I buckle Melly into her seat and we set off home. Once we've FaceTimed Josh, I'll be cooking some kind of comfort food to disappear into.

And attacking that basket of chocolate.

It took a while to get used to living in the middle of nowhere, but right now, I'm grateful for the peace. If I was in the city, there'd be reporters on my doorstep, and even though there's no one waiting when I get home, I still drive straight into the garage, which I haven't done since I moved here.

Melly skips from the garage into the house. At least she's

unaware of what's going on. All she knows is that we're about to call her father and that's enough to keep her happy.

I hope her life continues to be like this.

Once I'm inside, I join her on the couch.

"Can we call Daddy now?" She's so excited, and even as tired as I am, I muster a smile.

"We sure can. He's waiting for us to call."

I pull out my phone and FaceTime Josh.

It takes everything in me not to burst into tears at the sight of him.

"My girls."

"Daddy, I just got home from school," Melly says.

"Did you have a good day?"

She nods. "I had to go to the office for Mummy to pick me up. But the teacher said it was to keep me safe."

His lips twitch. "That's good then. My girl has to stay safe."

"I miss you, Daddy."

"I miss you, too. But I'll be there soon. I promise."

Leaving Melly with the phone, I head to the bathroom to splash water on my face. Between still feeling gross and the events of the day, all I want to do is curl up in bed with Josh. But he's thousands of kilometres away.

Melly hands me the phone when I get back.

"Daddy wants to talk to you. I need to go to the toilet."

I smile. "Okay. You go and do that."

Her footsteps thud down the hall.

"Hey, beautiful," Josh says. I smile at him. He scans my face. "You look tired."

"I am tired. It's been a really long day."

"Tell me what's going on."

I let out a sigh. "I found out where the photos came from."

"What? Where?"

I suck on my bottom lip, willing myself not to cry again. "Damon."

"That son of a bitch." I've never heard Josh so angry. "At least we know where it's come from. How did you find out?"

I take a deep breath. "He came in to apologise. He thought you would be the subject of the article."

He growls. "Are you two okay?"

Closing my eyes, I lean back on the couch. "I'm glad you turned off my social media notifications. I've had tweets from reporters, and plenty of people want to tell me what a bitch I am. The school's taking care of Melly."

"I'll organise some security. I should have done it the other day. You two need to be protected."

I blink rapidly. "No."

"I need to make sure you're safe." His tone is so anguished. "After what happened in Hawaii, I don't want anything else coming between us."

"It's not coming between us."

"Whether we like it or not, these things are going to wear us down. The sooner we're all together the better, and I'm working on that right now." He pauses. "At least, for a little while. I miss you like crazy."

I rock as I cradle the phone. "I miss you too. Want to have phone sex?"

Josh's strained laugh gives him away. He's as tired as I am. "You're sounding more like yourself."

"I feel more like myself now I'm talking to you. I'm looking forward to you coming to stay with us."

"Me too. Listen, I've got to get going, but call me tomorrow or I'll call you. If you're going to be stubborn about security, then I need to know what's going on and when to step in."

This is the part I hated thinking about. There was always a chance we'd end up with our carefree life being curtailed. I just thought we had more time. But Josh is right. We have to make sure this gets under control before it damages our relationship.

And that's all that matters.

CHAPTER FORTY-ONE

DELANEY

THANKFULLY, nothing more happens before Josh is due to arrive.

Damon hasn't been near the diner, to my relief. I've seen him in passing from across the street, but he hasn't tried approaching me. I think Pania put the fear of God into him. She's good at doing that.

The bell rings to say someone's walked in, and Jo has to nudge me to get me to look up.

Dark eyes greet me from the other side of the counter.

My heart races as I run around and into his arms.

All the pressure of the past few weeks flows from my body as I cry happy tears, his arms wrapped tightly around me. Josh is always what I need.

"Hey, baby. Miss me?" he murmurs, pressing a kiss into my hair.

"I'm so happy you're here. You didn't tell me." I pull back and slap his chest.

"I just wanted to see my girl." He reaches up and pushes a lock of hair behind my ear.

"Delaney. Get out of here." Pania's voice comes from behind us. I turn to see her smiling at me.

"Are you sure?"

She nods. "Nothing's more important right now. Go and spend some time together. Want me to pick up the munchkin?"

I look at the clock. It's a little after one in the afternoon. "No. We can go and get her. Thank you so much."

"It's obvious this is what you need. Call me later?"

I grin. "You know it."

Josh takes my hand and squeezes it. "Let's go for a drive. Then we can pick up Amelia."

I nod. "I'll just grab my bag."

He's waiting by the door when I come back out, and I walk into the sunshine hand in hand with him. I still feel like I could cry, I'm so happy, but I've had enough of crying lately.

His rental car sits outside the diner, standing out like a sore thumb because it's some expensive European thing. I let out a moan as I sink into the leather seat.

"You're a sight for sore eyes," he says.

"So are you. Why didn't you warn me you were coming?"

He chuckles as he starts the car. "I thought about it, but then I thought it'd be a nice surprise. Amelia's going to freak out."

"She really will. Where are we going?"

His expression's so hard to read, but he leans over and gives me a tender kiss. "That's a surprise too. I promise we'll be back in time to get Amelia."

"You've got my curiosity piqued, Carter."

"Then let's go."

It only takes a minute or two to work out that we're leaving the town centre and heading toward the mountain. As we hit the winding road, I know we're going to Richard's house. I'm not sure why. Josh will be staying with us, won't he?

What's going on?

I say nothing, but enjoy the scenery. With spring arriving, the road is lined with green trees and colourful flowers. It's a much nicer drive this time of year.

We pull up outside the house, and Josh gets out, walks around the car, and opens my door.

"What are we doing here?"

He takes my hand in his and leads me to the front door. I sigh a little at our return to this house. It's so beautiful. The cream stucco walls blend it into the background in the winter, and with its wall to floor glass on the top floor, the views must be amazing.

This is the home of my dreams.

Without a word, he slides the key in the lock and turns. After pushing the door open, he disarms the alarm and we step inside.

"Do you remember when we had our date here?"

I smile. "You mean when you burned the toasted sandwiches?"

He laughs. "Yes. And you fell in love with the kitchen."

Nodding, I squeeze his hand. "Oh, I remember."

"It's yours, Delaney. Well, ours. I bought the house."

My mouth falls open. "I ... we ..."

"I'm not saying you have to move up here. You're so close to work and school, and it makes sense for you to stay where you are. But later on, when you and Amelia are with me, we can come back here for holidays and reminisce about when we fell in love again."

Despite my earlier promise not to cry, I tear up. "Josh."

"And with you not wanting security, this is also a getaway if you're harassed. You can shut yourself up here and close the gates and get any time away you need."

My heart's so full, it might just burst. Right when I was dealing with all the hurt of someone I knew betraying me, and trying to cope mentally with the fallout over something so simple as people knowing about our daughter, Josh goes and does something incredible like this.

"You're crazy."

He laughs, wrapping his arms around me and kissing my temple. "Like I keep saying—crazy about you."

I raise my face, and a soft kiss turns into more and then I'm lost as the heat of the moment takes over.

And when we break apart, Josh presses his forehead to mine. "Want to explore?"

"Yes." I grin.

"Come on."

I didn't tour the house last time I was here. We got as far as the kitchen and the room where we watched the movie, but the house is so much more than that. The first place we reach is the kitchen where I run my index finger over the shiny appliances and across the marble benchtop. Josh almost has to drag me into the next room which I've seen before, but then he leads me upstairs to a large hallway with five bedrooms. And right at the end is the massive master bedroom, with a big bed and a huge bay window.

I was right about the breathtaking views.

"The deal includes all the furniture. Richard wasn't interested in getting it shipped out of here. The beds down the other end of the hallway are new, so we can swap this one out for one of those and have a new bed. It's all ours." Josh smiles.

"This is insane." I sit on the end of the bed, grab his hand, and pull him to me.

He takes a seat. "This house is important to me. It's the location of our first second-time-around date, and where I opened that letter. I don't want you to ever feel that if you come to live with me, you have to give up this town completely. We can holiday here."

"I love it." I chew on my bottom lip. "How much did you pay for it?"

Josh chuckles. "It doesn't matter. We negotiated a fair price. The settlement date is still a couple of weeks away, but Richard was happy to hand over the keys early. So, anytime you need to get away we can come up here."

"And you're still here for a few weeks?"

He nods. "I'm all yours."

I flop back on the bed. "Wanna come and show me, then?"

We spend so much time christening the house, we get to school just as the bell rings.

But I have no regrets at all.

———

HAVING JOSH HOME IS WONDERFUL.

It's like he never left and the past few months didn't happen as he slots into our daily lives effortlessly.

It helps that there aren't people waiting for days outside my place, hoping for a glimpse of him. It's peaceful, and while he gets stopped in the street sometimes for the odd selfie or autograph, he settles in like one of the locals.

Melly's happy she's got her daddy.

By the middle of the second week, he's well established. He drops Melly at school in the morning and picks her up in the afternoon. For the first time, I haven't had to rush anywhere, and I like it. Maybe a little too much.

All it will really do is make it harder when the inevitable happens and he leaves.

During the day, he sits at home on his laptop, working on something. I'm not sure what it is, but the little bits he has let me in on tell me it could be big. I don't really care what it is because he's smiling, and Melly is smiling, and I love him being there at night with us and waking up with me in the morning.

It's Sunday morning, and I've been lounging around in my pyjamas. The house is warm, so I can get away with wearing shorts and a tank top, my hair piled up into a messy bun so it looks like I've made a little effort when I haven't.

Josh has been with us for three weeks, and hasn't said anything about leaving yet. I've just decided to make the most of it until that day comes.

"Want to see what I'm doing?" Josh pats the leather couch beside him in invitation.

"Of course." I sit and lean against his arm.

"Reece and I have started a production company. We're going to make our own movie."

I stare at him. "What? When?"

"As soon as we can get this off the ground. We'll fund it together, but we're going to try and get some interest from one of the big studios for distribution. He's doing all the groundwork in LA, and he found us an office. He's even hired a couple of people to get us going and we're on the lookout for others who know more about how all this works."

I grin. "Josh, this is wonderful."

"I wouldn't have done it without you. If I hadn't made the break from Mac, I'd probably still be going from film to film without feeling like I was moving forward. I found our first story, and Reece has had a screenwriter working on it for months. All he needed was me in on it, and you were ... *are* my motivation for doing this."

I'm not sure what to say. I'm blinking and my eyebrows seem to operate by themselves as they rise.

Josh takes my hands in his. "I've wandered the world for so long when everything I ever wanted was here. I've made no secret of wanting you and Amelia to move to LA with me, but doing this means I'll be based there. No more running around."

What he's saying is huge. The last thing I wanted was to up and move to LA only to be left there while Josh travelled from location to location. It's not only a change in direction for his career—he's doing this for us.

If I didn't love him already, I'd fall in love all over again.

But there's something left unsaid, and I don't have to be a mind reader to know what it is.

"You're going back to the States."

He nods. "I have to be hands on for this. Reece can't do it all himself, and I can only do so much from here. All our contacts are in Los Angeles and so are the studios."

"It's okay. I knew you weren't here forever." I lick my lips. "When are you going?"

"I'll spend another week. I want you two to come with me."

I swallow hard, blinking back tears. "We can't. Not that quickly. I need to work out everything. There are business decisions with Pania, and it's a big change for Melly when she's settled into school here."

"I know. And if you want to stay here, that's fine too. We'll make it work."

His smile's reassuring, but I can already feel the chunk of my heart that is his leaving my chest. These past weeks have been the best of my life. It's all just been so normal.

"I have a lot to think about."

Josh pulls me into his arms. I breathe in that familiar earthy tone of his and it helps ground me when everything else in my life feels up in the air.

"Just know that I love you and Amelia. I'll do whatever it takes to make you happy and for all of us to be together. Wherever we end up."

I bury my face in his neck, unable to speak for the moment.

"Mummy," Amelia calls from her room where she's been playing.

I look up, and Josh palms my cheek. "Go and see what our daughter wants. I'll be right here."

He kisses me with so much tenderness, all it does is make it worse.

How am I going to go without this? Even for a little while?

CHAPTER FORTY-TWO

DELANEY

I FEEL SO empty when Josh leaves.

The move he's making is so good for him—for us, but I still have a business and a job to do. Melly still has school. We have our lives to get on with while I make the biggest decision of my life.

"Delaney." Pania's voice knocks me out of my thoughts. I've barely paid attention since Josh left a week ago, and I screw up my face as the smell of burning pancake hits me.

Flames leap up in front of my eyes.

The pan's on fire.

"Shit."

I pull the pan off the burner and drop it in the sink. It hisses as I pour cold water on it, copious amounts of steam filling the room.

"What are you doing? You never burn anything."

I frown. "Well, apparently today I'm making up for lost time."

Pania grasps my arm. "Breathe, girl. Breathe. It's Josh, isn't it?"

I nod. "I keep thinking about how good it was when he was here. We were all happy, and now I just feel lost."

She wraps her arms around my shoulders. "You're in love with him, Delaney. It's only natural."

"But I'm letting you down."

She lets go of me, meeting my gaze and scanning my expression. I know this woman, and I know she has something to say.

"Spill it, Pania."

"It's just ... this whole thing with you telling me about how Josh is following his dream and doing his own thing? I decided I should do the same."

I'm so confused. "I thought cooking was your thing."

"It was. But I've been thinking a lot lately about how much I also wanted to learn fashion design, so I applied to go to design school next year."

My mouth falls open. "Wow."

"I know it might feel like I'd be leaving you in the lurch, but—"

I shake my head. "No. It's wonderful. You're such a talented dressmaker, but this could really help you build a career in it."

She smiles. "Well, someone has to design your dresses for the red carpet."

I freeze. Even though I spent so long avoiding news of Josh, I still caught the odd glimpse of him on the news and I've seen him on red carpets at award ceremonies. I never thought about that being a part of his life. There's so much that comes with being his partner, and it's terrifying and exciting all at once.

"You never even thought about that, did you? When you move to be with him, and I'm positive you will, I'm sure you won't be sitting around some mansion all day mooning after him while he works."

I sigh, pulling away from her and sitting at the table. "I guess I knew how different our lives really were when we were in Hawaii. It's like a whole new world."

She nods. "Very different from this place."

"I just feel so lost. Ever since we came here and started the diner, I've known what I wanted. Now he's gone and thrown a big spanner in the works."

Pania shrugs. She pulls out the next chair at the table and sits beside me. "This is a huge opportunity for you, Delaney. Josh is following his dream, and maybe you can go to LA and grow your own. I'm sure he'd back you."

"I know he would." Knitting my fingers together, I squeeze them. "But I keep coming back to how we built this place from nothing. Gran's money started us off, but this diner has been a success because we worked hard. It feels like cheating if Josh funds a business over there."

"You're his partner and he loves you. What's his is yours. And what's yours is yours. Isn't that how it goes?" She laughs, placing her hand on mine. "You've been distracted from the moment he left. Go and claim that life you should have always had. We can find a manager for the diner, or ..."

"I sell it."

She nods. "Whichever you decide, I'm right behind you."

I meet her gaze, and see nothing but affection from my best friend. We've done everything together these past few years, which has made me super protective of her. We rise or we fail together.

We both need to choose to rise.

"Go home and have a think. I'll take over the cooking today, and then maybe we can meet up tonight for dinner and talk about it?"

"Are you sure?"

"I'm sure I don't want any more burnt meals because you're distracted." She smiles. "I've got your back. Always."

"Thank you."

"You're welcome. Now get out of here so I can get this kitchen re-organised."

I grimace. "Sorry."

"No harm done. I'll take care of it."

I get to my feet. "Come over tonight around seven?"

She nods. "I'll be there."

MELLY'S ASLEEP when Pania shows up at seven-thirty, and I have the wine bottle open.

"A woman after my own heart," she says as I hand her a glass.

"I figured we could both do with it after today."

She nods. "Given any more thought about what you're going to do?"

I sigh, leaning back in my chair. "I've thought of nothing else."

"You have to go, Delaney. Give him the chance to have his family together. And give yourself what you always wanted. You two are on fire when you're together."

She says that just as I take a mouthful of wine, and I spray it all over the living room as I nearly choke with laughter. "On fire."

Pania laughs. "I didn't mean you have to literally set fire to things."

"I don't really want to burn the business down before I make up my mind about it."

"Do you want my opinion?" She fixes her hazel eyes on me, and I know I'm going to get it whether I want it or not.

"Sure."

"I think you should sell. It's done well here, and you'll find a buyer. I can manage it until it sells, and most importantly it'll give you a little nest egg for your new life."

I nod. "Makes sense."

"I know you two want this to work, but maybe having the money of your own will give you a little peace of mind in case it doesn't."

Swallowing hard, I nod again. I hate that idea, but I've also been in a situation already in my life when I had nothing, and only the small inheritance from my grandmother got me started in business. Pania's right in that regard.

Besides, I've never not paid my own way. No matter how much Josh earns, I'll still want to contribute in whatever way I can.

"If I do this, I want to try and make sure that Trina and Jo still have jobs with the new owner."

Pania nods. "I think that's fair. I mean, worst case too is that it doesn't sell, and we find someone to run it for us."

I blow out a breath. "That is another option."

She smiles. "This is real. I can't believe it, but this is all real. I'm so happy for you."

"I can't quite believe it all myself." I bite my bottom lip. "I'll grab my laptop, and we'll start making some plans."

And just like when we originally planned to go into business together, we sit and drink wine while we dream of my future.

Regardless of what happens, we'll always be close.

She's the peanut to my butter. The Minnie to my Mickey.

Of everyone I know, Pania will be the hardest to leave behind.

But I know she'll always have my back as I'll always have hers.

BY THE TIME we're finished, Pania makes her way to my spare room to sleep off all the wine we've consumed, but I've got something else to do before I get some sleep.

I change into my pyjamas, and crawl into bed.

It's 1:30 a.m. in Los Angeles, and I flick off a text to Josh just in case he's awake. I know he's been working late nights on this new movie.

Me: *Are you awake?*

My phone buzzes with an incoming call, and I smile. "I take it the answer is yes?"

Josh laughs. "I lost track of time." He sounds tired, but happy to hear from me. The sound of his voice just makes me miss him.

"I've got news."

"Really? What kind of news."

I take a deep breath. "I'm selling the diner."

"Whoa." Now he sounds awake. I guess that's not what he thought he was going to hear.

"Pania and I talked it over tonight. Apparently you can't run a food business when you burn the food, so ..." I laugh.

There's silence for a moment. He's probably processing what I just said.

"Does that mean you've made a decision?" he finally asks.

I close my eyes, lying back on the bed and cradling the phone next to my ear. "Amelia has only ever known this as home, and she has friends that we'll have to say goodbye to, but I want to give her the chance to live her childhood with her father. She deserves that. It was never her fault that you weren't part of her life." I let out a sigh. "Besides, Josh Carter, I am absolutely, totally, hopelessly in love with you, and I want to be a part of your journey."

"You are my journey. Get your butt over here."

I lick my lips. "I'll apply for Amelia's passport tomorrow and we'll take it from there. I also have to talk to an agent about the sale of the diner. Pania's going to manage it until it's sold and then we'll see what happens. I want to try and help the staff retain their jobs."

Josh lets out a sigh of relief. "I hope you get everything you want. But I can't wait for you to get here. I love you so much."

"I burned food at the diner thinking about you today." I laugh.

"No way. Probably a good idea to get out of there, then. Before you burn the place down." He pauses. "Does this mean no more teasing about me burning the grilled cheese?"

"Maybe."

"The sooner you get here, the better. I'm looking forward to showing you the house, and you can meet Reece and—"

"Wait." I grin. "I can meet Reece Evans?"

Josh laughs. "I wish you'd stop fangirling over him."

"I'm sure I'll stop when I actually meet him and give him shit about how he was always too busy to meet me the first time around."

"He'll love it."

I sigh. "I should get some sleep, and you do the same. I'll start the ball rolling here tomorrow, and let you know what's going on."

"Okay. Love you."

"Love you too."

After the call is ended, I place the phone on the bedside cabinet and stare at the ceiling for a while.

Just because I've made up my mind doesn't mean I'm not scared. I'm terrified.

But I was no less terrified when I bought the diner and moved here.

That worked out well.

Surely, everything will get better from here on in.

CHAPTER FORTY-THREE

JOSH

"HAVE you got ants in your pants?" Reece laughs as I look at the clock for about the millionth time this morning.

"You know Delaney and Amelia arrive today."

He walks around my desk and grips my shoulder. "I know. Why don't we head over to the airport and have a drink or something before they arrive?"

"We?"

He grins. "I want to meet this woman. You've kept us apart for way too long."

I shake my head. "She wants to meet you too. But I'm not sure it's such a good idea."

"You're worried I'll steal her from you."

I laugh and stand. "That is one thing I'll never be worried about. She loves me."

Throwing on my jacket, I lead the way out of the office. Reece follows me as we walk to my car.

"If you want to come in my car, you'll have to sit in the back on the way to my place."

He shrugs. "It's easier going in one vehicle."

I smile. There's no shaking him. But it does make me feel good that he wants to make the effort to meet my girls.

My girls.

I've been so anxious for this day to come. And once they arrive, that's it. No more being apart. Where I go, we all go. We talked about what we would do if I did have to travel, and Delaney has agreed to her and Amelia coming with me if it's for any length of time. Amelia will attend school in LA, but we'll hire a tutor if we have to. And that won't happen until she's settled and made friends to come back to.

The only thing missing is Mom and Dad. Mom is champing at the bit to meet Amelia, but I managed to persuade her to wait a while and let Delaney settle in. I know that this whole life can be overwhelming, and my girlfriend doesn't need the extra stress.

It's not a long drive, but I'm relieved when I pull into the car park.

Reece orders a beer at the bar, but I want a clear head for today. I've been waiting for this for a long time.

"Nervous?" he asks as we take a seat. I do enjoy coming back to LA. The media aren't in my face as much as they are in other places, and we all but get ignored for the most part.

"A little. I just hope I make them happy."

He shoots me a wistful smile. "They love you. Neither of them will care about anything else other than being with you. I wish I had that."

"Stop chasing every piece of skirt you come across and maybe you will."

He chuckles. "I always used to think I made up for your celibacy. Now I have no excuse."

Silence falls over us. This is right up there as one of the most important days of my life. Delaney's given up everything she worked for to be with me. I have to make this worth it for her.

"You're a lucky man," Reece says.

Neither of us say anything else while Reece finishes his drink and I watch the clock. Every second that ticks down is a second closer to her.

I can't wait.

WHEN IT'S TIME, we wander down the hall to arrivals.

It might take a while for them to clear through TSA, but it'll all be worth it.

I blow out a breath, fighting my impatience to see my family. *My family.*

"Daddy!" Amelia's voice breaks through the noise and I look up. Delaney pushes a luggage trolley laden with bags while holding our daughter's hand against the side of the handle.

"Is that her?" Reece asks.

I grin at him. "There are my girls."

"Daddy."

Tears prick my eyes as Amelia breaks free from Delaney's grip and runs for me. I bend down, and she runs to me, throwing her small arms around my neck. Holding her tight, I stand as Delaney gets closer.

Her tired eyes are full of emotion as I slip Amelia onto one hip and use the other arm to embrace Delaney.

I press a kiss into her hair, so relieved to have both of them finally with me.

"I can't believe you're here," I whisper.

"We had couches on the plane, Daddy. I had a big sleep," Amelia declares.

"Did you?"

"She did. Me? Not so much. You're on child watch for the rest of the day." Delaney's lips twitch.

I chuckle. "That's fine with me. I brought someone with me for you guys to meet."

"Who, Daddy?"

Turning around, I grin at Reece.

"Amelia, this is my friend, Reece."

Reece winks. "Hi, Amelia. You're every bit as pretty as your daddy said you are." He takes Amelia's hand in his and plants a kiss on it. She's wide-eyed and giggles as he lets it go.

"So, this must be Delaney."

Delaney's eyes are so wide that it bugs me. I want that look of astonishment from her.

Reece smiles that charming smile of his, and leans over to peck her on the cheek. "I'm Reece."

"I know who you are." She beams as she looks at me.

"Enough of the hero worship. It's just Reece," I mutter.

She turns to me and cups my cheek. "Oh, poor baby. Someone's jealous."

I shrug. "Maybe."

"You're still my favourite." She's talking to me in a baby voice, and I just roll my eyes at Reece's laugh.

"Dude. I love her already."

"Don't get too carried away." I shoot him a pointed look. "Babe, do you have all your bags?"

She nods.

I lower Amelia to the floor. "Stick with your mother, and I'll grab the luggage."

Before I know it, I'm pushing the trolley while Reece loops his arm around Delaney's shoulders and holds Amelia's hand.

I could be annoyed, but all I can do is smile.

They'll be settled in before I know it.

***

AMELIA CHATS up a storm in the back seat of the car with Reece. She loves her new booster seat I bought during the week, and has to tell him all about it.

I reach for Delaney's hand across the centre console and she smiles as I link my fingers through hers.

"Love you," I say.

She leans her head back on the seat. "Better make this worth my while, Carter."

I laugh. "It will be. I promise."

"I love you too." She still looks tired, but at least she's smiling. "I had an offer for the diner too. A good one. I think I'm going to take it."

"That's fantastic."

Delaney yawns. "They'll keep Trina and Jo on for continuity. That was what really mattered to me."

"Sounds great." I change gear. "We'll be home soon."

She shuffles in her seat, leans back against the headrest and closes her eyes. "Home."

"Is this our house?" Amelia calls out a short time later when I stop and press the remote to open the gate.

"It is. There might even be a bedroom in it for you." I chuckle.

"Mummy, it's so big."

I'm half expecting a smart-arse comment from either Reece or Delaney, but neither of them speak. I turn to Delaney, but her head's to the side and it looks like she's asleep.

I give her arm a gentle nudge and she opens her eyes.

"We're here."

She raises her head. I know it's a lot to take in. The land is two acres, so there's plenty of space, and up the circular driveway is a two-storey house. The house itself has a ton of rooms. Six bedrooms, with the living spaces all upstairs. Downstairs is a large reception-type room which I've never used, but I think was designed for parties.

I pull up to the front door, and Max, walks out to greet us.

After we're all out of the car, I take Delaney's hand. "Max, I want you to meet Delaney, and this is Amelia."

He smiles. I've had staff here since I bought the house four years ago, and while I haven't been home a lot in the past, I've been able to rely on him to not only drive me to important events when I'm here, but also to help organise things around the property.

"It's a pleasure to meet you."

"Delaney, Max is my driver, and he sorts out things like getting people in to look after the grounds."

She nods. I didn't tell her I had staff. Ultimately, she'll be in charge of everything if she wants to be. It's her home too.

"I'll take the bags to the bedrooms," Max says.

Delaney nods again. "The smallest two cases are Amelia's."

He smiles. "They'll be in her room shortly."

"Thank you so much." She gives him that Delaney special smile that tells me she'll warm to him. I'm sure they'll be like old friends by the end of the week.

"Let's go inside."

Delaney's mouth hangs open as she looks around when we step in the door. It's not dissimilar to her reaction to Reece's place in Hawaii, and the houses do have some similarities with the sweeping staircases up to the second level.

"Josh. It's so much."

I wrap my arm around her waist. "It's ours. All ours. And together, I think we can make this the home it should have always been."

She leans her head on my shoulder. "This is insane."

"Come here," I say. She turns toward me, and I slide my other arm around her waist, pulling her close. "I know it's big, but it's private, and you'll have all the peace you need."

She nods. "I can see that."

"We can raise our family here, Delaney. We can turn it from a house into a home."

Her eyes meet mine. It's clear this is a lot to take in, but her smile warms my heart.

I lean in and kiss her, caressing her lips with mine.

"Ahem."

We break apart, and I turn to see Reece hand in hand with Amelia behind us.

"Why don't I show you where the bedrooms are? Then you can freshen up and we'll have something to eat," I say.

"That sounds like a great idea."

I hold out my hand for Amelia to take, and Reece follows as we climb the stairs.

"Left is to the kitchen and living room. Right to the bedrooms," I say.

Reece heads to the kitchen while we turn right, and end up in the hallway leading to our rooms.

Amelia's first.

I open the door to a newly decorated room. It's mostly pink—her favourite colour—with a chalkboard feature wall for her to draw on and, my favourite part, the black duvet on the bed with a large silver fern. She's half of me too, but I always want her to be in touch with her roots.

"Josh," Delaney gasps.

"This is my room?" Amelia asks.

"It is, sweetheart. I might have had some decorators in a while ago. Just in case."

Delaney walks in, brushing her fingers over the duvet.

"My bed is so awesome," Amelia squeals, and I laugh.

"I'm glad you like it. I knew it'd take some time to get your things over here, so I made sure that you had plenty of toys to play with, and I thought it should feel like home."

Delaney walks back to me, takes my hand in hers and squeezes it. "Thank you. It's beautiful."

"Having you here means I can spoil you."

"Not too much."

I know what she means. It'd be easy to go overboard, but I have to restrain myself where Amelia's concerned. Delaney, on the other hand …

"Come and see our room." I pull her by the hand out the door. "Are you okay, Amelia? We're just going down the hall to our room."

I'm not sure if she even hears me. She's opened her wardrobe and discovered where the toys are stored.

"She's distracted. Show me," Delaney says.

I lead Delaney a little farther down the hall and open the door to our room. She squeezes my hand again as we walk in the door.

The room's plainly decorated. I never put much effort into it when it was just me, and while I had Amelia's room revamped, I left our room as it was so Delaney could put her stamp on it.

She lets go of my hand, and opens the door to the walk-in wardrobe.

"I love it." She beams.

"It's all yours. Apart from that tiny part over there for me." I laugh.

She crosses the room and opens the French doors that lead to the balcony. It overlooks the back yard, and she takes an audible breath while she looks over the grounds.

I wrap my arms around her waist from behind and nuzzle her neck. "You like?"

"I love. It's just such a big house."

"Is that good or bad?"

She turns her head. "I'm not sure yet. We'll have to get used to it."

"It's yours, Delaney. Just as I am."

I loosen my grip and she turns around. Closing my eyes as she touches my cheek, I kiss her hand.

"I feel like I've waited forever for this," she whispers.

Opening my eyes, I press my forehead to hers. "I know what you mean. Now, we start our life together." I take a breath. "I've been thinking ..."

"Did it hurt?" She laughs.

"Maybe when you two are all settled in, we could talk about expanding our family. I don't know how you feel about it, but we were both only children, and I don't want Amelia to grow up alone."

Delaney lights up. "I love that idea."

I've never felt so complete.

AFTER A QUICK TOUR of the rest of the house, I lead Delaney and Amelia into the kitchen. It's on the same level as the bedrooms, and it's cosy and welcoming.

I chuckle at the sight of Reece at the table eating a sandwich. He has an innate habit of making his way to where the food is.

Delaney's eyes go straight to the appliances. I knew they would.

"There's someone I want you two to meet."

Mrs Becker walks out of the walk-in pantry and smiles at my girls.

"Delaney, this is Mrs Becker. She's the housekeeper and she organises all the jobs to be done around the house like cleaning and cooking."

Delaney's not often unreadable, but she is in this moment. I'm not sure she expected this, but then again, I know she's tired. "It's nice to meet you, Mrs Becker."

"You too." Mrs Becker looks at me. "Did you all want something to eat?"

"I'm sure Delaney and Amelia do. It's been a long flight for them."

"Of course."

Delaney shakes her head. "I'd really just like a coffee."

"I'll make you one. What does Amelia eat?"

Delaney shrugs. "Pretty much anything. Did you want something to eat, honey?"

Amelia nods. "A peanut butter sandwich."

"Well, that's easy to take care of." Mrs Becker gives us a smile and I guide Delaney to the table while the food and drinks are being made.

Amelia climbs onto a seat next to us.

"Are you okay?" I ask.

Delaney nods. "Just really tired. I'll have a drink and then nap, I think."

I kiss her temple. "Whatever you need."

I'm sure it'll take a little time for them both to settle in, but they're with me.

And that's all that matters.

CHAPTER FORTY-FOUR

DELANEY

FAIRY TALES DO COME TRUE.

I know because I'm living one. But something's missing.

My life is surreal. I'm with the man I love, feeling like the princess in the castle who's got her happily-ever-after with her prince.

Only, that's the point when the fairy tale stops. No one ever looks at what happens afterward. Do the prince and princess really stay together? Are they happy?

I feel like I should be, and I am. I've never felt so fulfilled and yet so empty. It's the strangest feeling.

It took a couple of weeks to decide on a school for Melly. At least that kept me busy. She had school visits last week, but started officially this week.

Josh works all day while he's getting this movie off the ground. He bought me a car, but I only drive to school to drop Melly off, and to pick her up afterward. I'm too paranoid to go sightseeing. What if I screw it up and am late to get her? But I don't want to hire a nanny like some other parents seem to do.

I'm in this huge house, which doesn't feel like mine. Every time I try to cook something, Mrs Becker appears as if she somehow knows

I'm touching her appliances and fusses that she'll make something for me until I leave.

I keep telling myself that it'll just take some time to work through everything, but it's been a month since we arrived, and every day's the same.

I'm glad when we reach Friday. Josh has made sure to take weekends off to spend with us, and I'm looking forward to him getting home.

My stomach grumbles. It's dinnertime, and I head to the kitchen. Of course, Mrs Becker's already in there, standing by the oven. Melly's sitting at the kitchen table with a cold drink.

"Delaney." She smiles. "I hope you're hungry."

"Starving. Josh should be home soon."

She smiles. "Amelia was telling me just how much she missed mac and cheese, so I made some for your dinner."

I smile. "That's very kind of you."

She nods. "I'm happy to make whatever you'd like. Just let me know. I'll leave you to your dinner."

Mrs Becker leaves the room, and I let out a long breath.

She's so kind, but all it does is make it harder to push back. I've never felt like this before, never had any problem standing up for myself, but this isn't a situation I'm used to. I'm out of my depth for the first time in a long time.

"Mac and cheese," Melly chants. She's so happy, and my priority is making sure she's settled.

"Hey, you guys." Josh slips his arms around me from behind and plants a kiss on the back of my neck.

"You're home," I say.

"Nowhere else I'd rather be." He nuzzles me under the ear, taking a gentle bite of the lobe before stepping back and heading to Melly. "Did you have a good day?"

"School is cool," Amelia says, bursting into giggles as he plucks her out of her chair and into his arms.

"Is it? First week went well?" He looks at me.

I nod. "She'll be fine. The kids all flock to her because they think she's a novelty right now, but she's already got her eye on a couple of them to be friends."

He chuckles. "That's my girl. Should we eat dinner before it gets cold?"

She nods, and he plants a kiss on her temple before setting her down.

I walk to her seat and spoon some mac and cheese onto her plate before taking my own seat and filling my plate. Josh smiles widely, taking the spoon from me and dishing up his own.

It looks lovely. Mrs Becker has gone above and beyond to take care of us, and I am grateful. I fill the fork and take a bite. It's loaded with onion and garlic, and when I make it for Melly, I leave all that out and add lots of bacon.

Melly pulls a face, and I know just what the problem is. This isn't *my* mac and cheese.

"Have a try."

She meets my gaze. Her lower lip wobbles.

"Amelia?" Josh's concerned tone hurts as much as Melly struggling. "What's wrong?"

"I want Mummy's mac and cheese." Two big tears roll down her cheeks. I know she's tired from her first week at school, and this on top has just broken her. She's in an unfamiliar place, she's started school with all new kids, and she's not got a lot around her to make her feel at home yet.

Standing, I walk around the table and pick up her plate. Scraping the food into the waste disposal, I run it to get rid of the evidence. I don't want to hurt Mrs Becker's feelings.

"Mummy?" Amelia asks.

"Hang on, honey. Let me just find a few things."

Walking into the pantry frustrates me. Nothing is where I'd put it, and it seems to take forever to find a loaf of bread and a jar of peanut butter.

"Delaney? Is everything okay?" Josh asks.

"It'll be fine." It's up to me to work this situation out. When I feel at home, Melly will be much more comfortable.

I spread the peanut butter on two slices of bread and piece together two sandwiches which I cut into triangles for her. It's been a while since she ate it like that, but it was her thing for a long time.

Placing it in front of her, I kiss the top of her head and she picks up a piece of bread and bites into it.

"Is that better?" I ask.

She nods, and I wipe her tears away with my thumb. Tomorrow will be a new day, and we'll all be at home together.

I sit back down, pick up my fork, and take a big mouthful of the mac and cheese.

No wonder Melly didn't like it.

"You know what? Forget this."

I stare as Josh stands, picks up his plate and mine, and takes them both to the bench.

"It's okay."

"Clearly, it's not. I can see your frustration. Let's go for a drive."

"Can I bring my sandwich?" Melly mumbles.

"Of course you can. We're going to get something else though."

He winks at her, and her whole face lights up as she sprays crumbs over the table. "Yay."

"Pizza sound good?"

She nods, and he plucks her from the chair and onto his hip. She's too big for me to do that with now, but Josh just makes it look effortless. And she loves clinging to him.

"Let's get going." He pecks her on the cheek.

"Come on, Mummy," she calls.

Her tone's flipped. She's gone from being miserable to sounding like this is the most exciting outing ever.

"I'll just take care of the rest of this." I pick up the dish and move it onto a shelf in the fridge before grabbing my bag and following Josh downstairs and into the garage.

He buckles Melly into her booster. She's got a sandwich in each hand, and a wide smile on her face. Her expression melts me. She looks at her father like he's the most amazing man ever.

I know that feeling. I'm sure it's the way I look at him.

Throwing my bag on the car floor, I climb into the passenger seat. Josh jumps in and starts the car.

"Let's go get some pizza," Josh says.

I close my eyes as we hit the road, and take a deep breath.

The car's quiet but for the smacking sound Melly makes when she chews, and I sneak a look at Josh.

He reaches across the centre console and takes my hand in his.

"Are you angry?" I ask.

"No. Why would I be?" he asks.

I shrug. "You haven't spoken to me since the dinner table."

"Amelia hated it. And I saw your face when you took a bite."

"It wasn't bad. It just wasn't that great for a five-year-old."

He indicates and turns a corner. "No, it wasn't. And Amelia has enough change in her life without anything else to deal with. Even if it's as simple as that."

For a moment, I just watch him. I should have told him how I was feeling, but I didn't want to put him under any more pressure. Now he's stepping in to take control, and the sense of relief is over-whelming.

"Where are we going?" I ask.

"A little pizza place I found a couple of years ago. I visit it far more often than I should when I'm home."

I smile. "No Australian baristas there?"

Josh pulls up to a red light and grins at me. "There's only one Australian barista who's ever stolen my heart."

"Really? She's a bit alright then?"

"Very. I think I might just spend the rest of my life with her."

The light turns green, and I'm glad Josh is driving because I can't focus. I know we're in a relationship, and plan to spend the rest of our lives together, but hearing those words still sets my heart fluttering.

It's not a long drive, but I have no idea where we are. I only really know how to get to the school and back, and we're a long way from the neighbourhood I stayed in last time I was here. Josh pulls into a small car park behind a building with a large sign outside that reads *Lorenzo's Pizza.*

"How did you find this place?" I ask

He shoots me a sheepish look. "I got lost, and then hungry."

I laugh. "That's so not like you."

Josh leans over and pecks me on the lips. "Best pizza anywhere. But then, you haven't made me pizza yet."

"That *could* be arranged."

"I hope so. What I think we need to do is go to the grocery store tomorrow and you can stock your kitchen your way."

I sigh. "You really do know the way to a woman's heart."

"Oh, I have an idea that'll really put a smile on your face later. Come on."

We get out of the car, and I open Melly's door. She's not happy until her father holds her hand and leads her toward the building. It's a wonderful sight. She really does have him wrapped around her little finger.

The aroma of pepperoni and oregano hit me when we walk in the door, and I find myself salivating.

"Josh." An older man with a wide smile approaches us. "It's been a long time. And who is this?" He looks between Melly and me.

"This is my partner, Delaney, and our daughter, Amelia." Josh turns to me. "Delaney, this is Lorenzo."

I take the hand the man offers and he raises it to his lips. "It's such a pleasure to meet you, Delaney."

"You too."

"I didn't know you had a daughter."

Josh grins. "It's a long story, but here she is."

Lorenzo lets go of my hand. "I have a spare booth down the back. Follow me."

We weave past crowded tables to a quiet corner of the restaurant, and I slide into the large red leather seat. Josh follows, and Melly sits on his other side.

"What did you want to order?"

Josh turns to Melly. "Do you like pepperoni?"

She nods, and he turns to me. "What about you?"

"I'm happy with whatever you order. I could eat a horse right now. Everything smells so good."

Josh laughs. "Lorenzo, could we please have the large pepperoni, and six garlic rolls?"

He nods. "Of course. I'll get that out as quickly as possible. Drinks?"

Josh looks at me. "Coke, please," I say. "And an orange juice for Melly."

"Coke for me too," Josh says.

"Coming right up."

"I love pizza," Melly says.

"I know you do, sweetheart." I turn to Josh. "This place looks lovely."

"It's pretty popular, but Lorenzo usually squeezes me in." He reaches for my hand. "Feeling better?"

"I am." Melly's announcement makes us both laugh.

"Straight to bed when we get home, I think." I'm not about to forget the tired tears. At least we've got the weekend together. That'll cheer her up.

It doesn't take long for the pizza to arrive, and Melly's eyes grow wide at the sight of it.

"It's so big," she says.

"I think the slices are as big as your head." I laugh.

"Let's test that theory." Josh picks up a piece and holds it in the air, looking between it and Melly. He nods. "Confirmed. I hope you didn't eat too much peanut butter. Be careful with this. It's pretty hot."

She giggles and he places the pizza on a plate in front of her.

I reach for a slice, and place it on my plate. After grabbing a garlic roll, I take a bite. The garlic is through the doughy bread, and I moan at how good it tastes.

"Moan like that again and we'll be taking this home." Josh murmurs in my ear.

I laugh, leaning my head against his. "These are so good."

"I hope you all enjoy your meal," Lorenzo says.

"It's fantastic so far," I say.

"Delaney's a cook. She owned her own diner back in New Zealand," Josh says.

Lorenzo grins. "Wonderful. Are you opening one here?"

I shake my head. "No plans to. I'm just adjusting to being here and settling Amelia in at the moment. I might have to become a regular customer of yours just for the rolls."

He chuckles. "I'm glad you like them."

Leaving us to our meal, he walks around the room making conversation with people on all the tables, and always with a smile on his face.

"He's such a nice guy," I say.

"Yeah, he is. He's the big reason I come here. It's always a family atmosphere, and I enjoy the company."

I shift my gaze to Josh. "Was it lonely? I mean, I know you have friends, but living in that big house ..."

He nods. "Sometimes. Other times, I liked rattling around in there. And then there were the times when Reece would come over and Mrs Becker would cook for him. I'm sure he'll start visiting you once he samples your cooking."

"I'd cook for him any time." I bat my lashes.

Josh studies me for a moment. "You don't have to get all starry-eyed over him."

"You know there's only one man who makes me see stars." I grin.

"Finished."

I look over at Melly. Her plate's already clean and she's licking her fingers. She beams a breathtaking smile at me.

"Did you want to try one of these rolls? They're very nice."

She nods. "Uh huh."

"Here you go." Josh hands her one, and she takes a big bite.

"They're yummy too," she exclaims, and my heart's so warmed by the sight.

She's happy again.

JOSH DEMOLISHES MOST of the pizza, but there's more than enough for the three of us.

Lorenzo approaches. "Did you want anything else?"

I shake my head. "We're full. But thank you so much. It was wonderful. I can see why Josh loves your food so much."

"I appreciate that." He turns to Melly. "How old are you?" he asks.

Melly holds up her splayed out fingers. "I'm five."

"Really? Would you like to meet my granddaughter? She's five, and she's having dinner here tonight too."

Melly nods.

He looks at me. "They're right over there. Do you mind if I take her over?"

Josh leans toward me "She'll be fine."

I nod. "It's okay with me."

Melly stands, takes Lorenzo's hand and he leads her to a nearby table. Another dark-haired little girl looks up as they approach, and her eyes light up when she sees Melly.

Josh slides his arm around my shoulders. "You're not happy."

When I turn, his eyes search mine. "We're still settling in."

He shakes his head. "That's not it. There's something missing. It's crept up, and I couldn't put my finger on it until tonight."

I blink back tears. "We'll work through it. This is such a big change for Melly and I."

"Look at her, Delaney. That's the biggest smile I think I've seen on her face all week."

I look over to where Melly's sitting with the other little girl. He's right. She's gone from tears in the dining room to beaming smiles.

"You've got enough on your plate, Josh ..."

"No. I want my feisty Delaney back. The one who puts me in my place and turns me upside down."

I give him a small smile. "And I thought I was the bossy one."

"Amelia didn't like the dinner Mrs Becker cooked."

I shake my head. "It wasn't the same as my mac and cheese. She's spent all her life with my cooking, and the food we get in New Zealand. A lot of things taste different here."

"Why didn't you make dinner?" His gaze is so intense. My stomach twists. He's trying to work this all out because he cares, but I still feel like an ungrateful naughty schoolgirl being told off by my dad.

I sigh, and he holds me a little tighter. He loves me, and I know that. I also know his change in career direction is putting pressure on him, and that's one of the reasons why I don't want to make a huge deal over it.

"I feel like a stranger in my own home."

His brows knit. "In what way?"

"Every time I step into that kitchen with the intention of making anything, Mrs Becker all but pushes me out. I know she wants to take care of us the way she's taken care of you, but I've never needed taking care of before."

He reaches up and brushes a stray lock of hair behind my ear. "You are the most capable person I've ever met. I needed her to make sure I had good meals and to run the household in my absence. It's your home now. Say the word and I'll help her find work somewhere else."

For a moment, I pause and just look at him. "You'd do that?"

He nods. "She's been good to me, and I wouldn't just throw her out, but yes. I'd do anything for you."

His expression softens, and tears roll down my cheeks at just how sweet he's being. I feel like I'm always crying around him, but the roller coaster of our life seems far from over.

"In the meantime, I'll talk to her tomorrow and make it clear she needs to give you the space to do your own thing. I thought it was weird you weren't cooking at all, but just assumed that you wanted a break for a while."

I shake my head. "I really do miss cooking."

"Well, there you go." He wipes my tears with his thumb. "I'm sorry I didn't work it out earlier. The last thing I ever want to see is you or Amelia unhappy. You two are my everything."

"I didn't want to worry you unnecessarily."

"You come first. No matter what."

He strokes my cheek as I smile. "That's better. Now I need you to say something really sarcastic or bitter to complete the Delaney experience."

"You're such a smart-arse."

"I do like the way you say arse." He says it with the r slightly rolled and it just sounds weird. "I also like *your* arse."

"Okay, you need to start talking your Canadian way again because this attempt at a Kiwi accent is really freaking me out."

"Made you smile." He kisses me softly, pressing his forehead to mine. "Just remember that what's mine is yours. Redecorate the house—make it a real home for us. And if it's too much, we'll sell it and buy something smaller."

I laugh. "You'd really do that?"

"Told you. Anything for you."

CHAPTER FORTY-FIVE

DELANEY

I'M NOT sure what he says to Mrs Becker, but the kitchen is clear in the morning, and I revel in the simple act of making French toast for breakfast.

Amelia's smiling again, and by the time Josh rolls out of bed, she's finished eating.

"Daddy!" she squeals. "Can we have pizza again today?"

He laughs. "You really enjoyed yourself last night."

She nods. "Maria is so much fun. She likes *Paw Patrol* too."

"Does she now?" He looks at me for guidance.

"It's her favourite cartoon."

"Oh." He plants a kiss on her head. "We can't go back today, but I'd be happy to talk to Lorenzo and maybe we could arrange a play-date."

"That would be wonderful," I say.

It's funny how one night fixes so much. There's a part of me that feels bad about Mrs Becker. She's a lovely lady, but this is my home.

The house is still ridiculously big and overwhelming, but every day I get a little more used to it. I've walked every inch of it, so at least I know it well now.

"After breakfast, let's go to the grocery store," Josh says.

"Really? I haven't even looked at the cupboards yet to see what's here."

"Do that first and then we'll go for a drive." He smiles.

It's the small actions that make me appreciate Josh all the more. He gave me time and then acted when he knew something was wrong.

I'm the luckiest woman alive.

———

MONDAY MORNING, I'm back in a funk.

Amelia's at school, and while I have a kitchen full of groceries, I'm not in the mood to cook.

I'm sure there are emails that need to be taken care of. Since I accepted the offer on the diner, there have been a few messages back and forward.

Josh bought me a new laptop when I arrived here. My old one had been through the wringer, doing all the work for the diner as well as my personal stuff. This one, at least, doesn't take forever to load.

I sit at the computer and load up all my tabs. I've barely touched social media since Josh and I got back together, and I know I'm asking for trouble, but maybe I can do some more work on muting and blocking what I don't want to see.

There's nothing too crazy recently. The fuss died down a lot after Josh put out a statement acknowledging Amelia as his daughter and disavowing the article about me.

But there is the odd thing that piques my interest.

Like the tweet with a photo of Josh and me. I've seen it before. It was taken the first week Amelia started school here. They don't show her or the school, but I had a hard time saying goodbye to her that first day, and Josh has me in his arms.

I know I shouldn't click.

The tweet reads: Ugh! Why is he with her? When will he be allowed to be with his real girlfriend?

His real girlfriend?

I click and click, falling down a well I shouldn't be falling down. It doesn't hurt. In fact, I think it's almost funny knowing what I know, but there are people who think Josh and Gabby are secretly married. Some think they have a child.

I wonder if Gabby knows about this. I'm sure she'd find it as amusing as I do.

A loud thud comes from behind me, and my heart races.

I turn to find Mrs Becker, a sheepish look on her face, quietly closing a cupboard door.

"Oh, sorry, Delaney. I didn't mean to disturb you."

I shake my head. "You didn't." Licking my lips, I stand. "Mrs Becker ..."

She smiles. "If you're worried about Josh talking to me about the kitchen, it's fine, love. I knew this day would come, and I'm glad that it's you."

I stare at her.

"Josh hired me four years ago, but I always told him that I'd leave when the time was right. My daughter's just had her fourth baby, and I think it's time."

For a moment, I don't know what to say. "You're leaving?"

She nods. "I'll talk to Josh tonight, but that's my plan. He's found the right one for him, and I'm so happy for the two of you."

I swallow hard. "Thank you."

"He was never one to bring girls home. Now you're here and he's happier than I've ever seen him. It does my heart good."

I smile.

"That little girl of yours is so precious. I'm glad I was here to meet the two of you."

"Me too." And I do mean it. Apart from the whole kitchen incident, I've seen what she does for Josh. If she's leaving, I'll need to learn some things from her.

"I'll give you all the details of who I get in to do what. Whether you get someone else in or you take it over, you'll need them."

All I can do is thank her again, and she gives me such a warm smile that I know she's okay.

And I will be too.

IT'S a quiet night as Melly and I eat alone, and she's asleep by the time Josh comes home.

He walks into the living room where I've been lying on the couch with my laptop, still engrossed in these crazy stories about my life.

"Oh my God, Josh." I place the laptop on the coffee table, leap up and throw myself at him.

"What?" He smiles, wrapping his arms around my waist.

"Did you know there's a Facebook group full of people who believe you're in a secret relationship with Gabby? Some of them think you have a hidden child with her."

He screws up his face. "What are you talking about?"

"It's amazing. They've taken every single story about you out of context. I'm some kind of decoy for whatever reason. Probably because you couldn't possibly be attracted to me."

His mouth falls open. "Delaney. Don't ever talk about yourself like that."

"I'm fine. I know the truth. I know how irresistible I am to you." I smile.

"You are."

I slide my arms around his neck. "I know just how much you want to put another big-headed Carter baby into my womb."

Josh laughs. "I love you, even if you are a little cuckoo. But stay away from those sites."

"I'm just trying to work out what to do with myself while you're working and Amelia's at school."

He gives me a tender kiss. "I've got something for you to try and solve that problem."

"What is it?"

"Give me a second, and I'll show you."

He kisses me again before disappearing back out the door.

I sit on the couch and wait.

"Tada." He brings in two boxes, one square, the other tall and thin.

"Open these."

"What are they?"

"This one first."

It's like Christmas, but the box isn't wrapped and when he hands it to me, I see immediately what it is.

I tear it open and pull out the camera inside. I've got no clue how to use it, but I'm sure I could work it out. I've never owned a proper camera. Maybe I could do a photography course.

He nods. "And the other box ..."

I put the camera onto the table and reach for the other box. Opening it, I slide out the contents.

"A tripod?"

"Well, I know how much you miss your diner, and I also know you're not keen on starting something new here with my money. So, I thought maybe you could vlog your cooking."

"Vlog? Like on YouTube?"

He nods. "People do all kinds of videos. You love cooking, so maybe you could vlog about it. You're so talented and you have such a way with words. My name might bring the vlog attention at first, but you'll keep your audience."

"A way with words like putting another big-headed Carter baby into my womb?"

His lips curl. "Something like that. Reece is doing one for the movie with some behind-the-scenes stuff planned. It gave me the idea."

"Don't you tell him that. He'll get a swollen head." I pause. "An even bigger swollen head."

Josh laughs, and flops on the couch beside me. "You already know him so well."

"I'm his biggest fan."

He leans over. "What about me?"

"It's always such a competition with you two. I have an unfair bias toward you, but that might just be all the sex you give me."

He runs his hand down my arm and takes my hand in his. "Wanna go get some now?"

"Soon. You need to talk to Mrs Becker first."

Josh frowns, scanning my expression. "What's happened?"

"Nothing bad, but she wants to talk to you. It's important."

His kiss catches me by surprise, but it's warm and tender with a promise of things to come. "How about I go and talk to her while you get ready for bed?"

"I suppose I could do that."

"See you real soon?"

I leave him to go see Mrs Becker, and make my way to our bedroom.

Stripping off all my clothes, I slide between the sheets. I do love this house. It's big and crazy, and not at all a house I thought I'd ever live in. But it's ours, and it's what we make of it.

Up until a few days ago, this didn't feel like home to me. But it's starting to now. And for the first time since we moved here, I feel truly like myself.

Josh joins me soon after. His expression is downcast. Mrs Becker has been a part of his life for a while, and I know he cares about her. I hate seeing him sad.

"You okay?" I ask.

"I'm guessing you know the news?" He tugs off his shirt.

I nod. "I do."

"I'll make sure she has enough to retire on. We'll give her a little nest egg."

I smile. "You're such a good man."

Josh drops his pants, and I grin at the sight of him. "Maybe I can show you just how good I am."

"Come here."

He slips into bed beside me, and I let out a contented sigh.

"There's something different about you," he says, cupping one breast.

"I think I finally feel settled in."

"That's good." He dips his head and sucks my nipple into his mouth. I hook my ankle around his and pull him closer.

His gentle touch down my back makes me shiver. He trails his fingers over my body and strokes my thigh, slowly drawing his hand closer to the apex of my legs. I part them a little to give him access. His long index finger swirls around my clit—tempting, teasing me in the way only Josh can.

"Fuck." He pushes me onto my back, and dives between my legs, his tongue working wonders as I lie back and enjoy it. Even the act of sex is more pleasurable now I've claimed our home.

I want a baby.

I cry out when Josh sucks on my clit, and I ride his face until I shatter into a million pieces as he brings me to orgasm.

My eyes are closed, and when I open them, he's looking at me with a curious expression on his face.

"Are you okay?" he asks.

"I'm not sure. Can we try that again?"

He shakes his head. "Maybe later." Planting a kiss on my navel, he makes his way up my body until we're almost face-to-face. "I need to be inside you right now."

"Hurry up then."

His eyes dance with mischief, and I grab hold of the headboard as he thrusts into me.

"Oh, God. Yes." I arch my back and push my hips toward him.

"This is the Delaney I've missed." His words spur me on, and he's right. Our sex life has been pretty subdued since we arrived. I'd put it down to being tired, but that wasn't it at all. I just needed to be me.

"Roll over."

Josh pulls out of me and grabs me by the leg, and I roll onto my stomach before getting up on all fours. He pauses for a moment.

"Josh?"

"If my Delaney is really back, I'm going to give her a night she'll never forget."

I laugh, gripping the pillow and moaning as he guides his cock back into me. "As if I forget anything."

He thrusts hard, and I let out a moan that's so loud it makes me glad we have such a large house.

"I gather you're enjoying this?" he teases.

"Give me one of those big-headed Carter babies." I laugh, but it quickly turns into pain as I faceplant the headboard.

"Shit. Are you okay?" He comes to a stop.

"Keep going. I need this." I push myself back up, and nearly die when he leans forward and grabs hold of my breast, his fingers caressing my nipples.

"I don't want to stop. You feel so good. But I think I'm going to ..." Josh lets out a groan, pulsing inside me. He slows again reaching around to finish me off. My body jerks with him still inside, and he lets out a moan as I buck in front of him.

I collapse onto my stomach, and he falls in a heap on top of me. All I can do is laugh.

He joins in, rolling off me and pulling me onto my side. "I love you, Delaney. You're nuts, but I love you."

"Love you too." I sigh.

He nuzzles my neck. "I have something else I need to tell you."

"What is it?" I'm still breathless, and in one of those moods where I could do this all night.

"My parents are visiting next week."

Total mood killer.

CHAPTER FORTY-SIX

DELANEY

THE THOUGHT of Josh's parents visiting fills me with anxiety.

Maybe it's because of my own relationship, or lack thereof, with my parents.

But they've been patient and given us a chance to settle into life together before coming to visit. And Amelia's owed a chance to get to know them.

That thought doesn't quell the nausea I'm feeling as Josh picks them up from the airport.

Amelia's excited. She knows Pania's mother as her *Kuia* who helped raise her at the start. But she's never had anything to do with my mother.

I suck in a deep breath when I hear voices.

Josh appears in the doorway, a big smile on his face. I rise from the couch, and he walks over to me, taking my hand in his. Into the room walks a short, dark-haired woman, and a tall man who I recognise as Josh's father. It's easy to see where Josh gets his looks from.

"Delaney, this is my mom, Rosalyn."

I draw in a nervous breath. "Hi, Rosalyn."

She smiles. "Hello, Delaney. You're even prettier than your photos."

I blush. I'm in love with this woman already.

"And this is my dad, Cal."

Josh's father steps forward, a huge smile on his face. It's okay. I know they're happy to see me, but it's Amelia they're really anxious to meet.

"Hi." I nod toward them. "And this is Amelia."

I turn my head, but she's not on the couch anymore. "Ouch." A sharp pinch to my thigh makes me look down. She's hiding behind my leg, her head peeking out around my skirt.

Josh laughs. "It's not like you to be shy."

"This is a really big deal for her." I bend, scooping her into my arms. This takes me back. When she was three, she went through a really shy phase, and as she did then, she buries her face in my neck.

"Of course it is," Rosalyn says. Enchantment's written all over her face. "Why don't we sit on the couch together?"

"Is that okay, Melly?" I ask.

She nods, and I take a seat, placing her beside me.

Rosalyn sits on the other side of her. "I've brought you a present."

Melly's eyes widen.

"I took a guess, but I'm sure this will fit." She hands Melly a package. Melly rips it open and her little mouth falls open. It's a pale pink cardigan.

"Mummy, look."

"I can see, sweetie." It's enough to bring tears to my eyes. I've knitted her a few things, and know just how special this is.

"I made it myself. Anything you need, Delaney, let me know. I'm so happy to have a little girl to knit things for."

I nod. "Thank you so much."

It takes about five more seconds for Melly to end up on her grandmother's lap.

She'll be just fine.

BY THE TIME we've finished lunch together, Melly's keeping her grandfather entertained on the other side of the room, regaling him with stories of All Black games and the haka.

"She's beautiful," Ros says.

I look up and smile. "She really is."

"There's so much of you in there, but I can see Josh. Especially around the eyes."

I nod. "I saw him in her every day from the moment she was born."

"That must have been hard for you." Her expression is so full of empathy. I'm sure Josh has told her my story.

"Very." I suck in a big breath. "She was a reminder of everything I'd lost. But at the same time, she gave me the courage to keep going. I'll tell you something else, too. I think she's almost guaranteed to follow in her father's footsteps."

Ros laughs. "We're in for a bumpy ride then."

"I'm sure."

She turns serious. "Josh told me about your mother. I'm so sorry that you couldn't get in touch with him. We would have been there for you."

I swallow hard. "Thank you. That means a lot."

"Oh, sweetheart." She wraps her arms around me, and holds me like a mother should. Is it weird that I've known her for an hour and she feels more motherly than my mum ever did?

I sniff. "It's really important to me that we develop a good relationship. Especially for Amelia. She doesn't really know what it's like to have grandparents."

"Oh, I think we already have that sorted." She lets go and holds me at arm's length. "I wasn't impressed when Josh called me, but once he explained the whole story ... well, I can't say I understand it all, but I don't have to. You two have worked things out, and now I have a precious granddaughter to love."

I smile through my tears. "She'll have you wrapped around her little finger in no time. That's what happened to Josh. I think he'd let her do anything right now."

She laughs again, wrapping one arm around my shoulders. "He's over the moon to have you two here. And I know we live on the other side of the country, but I'm only ever a phone call away if you need an ear."

"Thank you."

"His life isn't easy. But maybe he won't be so much of a nomad now he's got the two of you to come home to."

I nod. "I hope so. It sounds like he'll be more settled since he's formed his own business."

Her lips curl. "As long as he can keep Reece under control."

I laugh. "I'm not sure anyone can keep Reece under control."

"I think you're right."

CHAPTER FORTY-SEVEN

DELANEY

JOSH'S PARENTS stay for a week. And by the end of that week, I feel like they're my parents too. Amelia is like a pig in mud with all the attention. But once they're gone, and we're back into our regular life, I feel lost again.

It takes a couple more weeks, but I reach the point where I pull out the tripod and camera, and set them up on the other side of the bench in the kitchen. I'm still unsure about the vlogging thing, but it could be fun. Maybe if those fans online actually see me in Josh's house, they'll accept the truth. And if Josh appears on camera, it might hammer the message home even sooner.

I pull out all the ingredients to make mac and cheese. It's a basic dish and a good starter. And Melly and Josh love it. We can have it for dinner, and then have leftovers tomorrow.

"Hey, beautiful." I look up to see Reece walk into the kitchen. It's not like him to turn up in the middle of the day, but he's a big fan of my cooking. I don't mind the extra mouth to feed. It's like having a neglected puppy turn up on your doorstep when you're making meat pies.

He still jokes about stealing me away from Josh, and it's flattering.

It might be annoying if I thought he was serious, but he's also our biggest supporter. And Melly adores him.

"I love how you just walk into my house, Reece."

He chuckles. "You're cooking?"

I shoot him a look that I hope conveys how unimpressed with his skills of deduction I am. "How did you guess?"

He leans against the bench. "What are you doing?"

"Making mac and cheese."

His eyes widen. "Yum. I usually say you can't beat my mother's mac and cheese, but I bet yours is amazing."

"*I* bet you say that to all the girls." I shoot him a sly smile.

He turns to look at the tripod. "What's with the camera gear?"

For a moment, I pause, unsure whether this really is a stupid idea or not. "Well, I was thinking of filming myself cooking."

Reece nods. "Food porn. Nice. Cooking naked?"

I roll my eyes. "You never stop, do you?"

"Not often." His expression is thoughtful. "So, why are we doing some filming today?"

My cheeks burn. "Forget it. It's stupid."

"Seriously. What are you doing?"

I lean over the bench and chew my bottom lip. "Josh brought home the camera and tripod. He thought I might enjoy vlogging for a hobby."

Reece grins. "Nice. I'm having fun doing it for the film. I have plans to do some amazing behind-the-scenes videos. With this being a first for us, it's a good record of what we're doing."

I smile. "Josh told me. It sounds great."

"So does this. Good little opportunity to earn some money on the side too. I know you sold your business before coming out here."

My ears prick up. "Money?"

He chuckles. "You can monetise your videos. Get something out of it. I know Josh's motives would have been to encourage your interests, but why not make a little cash at the same time?"

That makes me feel a little better about it. I could sit back and try and find things to fill my time, but making my own money would make me feel more useful. Maybe that's partly why I've felt so lost.

"Just remember me when you're famous. Or give me a production credit."

"Production credit?"

He moves behind the camera and the little red light goes on. "Let's get started, beautiful. What are you cooking today?"

The weird thing is, Reece's presence calms me. He keeps me talking, asking me questions as I put the dish together. One by one, the ingredients go in, and he makes me laugh, which takes away the nerves—nerves which never made any sense in the first place. It's not like anyone is ever going to watch my vlog.

But Josh is right about one thing. I enjoy it once I get going, and it's not long before my dish is in the oven and Reece is pouring a wine for both of us.

"We just need to film the big food reveal. You need to prepare one earlier to speed things up."

I nod. "And I guess I need to find out how to edit video."

"Leave it with me. I'll sort it out. I'll do it tonight and have it back for you ready to upload tomorrow."

"If I ever do."

He cocks his head. "Delaney, you were amazing. Once you shook yourself out, everything just flowed. You've got to have faith in yourself. The camera loves you."

"Bet it adds ten pounds."

Reece laughs. "Don't be so hard on yourself. Trust me. It'll all be fine." He walks around the counter and pauses the camera. "Now, do I get to eat some of this when it's ready?"

"I made a truck load. You have no choice."

I breathe in the smell of melted cheese. My own stomach rumbles, and I have to remember to make a big deal of taking it out of the oven for the camera.

I spoon out two plates of food.

"This looks amazing. I love your cooking."

I laugh. "You have enough of it."

"Josh needs to be here for this."

I suck in a painful breath. I'd tucked that thought away myself this morning.

"Delaney? Are you okay?"

"I'm fine. It's just ... I'd love if he was here, but he's got a lot on his plate." I pause. "So do you, so why are you here?"

"I was hungry, and felt like some company other than your boyfriend." He grins. "Honestly, I love the shit out of Josh. He's like a brother to me. So having you and Amelia here is like having family. My family is half a country away."

I swallow hard.

"Josh is working hard, but you know he'd spend more time at home if you needed him to."

My eyes prick with tears, and I let out an anguished sigh. "I just don't want to get in the way of his dream."

Reece engulfs me in his embrace, kissing the top of my head. "Oh, honey. You're his dream. Everything else is just periphery. "

I meet his gaze.

"Trust me on this. Josh would drop everything for you. He'd take you and Amelia and live a quiet life if he thought you were unhappy."

I can't help but smile. It's not what I want him to do at all, but I appreciate the sentiment.

He laughs. "I love how much crap you give him. He needs it. It shows him that your love for him is real. It's not the make-believe bullshit that's out there. He knows you'll be there for him no matter what, and none of this ..." He waves his hand as if indicating the house. "... none of it matters."

There are days in your life when you hear something you need to, even if you didn't realise you needed it before you heard it.

Today is one of those days.

AMELIA SKIPS out of school toward me, a broad smile on her face. She loves this place. Sure, there's still a lot of curiosity about the little girl with the different accent, but she's making good friends and having fun.

"Is Daddy home?" she asks.

I shake my head. "Not yet. But I have mac and cheese for dinner, and I know that's your favourite."

"Can we have some ice cream too?"

I smile. "Of course we can. After dinner."

I tap her on the nose and she giggles.

Her question stabs me in the chest. But when I think about it, Josh has been late home all week. Not crazy late, but enough that she's asleep by the time he gets there.

Clearly, there are still things we need to work out. I love and support my boyfriend, but he needs to prioritise our daughter.

But I keep the mood light, and I drive her home playing that damned "Baby Shark" song in the car, which she very happily sings along to.

Despite the house being so big, our family area is cosy with the kitchen, dining room, and living room all open-plan.

Melly and I sit in front of the television to eat our mac and cheese. She chatters away about Josh joining us. She's painfully aware of his absence, and it hurts.

The pieces of our life have stitched themselves together only to fray at the seams.

"When's Daddy coming home?" she asks for the third time.

I stroke her hair. "I'm not sure, sweetheart. I'll text him, but him and Reece are very busy right now."

Reece, who skipped work to hang out with me.

I choose not to tell Melly that bit.

After dinner, ice cream, a bath, and teeth brushing, I read her a story.

I sit beside her on the bed until her shoulders slump. Her long eyelashes flutter as sleep claims her, and I smile as she snorts and rolls over.

"That's my girl." After a gentle kiss to her temple, I leave the room to get changed for bed.

I walk into our spacious bedroom, pick up the remote control, and flick on the TV.

Nothing keeps my interest, and I drift in and out of dozing, pushing myself to try and stay awake.

Hurry up and come home, Josh.

CHAPTER FORTY-EIGHT

JOSH

IT'S dark when I finally walk in the door.

All day long, I promised myself I'd be home early but, as happens most days lately, one problem leads to another.

We're in pre-production, but as Reece and I are running the show, we have a hand in everything right now. Although God knows where Reece disappeared to today.

The bedroom's dark, but I make out the shape of Delaney under the covers.

As quietly as I can, I pull open my drawer and pluck out a pair of boxers. All I want now is to have a hot shower and crawl into bed with my girl.

The hot water soothes my aches and pains, but does nothing to alleviate the heaviness of my heart. This whole thing is a lot harder than I'd ever imagined. I'm proud of what we're about to do, but it's exhausting. We've already learned so much for next time around.

After my shower, I dry off and slip into my boxers before sliding into bed beside Delaney. I bury my face in her hair. She smells of sunshine, something I've barely seen any of today.

Delaney rolls over to face me, and in the dim light of the room, I can barely make out her features but her parted lips and hooded eyes are clear.

She palms my cock through my boxers, and then gives it a gentle squeeze.

"Delaney." I love the sound of her name on my tongue.

She says nothing, stroking my length, her face an inch away from mine. But I'm barely holding on with the sudden deluge of touch.

"You smell so good." I kiss her, trying to distract myself from her hand and failing when she pushes my boxers down.

She rolls me onto my back, her strokes becoming more forceful.

"Yes," I hiss.

Dipping her head, she takes me deep in her mouth. It's warm and wet, and I close my eyes, running my fingers through her hair.

She takes me to the brink before I push her off and onto her back.

"It's been too long," she says.

"I love you," I whisper. "I'm sorry if I've been neglecting you. I don't mean to."

"Better make it up to me." Her eyes flash with desire. "I need you to touch me. Please."

"I never could say no to you."

Her lips curl into a smile as I cup her breast and run my thumb across her hardened nipple.

"I miss you," I say.

"I miss you, too." Those are words she should never have to say again. She's moved across the world to be with me. She deserves better.

Running my finger under the strap of her nightgown, I tug it down to expose her breast.

"Josh," she whispers.

Any exhaustion I felt disappears when I'm with her. I take her nipple into my mouth, and her gasp urges me on.

Brushing my hand down her stomach, I let out a moan when I find she's not wearing any underwear.

"I've been waiting." Her gentle laughter warms my heart.

"I'm sorry to do that to you." I raise my face to look at her, sliding a finger into her pussy. "I promise I'll make up for it."

Her breathy gasps spur me on as I stroke her clit. I can't look anywhere else but at her face when she closes her eyes, her body rising and falling at my touch. And then there's that moment when she comes, and a look of complete and utter bliss passes over her face. I fall all over again just watching her.

Her eyes spring open, and her lips curl into a devilish grin. She shoves me again onto my back. Her nightgown goes flying, and she straddles my hips, her heat engulfing me. She's perfect, even if she can't see it. Perfect for me.

"You're so fucking beautiful."

Her eyes flare with desire. "You're pretty hot yourself."

"Only pretty hot?"

"Okay. Amazingly hot. Will that do?"

I laugh. "It all sounds good to me."

She rocks her hips. Being inside Delaney is the best feeling in the world. I cherish it every time because I was without her for so long. But now she's home with me and I should be making the most of this —making the most of her.

I need Delaney more than ever.

Gripping her hips, I pull her down hard, and she leans over, her nipples right in front of my face. Her breathing grows heavy as I suck on them one by one.

"I love you," she says, but her words are lost when I pull her down to kiss her hard. I don't let her go, pushing my hips up to meet her. I'm so close, and when she drops her lips to my neck I lose all sense of myself.

My orgasm hits me hard, and I cry out as I come inside her.

Since she moved in, we haven't been strict on contraception, and maybe it'll catch us by surprise, but neither of us are too concerned.

She collapses onto the bed next to me.

"You're not usually that aggressive." I chuckle.

Delaney snuggles into my side. "You haven't seen Amelia in

nearly a week. We've been like two ships that pass in the night. Tonight, I'd just had enough. I need you."

"I'm doing a terrible job of all this."

She shakes her head. "This is new for all of us. We're a long way from where we were at the start."

I gaze at her. It's not like the last time; this time she's not using *new for all of us* to hide the way she feels. She means it.

"We are, but I need to do better."

"It'll balance out. Or you'll burn out and I'll end up nursing you back to health." Her eyes sparkle with mischief, but she's right.

"You'd make a sexy nurse. Maybe I'll buy you a uniform."

Delaney laughs. "I'll be your nurse. Any time. But please don't work yourself to that point. You don't need to, and you know that." She plants a kiss on my chest. "I'm going to go and clean up. Don't you dare move or fall asleep."

"I'll be waiting." I grin.

CHAPTER FORTY-NINE

DELANEY

HIS STOMACH GURGLES.

I bury my face in his chest and laugh. "You said you weren't hungry."

"Only for you."

"Does your need for me make your stomach grumble?"

"Maybe."

I pat his stomach. "You need food. Actual food."

He rubs the back of my neck. "I'd rather have you again."

Raising my head, I meet his gaze. "Josh, you can't do this to yourself. I'm completely behind you following your dream, but not at the expense of everything else."

His eyes search mine, and he slowly nods.

"If Reece had shown today when he was supposed to, that would have helped."

I frown. "He was supposed to be at work?

"This is our project. He picks and chooses his moments to show up."

I drop my gaze, smiling to myself.

"What's that smile about?" Josh's eyes are narrowed, as if he suspects I've been up to something.

"Reece was here today."

His mouth falls open. "He what ... when?"

"Around midday. For about two hours."

He runs his fingers through his hair. "What was he doing here for two hours?"

I pat his chest. "Well, we filmed ourselves having sex on the kitchen bench, and then in the walk-in pantry. And then there was—"

"Delaney," he growls.

I laugh. "He came to say hello, and noticed the camera setup. I was about to try this vlogging stuff. So, we made a movie, but it was food porn only."

Josh's expression is still tight. "Uh-huh."

"You don't believe me?"

He lets out an exasperated sigh. "Of course I do. Where's this video?"

"Actually, Reece is editing it tonight and bringing me back the finished product tomorrow." I don't miss him rolling his eyes. "But it was fun. He made it fun. I wish I'd done it with you."

His expression turns pained. *I've hurt him.*

"Josh," I whisper. "I want to do everything with you."

Leaning in, I kiss him, and he closes his eyes for a moment.

"I'll heat up some mac and cheese. There are leftovers."

His smile is so tired, but it lights up my heart. "I could eat."

"I'll sort it out." I peck him on the lips again and climb out of bed, grabbing my bathrobe.

I'm glad I woke. If I'd missed talking to him tonight, his absence would have festered and who knows what the end result would have been.

After scooping a plate full of mac and cheese, I slide it into the microwave and start it up.

"Hey." I close my eyes and lean back on his shoulder while he nuzzles my neck. "I thought I'd bring this to the bedroom for you."

"I missed you." His hands cup my breasts.

"I've been gone for thirty seconds."

Josh turns me around. His face is so full of love, I'm glad I groped him in the dark and didn't just let him fall asleep.

"I'm sorry," he says.

I shrug. "For what?"

"For getting carried away. It's why I need you. You keep me grounded, and you remind me of what's important."

I wrap my arms around his waist. Behind us, the microwave beeps, but neither of us move.

"Don't ever stop," he whispers.

"Never." I clasp my hands behind his back and give him a tender kiss. "I'm sure you'll feel better once you have some actual food."

"Your cooking is the best. Can't wait to see whatever craziness you made with Reece."

I laugh. "If he turns up here tomorrow, I'll send him to see you."

Josh smiles. "Thanks. Now, where's this food?"

Letting him go, I turn toward the microwave, and pull out the steaming plate. I place it on the counter as he retrieves a fork from the drawer.

He stirs the macaroni up, leaning against the counter as it cools.

"I'm sure learning a lot more about movie-making than I ever knew before. There's so much to it, but as we learn and work out where we can hire the right people, things will get better."

"I know it will. Just make sure we don't get left behind. Amelia asked for you today. She misses her dad."

He sighs. "I miss her, too. I'll make sure I come home earlier the rest of the week. Maybe I can pick her up from school some days."

"That'd be great. She's okay, but she notices."

Pausing for a moment, he fixes his gaze on me. "We cast my wife for the movie today. I'm hoping you approve of the choice."

I shrug. "As long as it's not Jessie Lane, I don't care."

Josh chuckles. "I wouldn't do that to you. We got Gabby. I know I've just made another film with her, but she's such a good actress, we have chemistry, and you like her."

I clap with excitement. "And I get to go shopping with Antonio while you guys are working."

Josh grimaces. "I hadn't thought of that. Better sort you out a credit card."

Sliding my hand over his, I shake my head. "I don't want your money."

"It's ours, Delaney. You have to get used to it." He scoops up a mouthful of the mac and cheese. "Oh my God. This is amazing. Exactly what I needed." He wolfs it down. I don't interrupt him because he must need it, despite saying he was happy to go to bed on an empty stomach.

"Don't make yourself sick."

He shrugs. "The more of this, the better."

"No. I mean, make sure you're eating properly. When was the last time you ate today?"

Josh pauses. "I'm not sure. Maybe around lunchtime I got something?"

"You're exhausted. You have to eat."

The corners of his mouth curl. "I know I do. Sometimes I just need a reminder."

"There's still plenty left. I'll pack you some of this for the morning. Make sure you eat it."

His smile widens. "Have I told you how much I love your bossiness?"

"Not lately."

He leans over and pecks me on the lips. "That's one of the things I always loved about you."

"Whatever."

"It's true. I was hooked the day you told me to do better."

My cheeks heat up. "You do better now."

"I try." He drops to one knee and takes my hands in his.

"What on earth are you doing?" I laugh.

"Something I should have done a long time ago. I love you. You could have rolled over and gone back to sleep, but your only concern is for me—for us. Since the day we got back together, you've just let me be me. I'm the luckiest guy alive, and I want to grow old with you."

I smile, tears pricking my eyes. "I love you."

"I love you, too. I don't have a ring because I'm so damned disorganised, but maybe we can go this weekend."

Sliding my arms around his neck, I close my eyes when he rests his head on my stomach. "I don't need anything too crazy."

"If it was up to me, I'd buy you the biggest damn diamond I could find, but you need to choose."

I chuckle. "You know me too well."

He looks up at me. "Will you marry me, Delaney?"

I can't help it. Tears roll down my cheeks as I look into the eyes of the man I loved and lost only to find again. "In a heartbeat."

He grins, rising to his feet. Sweeping me into his arms, he kisses me with so much love all it does is make the tears worse.

"You're supposed to be happy, not crying."

"I am happy." I sob. "I just never pictured being proposed to in the middle of my kitchen in the middle of the night."

Josh laughs. "Don't ever say I'm not spontaneous."

"I could never accuse you of that."

***

HIS SIDE of the bed is cold by the time I wake up. I knew it would be.

I reach for his pillow to breathe in his scent and a small piece of paper falls from it.

My darling Delaney,

Of all the things I've eaten in my life, I much prefer the taste of you.

All my love,
Josh

I laugh, hugging the paper to my chest.
We're going to be just fine.

CHAPTER FIFTY

DELANEY

OF COURSE JOSH'S idea of going shopping this weekend means a cross-country flight to New York.

He knows how much I love the movie *Breakfast at Tiffany's*, and even though I was perfectly happy to shop at Tiffany in Los Angeles, he insisted we go to the original store.

Not that I'm really complaining.

The weather's colder than we've been used to, and for the first time in ages, we're dressed warmly.

New York is somewhere I've never been before, and it's just so overwhelming and big.

But I'm not about to say no to shopping.

Josh, as always, spoils the shit out of us. We've got a car with a driver, and the poor guy is having to pack everything in the boot of the car. I don't envy him.

And then it's time.

We get dropped a short distance from the store because I want to see everything, but in the end, there's only one thing I really see.

I come to a halt, my eyes blurring over with what's in front of me.

We've been here for a while now, but this is a sight that's going to take some getting used to.

Amelia's hand in hand with her father. She's dressed in her jacket and the hat with the pom-pom that still desperately needs to be secured before it falls off. And she's looking up at him as if he hung the moon.

The thing that really drives this moment deep into my heart is the matching expression on his face.

None of this has been easy, but these two belong together. We all belong together. Maybe we're struggling to find balance, but we'll work everything out.

"Mummy," Amelia calls.

"Right behind you." I walk fast to catch up to them.

"Are you okay?" Josh asks.

"I am."

We reach the door and I take a deep breath. When I came to the States last time, I spent all my time on the West Coast. This was always something I wanted to see, but limited funds made it impossible.

Now, Josh has given this to me.

"Come here." He takes me by the hand. "They know we're coming."

"They do?"

"Nothing but the best for my girl. I love you, Delaney."

IT'S like a dream as I'm shown ring after ring.

They all kind of blur into one another after a while.

"I like this one."

I look at the one Melly's pointing at.

It's a huge teardrop diamond. I just stare at it for the longest time while Josh strokes my back.

"Josh, I can't. It's too much."

"You love it, right?"

I nod, unable to find any more words.

"Then that's all that matters."

I throw my arms around his neck, and he pulls me in tight. "I know this isn't the life you ever imagined for yourself, but we're together and that's what's important."

"I know," I whisper.

"Next week, when we're back home, I'll do some rearranging and even if it takes a while longer to get this movie made, I'll make things better."

I raise my face to look into his. "Are you sure?"

"More than sure. I just needed a wake-up call to tell me I was burying myself. This is all new for me too."

He looks at the salesperson. "This is the one."

My hand trembles when I try it on, and it's meant to be as it fits nicely.

"Perfect." Josh kisses my temple as I lean against him.

He takes care of it all while Melly and I go back outside for fresh air.

"Can I look?" Melly asks.

"Of course you can." I hold my hand down for her.

"Are you married now?"

I smile, shaking my head. "Not yet, sweetheart. This is a promise that your dad and I will get married."

"Will he marry me too?"

She's so earnest that I grin. "We should ask him about that."

Josh appears outside, and I don't even have time to catch my breath before he pulls me into his arms and kisses me.

His kiss reminds me of the first time. When we were younger and all the anticipation built to a crescendo that left my ears ringing.

"Let's go back to the hotel and order room service. We'll watch a movie with the kiddo until she falls asleep, and then have some us time."

That brings a smile to my lips. "I like that idea."

He looks down at Amelia. "Should we go inside where it's warm?"

She nods, that ridiculous pom-pom flying.

Josh hooks his arm around my shoulders, and takes Amelia's hand in his. "Let's get going."

This time, we walk together, Josh and I tangled around each other, Melly on his other side.

Our little family need each other so much.

More than we'd ever thought.

IT TAKES LONGER than usual to get Melly to sleep, but I'm not surprised. She loves her bedroom so much, and the thought of sleeping in a hotel doesn't impress her at all.

But finally, I get to snuggle on the couch with Josh and pretend the outside world doesn't exist.

"So, you like your ring?" he asks.

I raise my hand, tilting it to make the diamond sparkle. "It's perfect."

"Just like the lady wearing it."

He presses a kiss to my lips. It starts slow, but builds until I lean back and he's lying on top of me on the couch.

"I'm going to marry you, Delaney Carruthers," he whispers.

I look into his eyes and see all his love on display, nearly crapping myself when my phone on the coffee table starts playing circus music.

"What the hell is that?" Josh laughs.

"That's Reece. He's a clown so I gave him the appropriate ringtone."

"Why is he calling you?"

I shrug. "I don't know. Did you tell him why we were here?"

He shakes his head. "No, I wanted to wait until we were home so you could show off that engagement ring."

"Maybe I should answer it. It could be important."

He laughs. "Go on."

I reach for the phone and bring it to my ear, pressing the accept button as I do it. "Reece?"

"Delaney. What are you doing right now?"

I look at Josh. He's giving me some serious side-eye.

"Uhh, well. When a mummy and daddy love each other very much ..."

Reece roars with laughter. "Eww. Anyway, your views have gone nuts. Your video's viral."

"Really?" I sit up straight, pushing Josh off. "Like how viral?"

"Like a hundred thousand already and going up all the time."

I slap my hand over my mouth. "Oh, shut the hell up."

"It's true. You are an internet sensation."

I lean against Josh. "So, Mr Carter isn't the only rock star in the family."

"Far from it. I might have shared it on my social media."

Josh presses a kiss into my hair.

"Anyway, I just wanted to let you know. So you can get back to your sexy times. Have a good weekend."

"You too," I sing.

I place the phone on the table and smile at Josh.

"It's your fault for giving me that camera."

His eyebrows shoot up. "What's happened?"

"Apparently it's had about a hundred thousand views. Probably ninety thousand from your fans, or there's a ton of people out there with my mac and cheese recipe now."

He laughs. "That's fantastic."

"Thank you for giving me the idea in the first place. Maybe you could be there for the next one?"

Josh grins. "Next one? I plan on being there for every one."

And then he kisses me, and the views on YouTube are suddenly not that important anymore.

Mummy and Daddy have work to do.

CHAPTER FIFTY-ONE

DELANEY

Three months later

I'M SURPRISINGLY calm considering it's my wedding day.

Maybe it's because I don't have to go anywhere. We're getting married in our ridiculously huge backyard.

Josh, I have confidence in.

Reece is giving me away, and I'm not so sure about him.

At least I have Pania with me. She hasn't been studying for long, but there was no one else I could ask to design my dress. And I'm in love with it.

Cream silk hugs my curves just perfectly down to my ankles, and the neckline isn't too revealing, but my cleavage is on point.

"I'm here. Don't panic." Reece sweeps into the room with that charming smile that's enough to knock any woman off her feet. Except me. It doesn't work on me at all.

"Where the hell have you been? I know the bride's supposed to be late, but we should at least be attending the wedding on the same day," I say.

He laughs, before running his gaze down me. "You look beautiful, Delaney. You always do, but even more so right now."

"The charm offensive isn't working today, Reece." I cross my arms.

"I can see that." He sighs. "I'm sorry I'm late. Your groom had some last-minute things to give to me. Although, when I say last minute, it was my last minute and not his. He's uber organised."

I laugh. "You're terrible."

"But you love me. It's not too late to run away, you know."

"Not a chance."

It's hard to reconcile how starstruck I was by Reece at the start versus the easy friendship we've ended up with. I love Reece like a brother now, and he's a wonderful addition to our little family.

Reece turns to Amelia. "Hey, beautiful girl. I've got something for you."

"For me?" Her mouth falls open, and she places her hand on her heart. I swear to God this kid is going to follow in her father's footsteps. She could be nominated for an Oscar with the way she plays up to attention sometimes.

"Uh-huh. I've got something for your mother too, but I think you should go first."

He pulls a box out of the bag he's carrying, and I stare at it. I recognise the Tiffany box.

Amelia tugs at the ribbon when he hands it to her, and rips the lid of the box off.

"What it is?" I ask.

She pulls out something shiny. "Look, Mummy."

I take it from her. It's a gold bracelet. The heart charm on it sparkles in the light.

"It's beautiful."

Tears prick my eyes. "It is. Your daddy loves you very much, Amelia."

She frowns as I bend to place the bracelet on her wrist.

"You called me Amelia. Only Daddy does that."

I laugh. "I'm sorry. You're just looking very grown-up and beautiful today."

"Your mother's right, Melly. You're looking as gorgeous as your mother." Reece winks at her, and she giggles.

"Now for you." He pulls a larger box out of the bag, and my stomach flips. "He took forever to choose this. He wanted it to be something special that'd last a lifetime."

My hands shake as I take the familiar blue package.

"You okay?" Reece's tone is gentle. He knows how much today means to me. How much it means to all of us.

"I don't know if I've ever been so happy. But opening this makes me nervous."

He chuckles. "Josh is crazy about you. Open it."

I tug on the ribbon until it falls off and lift the box lid.

If Josh's gift to Melly was thoughtful, this one is off the charts.

I can barely breathe as I look down at the diamond teardrop necklace and matching earrings. They match my beautiful engagement ring perfectly.

"Let me." Reece lifts the necklace out of the box and waves at me to turn around. I place my hand to my throat, closing my eyes as he drapes it around my neck and does up the catch.

"Open your eyes, Delaney," he murmurs in my ear.

I swallow, tearing up at the sight of my gift.

"You're almost ready. But you'll need to change your earrings yourself because I'm not doing that. I'll take off your earlobe or something."

I laugh. "Thanks, Reece."

The door opens. Pania steps through and closes it behind her. I don't miss Reece catching his breath.

"Aren't I lucky? Surrounded by beautiful women," he says.

"So full of compliments today." I tug out my earrings and, one by one, my ears are weighed down by the heavier diamonds. But I can't wear anything else. I might never wear anything else.

"Just because you're getting married doesn't mean that I can't try and win your heart."

I roll my eyes, shoving his chest. "Good luck with that."

Pania cocks an eyebrow. "We should get this show on the road before Josh thinks you've abandoned him."

"Have you got the rings?"

He pats his pocket. "Everything's under control. Even with me pulling double roles."

I slide my arms around his waist. "Thank you for giving me away. I'm sorry if it makes more work for you today."

Reece kisses my temple. "Anything for you two. It's about time you got your wedding day. And I don't mind pulling double duty. I'd be pissed if anyone else was Josh's best man."

"I love you, Reece."

"Love you, too. So much that I'm not even going to make another joke about running away with me." He holds me out at arm's length, and there's a twinkle in his eye. "Let's go and get you married."

THE BACKYARD HAS BEEN TRANSFORMED.

A floral arch stands behind Josh, and the rows are filled with chairs with an aisle down the middle. A tent is over the whole lot to shield us from any press trying to get photos. Word got out a few days ago about our wedding.

I've handed my kitchen off to the caterers, and the big reception room we didn't know what to do with will finally get some use today.

I suck in a breath. It's like a who's who of Hollywood on both sides of the aisle. We kept the numbers low, but even now I still can't believe half the names Josh has added to the list.

Right up the front are Josh's parents, Gabby, and Antonio. Our family.

Pania leads Melly in front of us, and the two of them scatter rose petals as they walk toward the altar.

I raise my gaze and meet Josh's eyes. My breathing's deep as all my nerves rise to the surface.

"Stop trembling," Reece murmurs. "No one's going to bite."

"It's not them."

He squeezes my hand.

I've never seen Josh's face so full of raw emotion. His eyes drink me in as we draw closer, and I smile at him as if to tell him everything will be okay.

We made it.

We finally made it.

Reece kisses my cheek and passes my hand over to Josh before taking his place beside him. Josh links his fingers with mine and I let out a contented sigh.

"You look beautiful," Josh murmurs.

"You scrub up pretty good too."

He grins.

I'm not really paying attention to the first part of the ceremony. The thought of becoming Mrs Carter makes the butterflies in my stomach dance.

"And now for the vows."

Josh turns to me. "Delaney, I never realised just how lost I was without you. But finding you again has led me down a path with no regrets. I'm a better man for you, and I'll be a better husband for your love. You're my best friend, and the love of my life. How lucky was I to find those two things in one person? All you ever do is love me, even when I'm not sure I deserve it. I promise I'll spend my life making sure I'm worthy to hold your heart."

Tears trickle down my face.

"Are you okay?" The celebrant smiles at me, and I nod.

Reece reaches into his pocket and passes me a tissue. Behind me, I hear murmurs and "aww" sounds. I pat my face dry and smile.

"Delaney, if you'd like to speak your vows."

I nod again, and take a deep breath. "Josh, today we start our married life together, and nothing has ever made me so happy. You have given Amelia and me all of your love, and we both love you with all of our hearts. Whoever thought two crazy kids like us could get our shit together?"

Everyone behind me laughs.

"I swear that I'll always be here for you no matter what we face in the future. And I'll even teach you the rules of rugby and cricket if you pay attention for long enough."

Josh chuckles.

I turn to Amelia and take her hand, giving it a gentle tug for her to join us.

Josh squats in front of her. "I promised your mama that when we got married, I'd make a commitment to you too. And that is that I promise to always be a good father to you, Amelia. I'll listen, and make you your favourite hot chocolate with more whipped cream than your mother usually lets you have. I love you."

"Love you too, Daddy." She flings her arms around his neck, and he scoops her up, smothering her face in kisses.

She giggles, and my heart leaps at the sound.

Josh gently lowers her to the ground, and takes my hand in his again.

Reece takes a step forward and hands the rings to the celebrant.

She holds them in her hand and smiles. "Joshua and Delaney will now exchange rings to show their love and commitment to each other. A wedding ring is a circle—a symbol of a love that has no end. Joshua, please place the ring on Delaney's left hand and repeat after me."

My hand shakes as Josh takes hold of it, and he gives it a gentle squeeze before sliding the ring on and repeating the words. "As a sign of my love, that I have chosen you above all else, with this ring, I thee wed."

"Delaney, if you could place the ring on Josh's left hand and repeat after me."

I nod, picking up the ring and switching hands. "As a sign of my love, that I have chosen you above all else, with this ring, I thee wed."

"And now, by the power vested in me by the state of California, it is my absolute delight and pleasure to declare you married. I know you've been waiting all ceremony, Joshua, and it is now time to kiss your bride."

Josh grins, sweeping me into his arms, his lips crushing mine in a kiss that I'll remember for the rest of my life.

"I love you," he whispers.

Behind us, everyone cheers and any nerves I had about who our wedding guests were disappear as we turn together and face rows of beaming faces.

This is my life now, as crazy as it may be.

And the most important people in my life are right up the front to celebrate with me.

Best day ever.

THE DAY IS A BLUR.

There are photos. Oh, so many photos.

There's food and cake and dancing.

And then, Josh and I leave to spend the night at the Four Seasons hotel in the penthouse suite. By the time we get there, we're too distracted with each other to care about the decor.

We're a hot, sweaty mess tangled in the sheets, ready to shower and sleep in the small hours of the morning.

Josh and I have a week alone planned in Hawaii before Melly joins us with Josh's parents, Reece, and Pania. We wanted time for ourselves, but we also wanted to spend time with people we love the most.

Josh is still mucking around in the bathroom, and I pick up my phone and start scrolling through Instagram. We didn't put any restrictions on our guests about photos, and I still want to see if anyone has posted anything.

Josh's Instagram makes me smile.

He walks into the room, and shoots me a curious look as he climbs into bed beside me. "What are you looking at?"

"This." It's a black and white photo. My eyes are closed, and I have a smile on my face as my husband kisses my cheek. "Where did that come from? We need a print of that."

His breath is hot behind my ear. "Reece took it. He sent it through to me earlier, and apparently he's got a few candid shots he thinks will look great on the wall."

"Reece is very clever."

I smile at the post.

Today, I married my best friend and the love of my life. Turns out they're the same person.

The first comment is unsurprisingly from Reece. *No fair. I want a Delaney too. Can we clone her?*

I let out a soft moan as Josh nuzzles my neck. "Put the phone down. We're on our honeymoon, babe, and I want all your attention."

"I want sleep. I'm all champagned and danced and sexed out."

He laughs. "Come here and lie down so we can get some sleep then."

I put the phone back on the bedside cabinet and snuggle down with Josh.

After all this time, it's weird being married. But here we are.

Mr and Mrs Josh Carter.

DESPITE MY WANTING SLEEP, I can't.

I find myself staring at the ceiling until three in the morning. I'm sure it's the excitement of the day.

Whatever the reason, I have no ability to wind down.

I want that photo to be the background of my phone. Loading up

Instagram, I head to his account again. I screenshot the image and save it.

If I could bottle the feeling of the last few days, I would. Leaving New Zealand again left me unsettled, even with all the love and support I've had. But Amelia's happy, and now Josh and I are married. We're a family.

I smile again at Reece's comment. There are a ton of replies to it, and I don't expand them because I'm sure there'll be a ton of women propositioning him.

But I don't miss the next comment.

Really? You could do so much better than her.

Gold digger.

Hope you've got a pre-nup.

Fake news. We all know the studio's making you hide your real marriage to Gabby.

At that last one, my eyebrows rise. Apparently even a wedding isn't enough to prove a real marriage.

"Babe?" Josh's voice is thick with sleep. "What are you doing?"

"I just wanted a copy of that photo for my phone wallpaper. And then I started reading the comments."

He pushes himself up. "I need to get a social media manager to keep on top of that page. It's a big job, but there's no way I can keep control of all of it. It's run wild."

"So, you know what they're saying?"

He shrugs. "I can imagine. Maybe ninety-nine percent of the comments will be supportive, but there's always that element of asshole."

"Is that what you call it?"

Josh takes my phone from my hand. "They're all jealous because they'll never have what you do. And I'm not saying that because of my enormous ego, but because it's true. They'll also be jealous because you are fucking gorgeous and they know it. They're just mean."

I frown. "How do you deal with this?"

"I ignore it. My assistant used to skim through and check for any threats, but I haven't replaced her since I got rid of Mac. I need to hire someone to take care of it." He scrolls . "Some of this is pretty entertaining. The nasty comments have people replying and sticking up for us underneath them."

"Really?"

For a moment, he hesitates. "I don't want you looking at this shit, Delaney. It's meaningless. You got that? The only thing that matters is that you're my wife, and I will love you until the end of time. I don't care what random people on the internet say."

I nod. "I'll try not to."

"Look." He taps on the gold digger comment. Sure enough, there are a series of comments underneath it.

Jealous bitch, much?

Have you seen the photo he posted yesterday? They're in love and you're just sour.

"Hate only wins if we let it." He taps on the comment that says he could do better. I laugh out loud when I see Reece replied.

Are you serious? I'm fucking bitter I couldn't steal her from him. She could do so much better than Josh Carter.

"Reece has your back too. Always. I think if you had a sister, she'd have no chance."

I lean over and nuzzle his cheek.

"Look. Gabby posted too."

Congratulations Josh and Delaney. Beautiful couple. There's a row of heart-eye emojis, and I smile at it.

"Now, let's put the phone down and enjoy our honeymoon. Tomorrow, I'll send you the copy of the photo Reece sent me and you can use that for your wallpaper. It's much higher quality."

"Okay."

"Let's leave them to it and go back to sleep. I need my wife in my arms."

"Your wife." I grin.

Josh leans over and brushes his lips over mine. "My wife. I waited a long time to call you that."

"Me too. I'm still not sure what to call myself. Should I stick with Delaney Carruthers? Or should I be Mrs Carter? Or Mrs Carruthers Carter?"

"That's way too complicated a question to be asking in the middle of the night. Come here and snuggle with me."

It's too tempting an offer to pass up.

JOSH WAKES BEFORE I DO.

The smell of bacon from the room service breakfast really brings me to life. I stretch as I walk out of the bedroom, scratching my neck. "Morning."

Josh is sitting at the dining table, food in front of him. I bend and kiss him before sitting.

"I have something to show you." He grins.

"What?"

"The Delaney Carter Hawaiian fan club has arrived on the scene. I started going through deleting and banning some people, and I spotted this."

He shows me the screen and points at one of the comments I saw last night.

Really? You could do so much better than her.

"What about it?"

"The replies, babe. Look at the replies."

I slap my hand over my mouth.

Becky Foster: Oh, fuck off. I've met Delaney and she's amazing. And the way they look at each other? That's true love.

She's posted about half a dozen heart-eye emojis.

"Becky?"

Josh chuckles. "The one and only. She and I think her friends have spammed the negative comments. When we met, she said she worked in social media. Maybe I should employ her to help admin the page."

"You could do worse."

I laugh when I spot the new comment right underneath from Reece.

Leave him and marry me, Delaney.

"He needs to find something to do with himself for the week." Josh shakes his head.

"I don't know. Maybe he could join us early." I shoot him a sly smile.

He screws his face up. "I know you like his movies, but ..."

"I'm kidding. Maybe we need to find him a woman of his own."

Nodding, Josh puts down the phone. "I think you're right. He's really good at loving and leaving. He gets bored easily."

I reach over and cup his cheek. "This is why I know I made the right choice. I know I have your attention."

"You had it even when we weren't together. I love you, Delaney."

"I love you too."

EPILOGUE
DELANEY

Two years later

I KNEW my life would never be the same once I moved to Los Angeles to be with Josh.

That turned out to be an understatement.

Tonight, I'm attending my first Oscars ceremony, and the butterflies in my stomach aren't anything to do with the baby I'm six months pregnant with. Josh did end up impregnating me with that big-headed Carter baby after all.

"Mummy, you look like a princess." Amelia twirls in her own fancy dress. She's having a little Oscars party at home with Josh's parents.

"You look like a princess, too." I bend as far as I can and kiss her forehead.

"You really do look lovely, Delaney." Ros smiles.

"Thank you."

Ros and Cal arrived today for a few days. I'm so happy they're here as they'll either be celebrating with us, or we'll all pull together for Josh, depending on how tonight goes.

"There are my girls." Cal enters the room, and opens his arms for me.

I give him a hug. He's become the father I never really had, and I'm only sorry that the pair of them live so far from us.

"Don't you smudge her makeup," Ros says.

"I'm not kissing her." Cal laughs, then cocks his head at me. "Unless you want me to?"

"This makeup cost a lot to have done. Better not risk it smudging." He lets me go. "Maybe later." I wink and he laughs again.

"Oh no, all the kisses are for me." Josh wraps his arms around my waist—or rather what's left of it, and presses a kiss against the back of my neck. "It's time for us to get out of here."

"I thought Reece was coming with us."

He pulls away, and I turn to see him shaking his head. "Change of plans. But we'll meet him there. We'll all be sitting together."

I reach up and adjust the collar of his shirt. I'm so proud of this man. When he cut ties with Mac, I know he was confident enough to do his own thing, but still a little unsure. Since then, he's made such huge strides, and if his movie even wins one Oscar, it'll be massive.

It's got some crazy number of nominations, including Reece for best supporting actor, Gabby for best actress, Josh for best actor, and best movie. I'll be crossing my fingers for all of them tonight.

Josh takes my hand in his. "Come on, wife. Let's go."

I grin because I still love it when he calls me that. It feels so new, but I think that's because we still feel like newlyweds. Our marriage is solid, and we've worked hard to make up for the time that we lost. We've reached the point where the balance between work and personal life is right for us. And we plan on keeping it that way.

Max is waiting with a limo outside. It's not often that we get to travel like this, and the thrill is always there. I feel pampered just sitting in the car.

Josh and I sit thigh to thigh, his arm around my shoulders, his hand resting on my stomach as he waits to feel the baby kick. He or she hasn't graced him with their presence yet, but I sure as hell know that they're there.

"Are you nervous?" I ask.

He shrugs. "Maybe a little. We've got some tough competition, but the awards will go to deserving movies regardless. I'm just glad I get to share tonight with you."

It's nice to see Josh so fulfilled and content. This is the stuff dreams are made of, and we've made it. Even if this is as far as we get.

"I love you," I say.

"No regrets?"

I shake my head. "Not a single one. Though I might be regretting my shoe choice by the end of the night. I'm not sure Crocs are a good look on the red carpet, though."

He laughs, and presses a kiss to my temple. "I'll rub your aching feet tomorrow. Promise."

"I hope you know I'm keeping you to that. Especially if you win."

IT SEEMS TO TAKE FOREVER, but I'm so glad to be off my feet for a while longer before the car draws close to our destination.

"Ready?" Josh asks.

The limo pulls up, and someone opens the door. I nod. "As I'll ever be."

"You look beautiful."

I blush because I still do that when my husband compliments me. Even if he does it every day.

Josh steps out first, and then turns, holding his hand out for me to take.

His hold is firm, and as I step out of the car, he rests his other hand on the small of my back. It's those little things that make me appreciate him so much. He knows how nervous I am tonight.

This? This is a little overwhelming.

I've grown used to being in the public eye for the most part. I can handle someone coming to interview us. But this is the bit I'm not sure I'll ever be completely comfortable with.

Flashes go off everywhere as cameras take a zillion photos of us. Josh wraps his arm around my waist and looks into my eyes.

"You okay?"

"Of course I am. Temporarily blinded, but I'm fine." I grin.

"That's my girl." He gives me a tender kiss, and as always in that moment, it's just me and him. "Let's do this."

We don't get far before we're stopped by a reporter gushing over him.

I'm not angry or bitter, but if so much as one more eyelash gets fluttered at him, I swear I'm going to knock the bitch out.

Josh reaches for my hand and pulls me to his side. "Of course, I wouldn't be here if it wasn't for my wife, Delaney. Her love and support has made all of this possible, and I'm so happy to be able to share tonight with her."

The woman, who I don't recognise at all, looks like she just sucked a lemon. Then she flashes a brilliant smile and wishes us well, and we go on our way.

It seems to take forever as Josh keeps getting stopped.

"Delaney." I turn at the sound of Reece's voice. "You look amazing."

I take in the sight of my handsome friend, dressed in a black tux. "You don't scrub up too bad yourself."

He pecks me on the cheek. "Excited?"

"Terrified. But I'm here, and everything seems to be going well. We've stopped about five times for Josh to be interviewed, and my ankles will be mega-swollen by the time we get inside. But it's a wonderful night. Good luck."

He grins. "It's crazy to think we're even nominated. You're our good-luck charm."

I laugh, shaking my head. "No way. You guys just needed to get your shit together."

Reece squeezes my arm. "That's why I love you. You're so upfront with me."

"Always."

"Reece."

I turn my head to see my husband heading toward us.

He slips an arm around me. "It's good to see you, man. Let's head in."

My world has become so surreal with the number of actors and actresses who recognise me and say hello.

Our seats are near the front, and I'm so glad when I finally sink down into mine.

"You okay?" Josh asks.

I nod. "Sore feet, but I'll survive."

He takes my hand in his. "You know, even if I don't win this, I still win."

"How do you work that one out?" I laugh.

"I have you in my life. And I have Amelia. And in a few months, I'll have this one too." He places his hand on my bump. "I have the life I never dared to dream of. Thanks to you."

I shrug. "It's all your fault. Shouldn't have answered the door half-naked that first day."

"Is that what did it?" He leans in for a kiss.

"Uh-huh. I just couldn't stop myself after that."

"How about after all this, we go home, shower, and we'll re-enact that moment?"

I laugh. "I like that idea."

"I like the thought of showering with you. I'm in charge of the sponge."

Reece leans over me. "Can you two quit with the foreplay?"

"Jealous?" Josh asks.

"You know damn well I am." He grins.

I lean against Josh as he kisses my temple.

I love my life.

IT'S the craziest night of my life.

Reece and Gabby both win their awards, and I'm not surprised.

Their movie is beautiful.

It's the story of a damaged war veteran who comes home and struggles to settle back into regular life while also dealing with his wife's infidelity with his best friend while he was away. I cry every time I see it.

And then they get to the award for best actor.

Josh squeezes my hand, letting go only to applaud for each nominee.

"And the Oscar for best actor in a drama is ..."

I hold my breath.

"Josh Carter."

For a moment, it's like I don't hear his name. Around us, the room explodes, and I'm dragged into it by Reece grabbing my arm. I slam my hands over my mouth, and turn my head to look at the man I love.

I drop my hands as tears prick my eyes. He's done it. He's really done it. All the sweet things he said about being a winner even if he doesn't win are still so special, but now he really has it all. The family he wanted with me, and the accolade of becoming an Oscar winner.

He leans over, pressing his forehead to mine. Cupping my head with his hands, he gives me a hard kiss that leaves no one in any doubt that he's mine.

My chest swells with pride as we stand together. He shakes Reece's hand, but gives me one last lingering kiss before he squeezes my fingers and mounts the stairs to the stage.

I clap until my hands ache. He's worked so hard for this, and now he's been rewarded in front of all his peers.

Tears roll down my cheeks as he takes his award and I sit to watch my husband.

"Wow. This is amazing." He pauses. "I've thought about this

moment a million times since I started acting, but never really thought ... The first person I'd like to thank is my best buddy, Reece. I found the story, and he really did an insane job of pulling it all together and turning it into what it is now. I couldn't have done it without you."

I smile as he reels off a list of people involved in the making of the movie. He's just shining with pride, and I can't wait to show Amelia tomorrow morning.

"And last, but most importantly ..." Josh fixes his gaze on me. "Eight or so years ago, I met a beautiful girl in a coffee shop who told me to do better. And that's what I did. I love you, Delaney, and every-thing I do is for you."

My heart's in my throat as he speaks. I really thought if he won, his speech would just be thanks to Reece, his manager and the direc-tor. Never for a moment did I think he'd include me the way he has.

Tears prick my eyes, and I turn to my right as Reece nudges my arm.

"Let me guess. You didn't pack any tissues."

"I didn't even think about it."

"Here." He produces one from his pocket and hands it to me. I dab my eyes and blow my nose. He grimaces. "I don't want it back."

I laugh. "Thank you."

Josh soon rejoins us, and it's not long until it's time for the award for best movie. This is the big one. None of us dared to dream of this moment, but the way things have gone tonight, there's hopefully a good chance.

"And the Oscar goes to ..."

Once again, I hold my breath.

"*Coming Home.*"

My head spins.

Josh grasps my chin and pulls my face to his. "You okay?"

I nod. "I'm so proud of you."

He kisses me hard again, and I stand to make way for Reece to get past. Reece hugs me before following Josh and the rest of the cast and crew to make his way to the stage. I clap until my hands tingle, but my heart sings watching them step up and accept the award.

The director speaks. Reece speaks, winking at me as he hands the award to Josh. Josh looks straight at me and just blows me a kiss.

Tears roll down my cheeks, and the tissue Reece gave me is soon soaked and tearing apart.

When they rejoin me, I wrap my arms around Josh's neck and hold tight.

"We did it, baby," he says.

"You did. What are we doing now?" I ask.

Josh kisses my neck. "Now, we party."

***

"MUMMY."

I open one eye. Amelia leans over and places her face so close to mine, I can smell hot chocolate on her breath.

"Are you awake?" she asks.

"I am now." I groan. I've never been so glad to have such a comfortable bed. I feel like I've been drinking all night, but it's just that my very pregnant body is not coping with our very late evening.

"Daddy won."

"Daddy won big." I give her a tired smile, as big as I can muster.

"Daddy is the biggest winner of them all." Josh's voice comes from behind me. He throws his arm over my belly as he snuggles up. "I have my girls right here. That's all I need."

"And the bag with the statues in it that I managed to keep together all night."

He laughs. "At least one of us was responsible."

"Yeah, and I'm suffering for it this morning."

Josh raises his head. "I'll be down for breakfast soon, Amelia. Is Gran in the kitchen?"

She nods.

"Go on then. I'll come and see you soon when I've woken up properly."

I sigh as she runs from the room. "So much energy."

Josh rubs my stomach. "I'll go and get something to eat for both of us. Do you feel like coffee or tea?"

"Coffee. I think I need a pick-me-up today."

"Anything you want." He kisses the back of my neck right as the baby does a back-flip. "I think she's ready for breakfast, too."

"She?" We've had a very uncooperative baby as far as scans go.

He chuckles. "I don't know why, but I've just got a feeling I'm going to be surrounded by girls. Not that I'm complaining."

"Better not."

"Come here."

I roll over.

"Last night was amazing."

I grin. "It really was."

"You had fun?"

"Well, I wouldn't want to do it all the time, but I enjoyed it."

He grazes the back of his hand down my cheek, pressing a gentle kiss to my lips. "I'm glad I get to experience all this with you. Wouldn't be the same by myself."

"I'm so proud of you."

"None of it means anything without you, Delaney. You're my muse. I hope you know that." He sighs. "Do you think we should get out of bed and join our daughter?"

"Soon." I slide an arm over his waist. "Your muse could do with more kisses."

"She can have as many kisses as she wants. Maybe in the shower?"

I smile. "I like the way you think. Might wake me up."

"Oh, I'll wake you up alright."

He leaves me to doze while he gets the shower going. It feels like a second later when he returns to give me a gentle shake.

"Come on. This'll make you feel better."

He takes my hand, and helps me out of bed. Manoeuvring isn't easy, and there's still three more months of pregnancy to go.

I stand in the middle of the bathroom as he strips off my shirt and panties. Taking my hand, he helps me into the shower. I'm capable of doing it all, but this morning, while I feel sorry for myself, I appreciate the help.

The warm water dances on my skin, and I stand with it running over my face in an effort to wake up properly.

Josh wraps his arms around me.

"I love your pregnant body." He skims his hand, covered in body wash, over my baby bump. "Your breasts looked amazing in that dress last night."

"I thought *I* looked amazing—not just my breasts."

He grins. "Oh, you did, but that's what caught my eye."

"You're such a man."

Josh presses his cock against my thigh. I don't miss that he's hard. It's impossible to miss.

"What about now?" he asks.

"Definitely. Planning on doing something with that?"

He chuckles. "When we're out of the shower. I'm not sure shower sex would work too well right now."

"You mean because of this." I pat where the baby's growing. And she or he is really doing a good job of that.

"I know your centre of gravity is a bit screwy. The last thing either of us need is for you to fall in the shower. And you're slippery after washing."

"I'm not sure if you're complimenting or insulting me."

"It's always a compliment, Delaney. I value my life far too much to insult you." He presses a kiss just below my ear and I sigh.

"I wouldn't kill you if you did. The sex is too good."

"Glad I'm useful for something."

I grin, turning my head so he can kiss me again.

"I'll rinse you off and then help you out of the shower. Meet you in the bedroom?"

He reaches for the showerhead and runs the warm water over me. When he's finished, he takes my hand and holds it until I step out onto the bathmat and grab a towel from the heated rail.

"Don't get dressed. I have plans for you," he calls.

I rub myself dry before wrapping the towel around me and leaving to sit on the bed. I'm still tired, but not feeling quite so awful anymore. A good breakfast should help even more.

I laugh when my husband appears in the doorway, dressed only in a towel slung low around his hips.

"Is this what you like?" he asks.

"Absolutely."

He walks toward me. "Did thoughts of me keep you warm at night?"

"Maybe." When he reaches me, he bends over and plants a hard kiss against my lips. I grin. "Okay, yes. It wasn't Ryan Reynolds I thought of when I was alone. Except for that one time ..."

I laugh as Josh pushes me backward on the bed and drops the towel. "I'll make you forget he even exists."

"We're supposed to go down for breakfast."

He grins. "Oh, I'm going down alright. But breakfast can wait."

"You promised me a foot rub."

His eyes glisten with happiness. "Oh, baby. You're getting so much more than that."

THREE MONTHS later to the day of Josh's Oscar win, my water breaks, and when my contractions reach the point where I need to go to the hospital, we leave Amelia with her grandparents and Josh drives me to Valley Presbyterian Hospital.

Or rather, he intends to.

"I can't believe you got us lost. Again. Why can't you just use the GPS on your phone?" I grimace as another contraction hits. He needs to sort his shit out.

"I know where the hospital is, Delaney."

"Clearly, you don't." I pull my phone out of my bag. "We're on Addison Street. We're so naming this baby Addison if it's a girl."

Josh laughs.

"It's not funny, Josh. If you don't get us to the right place, I'm having this baby in the car."

I bark out directions as we finally head toward the hospital, and by the time we get there, I'm so over him that I'll be happy to leave him behind in the car.

I immediately change my mind after taking two steps.

Waves of pain hit me, and my knees buckle underneath me.

"I've got you." Josh scoops me up into his arms and carries me into the hospital.

"I love you." I wail.

"I know."

He murmurs the words in my ear and I relax as best I can until we're in the delivery room. Nothing else matters right now—just this baby.

She doesn't muck around, and she's born with just a couple of pushes. I shake, the shock of how quickly she's born leaving me a weeping mess.

She's here.

She.

Josh was right. He is surrounded by girls.

I look at my husband. Sharing this with him just makes my heart beat faster. He never got to do this with Amelia, never got the chance to see the moment she was born. With this baby, he'll get to do everything.

"Did you want to cut the cord?" the doctor asks.

Josh grins. "Yes, please."

Watching the joy on his face makes this day even more exciting.

After the baby's placed on my chest, I stroke the fuzz on the top of her head and hold my husband's hand as we revel in an experience we didn't get to do together the first time around.

It means everything.

"What are we going to call her?" he asks.

"I told you in the car. Her name is Addison."

He strokes her cheek. "Addison. I like it."

I widen my eyes. "I know. Addison Montgomery Carter."

He gives me the side-eye. "Why does that sound familiar?"

"Addison Montgomery was a character on *Grey's Anatomy*. McDreamy's first wife. You know how much I love that show."

He nods like he knows what I'm talking about, but he really doesn't.

"If you love it that much, maybe I should see if I could land an episode or two on it."

I grin. "I might watch you if you were on TV."

He laughs. "Just for you, Delaney. Always for you."

The look in his eyes shows me just how much he loves me. He's been like that ever since the night we got back together, and I hope I express my love for him in the same way.

"I think when she's a little older, we'll have to go on a trip to Glenderry. So she can meet everyone back there."

I smile. "I love that idea." We've been back once for a holiday after a year of living in Los Angeles, but not since then. I can't wait.

The thought of going home causes a swell in my emotions and I tear up. "You're making me cry."

"Only happy tears." He kisses my temple. "Only ever happy tears."

And I know, despite everything, that's all there'll ever be.

Only happiness forever.

ALSO BY WENDY SMITH

Coming Home

Doctor's Orders

Baker's Dozen

Hunter's Mark

Teacher's Pet

A Very Campbell Christmas

Fall and Rise Duet

Falling

Rising

Fall and Rise - The Complete Duet

The Aeon Series

Game On

Build a Nerd

Bar None

Hollywood Kiwis Series

Common Ground

Even Ground

Under Ground

Rocky Ground

Solid Ground

Ajax

Stand alones

For the Love of Chloe

Only Ever You

Another Chance

The Friends Duet

Loving Rowan

Three Days

The Forever Series

Something Real

The Right One

Unexpected

Chances Series

Another Chance

Taking Chances

Lifetime Series

In a Lifetime

In an Instant

In a Heartbeat

In the End

At the Start

ABOUT THE AUTHOR

Wendy Smith lives with her two children and three cats in Hastings, New Zealand, and she's not sure who's responsible for her grey hair. She's a multi-platform bestselling author, whose book In the End, written as Ariadne Wayne, was named one of Apple's best books of 2017. All her stories come with a quirky sense of humour, and she cries over everything.

Find me online
www.wendysmith.co.nz
wendy@wendysmith.co.nz